D0502256

GUN METAL HEART

Also by Dana Haynes

Crashers

Breaking Point

Ice Cold Kill

GUN
METAL
HEART

DANA HAYNES

MINOTAUR BOOKS
NEW YORK

GUN METAL HEART. Copyright © 2014 by Dana Haynes. All rights reserved. Printed in the United States of America. For information, address St. Martin's Press, 175 Fifth Avenue, New York, N.Y. 10010.

www.minotaurbooks.com

Library of Congress Cataloging-in-Publication Data

Haynes, Dana.
  Gun metal heart / Dana Haynes.—First Edition.
    pages   cm
  ISBN 978-1-250-00964-7 (hardcover)
  ISBN 978-1-4668-4872-6 (e-book)
  1. Women—Fiction.   2. Women engineers—Fiction.   3. Inventions—Fiction.
4. Spy stories.   I. Title.
  PS3558.A84875G86 2014
  813'.54—dc23   2014014597

Minotaur books may be purchased for educational, business, or promotional use. For information on bulk purchases, please contact Macmillan Corporate and Premium Sales Department at 1-800-221-7945, extension 5442, or write specialmarkets@macmillan.com.

First Edition: August 2014

10 9 8 7 6 5 4 3 2 1

To my incandescent wife, Katy

Acknowledgments

To Tamara Burkovskaya, former Senior Political Specialist at the U.S. Embassy in Bishkek, Kyrgyzstan, who provided a generous glimpse into embassy life. It proved invaluable.

To Tim King, research travel companion through the former Yugoslavia. It takes a special skill to spend that many days in the Balkans, in a rented subcompact, and not go nuts. You're a mensch.

GUN METAL HEART

One

The quiet man stood in the entrance to the taverna. The regulars didn't remember seeing him enter. They hadn't noticed the flash of too harsh, too white sunlight when the door opened. They hadn't smelled the tang of salt and seaweed invade the tobacco and hashish funk of the bar.

But there he stood.

He wore a cowboy hat, a denim shirt, jeans, and boots. The shirt was unbuttoned to reveal an off-white undershirt, and the sleeves were rolled up past tattoos and well-defined biceps.

One by one the patrons of the taverna noticed him, then went back to their beer and their boredom.

The quiet man walked to the bar, removed the cowboy hat—old and badly sweat-stained—and set it on the bar. His hair was black, almost shoulder length, and swept back. His face was leathery, tight, and deeply pocked. He had a thin, lipless mouth, exceedingly flat planes along his cheeks and forehead, and a nose that had been badly broken and poorly mended.

The old bartender, a pipe cleaner of a man, rubbed a filthy rag on the filthy bar and took his time looking up. When he did, he flinched at the sight of the customer's face.

"*Birra, signore?*"

The quiet man nodded.

The manager limped to the tap and returned with a pint. The quiet man reached into his shirt pocket and withdrew a much-bent photo. He set it on the sticky bar and slid it across.

It was a photo of Daria Gibron.

The old man peered at it, squinted, made a point of scratching his thin patch of hair. He looked up and shrugged.

"Seen her?" He spoke English.

"No."

"Sure?"

"*Sì.*"

The quiet man reached into the back pocket of his jeans and withdrew a folding knife, the handle carved of bone. He kept the knife closed.

The bartender peered at the knife, then up into the flat, reflectionless eyes, then back at the knife.

"Signorina Randagia?"

The quiet man looked skeptical. As if the name were unfamiliar.

"Gatta Randagia. It is what she calls herself, *signore*. Yes. I know her."

"She's here?"

The old man shrugged. "She's out."

The quiet man nodded solemnly and picked up his dirty stein with his left hand and sipped. "Out where?"

"*Cimitario.*"

"Graveyard?"

"*Sì.* For, ah old things, not people. Pieces . . . ?"

"Junkyard?"

"*Sì!*"

The manager grabbed a beer mat, turned it over to the blank side, and drew a map. He'd begun to sweat now. It wasn't just the unspoken threat of the closed knife. It was something intractable and menacing on the man's scarred face.

That, plus the *signorina*. The old man had feared her from day one. She was radiant, yet somehow she carried that exact same menacing air as this man.

The quiet man studied the beer mat. "Junkyard?"

"*Sì*. For aircraft. Old aeroplanes, *signore*."

"Why there?"

The old man wet his lips. "Running."

"From what?"

The bartender shrugged. "Who can say? The devil, maybe."

The quiet man drained his beer. He seemed to contemplate that. "The devil."

"*Sì*."

He pocketed the bone knife, shook his head. "Can't be two of us."

The bartender wasted no time in alerting the people in Caladri. The residents detested strangers. In a town in which the two main industries were the importation of illegal immigrants from Africa and illegal drugs from South America, a snooping foreigner is no friend.

Within minutes the grapevine spread the word that the stranger was looking for Signora Gatta Randagia.

Nobody could remember if the town had named her or if she'd coined the nickname for herself. *Gatta randagia*—stray cat.

The stray cat crouched in the shadows, fingertips on the ground, slightly forward of her hunched shoulders, the heels of both sneakers up off the dirt, and surveyed the battlefield.

It was only mid-July but already the weather had turned nasty on the Mediterranean coast. Where much of the region is sun-swept and touristy, Daria Gibron had picked a spit of land shoved uncomfortably between a barren strip of rocky coast and the Trenitalia railroad tracks, wedged like a broken rib up against the rest of northeastern Italy. The villages to the west were rich fishing waters and the villages to the east catered to a trendy, moneyed set. But on this rocky gouge of land, almost nobody had made an honest living in decades.

It suited Daria to a T.

The temperature was in the nineties and the humidity matched it. Yellow-white clouds filled the sky and turned the sea a mottled green, the kind of clouds that promise rain, just to taunt you.

Daria was hunched like a sprinter in a starting block. She squinted against the white glare and the painfully glinting metal all around her. Everywhere she looked Daria saw bits of things that once had been aircraft but which would never again have the word *air* associated with them. They were ground things now. Warped wings here, rusted fuselages there, piles of tread-bare tires and desiccated cockpits strewn about. The debris were dated between the 1950s and the 1990s. Some military aircraft, some civilian.

Daria's dark skin glowed with sweat. She wore ratty cutoffs and a short Violent Femmes T-shirt, sleeves ripped off and neckline badly and unevenly stretched out. Some boy had left it in her bed, but for the life of her she couldn't remember his face. Her sneakers were new. Her straight black hair was pulled into a ponytail. She wore fingerless black gloves with golden zippers that ran halfway up each palm: "borrowed" from a Parisian drug dealer the year before. Her only other accessories were bandages here and there, stretch tape wrapped around both wrists, and a red/purple swoosh of a lovely new bruise on her flank, under her left arm.

The junkyard had been built in the remnants of a mercury mine in a valley between scrubby hills. Almost no plants beyond weeds grew in the narrow valley. A flicker of a smile ghosted across Daria's parched lips. *What's a nice Jewish girl like you doing running in a place like this?*

She heard the squeak of shoe tread on aluminum and knew that the Kavlek brothers were on the move.

Daria bolted.

She pushed off with her right foot from beneath the truncated wing of a Phantom F-4F fighter. Her first goal was the stubby, roof-gutted Tornado dead ahead. Its cockpit had been blown out, avionics rusting in the thin haze and sun. A whacking great hole had been torn out of the top of the fuselage, likely from a midair collision or a missile rather than a crash landing.

The final goal wasn't the snub-nosed Tornado but the huge, mothballed Airbus A-320, just beyond. The narrow-body airliner was about 120 feet long, providing plenty of running room. It sat flat on the rocky ground, sans landing gear. If she could get inside that beast, she could buy herself some advantages.

An Israeli Army drill sergeant had once ragged her: "In an open-field flight, your advantages are eyesight, space, and liberty! Rob the enemy of them, and it's advantage you!"

Daria leaped from her cover, sneakers hitting the hard earth, legs and arms pumping.

A flash of skin to her left and above her. Mehmet Kavlek, the sturdier of the brothers, diving off the fuselage of the Phantom. He'd been above her all along.

Daria guessed that the husky Turk couldn't leap from atop the Phantom to the wing of the Tornado. He'd either land on the ground between . . . or atop Daria.

She threw herself forward in midair, ending with a tumble, shoulders first, then her back, her ass, her sneakers. Once her shoes hit the packed soil, she used her momentum and her bunched legs to leap.

Mehmet Kavlek thumped to the ground a meter behind her.

Where was the other brother?

Still running, Daria caught hold of the wing of the grounded fighter craft and swung her body up and to the left, one knee clearing the airlift surface of the wing. She grunted and used her momentum to roll along the surface, completing the roll on one knee and one foot.

She glanced back. Mehmet's meaty hands appeared before her eyes as he leaped for the wing.

Daria turned and ran, springing for the front half of the fuselage.

Ismael Kavlek made his appearance. Lighter than his brother, he sprang like a gazelle onto the horizontal elevator of the Tornado's tail section. A normal human would have smacked into the vertical stabilizer and rudder, but the whip-thin man raised one foot, kicked at the stabilizer, rerouted his momentum 90 degrees, and deftly surfaced atop the fuselage with Daria.

The roof was holed—too great a distance for even Ismael to reach her directly—but the bigger Turk had hauled himself up onto the port wing behind her, so there was nowhere for Daria to go but forward, toward the starboard wing.

She landed, knees bent, and hauled ass down the length of the wing, which sprang under her weight like a pirate ship's plank.

Behind her, Ismael Kavlek leaped—not *over* the hole in the fuselage but *through* it, head first, into the aircraft, landing in a somersault, springing to his feet, shoulder slamming open the flight-deck door. He was running perpendicular to Daria now.

The windshield was long gone. Ismael hit the pilot's seat with one boot, threw himself forward, out through the missing windshield, his right hand snapping onto a still-firm support post. His grip, plus his momentum, spun him clockwise. He let go in midair and landed deftly outside the aircraft, on the starboard wing.

Damn it! Daria gritted her teeth.

She dove off the end of the wing, using it like a springboard, and hit the ground. Ahead of her lay an aged, gray barrel of an obstacle: the remains of a Rolls-Royce Deutschland turbofan engine.

She could sprint around it, but that would take time. Daria sprang forward in a headfirst dive, hitting the top of the hot metal with both gloved hands, tucking her bent legs tight against her abdomen, and leapfrogged over it.

The Airbus now was five meters away.

Daria caught blurs of movement from the dumping ground's flag, from the squat African palm trees, from the sagebrush hillsides. Her mind shut out the irrelevant and reached for the stunted forward landing gear of the A-320 and climbed like a monkey through sharp, rusty holes up into the underbelly storage section of the airliner.

It was filthy inside, and rats scampered away from this strange, sweat-drenched alley cat.

Daria duck walked as fast as she could, forward to a service hatch. She used her legs for strength, shoulder to the hatch, and heaved it open.

Ismael Kavlek appeared behind her, through the landing-gear opening.

Daria hauled herself up into the single-aisle fuselage of the airliner, near the nose one. The passenger section gave her almost 150 meters of straight running space, and she dashed aft, leaping over debris where she could. She had spotted a blown-out starboard window, back near the bathrooms.

She heard Ismael's boots behind her and, simultaneously, Mehmet's boots thumped against the roof of the fuselage, over her head.

Daria dove headfirst through the smashed-open window.

Beneath her lay long weeds and rusty, razor-sharp bits of iron. She twisted in midair, landed on one shoulder, the banged-up rib punishing her. She rolled and was up again, as the bigger Turk jumped from atop the plane onto the tail, and from there to the ground.

He landed badly, skidding on his side into the weeds.

Daria caught sight of a Bell helicopter, a bubble-domed dragonfly, Korean War era. She angled for it. She heard Ismael mimic her mad dive through the starboard window and land right where she had.

Mehmet was on his feet, but huffing, and now it was a straightaway foot chase. The longer she could draw this out, the better.

The tail of the Bell was an open-air scaffolding affair, and Daria reached for it like it was a playground monkey bar, swinging beneath it, letting go, arcing five meters in the air, and landing on her feet, running, gasping for air.

The big Mehmet ducked and ran under the tail.

The lighter Ismael grabbed it with one hand and catapulted over it.

She hadn't gained a half second on them.

Daria reached a corridor between two gutted fuselages. She attempted a difficult, full-speed, right-angle turn, caroming off one of the aluminum frames, running full tilt, until her left leg simply gave out, her knee buckling in the turn.

She landed clumsily, face-first in the dirt, her chest taking the brunt of the impact, a mouth full of caked dirt. She tried to stop her momentum, but that only resulted in a tumbling roll that landed her, crumpled, against the gutted fuselage.

Ismael Kavlek rounded the corner but, unlike Daria, didn't try the right-angle turn. He leaped like a dancer, hit the fuselage with his boots, and ran two steps along the wall, literally running sideways parallel with the earth, his momentum defying gravity, until he pivoted in midair and landed, knees bent, in front of her.

Daria sat up against the curved aluminum, unable to catch her breath, chest on fire, now bleeding from her right cheek.

Mehmet Kavlek rounded the corner and, unlike either of them, simply let himself hit the fuselage with his shoulder, bleeding off his momentum. He was moving at only a jog as he reached his brother's side.

Daria squinted up into the white haze at the two men who loomed above her. She realized her hand rested next to a rusted spanner.

Ismael Kavlek grinned down at her. "Did you think—?"

The three of them were so intent on each other that the man in the cowboy hat and dusty boots seemed to appear as if by a conjurer's trick. One second later the butt of a sturdy Colt Python thudded into Mehmet Kavlek's temple and he dropped.

The quiet man turned the gun on Ismael, whose eyes bulged.

Daria grabbed the spanner and grunted, throwing it with her waning strength. It slammed into the raised arm of the newcomer, his aim shifting 10 degrees, and the .45 boomed, the bullet missing Ismael by inches, the sound deafening, echoing and reechoing back at them through the jungle of metal skeletons.

"*MercifulGodWhatInHell . . .*" Ismael yelped in Turkish.

Daria sprang to her feet, hoping to fake any remaining strength. Once up, she peered up into the ragged face of the newcomer.

"What th— You!"

The quiet man looked at her. If his arm hurt from being hit by a wrench, he didn't show it.

"*Diego?*"

Mehmet, on the ground, groaned.

The flat-planed face took in the three people. He turned back to Daria and nodded.

Daria huffed for air. One hand stole to the badly bruised rib under her left arm. "What—the hell—are you doing?!"

"Saving you."

She began to see red. "*Saving me? Sav—*" She ground her teeth. "Diego, you idiot! You almost killed this man!"

The quiet man mulled that for a second. He still hadn't lowered his Colt. "Yeah."

Daria wiped sweat from her eyes, tried to calm her beating heart. "Put away the gun. Do it now."

He did.

"I'm going to ask you again: What are you doing here?"

The man called Diego said, "I'm here to hire you."

Two

Dragan Petrovic had three meetings slated before noon.

He was on a committee that was hammering out a trade deal with Hungary regarding winter wheat. He was meeting with two ministers from the Pristina region regarding assigning more border officers to the road crossings into Bosnia. And he was part of the team crafting a bid for a European wine expo. It was going to be one of those days in the marble halls of the Serbian Parliament.

But before Petrovic did any of it, even before he got a chance to polish his wing tips or tie his tie, he was called upon to resolve a crisis inside his three-story Tudor home.

His eldest daughter, Sofija, had her driver's permit and wanted to drive to Novi Sad with her girlfriends. There were many things in Novi Sad to draw the attention of a gaggle of sixteen-year-old girls. All of them involved boys.

This, of course, led to an apocalyptic meltdown by Ana, the middle daughter, who suffered inequities the likes of which the writers of the Old Testament never imagined. The very idea of her sister driving to Novi Sad was a calamity of national importance. Then again, the same could be said of three events each day.

The youngest daughter, Ljubica, recently had discovered football. A ragamuffin with perpetually skinned knees and grass stains around her cherubic grin, she rarely spoke more than twenty words per day to her father. Which was fine by Dragan.

The member of Parliament did his level best to placate daughters number one and two, without countermanding his wife, Adrijana. He considered himself a decent father; certainly better than the abusive drunk he, himself, had run away from at the age of nine. He had found a surprising level of joy in helping to raise daughters. It was like gardening: he always assumed he'd hate it until he actually tried it.

Adrijana helped with his tie and Dragan checked the contents of his ubiquitous attaché case. He had everything he'd need for the day. His wife—lovely and lithe at forty—cast a critical eye over his suit and pronounced him acceptable for governing Serbia. As if any living soul could govern Serbia! They air-kissed at the door to their home.

Teodore, Dragan Petrovic's driver-bodyguard, had the armored Escalade waiting in front of the house. One of Teodore's soldiers would ride ahead on a motorcycle, eyes peeled for trouble.

Dragan sat in the back and read the London *Times* and *Le Monde*, translated on his iPad. Outside the smoked windows Belgrade looked dusty and dry, the citizens struggling to get started on another long, hot July day.

The SUV swung powerfully onto the bustling Kneza Milosa, wending deftly around the slower traffic. The neighborhood leading up to the Parliament building was embassy row.

Teodore took this route every morning. And, as every morning, Dragan Petrovic subconsciously looked up from his e-reader to observe the smashed edifice of the old Chinese Embassy as they passed by.

The building stood tall and devastated. Half of the building lay to the north of a side street, the other half to the south. No windows remained. The Americans had bombed the embassy in 1999. The rockets had landed at night. Five JDAM missiles, fired from the U.S. 509th bomber wing. Three missiles had landed on the north side of avenue Nemanjina, two on the south side.

The embassy was across the street from the Serbian Parliament building. The Americans had targeted a diplomatic building that was literally a stone's throw from the heart of the people's capitol. The affront had been unthinkable.

The Escalade glided past and Dragan kept his eyes locked on the devastation. He had been among the lawmakers who had lobbied, long and hard, not to tear down the lifeless hulk of a building. Better to leave it standing as a testament to the evil of America. Dragan Petrovic wanted to force his fellow lawmakers to drive past the shrine of Western aggression every single morning.

Most days, the Escalade slowed down to let the minister off in front of Parliament. But today Teodore followed orders and drove straight past the elegant building. The Kawasaki knew the new route and stayed ahead of them. First the motorcycle, then the SUV, turned into the entrance of a half-finished garage. An unmarked Crown Victoria sat in front, two men in civilian clothes and Ray-Bans, watching patiently.

The SUV glided into the inky black interior of the unfinished structure. One other car waited inside: an unremarkable Audi sedan. Teodore parked the Escalade ten meters from the Audi, hauled on the hand brake, unclipped his seat belt, and slid out of the car. As he did, the driver's-side door of the Audi opened. The sedan's interior lights had been disabled.

A woman stepped out of the sedan. She wore her hair pulled tightly back in a chignon. She had chosen a midnight-blue trench coat, finely pressed trousers, and boots with tall heels.

She crossed to the Escalade, her heels echoing in the parking lot. Teodore held open the rear left-side door, and she climbed in to sit next to Dragan Petrovic.

Her hair was so shockingly blond as to be nearly white. Her eyes were a silver blue, the lightest color eyes he had ever seen. And when she smiled, she seemed to light up the interior of the car.

Dragan straightened his cuffs.

"Minister." He noted that she spoke Serbian with an urban, Beograd accent.

He smiled stiffly. "Major Arcana."

The blonde nodded and continued to smile.

"Some would find your nom de guerre in poor taste," Dragan informed her. "I knew the real Arcan. I fought with him in Bosnia and Kosovo. He was a great man; a great military leader."

"Yes," the tall woman nodded. Dragan had difficulty placing her age. Late twenties? Early forties? "He also was a bank robber and a car thief and a thug. But some men rise to match the times, yes?"

Dragan ignored the dig against his long-dead friend and fellow freedom fighter. He willed himself to remain calm.

"Can you deliver?" he abruptly asked the smiling blonde.

She nodded. Her hair was held tightly in place; not a strand bobbed as she nodded. Her silvery eyes locked onto his.

"You are sure?"

Again, she nodded. And smiled.

A small leather pouch rested on the floorboard at Dragan's feet. He leaned forward now and retrieved the pouch. It was long and thin, twice the size of a number ten envelope. The flap was held down by a leather thong wrapped around a grommet.

He handed it over. The blonde took it, undid the string, pulled back the flap. She did not count the euros. She did not need to.

She resealed the bag.

"Thank you, Minister. You will hear back from me within three days."

With that she opened the passenger door of the SUV and climbed out. She strode purposefully across the empty parking structure and got into her Audi.

The car sat, windows darkened, as Minister Dragan Petrovic and his military escort left the unfinished building.

Outside Florence, Italy

The two Serb soldiers had a pretty good idea how long Vince Guzman would stay unconscious after being hit by the Taser. Still, they followed that up with a tranquilizer shot.

They moved him to an abandoned warehouse in Quinto, near Aeroporto Amerigo Vespucci. It was well built and sturdy enough to keep out kids and transients. It also lay under the approach vector for the airport, so the sound of descending jets helped mask noises.

It was dusk, and the road outside the warehouse was little used. Guzman sat in a metal chair, wrists flex-cuffed to the straight arms, ankles to the legs. His head lolled, and he'd drooled on his T-shirt. Adhesive pads were pressed against the insides of both elbows and both knees. All four pads bulged around thin tubes.

The Serbs were called Kostic and Lazarevic. Both had seen military duty and the insides of Yugoslav prisons. Both knew their jobs exquisitely.

Guzman moaned and came around. He raised his head and hissed painfully at the crick in his neck, which came from his head hanging loose for almost two hours.

The senior soldier, Kostic, had brought a thick, hardback Serb–English dictionary. It wasn't a simple tourist's dictionary; the conversation he was anticipating needed a broader range of words.

Kostic spoke in English. "Hallo."

"Hey. Hey!" Guzman jostled his beefy arms, straining against the white plastic cuffs. He peered around, teary eyes trying to focus on the warehouse, the metal chair, the brawny men in polo shirts. He really shook the chair now, putting his weight into it. The metal legs scraped on the rough cement floor, the sound echoing.

"The fuck is this! Hey!"

Kostic said, again, "Hallo."

Lazarevic said nothing.

Guzman struggled. "Get this fucking shit off me!"

Kostic ignored him. "You are hired. Are bodyguard. In Florence."

"What? Hey, I don't know what you guys are talking about. Get me the fuck outta this and let's talk. All right?"

Kostic said, "We do not have much time. Time is very bad."

"Time is bad? My time is bad, motherfucker! Let me up!"

Kostic said, "You enjoy American movies? Bruce Willis. Sylvester Stallone."

Guzman shot glares from one to the other.

"Action," Kostic said, then made a gun of his finger. "Bang bang."

"The fuck are you talking about?"

Lazarevic, his biceps and mustache bulging equally, stood with arms crossed and said nothing. Kostic said, "The hero is running, running. Always. Bad guys fire bullets. But they don't hit him. They hit walls, they hit street. Not Bruce Willis."

Lazarevic, unspeaking, uncrossed his arms and touched each of his elbows with his opposite hand.

Guzman didn't know the Serbian word for *elbow* but understood. He glanced down and noticed the square, white adhesive bandages on the insides of both elbows. Similar pads were adhered to the insides of both knees. Those plasters were adhered to his jeans, not to his skin. He blinked at the completely unfamiliar things.

"What the hell . . . ?"

Kostic was leaning against a metal worktable. He twisted at the waist and picked up something that looked, from Guzman's angle, like a multioutlet power strip. Wires and shiny silver tape dangled from it.

"You have interrogation before, we think. You are tough guy. It goes: You don't talk. We beat you. You don't talk. We beat you. Tonight, tomorrow, next day. Yes? You tell us what we need to know."

"Look, you bastard! I don't know—"

Kostic rode over him. "Hero in movies. Bruce Willis? Is not dodging bullets. There are no bullets." He waggled the long, narrow electric device in his right hand. He changed its angle. Guzman could see it was a cobbled together remote control with four toggle switches and a battery pack. "Are . . ."

He frowned, turned to Lazarevic. Lazarevic picked up the hardback dictionary. They had marked a page with a nude torn out of a girlie magazine.

The silent Lazarevic showed him the word.

Kostic said, "Squib. Yes. Small bomb. Very small. Goes boom in movie, it looks like bullet hits wall."

Guzman didn't have to act confused. "What?"

Kostic held the remote in his right hand and casually used his thumbnail to flip one of the toggles.

The small explosive squib adhered to Vince Guzman's left elbow exploded.

The small charge—the size, shape, and color of a cinnamon stick—smashed the elbow, sending bone chips up into Guzman's arm. The explosive, plus the bone chips, combined to shred Guzman's collateral ligaments.

In the blink of an eye, his left elbow became a permanently crippled bag of blood and sinew and floating bone fragments. The sleeve of skin, mostly unruptured by the directed explosive, acted like a sausage casing, holding his lower arm connected to his body.

Vince Guzman screamed. He flailed as best a bound man can, the chair shaking, metal legs beating a random tattoo on the cement. Every long muscle in his body went rigid. His head snapped backward and forward quickly, as if he were listening to a thrash-metal band.

He screamed until he puked, then screamed some more.

Kostic and Lazarevic watched. Kostic held the remote with the remaining three toggles. He didn't believe he would need to flip them.

Six minutes later, Vince Guzman sat quietly, head down, shirt stained with vomit and sweat, his trousers soiled, his left arm a soggy, seeping bag of morbid flesh. His bloodshot eyes locked onto the unfeeling mannequin's arm and hand flex-cuffed to the chair.

"Diego," he gasped, ". . . the job . . . Florence . . ."

Kostic nodded, pleased not to have wasted hours on an interrogation. "Diego. Is alone?"

A thick rope of drool and puke hung from Guzman's lips. "In trouble, he'll . . . go find Daria . . . always does . . ."

Kostic turned to his partner and translated. Lazarevic frowned. "Daria?" He went down on his haunches, attempting to make eye contact with Vince Guzman. Guzman just stared at the plastic-looking, gray-white hand cuffed to the chair. "Is woman? Daria? Is trouble?"

"Y-yeah . . . she's all high and mighty but . . . yeah." He sniveled snot. "She's trouble."

"Her name?"

"Gibron. Daria Gibron."

Kostic stood straight. Vince Guzman, a lifelong tough guy, spat out a sob. His eyes never left the lifeless handlike thing attached to his arm.

Lazarevic drew a Russian-made .9 auto and waited for the next jetliner to roar overhead.

Sandpoint, Idaho

Todd Brevidge thought the three worst ideas of the past decade had to be: trading Jeremy Linn to the Houston Rockets, a Broadway musical based on the Spice Girls, and moving the Research and Development Division of American Citadel Technologies to Sandpoint Freaking Idaho. And not in that order.

Brevidge guided his Ferrari F430 through the streets of the sleepy town.

Todd Brevidge stood out, in his Hong Kong suits, seven-hundred-dollar Tom Ford shades, and his Ferrari, for which he'd paid extra to make sure the hot-hot red was the exact color of his favorite escort's lingerie. At thirty he was considered a prime shaker and mover in the high-tech industry; in five years he'd be an elder statesman.

And here he was. In Idaho. The Siberia of the West.

Brevidge made nine hundred grand a year after stock options. He'd been with American Citadel since it was a three-room office suite behind an AM/PM Mini Mart in Modesto. Since before the four international buyouts. He'd been loyal from the start. For which he'd been exiled to this gulag of country music and Big Gulps and mud flaps.

Brevidge roared into the five-space parking lot, the Ferrari purring, and climbed out.

He understood moving research and development away from Silicon Valley, away from the prying eyes of the competition and the high-tech media and the various federal government oversight agencies.

Special Projects was on the verge of some incredible breakthroughs. Not the least of which were Mercutio and Hotspur. It was time American Citadel got to sit at the grown-up table, and Todd Brevidge had been instrumental in making that happen.

He walked into the entirely unassuming office with its entirely unassuming lobby. The only people present were the morning guard, who nodded his greeting, and the chief engineer for the Hotspur and Mercutio projects, Bryan Snow.

Snow looked, as usual, like a guy in costume playing Buddy Holly, with black plastic frames and a maroon cardigan and—literally—blue suede shoes. He wore jeans with the cuffs rolled up, and Brevidge wondered when that trend had reappeared.

Snow adjusted his retro glasses. "Good morning."

"It will be," Brevidge said, "if engineering holds up its end of things."

Snow shrugged and smiled sheepishly. "We will."

Brevidge glanced around, then stepped to the elevator. He hit the retrieval button. Above the elevator, only three floors were marked. Brevidge checked his watch and waited. The elevator dinged open. Snow stood with his fingers sheathed in the rear pockets of his jeans.

"You guys have no idea what's at stake." Brevidge appeared to be addressing the digital readout of floors on the panel over the elevator door.

"I think we do," Bryan Snow replied softly.

Brevidge spat out a mirthless laugh and adjusted the Bluetooth earpiece he wore at all hours, even when he wasn't taking calls. He stepped into the elevator and Snow followed. The controls inside included three large, round plastic buttons, beside three numbers, 1, 2, and 3. Next to the 1 was a star, which denoted the lobby. Brevidge didn't hit any of the number buttons. Instead he pressed the knuckle of his forefinger against the star. He applied pressure.

After a second's delay, the star depressed.

The door slid closed and the elevator descended to a basement that was not represented on the elevator controls, on the building schematics, or in the blueprints on file at the Sandpoint Fire Department.

"This demo is make or break, man." Brevidge shook his head ruefully.

"I mean it. Make or fucking break. No third option. Besides the buyers, do you know we've got brass here?"

Snow toed the floor of the elevator, as if trying to draw a line in the sand. "Yes."

"You know that? You know we've got actual management in the building today? Really, Bryan? See, I don't think you did know that. I don't think you're cleared to know that the guys who sign the paychecks are actually here in—"

The door hissed open and revealed the gaunt and spectral form of Cyrus Acton. Of the American Citadel board of directors.

Snow looked down at his suede bucks and cleared his throat. "Todd, you know Mr. Acton? He got here about an hour ago."

Cyrus Acton was pale and bald and appeared to have been manufactured by the process of stretching human skin over chicken wire. He wore a somber suit, a plain black tie on a plain white shirt. No Bluetooth for him.

He said, "Todd." His voice had been bled of all emotion. "Good morning."

"Mr. Acton." Todd ginned up a grin. He couldn't believe that geek Snow hadn't warned him! Asshole! "Good to see you, sir! Your flight was okay?"

Mr. Acton nodded. The overhead lights glinted on his liver-spotted pate.

"Outstanding, sir. Well, we're ready for the demonstration."

"You're sure?"

Brevidge grinned. "Oh, hell yes, sir. I was just telling Snow here, we're absolutely gonna knock their socks off. The minute the buyers get here, have we got a show for them!"

"They are not," Mr. Acton intoned.

"Ah . . . not . . . here?"

"Buyers," Mr. Acton said. "They are not yet *buyers*, Todd. They have examined the merchandise. They have weighed their options. And they have chosen not to invest in the American Citadel product. They continue to cite these utterly outrageous sanctions from the State Department." Mr. Acton looked like the word *sanctions* tasted chalky.

"Ah. Right. Of course."

"The people who sanctioned our company are the kind that have kept America weak," Cyrus Acton continued. "They would put onerous regulations ahead of American jobs. It's our responsibility to convince our guests to look beyond the sanctions."

Brevidge beamed. Convincing people to do *otherwise* was as good a description of the art of the sell as any he'd ever heard. And when it came to that, Todd Brevidge was the Beatles of sales.

"When they see what we can do, they'll change their minds. Guaranteed!"

Mr. Acton smiled. His face was long, his cheekbones prominent, his chin pointed. "Guaranteed?"

Todd felt his underarms begin to perspire. "Absolutely. Positively. Completely."

Mr. Acton smiled. "That's what we in management like about you, Todd. We appreciate your uncompromising faith in the product."

Brevidge grinned and shot the engineer, Snow, a look. "Then give me twenty-four hours, sir. And I think I can make wholehearted believers out of the buyers. You could stake your life on it, sir!"

Mr. Acton smiled. He patted the young salesman on the shoulder. "Oh gosh, no, Todd." He laughed. "We'll stake yours."

Three

Daria and the quiet man, Diego, retired to her rented apartment in the tiny village. The town consisted of one paved street that paralleled the highway to Genoa and a second paved street that led down to the docks.

Daria stripped, removed her various bandages, and showered. Gingerly.

She threw on panties and an old T-shirt and padded out to find Diego leaning against the wall, glancing out the room's single small, dingy window. He set his hat upside down on the room's cheap, chipped chest of drawers.

Diego was Mexican; born and raised in Mexico City. He was of Indio blood, claimed to be an Aztec, but only if he was drunk enough to speak in complete sentences, which was rarely. He'd spent his teens in East LA. He'd been a hoodlum (good at it), and after 9/11, a soldier (excellent at it). When soldiering hadn't turned into a career—something about decking a superior officer—Diego had gone back to the family business, thugging.

Diego stopped inspecting the town's one dusty street as Daria stepped out of the bathroom. She tossed a tube of ointment, a box of cotton balls, and adhesive plasters onto the bed. She perched on the side. "Make yourself useful."

Diego walked over and sat on the bed, too. He applied astringent to the cut under her right eye, drawing not a sound from her. He rooted through the box, found two small plaster strips, and fashioned them into a butterfly bandage.

"There. Rib?"

Daria glowered at him, but glowering just tugged at the butterfly bandage. She twisted sideways, raised her left arm over her head and lifted the T-shirt over one breast. Any casual observer could tell that Diego had seen all the important bits of Daria Gibron before today. Usually wounded. He leaned forward and peered at the zucchini-shaped bruise on her flank. He probed it none too gently with a blunt finger. His hands were small but rigid and scarred from boxing.

"Not broken. You'll heal."

He affixed a square of cotton over the bruise with adhesive tape. It wouldn't speed up the healing process but would keep her clothes from annoying the sensitive bruise.

She lowered her shirt.

"What was that, at the junkyard?"

Daria pointed to the cheap plywood chest of drawers by the bed, atop which sat Diego's old hat along with a half-full bottle of cheap Czech vodka and two mismatched coffee cups. Diego eased off the bed and poured them each a generous portion.

Daria sipped hers, rib protesting even the act of swallowing. "It's a sport. It's called Parkour."

Diego snorted, or appeared to snort. It was silent. "Looked like gang rape."

"Ismael and Mehmet? God, no!" The very notion made her laugh. "They're sweethearts. They're teaching me Parkour, or free running. The idea is to move as fast, and as creatively, as you can over a broken, obstructed course. You don't dodge the obstacles, you incorporate them."

Diego again checked out the street scene through the one window. He wasn't looking for specific trouble; it was the habit of a lifetime. "Why?"

"For the lads? To get on YouTube, to impress other boys, to impress girls. Mostly to impress girls."

"An' you? Another of your martial arts?"

Daria laughed, and of course that hurt, too. "No! The Kavlek brothers are nineteen and twenty-one. You saw: I didn't last five minutes evading them. No chance at being truly competitive at Parkour at my age. I'll never be of their caliber."

He thought about that and sipped his vodka. "You mind me asking . . . ?"

Daria drained her cup. She had known Diego for ages; their relationship dated back to her years in Europe. Initially she had thought of him as a necessary evil, a way of establishing a cover as a gunrunner. Over time that relationship had somehow changed into respect and, perhaps, at some level, friendship. Or at least comradeship. One or two of their jobs had gone south, and every time, Diego had proven himself to be a stand-up guy. Thief he may be. Thug he may be. But a good guy, all the same.

Diego leaned on the wall. His hips were narrow, his shoulders wide.

"Last winter, I was sick," Daria spoke into her chipped coffee mug. "A kind of flu, but more than a flu. I got better. I started working out. I ran. I lifted weights, kickboxed, climbed rocks, went back to archery and fencing. All my old bad habits."

Daria glanced up at his scarred face. She knew that some of the scars were from childhood acne. Some were from a razor fight in an alley in Ciudad Juárez. Some were from a roadside bomb outside Falluja.

She stared up at him, and Diego took the stare from those raven-black eyes the same way he'd taken punches. Without comment.

"I'm not one hundred percent. My body got better but my mind . . . my reaction time, my instincts. They haven't come back."

"And this . . . ?"

"Parkour. It's all about split-second decisions. About judging bad alternatives and picking the least bad. Or sometimes the least likely. Or the least predictable. It's also fun. And, just maybe, it's working."

"And the bruises?"

Daria smiled up at him and twisted her long brown legs into a yoga position, feet under her, knees akimbo. "Do you fret over your bruises?"

Diego allowed himself a shallow smile. The number of people on earth who got to see that smile could be counted on two hands.

"So tell me what you need me for."

Diego poured them both another couple of shots. "Remember Vince?"

Daria rolled her eyes. Vince Guzman, a beefy American, had been Diego's friend and partner in crime since childhood. A Los Angelino and half Latino, Guzman was younger and considerably dumber than Diego. But by the time they were in their midteens, the two were joined at the hip. Guzman wasn't terribly bright, and he was nowhere near as reliable as Diego. But Diego had a blind spot for him. Always had.

"And how is Vince?"

"Missing. In Florence."

"Best tell me about it."

Diego was quiet for a while. He sipped his drink. He never liked talking. "Vince got us a job. Bodyguarding an engineer, protecting her invention."

Daria came close to spitting vodka across the room, and her rib snarled at her. "You two? Bodyguards?"

"We're good at it. Who'd fuck with us?"

Daria blinked at him. Diego flickered that smile, on and off. He actually seemed to blush. "We'd have gotten around to stealing the thing eventually."

"That's more like it."

"Figured the engineer was paranoid. We'd take her money. Hang in Florence. Good enough work."

"But . . . ?"

Diego shook his head. "Not paranoid. Bad guys."

"*Bad* bad?"

He said, "Way bad. Russians. Organized. Good weps, expensive comms. Chain of command. Training." He shrugged. "Paramilitary."

Daria sipped, waited.

"Russians had tatts. Scorpions. All white."

She coughed, the caustic liquor hitting the wrong tube, her rib spasming and sending sparks of heat through her frame.

Diego waited.

"You're joking! *Skorpjo?*"

He sighed. "'Scorpio?' You know 'em." It wasn't a question.

She wiped her lower lip with the back of her hand. Diego took the opportunity to pour her another shot.

"Not Russians. They're Serbians. *Skorpjo*. Also known as White Scorpions. They were a military unit during the Yugoslav civil war, in the nineties. Racist. Exceedingly violent. Went freelance after the peace accord. You and Guzman are messing about with very bad people."

Diego nodded, knowingly. His movements were spare, his face passive. "Figured. Fuck."

He sounded forlorn.

"So what happened?"

Diego said, "Vince's gone missing."

"You think *Skorpjo* sussed him out?"

The quiet man shrugged.

Daria rose and crossed to him. She placed a hand on his shoulder. Diego normally hated being touched. "Look, I know you and Guzman have been friends forever. But are you certain he's missing and hasn't just cut a deal with the White Scorpions? You have to admit, it's not out of the question."

The Mexican stared out the window a bit. He shook his head softly. "Sure. Vince could sell someone out. Not me. I don't think."

Daria leaned in and kissed his badly scarred cheek. She had always admired loyalty. "How'd you find me?"

"Viking."

She laughed. Fredrik Olsson was Europe's preeminent fence and criminal transportation coordinator. He traded in information. Of course he'd known how to find Daria.

"I'm sorry. I'm not one hundred percent. I'm still recovering."

Diego said, "Don't need muscle. Got muscle."

"Then why come find me?"

He turned to her. He looked as if the obvious simplicity of the question surprised him.

"Because you're smart. I need brains."

"You're a dear."

"You'll help?"

Daria pondered the situation. Diego stood and let her get there.

"Truth is, I might've gotten all I can out of Parkour and working out. I have to get back into the game eventually."

He nodded.

Daria squeezed his shoulder. "One question. This thing in Florence. Any chance of gratuitous violence?"

"You an' me?" Diego drained his vodka. "Don't see why not."

Four

The point of being a spy is being able to blend in.

The three Americans were foreigners in France. But meeting in a McDonald's gave them complete anonymity. Plus clean bathrooms.

Owen Cain Thorson was there first, in a booth, with a tall Diet Coke. He'd had to ask for ice. He wore black jeans and boots, a black T-shirt, and a black motorcycle jacket. It was too hot out for a motorcycle jacket, but he wore it well.

The other two spotted Thorson upon entering. Jake Kenner also was blond, but bulkier, and he favored tight T-shirts that displayed his pecs and treelike arms. Derrick Saito was cautious and quiet, with a physique built for speed rather than size. Kenner ordered coffees for them both as Saito slid into the booth opposite Thorson. A lot of the patrons were Americans, expatriated Americans, and American wannabes. The three men did not stand out.

Kenner brought the coffees and slid in. "Dude."

Owen Cain Thorson shook their hands. "Guys."

Saito scanned the room without appearing to do so. He said, "You looking good."

"Thanks."

"I mean . . . you know." Saito shrugged. "Considering."

Thorson did look good. He was a blue blood, of very old money and very staid politics. He had been the sixth generation of Thorsons to serve in the U.S. Army, and none had rotated out as anything less than a colonel. He was the third Thorson to join the CIA. One of them had retired as agency director.

Thorson was the kind of all-American male who always looked good.

Truth be told, though, he wasn't his usual matinee idol self. His haircut was a little off. His complexion a little waxy. His eyes darted more than the guys remembered.

He'd had a bitch of a year.

Saito sipped coffee and grimaced. It was bitter. He shook out two packets of sugar and poured them both in.

Kenner grinned, clearly thrilled to be there. "Fuckin'-A, man! I thought you were freaking crazy. I never figured Langley would give us jack. But we asked around, and hey, you were right."

Thorson nodded. His heart was racing, but he'd perfected his poker face, and he was sure the other two couldn't tell.

Derrick Saito tried his coffee again, grimaced again, and reached for more sugar. "There's enough brass at Langley who hate that dyke. It didn't take me more'n a day to find the right guy."

"But you were careful?"

Saito shrugged off the question as stupid.

Kenner leaned over the table. "She's living in Italy! Crappy little town on the Mediterranean. Caladri. Deal they cut with her was: She stays off the grid, the Agency leaves her the fuck alone. She starts poking her nose into Agency business, the Agency fries her ass."

Thorson said, "Sure."

"Get this, bro: NSA's been monitoring all comms from her known contacts. There's this guy called Diego. Mex gangbanger, former GI. The bitch and him pulled off some shit around Europe before she moved to Los Angeles. NSA reported—*today*, man—to-fucking-*day*!—that this Diego's in Caladri."

Thorson's heart hammered. "Yeah?"

"Caladri was a one-horse town before the meat shortage!" Jake

Kenner laughed at his own joke. "No way this beaner is there on accident. NSA reports to the Agency. Agency checks with Eye-talian intelligence. Wops say Diego runs with another gangbanger named Guzman, and says the two of them are pulling some scam in Florence. So the smart money says the bitch either stays put in Caladri, or she pops up in Florence. Either way, we got her ass in the crosshairs. Yo?"

Kenner offered a fist. Saito reached up and bumped knuckles, but he did so with the distracted air of a man who would rather not have made the gesture but knew that if he didn't there'd be this weird tense moment, and who needed that?

Owen Cain Thorson said, "I could use you guys. Ten thousand dollars. Each. Interested?"

Kenner said, "Shit, yes! Charges against us were bullshit! We should be on Agency time, right now! What they did to you? Double bullshit! Be good to show the suits in Langley that they took a dump on the wrong peeps. I'm in, man!"

Saito sipped his coffee and nodded.

Owen Cain Thorson smiled and gripped their hands. His hand shook, and both of the men noticed. Thorson did not.

He was within days of meeting Daria Gibron. The same Daria Gibron who had ambushed him in Manhattan. Who had embarrassed him. Embarrassed the Agency. Embarrassed the U.S. intelligence community. Who had gutted his career and his family name.

He felt the pressure of the Glock automatic tucked under his arm. It felt as if God was reaching down with a single finger and nudging Thorson's heart.

Jake Kenner gulped all of his coffee in one swig, his Adam's apple bobbing, then belched. Saito eased out of the booth, and Kenner followed.

Kenner said, "We gonna do this bitch?"

Thorson stood. "Yeah," he vowed. "We are."

Five

After lunch, Diego got in his rental and drove back to Florence. Daria said she had business to wrap up and would join him the next morning.

She grabbed a scruffy white canvas bag, tube-shaped with canvas handles, slung it over one shoulder, and walked away from the grotty little village of Caladri and its loathing of outsiders. Daria knew the name was from the Lombardi dialect and translated as House of Thieves.

She tightened her shoelaces and crab-climbed her way down the craggy rock face to the shore. There were no sandy beaches here and no commercial dock.

Daria wore a wash-faded pink bikini bottom under her cutoffs. She retied her black, straight hair into a tight ponytail, stepped out of the bleached-white shorts, toed off her shoes, and dove into the sea, avoiding the rocks, but not by much. The July water was warm and briny, slate green, and only shallow waves today. Daria swam the breaststroke, knowing that would punish her bruised rib but also would loosen up the muscles that articulated her ribs. A fair trade-off. She swam for five hundred strokes, not knowing how far that took her and not caring. She counted metronomically in her head, all other thoughts abandoned. At five hundred, she paused, treading water, panting. She used her arms and legs to rotate 360 degrees. The ghostly outline of a freighter passed in the distance. The rocky shore of Caladri loomed, the hills above the mercury-stunted valley dense with dark-green vegetation. The trees of the Italian coast, this far north, would provide good cover for an ambush.

She swam back to the jagged black rocks. It took timing and dexterity to let the waves lift her high enough for a single-handed grab at the flat outcropping from which she'd jumped. It was an uninhabited and uninviting cove, and she hadn't worried about anyone finding her shorts and shoes. She cleared the volcanic rocks, bloodying only one knee in the process. She sat on the rock for a few minutes, letting the sun dry her cropped T-shirt while she regained her breath.

One year earlier she could have swum ten times that distance without pausing for breath. There were a lot of things Daria could have done a year earlier.

She stood and snugged into the cutoffs, sun-faded to the color of a drowned man's lips. She pulled on the low sneakers and untied her hair.

She started uphill, quickly passing from Martian rocks to scrubby growth to the railroad tracks leading west to Genoa. Beyond that was the tree line. She hiked up a nonexistent path. She braced herself with her palms on tree trunks, climbing higher. Twenty meters short of the actual path that led into the smugglers' village, Daria veered upward again, hiking counterclockwise, ever upward. The salt from the sea dried on her skin and itched. She soon sweated it off. She hiked a zig-zag path up the grueling face of the bluff, stepping over fallen branches, hearing small creatures, unseen, skitter out of her path. She used her arms as much as her legs for some of the rougher bits, hauling herself around precarious cliff faces scoured by African winds and Atlantic gales.

Her breathing became ragged.

At almost three hundred feet above sea level she found the remains of a servants' path, about a third of which was roughly paved with stones. Her progress improved. The gradient became much kinder.

The stone path led to a relatively flat pasture that canted gently toward the cliffs. Three black Arabian horses lived there that summer.

They eyed her the way that toughs guarding their own turf eye any passing stranger, in any town on earth.

Beyond the green pasture was a narrow road of crushed white oyster shells, which wound its way amid sculpted tufts of emerald lawns and truncated bits of Greek statuary, a torso here, some disembodied heads there. Well hidden among the statuary were CCTV cameras. Daria had clocked them on her first approach, weeks earlier.

Beyond a freshly painted stable and a voluminous garage she spotted the great house, four stories tall, all weathered stone and rounded turrets and terra-cotta roofs. It was immense and formidable, designed to weather Mediterranean storms.

The breeze this high up was fresh and cool. Daria's hair had dried straight back off her skull, strands tickling her shoulder blades. She nodded casually to the grounds crew, chatted with a few. Her Italian was good enough that she could do a Sicilian accent, and everybody down in the village and up in the converted castle assumed that that was where the mysterious *Gatta Randagia* was from. Israeli by birth, she could pass easily enough.

The house staff was less convivial than the grounds crew and eyed her with the exact same hostility as the Arabian horses. She nodded to a few of them, expecting and receiving no responses. She hadn't bothered making friends in the great house.

Her stretched-out Violent Femmes T, ripped cutoffs, and battered sneakers drew an unctuous glare from Anton, chief assistant to Signore Giancarlo Docetti.

Anton certainly didn't mind Signore Docetti having amorous dalliances. He'd have thought it odd for a financier of Signore Docetti's stature *not* to have mistresses here and there.

He didn't mind Ana, the current Signora Docetti, either. The young, tall, and angular beauty—almost thirty years younger than the *signore*—recently had made the climb from fashion runway to TV presenter. She was using *trophy wife* as a base camp before her final assent on Mount Hollywood. Anton didn't begrudge her this. It was Italy.

And he didn't even mind the romantic interludes of Gianni Docetti, the twenty-year-old son, the racing enthusiast and constant fodder for

31

the more lurid Italian media. Docetti the Younger could (and did) sleep with whomsoever he wished.

Still, Anton did not like Daria, the solidly muscled stranger with the hobo's clothes, tightly defined muscles, sun-bronzed skin, and jet-black eyes. Anton mistrusted the misfit.

Anton had yet to figure out whose romantic dalliance she was: Signore Docetti, Signora Docetti, or Docetti the Younger? Based on when the woman visited, anyone was possible. Any two were conceivable. Even, God forbid, the trifecta.

Italian, Anton might be. But even Italians draw the line somewhere.

A little girl. A soldier. The Gaza Strip. Bombs, blood. Callused hands, long pianist's fingers, nails shredded and bloody, reaching for her. Scrambling for her. Diggers above, screaming for help. The smell of charred human. The life flickering and dying in a woman's pitch-black eyes. Lips silently breathing apologies.

Gasping, sweating, eyes ablaze in sheer terror, Daria awoke.

She was not buried alive. She was not caked in blood and mud, ribs squeezed by debris. She was not straining for a hand always out of her reach.

She lay in a warm, king-sized bed, amid Egyptian cotton sheets.

She waited for her heart to stop thundering and eventually drifted back to sleep.

Afterward, Daria lay in bed with Gianni, Docetti the Younger, one hand behind her head, one naked leg bent, knee up, and listened to the youth with the creamy skin and rocker tattoos use hand gestures to describe the feeling of speed. Gianni sat up in bed, sheets spooled around his long, rangy body, and he dazzled Daria with his stories: the rush, the crazed fans, the gorgeous girls and equally gorgeous boys, the competitors giving their all.

Daria listened, amused. She had always liked athletes. She was intensely competitive by nature and was attracted to people who lived for challenges.

When he grew tired of talking, Gianni Docetti reached over and adjusted a stray strand of straight black hair behind her ear. She smiled up at him.

"Someday you'll have to tell me about the nightmares, *Gatta*."

She reacted without thinking. "I don't have nightmares."

Gianni smiled down at her. "You do. Almost every night we're together."

Daria squirmed in the sheets. "I wouldn't worry about it."

Gianni Docetti was very young and very self-centered. But he knew when he was being dismissed. He let her get away with it, leaning over and kissing her hard on the lips. Daria snuggled deeper into the covers, let the moment go where it would.

After they'd made love twice, Gianni took a shower. Daria slipped into a silvery silk blouse that smelled of Ana, the current signora Docetti. She buttoned as many buttons as the Italian version of modesty required, then stepped out onto a flagstone balcony that overlooked the sea. She borrowed Gianni's mobile phone; she'd thrown away her own phone after last winter's contretemps, well aware that a steeply increasing array of Western intelligence agencies would be monitoring her communications. In theory, none of those agencies knew about Casa Docetti.

Someday you'll have to tell me about the nightmares.

For a while, after last winter's illness, she had thought her childhood curse of nightmares was diminishing a bit. The reprieve hadn't lasted, though.

She decided not to worry about it today. She used the international prefix for the United States, then called the one person she knew who might be willing to take her call. And not inform the CIA.

Six

The last thing John Broom wanted to do was miss the staff meeting. He knew they were important. The chief of staff for Senator Singer Cavanaugh had informed John of this time and again.

Good service to the senator and his constituents began with good teamwork. And good teamwork required staff meetings. Lots of staff meetings. Long staff meetings.

John had assured Calvin Pope, the chief of staff, that he would make attending staff meetings his new priority.

He'd assured Calvin of this in February. Also in April.

As of July, that hadn't happened yet.

John Broom had joined the senator's staff in December, following a ten-year career as an analyst at the Central Intelligence Agency. John's specialty at the CIA had been the study of weapons and weapon platforms, along with military and foreign policy. Anyone can read the papers and talk about a war that is raging. John could talk at length about the next war to break out.

His time at the CIA had ended with a flourish: an investigation into stolen canisters of recombinant influenza. It had resulted in John being sent into the field of play, where guns were fired. Lots of guns.

Prior to last November, John had never heard a gun fired in real life. After November, John vowed never to be near a discharged gun again. John liked to tell people, "It's not that I'm a coward . . . no, wait. It's exactly that. I'm a coward. No more guns."

Thus, the new gig was perfect, a desk job inside the Beltway serving Senator Singer Cavanaugh, D-Louisiana, former war hero, former prosecutor, former FBI director, and longtime chairman of the Joint Committee on Intelligence. Precisely the kind of guy who needed to know about weapons, weapon platforms, military policy, foreign policy, and the next wars brewing.

At 10:05 A.M. Tuesday, John sat atop his cluttered desk in the Dirksen Senate Office Building, just north of the Hill, struggling to open a packet of peanuts. From his perch he could scan television channels on his desktop computer and Web sites on his tablet computer and keep an eye on the door that he and three other staffers shared in the tight, ill-ventilated office. He also kept a thin Moleskine notepad open on his lap, jotting notes in his precise handwriting. His eyes flickered from image to image and occasionally back to *The Wall Street Journal* open on his desk. He also could see the few dozen Post-it notes he'd spread about, all with Really Important Information he was sure he would need at some point in his life.

He could see shadows in the office corridor before anyone reached his door. Ever since his encounter with guns (lots and lots of guns), John had favored being able to see doorways.

The doorway was filled now by an intern, one of four they had that summer. She was twenty, cute, black, petite, and dressed as professionally as her meager budget would allow. She rapped tentatively on the door before entering, a laptop clutched to her chest, a lapel pin that logged her as a staff member glistening under her dark black, chemically straightened hair.

"John?"

"Hmm? Oh, hi, ah . . ."

John knew the interns' names, of course. He had written them down on one of his Post-its, in order to memorize them. Piper, Paige, Bryce, and Ryder. Easy. Two guys, two girls. Two black, one white, one Asian. Tulane, Louisiana, U–New Orleans, Notre Dame, and Northwestern. Straight, straight, straight, and bi. Liberal, liberal, liberal, and bemoaning the fate of Leon Trotsky. Too young to contemplate as bed partners. (Also, again, two of them guys, not John's flavor, but hey, he didn't judge.)

John Broom was a man who could talk to you at length about the Treaty of Westphalia. Memorizing four names—as his dad always said—wasn't rocket surgery.

He smiled at the intern. "Hi, Bryce."

"It's Piper."

John thought, *Crap!* "I know. What's up?"

"I wanted to let you know it's ten o'clock."

He smiled. That was considerate of her. There were only three wall clocks in the crammed office, plus a half-dozen computers, all of which displayed the time. His eyes flickered from TV monitor to tablet computer to *The Wall Street Journal.* "Thanks. Hey, did you get that itinerary for the Soviet thing?"

She blinked in surprise. "Soviet?" She'd been born after the Wall fell.

John looked up. "The People's Democratic Blah-Blah thing."

"Oh. I think you asked Ryder for that. What is it?"

John thought she'd just called herself Ryder. "Ah, it's a new party in Novosibirsk. They're making some electoral inroads around Kiev. There's a big gathering coming up. I wanted to know who's speaking."

Piper seemed to absorb that. "Is it important?"

John smiled at her. He used his teeth to try to open the peanut packet. "I don't know."

"Oh. Anyway, it's ten."

"Okay."

"Here." She summoned a bit of confidence and stepped fully into the office, hand out. John handed her the packet of peanuts. She set down her laptop, deftly split it open, and handed it back. "Is that what you're working on now? The Soviet thing?"

"Where?"

She blinked around the room. "Well . . . here."

"No." He ate a handful of peanuts, offered her the packet. She shook her head. John nodded to the newspaper. "The *Journal* has an article about the president pushing for a larger presence of the Navy's Fifth Fleet in the South Pacific."

He waggled the tablet computer in the air. "Sky News is reporting that a Spanish transit union is scheduling a nationwide strike."

He ate a mouthful of peanuts and nodded to the TV screen. "And an Egyptian court wants the military to reopen the border with Gaza, but the military is balking, which is just plain weird."

He chewed his peanuts. He shook his head. "Weird . . ."

Piper had been staring at his eyes but hurriedly looked away when John realized she was still standing there. "Um . . . why?" she said, "Why weird?"

John offered her the packet again. This time, she took a single peanut. He said, "Which one?"

"Any of them. Why does the senator need to know about them?" She ate her single peanut.

"I don't know."

"You don't know?"

John shrugged. "No. He might not. I won't know until I look into them. If he doesn't, well, no loss. If he does, I'd rather have talking points before he needs them than after he needs them. You know?"

"Sure," she said. "That's why you're missing the meeting?"

"Which meeting?"

"The ten o'clock meeting."

John said, "Is it ten o'clock?"

Piper thought about a half-dozen replies but bit them all back.

John stood up and retrieved his suit-coat jacket from the back of his chair. The jacket was matte black and the lining tamale red. It was the precise same red as the swirls of his tie. The red also appeared as a thin line in his pocket square. Piper, Paige, Bryce, and Ryder played a kind of drinking game in the evening, based on what color combinations John Broom would wear the next day to work, and whether the lining of his jacket, or his pocket squares, would match his ties.

John gathered his tablet computer and the intern gathered her laptop.

"I can't miss this meeting," he told her. "It's important. Calvin places a lot of importance on team meetings."

"He does," she conceded.

"It's bad form to miss these meetings."

Piper nodded.

"Really, missing the meeting would be bad."

John's phone vibrated while they were still six paces from the senator's conference room door. John whisked it out of his trouser pocket. He frowned at the extra-long overseas number on display.

"John Broom."

The voice on the other end said, "Hallo, Mr. Broom."

John froze. Piper took two steps before she realized he wasn't moving. She turned back.

John gulped.

The voice on the line said, "Is this a bad time, p'raps?"

Piper raised her eyebrows.

John held the phone against his chest. "Tell Calvin I'll be missing the meeting."

Daria felt the breeze, salty and warm, off the Mediterranean. Anton brought her an iced Sorrentine limoncello and a dull glower.

She smiled as the voice over the international call said, "Thought we agreed to use first names."

"Right you are. Hallo, John."

"Hi, Daria."

"Surprised to hear from me?"

Gulls arced overhead, not flapping their wings but riding the thermals.

"I was not part of that bullshit with the CIA," John Broom shot back quickly. "I hope you know that. I fought hard for them to understand that you weren't the bad guy. That you saved lives. Lots of lives."

"I do know that, John. Just as I know that the CIA, and the other agencies, agreed to leave me alone so long as I stay low and don't interfere."

She sipped the icy drink. She listened to the two beats of silence. John said, "Uh oh."

She barked a quick, musical laugh. "'Fraid so. Friend of a friend might be in trouble. I'm getting involved."

She hooked one bare heel up on the seat of her chair.

"You need any help?"

"A bit, and I wouldn't bother you, but some rather bad players appear to be in Florence. They shouldn't be. This isn't their patch. D'you know of the White Scorpions?"

One of the gulls dive-bombed the flagstone balcony, a baleful eye on Daria's sunny yellow drink. "The old Yugoslavia?"

She was impressed. "Ten for ten. Serbia, to be precise. Paramilitary death squads during the Yugoslav civil war."

"They're in Florence?"

"Apparently." She closed her eyes to dredge up the details Diego had shared. "There's an engineer from Rome named Gabriella Incantada. She hired a friend of mine to protect something she invented. She was planning to sell this thing—don't know what it is, alas—at the Hotel Criterion in Florence. My friend said *Skorpjo* blokes started showing up."

"In Italy?"

Daria said, "Quite. And while I've no idea who Gabriella Incantada is, nor what she invented, my friend said it's military in nature. A weapon, he thinks. Possibly—"

The voice over the phone line said, "Avionics control suites. Interfaces for aircraft."

Daria grinned and sat lower, knee raised higher. "And you know that . . . ?"

"Because I looked it up while we were talking. Gabriella Incantada makes aviation control circuits."

"Splendid." She sipped the drink. Gianni Docetti appeared from his bedroom, wearing a towel low around his hips and a broad smile. His muscled body had about 5 percent body fat and maybe fifteen tattoos. He carried a rolled-up map. He laid it out on the table before her. It displayed the topography of northern Italy.

"Not so splendid. First, I'm no expert on Serb gangsters, but they're supposed to be a force in Central Europe. Florence isn't their turf. Second, I think they go in for the kidnap-and-ransom game, plus murder for hire, knocking over banks, drug trade, prostitution. But weapons-grade avionics?" He paused as if thinking. "Yikes."

"Indeed. As you say: Yikes."

Gianni picked up his own drink and swigged it. He ran a hand through his wild mane of sun-bleached hair and inhaled the salty sea air. He studied the map, one blunt finger tracing the straightaways and noting the wicked switchback hills.

John said, "Okay. Daria? I'm on this thing. Can I get back to you on this line?"

"No," she said, setting down her drink. "It's not my phone. And I'm helping a friend. That's all. Thought you should know that the White Scorpions are trading up. Do with this information as you will, John Broom."

"But I—"

"*Ciao.*" She hung up and set the mobile on the round glass-and-iron patio table.

Gianni bent at the waist, a hand on the back of her head, and kissed her deeply.

"Hmmm," he said, grinning. "*Mia Gatta.* You taste like lemons."

"Really." Daria whisked away his towel. "And what do you taste like today?"

Seven

The hidden basement level of the American Citadel Electronics R&D offsite facility had a simple layout: a conference room, a control room, and an observation lounge. The last two were set up like a movie theater with a projection room: people inside the control room looked out through a long, narrow window at the backs of the heads of the people in the observation room. A giant array of plasma screens occupied every square centimeter of the far wall. Todd Brevidge had once watched a NASCAR race on that wall of screens, shot from the perspective of a driver, and had almost puked. The system's vivid detail was unmatched.

The two potential buyers arrived first, followed by more honchos from Corporate. Everyone flew into the one-runway airfield to the north and west of the town, perched on the upper curve of the question mark–shaped Lake Pend Oreille.

The newcomers were escorted to the basement observation room of the American Citadel office. Neither of the guests asked why they had been spirited to the remotest realms of the contiguous forty-eight for this demonstration. They knew why.

The guests were easy to identify. One man, white; one woman, black.

He in his sixties; she in her late forties. Both held themselves ramrod straight, arms either at their sides or one fist wrapped around one wrist, behind the back. Tight haircuts. Stiff and formal. In real life the buyers would wear stars and bars on their clothing. The building in which they worked would have five sides, not four.

But during their stay at the American Citadel R&D offsite facility, the white man and the black woman would be called Mr. Smith and Miss Jones. No rank. No insignia. It was the only way to get these two top officials to venture into the American Citadel infrastructure. Just doing so violated half a dozen restrictions placed on the company by the U.S. State Department, the U.S. Department of Defense, and the U.S. Department of Commerce.

Six months earlier American Citadel technology had been discovered in the bunkers of soldiers in Sudan and Somalia. Six years before that, American Citadel technology had been used against Allied troops in Iraq.

The company had been saddled with massive and (in the minds of the brass) unfair trade restrictions ever since. A half-dozen federal criminal investigations were ongoing.

Which is why Mr. Smith and Miss Jones were flying in under the radar today.

Cyrus Acton, the tall, gaunt member of the Citadel board of directors, greeted the guests warmly.

Bryan Snow retired to the control room with two of his technicians who, in the parlance of American Citadel research and development, were called *pilots*. Together they ran through one last diagnostic check of all the systems.

Before the demonstration began, Mr. Acton took Todd Brevidge by the elbow and moved him aside. He winked conspiratorially. "There are those on the board who don't think you're ready, Todd. I am not one of them. I am your guy on the board. You know that. Right?"

"Absolutely, sir. I've always known that."

As always, the gaunt man overenunciated his words, as if he'd had a stroke or was mildly drunk and compensating. "Todd, the buyers today are different from most. Do you know why?"

"No, sir?"

Mr. Acton licked his very thin lips. "They have already said no thanks to our product and have placed orders with our competitor."

Todd nodded. Of course he knew that. They were swimming upstream with today's sales pitch, and nobody knew that better than Todd Brevidge!

"They want the competitor's product!" Mr. Acton hissed. "Todd. Today is our opportunity—you'll note the singular, yes? *Opportunity.* Today is our opportunity to turn them around. These idiotic sanctions, the wholly discredited criminal investigations. Today we can put all that behind us. Today we can show them that American Citadel makes the finest product on the planet and that their agreement with the competition is . . ."

Mr. Acton paused, leaned in, and spoke the holy curse. "*Bad for business.*"

Todd Brevidge said, "Believe me. After this demonstration they'll fall on their knees and beg for our product."

Mr. Acton gripped his elbow. The grip itself was incredibly weak.

"Make me proud, Todd."

"Yes, sir. You just wait."

Mr. Acton blinked down at him, nodded once, and joined the others in the observation room.

Todd Brevidge excused himself to the men's room.

Now seemed like an ideal time for a line of coke.

In the control room, one of the pilots checked to make sure all of the internal communications were off. He turned to Bryan Snow, who sat in the center chair. "Is Brevidge gonna have a heart attack or what? Brown noser looks ready to barf."

Bryan Snow adjusted his seat. It was designed more or less like the captain's chair on the *Star Trek* series. Before him were flat-screen monitors spread out in a 200-degree semicircle. Beyond the screens were the workstations for Snow's two in-house pilots. Snow adjusted his hipster-framed glasses and began scanning his monitors. He had three keyboards within reach, like a guy playing a synthesizer.

He slid on a headset that had a voice wand attached and punched in the number that he had marked *Truck* on his console. "Ah, Home Team here. You reading me, Away Team?"

After a one-second pause, a voice came back over the line. "Away Team. Five by five. We good to go for the demo?"

The voice was crystal clear. Remarkable, since it came from the cab of a truck-and-trailer rig parked in a rest stop eight thousand miles to the east.

"The demonstration is a go. Stand by for prep."

Snow disconnected the line and adjusted his black plastic eyeglasses. He turned to his two in-house pilots. "Let's see if we can't give Brevidge a ride he'll remember. Optics?"

One of his pilots said, "Optics read good."

"Audio?"

"Audio nominal."

"Avionics?"

"Green across the board."

"Comms with Away Team are good," he informed his guys.

The Away Team sat in the cab of a truck-and-trailer rig parked at a rest stop. They were thousands of miles from Sandpoint, Idaho. They, too, were called pilots. The gig allowed the two pilots to be airborne without ever leaving the ground. Instead of scratchy long johns and five-point safety harnesses that dug into their crotches, the pilots flew their aircraft while wearing jeans and polo shirts and listening to Aerosmith on the CD player.

For natural-born flyboys, the American Citadel gig was sweet.

Three more members of the American Citadel inner circle had joined those in the observation lounge, along with Cyrus Acton and Mr. Smith and Miss Jones.

Todd Brevidge waited in the corridor and steeled himself, pumped his fist in the air twice for confidence, straightened his tie and his cuffs, then strode into the low-ceilinged room. Through the observation window leading to the control room, his chief engineer, Snow, gave him the thumbs-up.

Brevidge held a Nextel walkie phone, keyed to the control room. "We're good in here," he said quietly, then turned to the newcomers. "Folks?"

He waved to the high-definition plasma wall, getting his P. T. Barnum on. The entire western wall of the observation lounge lit up with dozens of screens stretching from floor to ceiling, and from wall to wall. Each screen could present a different image. But now they were slaved, offering one gigantic, panoramic view of a distinctly European city, complete with a massive dome and ornate tower of green and pink and white.

Todd Brevidge turned to the buyers and the brass. "Folks? Welcome to Florence, Italy."

Eight

Italy

Daria packed all of her belongings into a surplus army duffel bag and hiked to Santa Margherita Ligure, the nearest train station to Caladri.

Her belongings consisted of shorts and tees and some raggedy underthings, plus toiletries and a used paperback. Aging sneakers. Two bikini tops and two bottoms, all mismatched. The black kidskin wrist gloves with the tiny gold zippers along the palm. Plus a steel straight razor, circa 1920, with a hollow steel handle stamped with the word *Savila*. Daria had modified the hinge of the cutthroat razor so it would lock open. Deployed, it gave her almost eight additional inches of lethal reach.

Everyone has their own definition of travel essentials.

She planned to switch trains at Pisa. About thirty kilometers outside of town, she realized she had the six-seat train car to herself because she looked like an unkempt wild child in her ratty attire and densely packed musculature. Priority number one when she got to Florence would be to purchase some girl clothes.

Daria had plenty of money for shopping. She had squirreled away a couple hundred thousand in dollars and euros at banks throughout the world. Each was under a different false name, the IDs provided by a grateful Estonian gangster who had owed her big-time. During Daria's exile in Caladri, she had occasionally hitchhiked to Genoa to use a random ATM to make sure her accounts were safe.

That winter's unfortunate imbroglio had resulted in Daria crossing swords with the United States Central Intelligence Agency, the Israeli Defense Forces, French intelligence, and Italian law enforcement. Plus a shadowy, pro-Israel cabal that, a very long time ago, had saved Daria's life and childhood, and had given her the closest thing she would ever have to a family.

These things happen, she realized. One minute you're living in Los Angeles, minding your own business and wearing Gucci. The next, you're smashing an international conspiracy to kill thousands, your "wardrobe" can fit in a duffel bag, and you've become the Typhoid Mary of Western intelligence.

Comme ci, comme ça.

Repairing her reputation had to become Daria's top priority.

Right after buying girl clothes.

The woman who called herself Major Arcana hired caterers to drive out to the rented Tuscan villa and to set up coffee and pastries and fresh fruit and juices. All for her team. She firmly believed that breakfast was the most important meal of the day. She also believed that a good leader instilled a sense of well-being and togetherness within her team.

It's the little touches. Like a thoughtful breakfast.

The setting was an olive farm two kilometers outside Florence, in the gently rolling hills overlooking the Arno River. The farmhouse was only one story and rambling. Wings had been added haphazardly over eighty years.

The team consisted of former soldiers. Most were Serbs, but the crew included several men from countries previously associated with the Soviet Union. None of them currently served any nation's military. Most of them had been dishonorably discharged. Most had served time in prison.

The blonde was not a member of the White Scorpions but had convinced its financiers and hidden power brokers that their cause was hers.

The *Skorpjo* soldiers queued up for the food and coffee, then picked web-and-tube deck chairs under umbrellas. The blonde waited until they had tucked into their food before getting down to business. She wore shockingly white trousers and a fitted white, double-breasted suit with no blouse beneath, stilettos, and no jewelry. Her hair was platinum and her skin very pale and unblemished. Her eyes were so light blue as to resemble quicksilver in the Tuscan sunshine. She was tall and languid and cool.

She stepped out onto the patio, and all eyes turned to her. She spoke fluent Serbian with a city accent. "It's time to tell you about our target. Here are the basic facts: An Italian aerospace designer, Dr. Gabriella Incantada, has created a device. She is unveiling a prototype of the device today to some backers. It's happening down there."

She pointed to the oatmeal walls and terra-cotta roofs of Florence, sprawled out on the valley floor like a mediaeval tapestry.

"Dr. Incantada hopes to sell the device to any of a dozen governments around the world. I have blueprints of the venue. One of our teams shot an estimated forty-five hours of video: day, night, morning, afternoon, weekdays, and weekends. That team has distilled the images into the data we will need for the job.

"We have unimpaired access to the communications frequencies used by the Florentine police. We have their computers. Some of the potential buyers have hired their own private bodyguards. We have access to their communications and protocols, too."

This was the first time that all the individual teams had met. The blonde liked to keep her chess pieces apart during the early phases of any campaign. She turned now to one of the tables and asked a team about handling Florentine police. A couple of clever diversions were planned to keep the patrol cars away from the real target.

She asked another table about transit plans, after the mission. Every contingency was covered.

"We should expect some opposition. Mr. Kostic? How went your interview with the American?"

Kostic and Lazarevic had been sitting at their own table chain-smoking and leaving the butts in their drained coffee cups. Kostic sat forward and fiercely stubbed out his Syrian Alhamra cigarette; cheap to buy but so poorly rolled they tend to dissolve as they are smoked. As usual, Kostic's polo shirt was dusted in ash.

"We talked to the American. Nothing we cannot handle."

The smiling blonde studied him a moment. She didn't move: her smile didn't falter; her eyes didn't narrow. But the air pressure on the patio seemed to change. A couple of soldiers glanced at the sky to see if the weather was turning.

She kept her eyes on Kostic but turned her head to take in the other tables. "The American talked?"

Kostic lit another Alhamra from the dwindling pack. "You were right. The Mexican and the American were hired to protect this Incantada woman. The American is out of the way. He said the Mexican likely will go get help. Guzman said that means an Israeli woman, a gunrunner and soldier. Whenever Diego's in trouble, that's who he turns to."

The blonde tilted her head. "And is this gunrunner and soldier by any chance named Gibron?"

The Serb hitters exchanged surprised glances. "That's her name, yes. You know her?"

Major Arcana laughed, exposing her canine teeth. "Not officially, no. But we've traveled in the same circles. Her reputation is . . . the word *impressive* doesn't do it justice. If she's helping the Mexican, well, this whole thing just got a bit more fun."

Lazarevic said nothing. He never did. Kostic picked loose tobacco off his tongue and said, "Israeli is dangerous? Worth attention?"

The blonde bit her lower lip. "Yes. She's dangerous and worthy of our attention. But I think we stick to our plan. If she chooses to get involved . . . well . . ." The blonde amped up her smile. "Cool!"

Diego met Daria at the squat, utilitarian, and ever-bustling Santa Maria Novella train depot in Florence. A steady stream of people flowed through the station. The flow vectored away from Diego the same way leaves in a river divert around a half-submerged boulder. He wasn't large, and he didn't glower or threaten. People just avoided him.

Daria, in sneaks, cutoffs, and a ratty T-shirt, threw her duffel over one shoulder and kissed him on the cheek. "*Buon giorno.*"

His head bobbed in a subtle nod. "Hey."

"First, find me a clothing store. Then get me a gelato. Then tell me about Gabriella Incantada and the thing she invented."

Daria knew Diego had an old-fashioned sense of propriety. She likely had much more money at her command than he did, but she knew he'd insist on paying, because it was his gig. She chose the Spanish retailer Zara, because the clothes were inexpensive but looked posh, and because Diego wouldn't know the difference. She found a short, sleeveless sundress in bright daisy yellow and white and black patent sandals with ankle straps. She picked out some panties. In the dressing cubicle she did her hair in a French braid and slid on a pair of expensive, designer sunglasses she'd nicked from Signora Docetti the Current.

She applied enough makeup to cover the cut under her eye. That, plus sundry bruises here and there.

Out on the bustling Via Lambertesca, she let Diego buy her a sturdy but tiny black leather backpack, engraved with the fleur de lis sigil of Florence. The bag was large enough for a wallet, a lipstick, and the cutthroat Spanish razor. Just the basics for a day on the town.

Around them, Florence zipped along at a frenetic pace. Tourists flowed like storm-swept creeks, running over their banks and splashing into museums and shops and restaurants. The lanes were tight and only rarely intersected at right angles. African refugees hawked bright, cheap tchotchkes and buskers performed under gaily painted awnings, occupying the exact same spots their kind had for centuries.

Daria linked arms with the slight man in the cowboy hat and aged boots. "So, what's the play?"

"Supposed to meet Vince. He's not at the hotel room. His shit's still there."

"And you checked the local bordellos and drunk tank?" Daria didn't think much of Vince Guzman, and she saw no reason to hide it.

Diego pulled a pack of Camels from his back pocket, plus an old steel lighter. "Yeah. No sign. But the guys with the white scorpion tatts are all over the place."

Daria mulled that. "Show me the engineer's hotel."

The meeting was set for the Hotel Criterion de Medici, a boutique establishment carved into the hollowed-out, historic shell of an ancillary building adjacent to the sprawling, green Palazzo Pitti. A New Zealand hotel conglomerate had purchased the building and transformed it with enough coaxial cable, Wi-Fi, and blade servers to run a small offshore bank. But the edifice remained undisturbed and elegant, and the hotel's nine large en suite rooms and five-star kitchen provided old-world elegance and style.

It also was out of the way, down a twisted alley to the south of the Ponte Vecchio, the famed pedestrian bridge with its hobbit-sized jewelry hutches and maddening throngs of tourists. You'd never stumble on it by accident.

The owners of the Criterion de Medici had decided the economic doldrums were coming to an end and it was time to expand. The New Zealand conglomerate bought a three-story building adjacent to the hotel. It, too, had been an outbuilding for the old Pitti Palace, part of the livery and stables for the royal court. The place was old and unsafe. Interior work had begun and the face of the building had been surgically removed, exposing the rooms within. The entire façade was covered in a kind of cheesecloth, a square slate-gray shroud, three stories tall, that blocked off the potentially dangerous construction from guests entering and leaving the Criterion.

The result was to create one beautifully restored, seventeenth-century façade adjacent to a grim and grimy scrim, making the old livery building look like the Ghost of Architecture Past.

It also made for half a dozen extremely easy routes into and out of the upscale hotel, all of which bypassed the lobby.

Daria wanted a gelato and Diego bought. He got himself a coffee to go, American style. This was something new for Italy, Daria noted.

Even two years ago one would never have seen a lidded coffee cup with a cardboard sleeve. She decided she wouldn't get violent about it until a Starbucks popped up in Venice's Piazza San Marco.

Diego waved the cup forward and to their right. "Place is just over the bridge. Near the palace."

Daria took a long lick of *stracciatella* and her eyes fluttered in near-sexual bliss. "Near the palace? Risky," she said. "City police, state police, and private security from the national registry of historic places."

Diego nodded.

Daria reached into the tiny backpack over her left shoulder and withdrew a sheet of printer paper that she had folded twice.

"I looked up your Hotel Criterion, last night. Posh. Not many rooms."

They were about a third of the way over the ancient Ponte Vecchio. Normally going was tough across the bridge, which was more narrow than the streets on either end. People parted naturally to give the Mexican his space. Daria found it easy going by drifting in Diego's wake, riding his fear factor.

A portable wooden stage had been set up, off near the edge of the bridge, for street buskers. In this case, a man in a ratty Uncle Sam costume and three girls in red, white, and blue. Uncle Sam held out a top hat for donations.

"*My country 'tis of thee,*" the girls sang sweetly. They wore pigtails. They sounded like Americans. Most of those donating coins looked like Americans, too. "*Sweet land of liberty . . . !*"

Daria had stopped walking. She watched them.

Diego sipped his coffee, his eyes shaded by the hat. "A year ago, you were living in the U.S. You looked happy."

"I don't much want to talk about that."

He nodded.

Daria snapped herself out of her reverie. "Now I'll have that song stuck in my head. Lovely."

"Hotel's just ahead." He deftly changed topic, and Daria wrapped her arm in his.

"While I was living in the States, I had a side business as a translator. I stayed at a dozen boutique hotels like this. They're pretty much of a kind. I can find my way around inside all right."

Diego let it drop. "Guzman and me dogged this engineer for five days. Between here and an industrial plant out near San Jacopo."

Daria licked ice cream off her knuckle. "East of here on the Arno."

"Yeah. They moved between San Jacopo and the Hotel Criterion. Made the same trip every day. In a Hyundai."

Daria looked startled. "Good lord. Neither fast nor armored. Terrible transport."

Diego motioned toward the sea of bobbing heads before them. "Engineer's old. Walks with a cane."

Daria absorbed that. "The Serbs could have snagged this Gabriella Incantada anywhere between San Jacopo and the hotel. Anywhere along the SS67, really." She had a basic familiarity with the highways that feed into most northern Italian cities. "Meaning the engineer isn't the only target."

Diego said, "Nope," and tossed the lidded cup into an iron garbage can filled to more than overflowing. "Something they want at the hotel, too."

"When do you expect *Skorpjo* to hit?"

"This afternoon. Rental on the Hyundai expires tomorrow."

Daria would have liked more time for surveillance. "Then let's see what there is to see. Shall we?"

Thirty paces behind them, a Serb soldier in a muscle shirt, hair slicked back, watched the two of them pass and took pains to ignore them.

When they were out of earshot he spoke into a microphone worked into the leather bracelet attached to his wrist.

"Got the Mexican. He's with a chick: five-six, black hair. Hot. This Daria of yours?"

His earpiece crackled. Major Arcana said, "Yes. My Daria."

Nine

Daria decided to do a solo reconnaissance of the Hotel Criterion de Medici. If the Serbs had taken Guzman, then they would know about Diego. The Mexican held himself as taut as razor wire. He didn't exactly melt into crowds.

They stopped at a new hotel—one Diego hadn't used before—rented two rooms and stored Daria's duffel and her shopping bags. Next they hit an electronics shop and bought two cheap mobile phones with prepaid plans and plugged into each other's speed dial. "If Guzman's watching, he'll see me and know the game is rigged. We'll meet you back here, or I'll call."

Diego nodded. He didn't argue. She kissed his gouged cheek. "Be good."

Daria located the alley. With no big-name retail outlets and no museums down there, the going was much less crowded. Daria slipped into a bookstore and emerged moments later with a tourist's map of Florence. She slid the stolen pair of sunglasses over her raven-black eyes. Leaving the crowds behind, she held the map up to partially obscure her face and walked cautiously into the alley.

The buildings facing the alley were uniformly three stories tall, and the alley itself was narrow and curved in an S-shape. It was impossible to get a good angle on the hotel because of the tightness of the quarters. There was room for precisely one car in front of the hotel's revolving doors, and a uniformed youth stood at attention, ready to move any guest's vehicle to a valet parking garage.

The building directly to the left of the hotel—as you faced it—was under renovation. The façade was covered in a huge swatch of porous gray cloth that billowed slowly and rhythmically, with the effect of making the mummified building appear to be breathing.

A van parked half a block from the derelict building bore tinted windows and the logo of a painting company. Daria paused as she passed the van. She tucked the map under her arm, leaned one hand on the side of the van, and raised one foot to fiddle with her ankle strap.

Men waited inside the van. They were Americans. Former CIA operatives Owen Cain Thorson, Derrick Saito, and Jake Kenner. Kenner was at the wheel, with Thorson in the shotgun position. Saito sat in back, manning the camera monitors.

Thorson willed himself to sit still. Sweat beaded on his brow. The windows were darkly tinted. The van was equipped with a tall, narrow side mirror, slightly wider at the top than the bottom and shaped more or less like a standing coffin. A small, round, convex second mirror had been adhered to the bottom of the mirror.

Kenner leaned forward to see around Thorson's torso. "Jesus! That's her!" he whispered.

He eased slowly back, praying the Gibron woman wouldn't feel the vibration as she leaned against their van. He turned his head to Saito in the back. "Don't fuckin' move, dude. She's touching the van!"

Daria Gibron was reflected in the coffin-shaped mirror. Thorson knew her. He felt he knew her better than any soul alive. He had seen her that last November in New York. Also in Milan. And a thousand times in his nightmares. He had studied her photo at least once per day.

All during his quick, quiet, and dishonorable removal from the ranks of the Central Intelligence Agency, Thorson had studied the photos daily. At home he'd glued a photo of her on the ceiling, over the bench where he pressed weights. He looked up into her obsidian eyes as he counted off reps.

Today she wore her hair tightly back and braided. She wore very dark sunglasses. She looked more tanned than before, and more fit. The muscles beneath her bare shoulders looked as solid as the meat of a walnut.

Thorson's hand shook, in tiny, involuntary spasms. He was entirely unaware of it.

Daria Gibron leaned one hand on the side the van, bent one knee, and raised her foot behind her. She adjusted the ankle strap of her sandal.

Kenner hardly breathed. "Too many eyes on the street, man. Would love to cap her ass, but not here." He licked his suddenly dry lips.

Thorson's eye flickered to the round, convex mirror at the bottom of the coffin-shaped mirror. Daria looked distorted and mutated, her head and legs tiny, her chest and shoulders comically wide. She looked monstrous. Like the images in his nightmares.

"We don't cap her out here on the street. Right, man?"

Thorson stared at the mirror.

"Yo. Owen?"

Daria set her foot back on the pavement. She removed her hand from the side of the van. She straightened her sexy little dress and walked on. They could watch her through the windshield now. Other pedestrians hustled by. A hummingbird flitted into view and disappeared.

Kenner exhaled. "That was fucking intense!"

He laughed.

He glanced at Thorson. "We're not. Right? Not capping this bitch, here 'n' now?"

Thorson realized his friend was speaking. He blinked sweat from his eyes. His right hand cramped. "What?"

"Gibron. We're not doing her in broad daylight. Right?"

Thorson nodded. "Of course."

"Then . . . you won't need that, man."

Confused, Thorson frowned. Kenner nodded downward.

Thorson realized he had drawn his Glock. His finger was not indexed safely along the side of the weapon. It was tight, flush, against the trigger.

"No," he said, and slid the weapon into his holster. "Of course not."

Ten

The last committee meeting on the Hill ended at 9:00 P.M. Tuesday. John Broom asked for a quick meeting with the senator following that.

Senator Singer Cavanaugh escorted John and Chief of Staff Calvin Pope into his cluttered office on the top floor of the Dirksen Senate Office Building, one of the three grand sisters along Constitution Avenue, along with the Hart and Russell office buildings.

Cavanaugh looked like he fit in the ornate building. He had turned seventy and stood six foot six. He was thin and exceedingly Southern, with a mop of white hair and bushy eyebrows, a hawklike nose, piercing blue eyes, and a fondness for seersucker suits and black bow ties. He'd had a mild stroke the summer before and walked with a cane. The cane was wooden, a little too short and slightly bowed.

Singer limped into his office. It was going on hour number fourteen for that particular day, which was *not* a particular day.

Calvin, a longtime political insider in Washington, had opposed this impromptu meeting. In fact, he had said no when John first requested it and was more than a little annoyed when John took his request up with the highest authority in the land—Miss Clara Beauchamp, Singer's long-suffering secretary.

During her many decades of service to Singer Cavanaugh, Miss Clara had been his Negro secretary, and his colored secretary, and his black secretary, and his African American secretary. She herself had eschewed these labels; she was simply the person you needed to respect if you hoped to see the senator.

Over the years, a few people in Washington had disrespected Miss Clara. None of them currently worked in Washington. Or ever would again.

The three men gathered around Singer's antique oak desk, which was piled so high with documents that a person was at risk of injury in an avalanche. Singer poured each man a finger full of bourbon without asking what they wanted, then eased his aching, scarecrow body into his old slat-back chair.

Calvin said, "Better be good, John. We've got a hearing first thing tomorrow on military base closings. And the California delegation is loaded for bear."

John understood the art of playing nice. "Thanks, Cal. I appreciate this."

He turned to the older man. He took a breath, leaned forward, elbows on his knees. He had a fine needle to thread here, and he knew it.

"Senator, I have a source who confirms that a violent paramilitary and criminal organization that operates in Central Europe has extended its reach into Italy. Florence, to be exact. And that this group has an interest in stealing military technology."

Singer Cavanaugh sipped from his heavy-bottomed glass but otherwise did not react. Calvin Pope rolled his eyes and began to interrupt, but John had anticipated that and cut him off with a smile and a nod.

"I know what you're about to say, Cal. Eastern Bloc mafia types moving into Western Europe is old news. Happens all the time. And you're completely correct."

That wasn't what Calvin had been about to say, but the transition, and the smiling compliment, caught him off guard.

John turned back to the senator. "There are four pertinent facts that take this out of the ordinary, sir. First, this gang, the White Scorpions of Serbia, isn't just a bunch of bank robbers and drug lords. They're politically motivated. They were a Serbian military unit during the breakup of Yugoslavia in the nineties, and they remain politically and ethnically motivated today."

Calvin inhaled to jump in, but John pretended not to notice.

"Second: my source tells me the White Scorpions, or *Skorpjo*, have targeted an Italian weapons manufacturer, a Gabriella Incantada. Her firm is small, but they've provided some key avionics technology for fighter aircraft used by Italy, France, Spain, and Germany. My source doesn't know what *Skorpjo* has targeted to steal, but I'm certain it isn't something we want on the black market of Eastern Europe. Third: During the breakup of Yugoslavia the White Scorpions were part and parcel of the ethnic cleansing of places like Sarajevo and the Muslim enclave of Srebrenica. These guys were complicit in genocide, then faded into the woodwork before the war crime tribunals at The Hague could get started. These are not people we want stealing military tech in Western Europe."

Calvin leaped in this time. "Fine! Good, John. So a simple call to Interpol to alert them, and it's out of our hands. Right? We cc State, and probably the CIA, just to stay on the safe side. There we are. Meeting adjourned."

Singer Cavanaugh swirled the remaining bourbon in his glass. "And the fourth thing?"

Calvin looked up. "Sir?"

"John said there were four things."

John stayed bent forward, elbows on his knees, eyes locked on those of the wily Southern gentleman. "Fourth: My source is pristine. Absolutely the best. But we cannot inform Interpol. We cannot inform State. And we definitely cannot inform the CIA. Not unless we want this thing to go way south, way quick."

Calvin groaned and ran both hands through his thinning, ginger hair. "Oh, come on! Either the source is good or he's not, John! Either way, we've got bigger fish to fry."

Singer set down his glass on the few square inches of bare space on his burdened desk. "Calvin, are we ready for the base closure folks tomorrow?"

Calvin thumped his fist on the side of the desk for emphasis. Several piles of reports wobbled. "Yes! We have initial reports from all parties. Clara will have talking points in your take-home folder. We're ready to go. I want to liaise with the Congressional Black Caucus in the morning, see where they're leaning vis-à-vis jobs. But otherwise we're good to go."

Singer nodded and made a vaguely pianolike flourish with his long fingers. "Fine, fine. Thank you. Gentlemen? Let's call it a night. See you at six. John: talk to you a second?"

Calvin hustled around the office, gathering documents, pleased to have fulfilled his role as guardian of Singer Cavanaugh's time. He made a gun of his forefinger and thumb and shot John in the gut. "Hey. Let's find some time tomorrow morning to talk about team meetings. Again." He gave him a *chck* noise with his cheek, plus a wink. He hustled out of the office.

Singer Cavanaugh lumbered up, retrieved his much-abused Blackstone bag, and began stuffing it with folders.

John stood, too.

The senator said, "So. Daria Gibron. I'm figuring?"

Clara Beauchamp, early eighties and as plump as a beignet, had filled Singer's take-home folder with a fat stack of documents. John offered to carry it down. Singer had prided himself in taking the Metro home every night up until his stroke. Now he begrudgingly admitted the need for a driver. Singer being Singer, he'd turned down the various Cadillac options and opted to lease a Smart car. Then a Volt. Just to see how they worked.

John and the senator took the elevator to the ground floor of the Dirksen Senate Office Building. Singer said, "Talk to me, son."

"Daria Gibron is my friend, and she may be the bravest person I ever met. But she's mad, bad, and dangerous to know. Your office wants nothing whatsoever to do with her."

Singer grunted. "You don't chair the Joint Committee on Intelligence without hearing about things like that nonsense with your Ms. Gibron in Milan, son. Tell me your version."

"I trust her. But I did so well before Milan. She was involved in that Vermeer 111 crash in Oregon a couple of years ago. She saved lives, including federal agents. She was involved in an imbroglio in Montana last year. Again: She saved lives, including federal lives. Then the thing in Milan."

The elevator thumped to a halt. Singer Cavanaugh said, "Before Milan was Manhattan, son."

John blushed. He hated that the senator was that much smarter than himself. Hated it and loved it. "Yes, sir. It was amazing. Daria pretty much devastated a wide swath of the CIA's best thinkers. It was like watching the absolute best high school basketball team in the entire nation go up against Michael Jordan in his prime. She didn't beat us; she took us to school. At some point it went from excruciating to boring."

They walked through the almost deserted main hall of the Dirksen Building. A uniformed guard at the front desk nodded. Singer nodded to the guard. "How close is Wendy?"

The guard blinked in surprise. "Sir? My wife?"

"She's due?"

John watched—thunderstruck—as the guard reeled. "Ah . . . yes, sir. My wife's due tomorrow, sir. We're . . ."

Singer Cavanaugh patted the man on the shoulder. "Your first?"

The guard said, "Yes, sir."

Singer turned to John. "Man's here doing his duty. His wife's dilating. Swear to God, John, I wish the antigovernment people would spend one day—one day—watching real people do their jobs."

He turned to the guard. "Get some rest, son. I'm not joking. You're gonna need it."

He limped out the door, John in his wake.

"Daria?" the senator said over his shoulder.

John said, "I trust her. With my life. But I don't want her anywhere near you or your office. Her heart's in the right place, but she's a hand grenade in high heels."

Singer laughed. "Keep looking into this thing. Take whatever precautions you think are necessary. But you let me worry about the office, son."

Eleven

Florence

Daria and Diego had a couple of hours to kill before the engineer from Rome arrived. They went back to the new hotel. Daria knew from the past that Diego had rules about sleeping with business partners, so instead she took a quick nap, then joined him for cappuccinos and croissants, not far from the famed Ponte Vecchio and within sight of the tip of Giotto's famous tower.

He stirred a packet of brown sugar into his coffee. "Ideas?"

Daria watched the parade of tourists. "There was a painters' van in the alley outside the hotel. I leaned against it and used my thumbnail to pull back a temporary, magnetic sign."

Diego said "Surveillance."

"Hmm. Serbs or not, I can't say. But they were either there for your engineer or for you."

The Mexican placed his cowboy hat carefully on the small metal table, brim up. "We got a play?"

Daria cupped his hand on the table with her own. She smiled. "I'm a simple girl. I say we blunder in and see what happens."

Diego dug euros out of his jeans pocket. He nodded once. "Let's play."

● ● ●

Tuesday afternoon, the lobby of the Hotel Criterion de Medici was all but vacant. No guests checked in or out.

The lobby had black-and-white parquet floors and tastefully done murals of grape leaves and golden Tuscan fields. A largish aquarium burbled. A seating area included a low leather couch and a matching chair, a coffee table, a TV, and an array of tourism magazines artfully fanned out. The two people working the concierge desk wore navy blazers with golden emblems over their hearts.

A woman stood at the door, wearing a lavender sweater set, skirt, and hand-stitched Gucci pumps. She held a portfolio binder clutched to her chest in both arms. She was blond, very pale, with eyes so crystalline blue as to appear almost silver.

She tucked a strand of ice-blond hair behind her ear and spoke into the mic embedded into her wide, ornately carved bracelet. Her Serbian was flawless. "Time to intercept?"

Her man on the Ponte Vecchio responded. "Hyundai's nearing the bridge. Ten minutes to get through the crowd."

She turned and nodded to the two behind the concierge desk. They checked the Russian SR-2 Veresk semiautomatic weapons under the counter.

Half a block away, the white van with the magnetic logo waited. Owen Cain Thorson kept his eyes on the shrouded building to the left of the hotel. The buildings shared a wall.

"Through there," he said. Derrick Saito and Jake Kenner followed his eyes. "She'll get into the hotel through there."

"Yeah." Kenner chewed a massive wad of gum. "Looks good. We wait for her in there?"

"Saito and me. You stay with the van. Let us know if you see her out front."

"That's a big ten-four, man."

Owen Cain Thorson turned and looked intensely at his friends. He looked cool and calm, but a muscle near his jaw joint pulsed.

"Either of you get a chance to grab her at gunpoint, do it. She looks like she's bolting, it's okay to take her down."

Saito said, "Got it."

"It's all right to beat her. It's all right to wound her. But guys? I get some time with her. One on one. You'll get a chance to do . . . whatever you want to do. For as long as you want. But in the end, I kill her. Are we crystal?"

Sandpoint, Idaho

Todd Brevidge waved to the walls of screens, which showed a bustling, sunny streetscape. "Look at the detail. The filigree on the building. Here, see? And you'll notice . . ."

He pointed to the upper-left-hand corner screens of the full wall. "No loss of focus in the corners. The image is sharp throughout. The lens that allows for that? Developed for NASA. We have the patent on that."

The brass from American Citadel administration had picked plush black leather seats with attached drink tables. The buyers, Mr. Smith and Miss Jones, remained standing. Once Cyrus Acton realized that, he, too, stood to watch the demonstration.

Brevidge lifted his walkie phone to his lips. "Give me the van."

In the control room, Bryan Snow sat in a high-backed swivel chair with left-hand and right-hand trigger grips, and he adjusted both. The twin grips looked like the weapons grips on an American warplane. His two pilots manned their stations. Snow had been most specific in his designs for the control room. He could see every screen, plus both technicians, without hardly turning his head. He could touch all three elevated keyboards without reaching. Arrayed before him was an arc of plasma screens, each exactly ninety-four inches from his face.

Most were black. One was lit. It showed the same urban scene as the wall of screens in the observation room: a tight, curving alley and three-story buildings of old stone and aging brick.

Snow used the trigger grips as the image on his one lit screen shifted. He glanced through the narrow window into the observation theater. The wall-sized screen therein mimicked his screen.

• • •

Daria Gibron was no one's idea of a world-class strategist.

When walking into a blind situation, she sometimes liked to imagine the scene was a snow globe: best thing to do is turn it upside down and shake it a bit, see what changes.

She knew Diego's first priority would be finding Vince Guzman. Daria had no problem helping with that, but she had some passing understanding of *Skorpjo*, and she feared Guzman could be beyond rescuing. The White Scorpions hovered in the nebulous space between terrorism and organized crime—a Talibanized mafia. Daria had no love lost for their ilk. She didn't know what the bastards had targeted to steal, but she had a gut sense that Europe would be a little better off if they failed. And for the foreseeable future, Europe was her home.

She and Diego once again approached the famous bridge, which was packed shoulder to shoulder with pedestrians. They could just see the roof of the rented Hyundai, slowly approaching from behind them.

Daria wore her new sundress and gladiator flats that laced around her ankles. She hitched the little black backpack over one shoulder.

Diego said, "We do this, you want my gun?"

"The Colt? Please! I'd hurt my back just trying to lift that bazooka."

Diego absorbed that, his lips thinning. She took the man's arm.

"Don't worry. A gun will show up if I need one. They always do."

He shook his head and gave her an almost smile. It was more emotion that most people got from him.

Daria said, "Did you clock the thug on the bridge?"

"Muscle shirt, scorpion tatt?"

"Poor lad looked bored. Shall we make introductions?"

They split up without discussing it.

The guard's inner forearm tattoo was obvious from twenty paces away when he lifted his left hand and spoke into a wide metal wrist cuff. Daria surfed a tide of tourists, tacking closer to the watcher and, now, to the slowly creeping Hyundai with the electrical engineer and her team.

When the car was parallel with the Serb watcher, Daria skittered out of the crowd. She drove the sole of her strappy sandal into the man's knee, hyperextending the joint. The pain was excruciating. He crumbled, but Daria danced forward, into his path, partially catching him and keeping him vertical as she whipped off his wrist mic. From her new angle, she could see the man wore an earjack with a twisty wire that dove down his back into his muscle shirt.

Daria caught a glimpse of the woman driver of the Hyundai, who frowned at the flow of tourists around her vehicle.

Diego appeared as if by magic. He wrapped one fist around the man's neck and held him up and out like dry cleaning.

Daria made the universal *roll-down-your-window* sign, and the driver, unsure of what was going on, did so.

"Hallo." Daria spoke Italian and bent at the waist to made eye contact with the four people, including a very large and elderly woman in the front passenger seat.

The woman leaned forward and squinted through very thick glasses. "Mr. Diego? What is going on here?"

Diego shook the Serb and the man's head bobbed. "Bodyguarding."

Daria said, "My name is Daria Gibron. I'm Diego's friend. The fellow in his hands is a member of Serbian organized crime. A gang of his is awaiting you at the hotel."

The *Skorpjo* watcher gasped for breath. "Fucking . . . whore . . . !"

With no real effort, Diego shoved the apparently weightless man forward and down, bouncing his forehead off the Hyundai's bonnet. His eyes rolled up into his skull. Most tourists had noticed only the traffic congestion caused by the unmoving car. But some of them began to see the action. A murmur shot through the crowd.

Diego gave Daria a little apologetic shrug. "Don't know what he said. Sounded rude."

The elderly woman struggled to lean forward, her jowls quaking. "Mr. Diego, I don't understand. Who is this woman?"

Daria answered for him. "In the American parlance? The cavalry."

Gabriella Incantada turned stiffly to the men in back. "I knew something was wrong at the hotel. I knew it!"

"Dr. Incantada, more mafia types are waiting up ahead. They plan to steal your invention. Mind you: I've no idea what that is. But we think they have a friend of ours. Now, may I take sixty seconds to make a suggestion that could benefit us both?"

The Criterion is a small, intimate hotel. Daria knew that the thieves' plan had to include getting Gabriella Incantada and her team isolated from the hotel staff. That most likely meant the second-story conference room, which would be soundproofed for audiovisual presentations. During yesterday's walk-through of the alley, Daria had noted the livery building under renovation to the left of the hotel. She figured that to be the thieves' likely exit. That's how Daria would have pulled off this particular caper.

Her best bet for finding out what happened to Vince Guzman, and screwing with the White Scorpions, was to get the engineer and her creation bottled up inside the hotel and to grab someone higher up on the food chain than Mr. Muscle Shirt on the bridge—the man fairly screamed off-the-rack ruffian. Which meant convincing the Serbs that all was well until they could get into the hotel and up to the conference-room floor.

Daria outlined her plan to Gabriella Incantada, who was surprisingly accommodating. Daria took the driver's hat and blue blazer, which were oddly mismatched with the bright yellow sundress and sandals. She couldn't very well ask the driver to doff her trousers midway across the Ponte Vecchio. Although, to be honest, she had made racier suggestions in equally crowded venues. Just never in the middle of a fight.

Everyone got back into the car except the well-paid driver and the now unconscious hoodlum. Daria would have loved to keep the ear jack, but she didn't speak Serbian and couldn't see any advantage in keeping it. Both the bracelet and the power pack arced gracefully into the Arno River.

Daria got into the compact and drove to the hotel. The white van with the painters' logo was there again.

Inside the painters' van, Jake Kenner spoke into his earjack, the microphone dangling from a wire. "Engineer's here. No sign of Gibron."

He registered that the engineer's driver was a woman; he looked at her without truly seeing her.

On the second floor of the livery building, Owen Cain Thorson hit his comms. "She's coming. Eyes open."

Sandpoint, Idaho

Todd Brevidge stepped to the south-facing wall of the observation lounge and touched two large, square, flat drawers that resembled nothing so much as the sliding trays in a city morgue. He inserted a titanium key into a slot between the two drawers, turned it counterclockwise 90 degrees, then typed in a command on a recessed keypad.

The two drawers *snicked* open. Todd pulled them all the way out.

Inside one sat a sort of model airplane that resembled a hawk. It was almost a foot long, and had a two-foot wingspan.

Todd reached into the other drawer and pulled out a hummingbird.

"Folks?" He beamed around the underground observation room. "Meet Mercutio."

The whole thing fit on the palm of his hand and was more or less the size of a can of beer. It wasn't a hummingbird, of course. It looked a bit like the Apollo mission moon landers of the late 1960s, or maybe a shuttlecock, but one with four arms that stuck straight out an inch. At the end of each arm was a flat plastic doughnut, and inside each doughnut hole was a tiny plastic propeller.

"Our primary competition is building micro air vehicles, or MAVs. I'm told their small surveillance MAVs are the size of, oh, a large microwave oven. Here's ours. It's—simply put—better."

He studied the shuttlecock thing sitting on his palm. "Mercutio is our latest in surveillance drones. With a lithium/hybrid battery it can stay in the air for up to three hours. It makes as much noise as an electric toothbrush while consuming one-third the energy. It pivots through six degrees of freedom—up, down, right, left, forward, and backward— and it's too damn quick to see."

The senior buyer, the general working under the name Mr. Smith, wore a salt-and-pepper flattop and a bristly mustache. He stepped forward and peered into the second case. "And this MAV? The hawk?"

Todd grinned. "Ah. Hotspur. See, Mercutio, here"—he hefted the shuttlecock—"gives us eyes and ears. And we'll demonstrate that in a moment. But his big brother, there? Hotspur?"

Todd paused for dramatic effect. "Hotspur gives us talons."

Florence

The Hotel Criterion had only one parking place in front for guests checking in, or for taxis. Daria pulled up. Dr. Incantada made an elaborate show of getting her rheumatoid-ridden legs, then her elaborate cane, out of the car. Every eye was on her. Daria slipped out of the compact, keeping low, as if rummaging around the floorboards for something.

Dr. Incantada limped around the car to her and peered through her distorting lenses. "Are you sure about this?" she asked in Italian.

A hummingbird flitted nearby, held position a moment. No one from the Hyundai paid it any attention.

Daria said, "Yes. Trust me, Doctor."

The high-tech designer's entourage entered the hotel, Daria tucked into the middle between the two men, arms laden with metal boxes.

A beautiful blond woman in a twinset and perky ponytail greeted them. She held an embossed portfolio against her chest. She wore pearl earrings and an understated single strand of pearls around her neck. She wore a silver bracelet.

It was identical to the bracelet Daria had taken off the watcher on the bridge.

Daria made eye contact with the blonde.

Daria's hand snapped out and captured the blonde's wrist.

"May I?" she said, and with the deft flick of her thumbnail the clasp on the comms bracelet popped open, and the bracelet tumbled to the floor.

The blonde didn't look startled or shocked. She didn't gasp or back up. She didn't complain or argue. She didn't feign ignorance or innocence. She smiled at Daria and nodded approval.

"Practiced that with garter belts, have you?"

The blonde tried to shove her leather portfolio into Daria's face. Daria easily blocked the useless blow with her left forearm and stepped into the paltry attack, right forearm rising, aiming for the blonde's ear. A stunning blow, one that combines pain with a momentary failure of the inner ear and the body's gyroscope.

The blonde refused to play along.

Daria swung her elbow and missed.

A bit late, she realized the leather portfolio had been a feint. Daria had blocked it and stepped into the fight. The blonde pivoted to her right. Daria pivoted to her left. It was as if the women were dancing around a maypole.

The blonde grabbed the lapels of the driver's jacket and pulled her in. She extended one leg, hip-checked Daria, and sent her spinning to the floor.

Daria hadn't seen the judo throw coming. Her momentum had driven her in, toward the opponent. The blonde had used her momentum against her.

Someone's elbow did crack into someone's ear. But it wasn't Daria's elbow and it wasn't the blonde's ear.

And Daria lay on the carpet of the hotel lobby, out like a light.

Sandpoint, Idaho

"This is all happening in real time," Todd Brevidge assured the buyers. Cyrus Acton and the rest of the brass from Corporate stayed in the background, enjoying the show, but less awed by it; they'd seen the beta test runs.

"Now. Watch this." Brevidge raised his walkie phone and spoke to the control room. "Audio, dude."

A computer-generated rectangle appeared atop the video feed from Italy. The rectangle was long and low and bisected by a horizontal hairline.

The image itself zoomed from the white van to a Hyundai discharging four people: two men in ill-fitting, cheap suits, an older woman unfolding an aluminum cane, and a driver.

The older woman, jowly and all but disguised by gigantic glasses, spoke. "*Sei securo di questa?*"

The spiky sine wave of an audio signal appeared in the narrow computer-generated box. Words appeared, attached to the box, reading SUBJECT 1.

The audio box snapped up into the left-hand corner of the wall-wide screen, lining up with an unseen grid.

Another voice from the street—someone else from the Hyundai party—said, "*Sì. Fiducia, Dottore.*"

A new audio box popped up marked SUBJECT 2.

"There." Brevidge grinned. "With a couple of words, Mercutio can acquire the voice prints of up to two hundred and thirty different people. Now, if this old lady were to walk into a cocktail party with hundreds of people talking, laughing, music playing, whatever; Mercutio could pick her out in under ten seconds. From her voice print alone."

The guests nodded their approval.

"Once we have an audio print, there's no way anyone can shake us." He spoke into his handheld. "Translation?"

Words began appearing on the audio boxes, in a tight, conservative typeface.

INCANTADA: Are you sure about this?
SUBJECT 2: Yes. Trust me, Doctor.

Todd said, "And if that wasn't enough . . ." He spoke into his phone. "Face."

A computer-generated frame appeared around Dr. Incantada's face. The frame zoomed off to a far corner of the screen, taking an after-image of her face with it. The image flickered a few times, then locked in place.

"Facial recognition software," Brevidge said. "Should the lady choose not to speak again: Big deal. Mercutio never forgets a face."

Both buyers were reacting now, as they studied the face on the screen.

Brevidge had picked his moment well. "Oh, yeah. I see you've met our guest today. Dr. Gabriella Incantada. Folks: Our competition. I understand Uncle Sam has considered putting in an order for her invention, over ours."

Mr. Smith and Miss Jones looked none too happy about this development.

Todd Brevidge straightened his tie and gave them his best canary-fed grin. "This would be a good time to ask for the taxpayers' money back."

Florence

The livery building had been gutted but the floors were still standing. The accoutrements of construction workers were everywhere, from paint cans and long-handled paint rollers to a bolted-down table saw to fat pink rolls of insulation, still tightly ensconced in shrink wrap. The floors were covered in sweet-smelling sawdust and wood chips. A garbage chute was set up on a second floor: a glassless window covered by a wooden frame, outside of which hung a long plastic tube, three feet in diameter and looking like a giant vacuum cleaner hose. It dove down two floors to a paint-scarred orange Dumpster in the pedestrian alley behind the building.

On the ground floor, the rehabilitation project had left no obvious or easy means of egress from the livery building to the hotel. But several shared walls had been breached on the second and third floors.

Derrick Saito silently prowled the floor, glancing quickly out through the windows in back or through the billowing shroud up front.

Owen Cain Thorson settled down, sitting on a roll of pink insulation wrapped into tight logs. He gripped his Glock in his right hand. In his left he held a badly creased, sun-faded photo of Daria Gibron.

His hands shook.

The blonde working under the nom de guerre of Major Arcana had carefully orchestrated the theft of Gabriella Incantada's invention.

Controlling the concierge desk had been step one: They had allowed guests to check out but not check in. The Hotel Criterion was down to just one set of guests, occupying a third-floor suite.

The so-called major thought she had accounted for every contingency. She hadn't anticipated the engineer's driver pulling a stunt like that. From the way the black-haired beauty moved, she was well trained. Krav Maga, the Israeli martial arts form, the major thought.

Which meant the unconscious woman at her feet was Daria Gibron, friend of the Mexican.

The major blinked at the woman sprawled on the brown-and-gold miasmic carpet. Then grinned up at Dr. Incantada. "Cool! You made a new friend!"

The major spoke fluent Italian, and with a Roman accent not dissimilar to Gabriella Incantada's own.

"I require your case, please."

The Serb soldiers circled the concierge desk from the left and the right, both ratcheting their machine pistols solely for the shock value of that distinctive sound. Gabriella Incantada's two technicians flinched, blood draining from their faces.

Dr. Incantada peered up through her coke-bottle glasses at the strangely grinning blonde in the ponytail and cute little sweater set.

"Who are you?"

The blonde clicked her teeth. "A huge fan of your work, Gabby. Can I call you Gabby? The case, please."

Dr. Incantada studied her. She glanced at the strange Israeli woman at her feet. The engineer looked more annoyed than frightened. She looked down at her case. It was a classic doctor's bag, flat-bottomed, pebbled leather, with a single arced leather handle and twin straps over the top, to either side of the handle.

She considered her options.

They had agreed that Diego would stay outside and keep an eye on everyone. *Skorpjo* likely knew what Diego looked like. Daria could make the approach to the hotel more quietly on her own.

Diego scored a pair of binoculars from a tourist shop. He stepped into a restaurant and walked back to the men's room, then picked a lock to get upstairs and onto the roof. From there he could watch the Hotel Criterion and Daria's back.

He was watching her back now, all right. It lay unmoving on the lobby carpet, at the feet of Dr. Incantada. Diego couldn't tell from his angle if Daria was breathing.

He adjusted his cowboy hat, lipped a silent prayer to St. Jude, and reached under his denim shirt for his Colt .45.

Twelve

Sandpoint, Idaho

The Pentagon contingent stared at the computer-generated image of Gabriella Incantada. They realized that the timing of the American Citadel demonstration had been no coincidence. There was a reason they'd both been spirited into Canada, east across the continent, and then back into the United States, despite the very strict rules of the U.S. State Department regarding business dealings with American Citadel Electronics, LLC.

Todd Brevidge was enjoying the theatricality of the show. "Mercutio's optics have already been demonstrated. Now that we have Dr. Incantada's face on file, Mercutio could follow her anywhere."

Brevidge waited a second for the guests to absorb this.

"Its audio capability also has been demonstrated. Combine the face-recognition software with the voice-recognition software, and Mercutio becomes the ultimate bloodhound. We could follow Dr. Incantada into that huge crowd outside the cathedral, right now, this very second, and she'd have no possible hope of eluding us."

Mr. Smith and Miss Jones eyed each other.

Mr. Smith caught Brevidge's attention. When he spoke his voice was a guttural Southern drawl, a raspy blend of cigarettes and a career screaming at soldiers. "Dr. Incantada promises the same thing. And her price is a hell of a lot more reasonable."

Brevidge forced a laugh. "Well, sure. Cut-rate prices for cut-rate material. You get what you pay for. Our product is expensive. But what it delivers—our nation's safety, our enemies' heads on spits while our pilots sit in comfort, far from the enemy—is worth the price."

Miss Jones raised an eyebrow. "Dr. Incantada made much the same argument. But again, at two-thirds the price."

Brevidge was about to counter, but the man they were calling Mr. Smith cut in. "You're controlling the drone's movements from here?"

"Yes and no. Our chief engineer and his pilots, in the booth behind you, have given the Mercutio you see on this screen a task. He told it to study the automobiles and the people in that alley in Florence. We also have a truck-and-trailer parked just outside of Florence for the transportation and maintenance of the drones. The truck has two more pilots, who can control the drones as well. Either way: if this was Fallujah or downtown Tehran, you'd have birds in the air but pilots who are safe and sound."

The Pentagon brass seemed to approve.

Todd waved toward the screens. "For this mission, my chief engineer can override that task and zoom Mercutio number one into a specific target, like the white van, or a specific person, like the old broad with the cane."

Miss Jones stepped in. "'Mercutio number one'?"

"Ah!" Brevidge held up one finger, so pleased that someone had pounced on the line he'd laid out for them. "Did I forget to mention: this Mercutio doesn't fly alone."

He lifted the walkie phone. "Snow?"

And the wall-to-wall, floor-to-ceiling plasma screen split instantaneously, morphing from one huge Florentine image into eight images, four across, two deep. Each showed the alley or the architecture of the southern side of Florence, but from differing heights and differing angles.

"We didn't send one Mercutio for this demonstration. We sent eight. And the data stream from all eight merges at a dedicated satellite and bounces right back. Which means the voice-recog and face-recog data that one micro-drone has, all eight micro-drones have."

"Folks?" Brevidge patted down his silk tie and pivoted on the heel of his shoe. "I said Mercutio is a bloodhound. That's not quite accurate. It's a pack of hunting dogs."

Mr. Smith said, "Will we get a demonstration of Hotspur?"

Todd glanced at the American Citadel brass in the back of the room. "Well, not from Italy, no. While Mercutio is a surveillance suite, Hotspur is an aggressive weapons package. We can't exactly go blasting away in Florence. However, we have a demonstration range in an abandoned mine, about two hours south of Sandpoint, which we'll be switching to for a live demonstration in about thirty minutes."

Miss Jones said, "What sort of weapons package?"

"Depends on the configuration," Todd swiveled to her. "Guns or miniature guided missiles. Because of weight restrictions on the drones, we use only small-caliber weapons. But the bullets are incendiaries, and the missiles are our own design, which we'll show you when we switch to the demonstration range a little later this morning. The beauty of the Hotspur weapons suite is that we can configure the MAVs for whatever opposition we expect to face."

Cyrus Acton glowed, watching his protégé, Todd Brevidge, completely in his element.

Miss Jones nodded, eyes darting to the screen. "But you have a set of these Hotspur drones on scene? In Florence?"

"For demonstration purposes, yes. We wanted you to notice that the hummingbirds and the hawks are floating around over this very crowded city and nobody's paying any attention to them. They're just too small and too fast, and they were designed to be mistaken for actual birds.

"We'll show you the visuals from Hotspur's perspective, too. While Mercutio can hover like a helicopter, Hotspur swoops. I say that as a warning; with the high-def screens, it can be a little disorienting. For instance, you won't get an image as stable as this."

He spoke into his walkie. "Give us a close-up of the lobby, dude."

One of the Mercutio MAVs zoomed in on the front window of the

Hotel Criterion. Through the glass, they could see a cluster of people standing about.

From the back of the room, Cyrus Acton said, "Todd . . . ?"

"Ah. Yessir?"

Acton pointed over Brevidge's shoulder at the screen. "What's going on there? In the hotel?"

Todd turned. Through the plate-glass window of the hotel, he, the brass, and the buyers could see Dr. Incantada and her two assistant engineers. Standing opposite them were members of the hotel staff.

It took Todd a moment to realize that the engineer's driver lay on the floor. Unconscious or dead.

And that two of the hotel staff carried submachine guns with folding stocks and dual handles.

"Whoa," Todd said. "Whoa whoa whoa what the hell?"

Mr. Acton had surged forward, now standing between Todd and the buyers.

Todd lifted his walkie. "Snow, are you getting this?"

The voice came back quickly from the phone. "Sure am."

"What the . . . is this a robbery? Snow, get us audio."

A second later, and the people in the observation lounge began to hear electronically enhanced voices. Audio signatures popped up on one of the screens, logging the speakers as INCANTADA, DR. GABRIELLA and SPEAKER 3.

Speaker number three was the tall, pretty blond woman. She was speaking in Italian.

From the control room, one of Snow's pilots made an adjustment to the audio. As the blonde spoke, an English translation of her words appeared beneath the sine wave of her audio signature.

SPEAKER 3: I'm waiting.

INCANTADA: Who are you?

SPEAKER 3: For the sake of today's fun, I'm using the name Major Arcana. It's a joke, but don't feel bad if you don't get it. Now, my friends in Belgrade have need of some of your technology, Doctor . . .

Florence

Daria lay sprawled before the blonde's Gucci pumps. The peaked driver's cap lay on the floor, upside down. Daria's hair fanned out, obscuring her eyes, which were open. She was awake and listening to the conversation above her. She did not move.

The blonde calling herself Major Arcana turned to the elderly woman with the pebbled leather doctor's bag and three-footed cane. "My friends in Belgrade have need of some of your technology, Doctor."

Dr. Incantada's eyes grew large, magnified by her thick lenses. She gripped her steel case in the hand not holding her cane. She looked pugnacious.

Major Arcana bent at the waist and picked up the communications bracelet Daria had stripped off her wrist. "I've got two friends with me, and you've got two friends with you. The big difference is: my friends have submachine guns. And I've asked my friends to shoot your friends in the kneecaps should you be reluctant to cooperate."

The two engineers started to protest, but a glance from the woman's silvery blue eyes shut them up.

"May I have the case, please?" The major held out her hand. "Doctor?"

Gabriella Incantada paused a second, then handed over her doctor's bag.

The blonde took it from her. "Thank you. Now my sources say the command mechanism for this device is already in the hotel safe. And you have the combination?"

Incantada studied the younger woman. Jowls quivering, she recited the fourteen-digit alphanumeric code. Major Arcana didn't bother writing it down.

"Splendid! Dr. Incantada? Gentlemen? We are heading upstairs now. I have locked the front door and the telephones are disabled. I wish you to stay here for exactly twenty minutes. Can you do that? Twenty minutes. Then please feel free to holler all you wish."

She turned to the stairs, and her two Serb soldiers backed up, machine pistols locked on the engineer, her men, and the unmoving form at her feet.

Sandpoint, Idaho

Mr. Acton grabbed Todd by the shoulder and hissed. "We have to do something!"

Todd turned on the emaciated man. "Ah. Sure. I mean: Yeah. But . . . I don't know what we can do about it. This is happening in real time!"

The representatives from the Pentagon stood back and watched the interplay.

Acton leaned in closer. Brevidge could smell Aqua Velva. "It's one thing to convince Incantada's buyers that our product is better. But we cannot have her product out there, competing against us. Especially in Eastern Europe! You heard that woman! She mentioned Belgrade! That's the Balkans!"

"Sure. I know." Brevidge could see the two buyers watching it all. "But even if we tried to contact the Florence cops, I don't think we could stop this in time! It looks like Incantada's driver is already dead. Jesus, man, we gotta—"

"Think of something, Todd!"

The salesman's brain reeled. He turned again to study the screen. The mysterious blonde and her armed men were gone. Dr. Incantada's party stood, paralyzed, the woman driver lying on the floor.

Todd lifted his walkie. "Snow? Dude. You got any brilliant ideas, now'd be the time."

In the control room, Bryan Snow adjusted his voice wand first, then his Buddy Holly frames. "You know? I think maybe I have an idea."

Daria, her cheek against the carpet, watched the blonde and her soldiers hit the stairs.

She'd just had her ass kicked by a Barbie doll.

As soon as the opposition rounded the curved stairs, Daria sat up painfully. She hauled herself to her hands and knees. Dr. Gabriella Incantada and her engineers stood, stone-scared.

The engineer said, "Are you all right?"

Daria said, "No."

"Those people. They took my module."

Daria's ear was in flames and pain radiated from her skull, down her neck, to her back. Her vision blurred.

Think, bitch! Daria cursed herself. *Get on your goddam feet, Gibron! Move Move Move!*

She clamored clumsily to her feet. She almost toppled but managed to right herself.

Dr. Incantada said, "My module—"

"Is it dangerous?"

"I should think so, *signora*. There are three of them. They have guns."

Daria screwed her eyes shut and ground her teeth together. When she opened her eyes, the room had stopped spinning. "No," she hissed. "This module thing. Is it dangerous?"

The engineer shrugged her shoulders and her fleshy arms bobbed. "With the right technology. And the right knowledge. Yes."

Daria said, "My backpack?"

The doctor pointed to the pile of boxes. One of the technicians had been carrying it since Daria had shrugged into the driver's jacket. Daria scooped it up, unzipped it, and withdrew the cutthroat razor of Spanish steel. She doffed the jacket, let it unfurl around her sandals. She slung the backpack over her bare shoulder. "Stay here. If Diego comes, do as he says."

Gabriella Incantada said, "Where are you going? Are you just leaving us down here?"

Daria said, "Yes," and headed for the stairs. "Stay here. You'll be safe."

The major and the Serb soldiers sauntered confidently into the second-floor conference room of the Hotel Criterion. The room was simple, minimally adorned, the walls and ceiling and carpet a dull mushroom color. The room featured an array of audio and visual implementations designed for a state-of-the-art visual presentation. The room was outfitted with high-speed Wi-Fi and high-definition computer screens. The Criterion had become a favorite hotel for upper-level business executives, who wanted only the best for their presentations.

Major Arcana brushed aside a framed black-and-white photo of some Italianate architecture. Behind the frame was a wall safe.

She tapped in Gabriella Incantada's code. As she did, one of the soldiers moved to a wall and began pounding with the butt of his hand. Within seconds his thumping took on a hollow sound. He'd reached a hollow space behind the wallpaper.

The major reached into the safe and removed a device the size of an e-reader. She turned and set it down on a conference room table next to the maple-colored doctor's bag. She undid both buckled straps, on both sides of the handle, and opened the top of the bag. She removed a complicated electronic mechanism. She used a coaxial cable to connect the e-reader-sized device to the control circuits inside the attaché case.

She had retrieved her communication bracelet from the floor of the hotel lobby. She spoke into it now.

"We are go, this end."

Daria couldn't believe how badly the confrontation in the lobby had gone. True, she had been the one to tell Diego that she was out of practice. That she hadn't faced a real foe since contracting the Pegasus-B super flu that last November outside Paris. *I'm not one hundred percent*, she had told him.

Then the cute-as-a-button blonde with the perky ponytail stomped her like a bug.

Daria hadn't even gotten in a single blow.

Her head ached. *Good, you bitch. I'm glad your head hurts*, she groused. *Had it coming.*

At least she knew what she was up against now: No more surprises.

In the second-floor conference room, Major Arcana typed instructions on the keypad she'd removed from the stolen doctor's bag.

One of the Serb soldiers reversed his machine pistol and used the folding stock as a hatchet. He began hacking away the room's wallpaper, revealing a door-sized entry from the hotel conference room to the livery building beyond.

The other Serb guarded the conference room door. Nobody expected

Dr. Incantada or her people to show any bravery, but there was still one other party checked into the hotel.

The guard at the door watched his partner gouge a door in the far wall.

"Pssst!"

The guard heard a beckoning voice from the hallway and turned back.

The black-haired woman in the brief lemon dress swung at him, as if to slug him in the chin. The Serb stepped back out of her reach. The blow didn't even land.

He grinned and raised his machine pistol.

Or *tried* to raise his machine pistol. His arms refused to obey his brain. He paused, still grinning, and felt the earth tilt a little.

He looked down at his hands, and at the SR-2 Veresk.

His shirtfront was drenched in blood. More blood poured down. Apparently from his throat. How odd.

His legs buckled.

He dropped his auto, but it never hit the carpet. The dark woman knelt and plucked it out of the air.

In the conference room, the second Serbian thug hadn't seen who had injured his cohort. He tried firing a prolonged blast blindly out the door. The bullets tore the holy hell out of the far wall and the industrial carpet in the hallway.

"It's Gibron!" the blonde said, fingers flying over the keyboard and the command module. She produced a high-speed, male-to-male USB cord and connected the Incantada device to the conference room's computer tower.

Daria fired from the corridor into the conference room. She fired blindly, but on single-shot. She could *ping* Major Arcana and the Serb for an hour, pinning them down, as Florentine police responded to the sound of gunfire. The tactical advantage to a standoff lay completely with Daria.

Wrong weapon, the blonde said to herself. She savagely hit the last few keys on the keyboard, then spoke into her wrist cuff. "Transferring . . . now!"

．．．

In the control room in Sandpoint, Idaho, Bryan Snow heard a familiar voice coming from his earjack. He swallowed the shit-eating grin that tried to manifest itself. He hit a knuckle-buster combination of keys on his master control. A second later, both of his in-house pilots reacted as their monitors died.

In the Hotel Criterion conference room, Major Arcana stabbed the Enter button on the Incantada device.

In Florence, three hawks floated on the city's thermals, gracefully arcing over the southern half of the ancient city, the Arno and her bridges.

One of the three hawks broke its preprogrammed gyre and began descending toward a narrow alley.

The hawk was ceramic and plastic and glass and metal, but not much metal, at least on the outside. It was invisible to radar, which is calibrated for solid, metal things.

It turned out to be Hotspur.

A miniaturized version of a Hellfire missile screamed away from the first Hotspur drone. Relieved of a third of its mass, the mechanical hawk banked sharply and rose.

The missile smashed through the glass, into the lobby.

Whereas the Lockheed Martin Hellfire II weighs in at a tad over one hundred pounds and is sixty-four inches long, the American Citadel variation weighs less than ten pounds and runs only ten inches in length. The Hellfire employs high-explosive antitank technology that uses pressure—not heat—to punch through armor. The American Citadel missile relies on heat more than pressure. It also features an external blast fragmentation sleeve, which disintegrates on impact and vastly increases the carnage caused by an explosion.

The missile set the lobby on fire. The concierge desk ignited. The carpet ignited. The decorative chandeliers exploded. The wallpaper and the comfy couch and the aquarium and the big-screen TV and the magazine rack and the three engineers from Rome burst into flames.

Dr. Incantada was dead before she felt anything.

The swirling fireball, a tornado of flames and anger, ate up all the oxygen in the lobby and, seeking further fuel, spiraled up the curved stairs.

Sandpoint, Idaho

Todd Brevidge and Cyrus Acton watched the hotel lobby disintegrate, watched the charcoal-gray cloud billow from the ruined plate-glass window.

They realized they had seen the first-ever live field demonstration of their own weapon.

Brevidge shrieked. *"Jesus the fuck is that! Christ! Snow! We fired! We fired a missile! Holy shit! The fuck is happening?"*

He realized he hadn't lifted the walkie-talkie, though Snow likely had heard him through the observation room window.

He shouted into his hand-held. *"Snow! Do something!"*

Next door, in the control room, Bryan Snow bit back his grin. His two pilots had popped out of their chairs as if they had ejector seats.

"Wow, Todd." Snow tried to sound surprised. "Not sure what the heck just happened."

In the observation lounge, the Pentagon officials glared at the carnage on the screen.

The colonel, Miss Jones, initially thought she was watching a computer-generated illusion on the screens, part of the American Citadel sales pitch. She cracked a smile and shook her head at the salesmen's gall. Then she noticed that the general wasn't smiling.

The general, Mr. Smith, had seen his fair share of war and knew a missile strike when he saw one.

Florence

The walls in the second-story corridor shook and plaster rained down from the ceiling.

Daria was an Israeli. In her short life she had been in way, way too many buildings hit by mortar fire. She knew instantly what had happened.

What she didn't instantly understand is why her heart rate flashed upward into the danger zone. She felt cold sweat prickle her body; felt her long muscles go rigid with fright.

Images pinballed madly in her mind's eye. *Bombs, blood. Long pianist's fingers, reaching for her. Scrambling for her. Diggers above, screaming for help.*

Daria grit her teeth, eyes screwed shut. She tried to make fists and felt the Russian submachine gun in her grip. She'd forgotten she was holding it. She drew an odd comfort from its cool, slightly oily utilitarian solidness.

She hunkered low on the carpet, back hunched, arms up over her head. *Snap out of it!* she bellowed silently. This was hardly her first bombed-out building.

The flame tornado corkscrewed above her, seeking ever-higher floors.

The walls cracked, plaster disintegrating, and Daria felt the floor cant beneath her knees and felt the panic attack ebb.

In the conference room, Major Arcana had been braced for the explosion. She remained on her feet. She stuffed all the stolen mechanisms into the doctor's bag and rebuckled both top straps. She thrust her chin in the direction of the door her soldier had carved in the wallpaper.

"Let's go."

Thirteen

The Hotel Criterion de Medici died badly.

Flames leaped from the lobby. Shrapnel and bits of the building littered the street. One pedestrian caught fire, totally engulfed, arms pinwheeling, leaving afterimages of flames etched into the eyes of on-lookers.

A car outside the hotel had veered out of control and careened into a white van.

Diego dashed down from his rooftop vantage point after seeing Daria beaten in the fight. He'd missed her rising again and following the blonde and her men up the stairs. Now, out on the street, the plasma bubble of superheated air lifted Diego off his feet and threw him back six feet into the window of a pharmacy.

He lay amid the display shelves, safety glass pebbling all around him, and shook his head to clear the shock. He gaped as a roiling mushroom cloud of dense gray smoke billowed out of the alley.

As far as he could tell, the epicenter of the explosion came from the lobby—exactly where he'd last seen Daria Gibron.

In the livery building, Owen Cain Thorson and Derrick Saito were knocked off their feet behind the rolls of insulation.

Seconds later, Major Arcana and her Serbian soldier entered through a hole in the wall.

"Stand guard. Nobody steps through from the hotel. Understood?"

The Serb ratcheted the slide on his machine pistol.

The blonde marched across the second floor of the livery building. A weird, shimmering gray light leaked through the shroud that was the building's façade. She found a bolted-down table saw with upright, discus-shaped blades. She set down Incantada's pebbled leather bag and reopened it. She lifted out a tablet computer, the size of an e-reader, notched it against the doctor's bag at a forty-five degree angle. The screen included a pinhole camera.

Arcana typed in a set of commands. A second later, the screen lit up. It showed a bright, white room, equipped with comfy chairs and drinks tables. Seven people were present. In the foreground stood a dapper young man and an exceedingly gaunt gentlemen. Standing behind them was a white man in his sixties with a flattop and a black woman in her forties.

Arcana gave them her best smile. "Delegates from American Citadel, representatives from the Pentagon: Welcome to sunny Florence!"

Sandpoint, Idaho

Everyone froze: Todd Brevidge and Cyrus Acton in the foreground, Mr. Smith and Miss Jones behind them, the three other senior brass from American Citadel still seated in the leather chairs.

The blonde's lovely face took up nearly half of the full wall of screens. Miss Jones had a fleeting memory of the Wizard of Oz, addressing Dorothy and her companions.

"We are joined today by celebrities," the woman said. She spoke English, Americanized and Midwestern. "Our guests are General Howard Cathcart and Colonel Olivia Crace. Both U.S. Army, both attached to a Pentagon weapons procurement division. General Cathcart, Colonel Crace, care to say a few words?"

The Army officers stood rooted, aghast. When they saw the hotel lobby in Italy incinerated they thought they were observing a worst-case scenario. Hearing their names spoken out loud by the psychopath responsible for the slaughter made things much worse.

"General, Colonel, please understand the following: I have command of the Hotspur and Mercutio drones. I'll be giving you back control of them real soon. In the meantime, I'm recording your images, there in your supersecret hideout in Sandpoint, Idaho."

Everyone in the observation lounge reacted to this news.

"General Cathcart: Gabriella Incantada is dead. So are her chief engineers. I'd taken the liberty of emptying the Hotel Criterion before stealing this technology. But you need to know that one set of guests never got the message to leave. They were meeting Dr. Incantada here. They represent the Russian air force."

General Cathcart's fists clenched.

"Here's the deal: American technology just blew up a hotel in a NATO country, killing Italian scientists and Russian military attachés. It was yet another deplorable American drone strike, like the ones that have riled up world sentiment in Pakistan and Yemen and elsewhere. Only this time, it's in the heart of a major European tourist attraction."

General Cathcart surged forward. "What in God's name is going on here? Who the hell are you?"

"I'm the woman who has your facial recognition imprint and, thanks to that outburst, your voice print, sir. Linking you to a company that's facing some pretty stiff sanctions and criminal charges. Tsk. Not good, General. Not good."

Cathcart fairly vibrated with anger.

"Now, you're about to regain control of your systems in, say, thirty seconds. When you do, I want you to consider something. My friends and I have the voice and face data that link you to the deaths in Florence and to business dealings with American Citadel. I've already transferred this data for safekeeping. My friends and I wish you no ill will. You're free to go about being the World's Policeman and protecting Truth, Justice, and the American Way. Amen and God bless. However, there's a certain black-haired bitch who's messing up my operation. She, too, knows all about you guys. Her name is Daria Gibron and, General?

If you check with your buddies at the Central Intelligence Agency, you'll find her filed under Complete Pain in the Ass. Do what you will with her; the U.S. intelligence agency won't coming knocking on anybody's doors."

General Cathcart and Colonel Crace exchanged looks. Todd Brevidge and the brass of American Citadel were still in severe shock.

"Alrighty then!" the blonde beamed. "This is Major Arcana, signing off. Peace out."

She made the V sign with her fingers and disconnected the line.

Behind the Pentagon officials and the brass, in the control room, Bryan Snow again hit his combination of shift-command-option and three letters. As he did so, his pilots' workstations began to light up again.

Fourteen

Daria felt the floor ripple beneath her legs and the hotel groaned, a long, low, ominous sound that was as much felt in the sternum as heard.

Whatever that brief panic attack had been about, it had passed. Leaving Daria more annoyed than frightened.

She rose and dared a glance into the conference room. The man whose throat she'd sliced open still hadn't quite died; he lay, gasping, twitching, both hands around his throat, holding back the weakly pulsing streamers of blood.

A whacking great hole had been torn in the far wall. The building under construction lay that way. She stuffed the razor blade into her backpack, knelt, and grabbed the nearly dead mobster's Makarov. She had never held a Veresk submachine gun and didn't trust unfamiliar weapons. But she gathered the leather strap, letting the machine gun join her backpack over one shoulder.

The hole gouged into the wall looked inviting. The floor under Daria's sandals vibrated and smoke began billowing into the conference room.

She stayed down on one knee, left hand bracing her right, and pointed the .45 at the impromptu door. She squinted and fired two rounds through the wall to the left of the gaping hole, and two rounds to the right of the gaping hole.

Another machine pistol clattered to the ground and the second Serbian stumbled into view, holding a bloody hand against his belly.

He glared hatred back into the conference room and began to cough up blood. Daria put a fifth round through his sternum.

She rose fast and hit the hole in the wall just as the conference room ceiling began crashing down behind her.

The dank gray shroud over the livery building billowed like diseased lungs, stirring up dust devils on the second floor. Sawdust eddies undulated across the floor in long sinuous S-shapes like sand in the Sahara.

Daria knew the structure wasn't going to last much longer. It had been anchored on its left side by the Hotel Criterion, which was collapsing. The more stable but blast-gutted building would bring down its less stable neighbor.

Daria spotted the blonde running pell-mell across the livery building. Daria shouted, "That'll do!"

She planted her sandals and raised the Makarov pistol.

The blonde stopped running.

Daria shouted "Weapon down!"

The tall woman dropped her handgun.

Daria said, "The bag, too! Give me what you stole and I let you walk out of here!"

The pale woman turned over one shoulder and grinned back. When she spoke, it was in English. "Why do you want it?"

Daria almost laughed but remembered the likely fate of Dr. Incantada and her staff, whom she'd left downstairs in the lobby. "I don't. Want it, that is. I don't even know what the fuck it is. I've just decided you shan't have it. Set it down."

She thought the blonde might have more surprises up her sleeve. To her left sat a large, industrial table saw. Its legs had been bolted to the floor. The surface held one upright, jagged-toothed saw and four or five loose, plate-shaped saws. There was a T-square on one end of the table, and the whole thing was rigged to a portable gas-powered generator. Not all of it was bullet-proof, but some of it was, and Daria angled that way, putting the contraption between herself and the tall blonde.

Sandpoint, Idaho

Bryan Snow tried to look as confused as his pilots. "You guys know what happened?"

They did not.

"Wow. Well, okay, run full diagnostics. Right now." He adjusted his voice wand. "Todd. You folks all right in there?"

The seven people in the observation lounge looked utterly stunned. The newly identified General Cathcart and Colonel Crace could feel their careers slipping from their fingers.

Cyrus Acton tried to fake a semblance of control. "Ah. Well. We don't . . . this wasn't a contingency for which we were prepared. Obviously. We couldn't have been. There's no way—"

Cathcart had spent the better part of three and a half decades taking command of shit storms. The worse the situation, the more he felt at home. "The dark-haired woman. Gibron? That was the driver. Do you still have her voice print?"

Todd Brevidge was sweating profusely in his very fine suit. "Ye-yeah. Sure. I mean . . . yeah." He picked up his walkie. "Snow? Get us Target Number Two."

A moment later and Bryan Snow's voice rang from the overhead speakers. "One of the Mercutios is picking up her audio signature. It's coming from the building to the left of the hotel. Hang on."

The Mercutio drones began refocusing on the frontless livery building and the images began appearing on the wallwide screens.

"Targets Two and Three," Snow said over the PA. "The driver—Gibron?—and the blonde."

Colonel Crace said, "Find the source!"

The screen images from the war zone in Florence shifted. One of the monitor screens—it was denoted MERCUTIO-4—zoomed in on the building under construction adjacent to the flaming hotel. The drone's cameras zoomed in on the middle of the building—the center of the second of three floors.

The general snapped, "Can we get visual?"

The image on the screen shifted sharply to infrared. Two images stood out in sharp contrast behind the slate-colored scrim over the building façade. Both were human. One held a gun, one arm supporting the other, in a classic military stance.

The audio signature appeared across the bottom of the monitor screen.

They heard: "I don't. Want it, that is. I don't even know what the fuck it is. I've just decided you shan't have it. Set it down."

The voice spoke English but sounded foreign. Nobody in the underground rooms in Sandpoint could pinpoint the origin of the accent.

Todd Brevidge might have been in shock, but a lifetime in sales began to reassert itself. "I told you we couldn't lose anyone."

The second figure spoke, also in English. Everyone in the observation lounge recognized the California Valley girl cadence of the so-called Major Arcana. "They're the control modules for Dr. Incantada's creation. And I have a very reliable buyer in Belgrade who will pay top dollar for it. You don't even know what it is. What say I buy my way out of this for, oh, a hundred grand in euros?"

General Cathcart had taken command of the situation. It was in his genes. "The driver, this Daria Gibron, is trying to steal the command unit: retag her as Target One and Major Arcana as Target Two. Did we get a visual on Gibron?"

Another of the monitors in the observation room popped to life and showed a recording from several minutes earlier. It showed Daria twisting out of Dr. Incantada's Hyundai. Bryan Snow froze the frame and the facial recognition filters began taking minute measurements of the eyes, nose, lips, cheeks, hairdo, and jawline; as well as the color of her skin, hair, and lips.

A computer-painted illustration of Daria's face magically appeared on the screen.

"Aaaand . . . we have her," Snow said, over the ceiling-mounted speakers. "I'm running her image through international criminal databases."

Todd Brevidge preened a bit, trying to regain a fraction of control. "Which, obviously, we've got."

The military officials glanced witheringly at him.

"It's, um, all part of the software package. We throw it in. Gratis."

Everyone heard Daria Gibron say, "Not interested. Drop the bag." Her voice was pitched low and carried the odd cadence of a myriad of accents blended together.

Colonel Crace pointed at one of the wall monitors. "Wait . . . who's that?"

A third amorphous but human form appeared on the infrared image.

Owen Cain Thorson forced himself to rise. His head was ringing. He must have cracked his skull in the fall. He heard voices. His hand squeezed, and he was pleased to feel the comforting weight of his Glock.

He pushed himself to sit up.

There were two voices. Both female. Both spoke English.

He recognized Daria Gibron. The edges of his vision began to turn crimson.

To his left, Derrick Saito rose, too. He maneuvered himself up onto his knees. Neither had been noticed by the women.

Fifteen

Daria kept her focus on the tall blonde. "Why did you bomb the hotel?"

"Lots of reasons. One of which was: Because I could."

Daria said nothing, just watched her.

"You're Daria Gibron, aren't you?"

"You know who I am?"

"I know you could use a payday, honey. You've got no stake in this, outside the basic mercenary one."

Daria said, "Vince Guzman?"

The blonde had the audacity to look a little chagrined. "He's probably dead. The Serbs interrogated him, and they lack subtlety. This one guy, Kostic? He uses really, really small explosives, called squibs. They do a hellish amount of damage but highly localized. Pulverize bones and meat but cauterize arteries. He is the fastest interrogator I ever met. Sweetie, you should meet this guy."

Daria was thinking: *Why is she telling me all this?* She glanced about and caught a reflection in the upright metal blade of the table saw.

She twisted, down to one knee, hands extended, right hand braced, and fired without aiming.

A man's head snapped back behind the log of insulation. Daria saw straight black hair, a wiry frame, and Asian features. She could tell she caught him.

That's when she glimpsed the second man, moving laterally.

Guided by the telemetry of Mercutio-4, one of the three Hotspurs slid down into the alley, lined up, and spat a single bullet into the livery building.

The .22 caliber bullet sliced through the gray shroud over the missing facade. It would have sliced through Daria Gibron but a second earlier she chose to kneel and spin. Instead, the bullet smashed into the vertical blade of the table saw.

It was by no means a heavy bullet—the makeup of the Hotspur MAV meant it couldn't contain anything dense. To make up for the light load, the hawk drones had been loaded with pyrophoric rounds. When the bullet hit the table saw it heated up to more than 2,000 degrees. A fireball like some kind of magician's trick erupted in midair.

The discuslike saw blade shattered; replacement buzz saws clattered to the ground around Daria. The table bucked, two of its bolted-down legs ripping free of the floorboards.

Diego had climbed out of the pharmacy window. He wasn't even aware of reaching for his cowboy hat on the sidewalk.

He looked up and watched a mechanical hawk spit a single round into the shrouded livery stable. Two more hawks circled.

Diego made the sign of the cross. "Holy Mary," he whispered.

Daria covered her head as a fireball erupted and bits of table saw spun about the ill-lit room. Sniper outside, new gunman within. Daria was beginning to believe she hadn't thought this through.

The shot from outside had been disturbingly close, which suggested the sniper had drawn a bead on her. Which, in turn, suggested an infrared scope.

There was no way to triangulate the floor plan in order to use the heavy table saw to hide herself from the blonde, the sniper outside, and whoever was behind the rolls of insulation.

Daria heard a *ziiip* behind her, and another .22 slug smacked into one of four vertical support pillars holding up the ceiling, the third floor, and the roof above. A large bubble of dust and cement debris bloomed on the far side of the pillar.

The concrete of the pillar caught fire.

At what temperature does concrete burn? Daria wondered. *Answer: pretty fucking hot.*

She heard the blonde laugh but, ducked down as she was, no longer could see her. "Hilarity ensues!"

Daria was so pleased that the benighted bitch was enjoying herself. "Friends of yours?" she shouted.

"Outside, yeah. Inside? The guys you're shooting at? Them, I don't know."

Daria tried to keep her eye out for the man she'd glimpsed behind the bales of insulation, but light coming through the billowy shroud over the façade shifted the shadows, and waves of sweet-smelling sawdust slithered across the floor. Plus, there was the blazing pillar, like something from the Book of Revelations.

Pyrophoric rounds are scary but, in this case, played to Daria's strengths: if the shooter was peering through the shroud using infrared, then the pillar just became a lot hotter than Daria's body. She now was essentially invisible.

Hunkered down, she shouted over the roar of flames. "You brought rocket launchers and a sniper. Not fair!"

The blonde laughed again. "Sniper? Oh, babycakes! You've seen the movie *The Birds*!"

Daria watched the felled logs of pink insulation. One man was down; she could still see his raised knee from when he'd fallen over backward. Where was the second man? "Sorry!" she shouted to the blond woman. "Never saw it. Please leave the bag on the floor and scoot."

The exterior gun had gone silent.

The blonde shouted back. "I'm . . . wait. You never saw *The Birds*?"

Daria fired off a round in the general direction of the rolls of insulation. In the most unladylike manner, she ducked her head clear to the floor, still on one sandaled foot and one knee, with her ass facing the ceiling. Undignified, yes, but it gave her a quick glimpse under the table saw. The blonde was hunkered into a corner that likely led to an office or a bathroom. Beyond her and to her left, Daria thought she caught a glimpse of the foe's exit strategy: one of those long refuse tubes used for chucking rubbish out of a construction site to a bin below.

"Seriously?" The blonde's voice echoed in the shifting shadows. "Alfred Hitchcock? Tippi Hedren, Rod Taylor? The monkey bars?"

Another bullet zipped through the building's scrim and whistled through the second floor, hitting nothing.

Behind Daria, a deep American voice said, "Guns."

The man behind the insulation rolls was no longer behind the insulation rolls. He'd moved in such a way as to put the flaming pillar between them. That's why Daria's peripheral vision had failed her. She heard a clack and identified it as an American-made Glock.

"Guns. Now."

She set down the Makarov.

"Machine gun, too."

She unslung the weapon, laid it down.

"Stand. Kick the guns my way."

Daria stood, but stepped away from the guns rather than kick them. That put her closer to the table saw bolted to the floor.

The man stepped more clearly into view. Six-two, she guessed, and blond. He was built like a serious athlete, wearing all black. Handsome; no question. He handled the Glock as if it were a natural extension of his arm.

He looked simultaneously grim and self-satisfied.

Daria saw the laughing woman step out of her cover but not far enough out to recover her own Makarov. "Hey, big fella," she called out. "I'd say I have dibs on Miss Gibron here, but if you want to play through . . . ?"

"Shut up."

"Look, sweety pie. I don't know who you are or what your interest is in all this. But that's not a sniper out there. It's a state-of-the-art suite of micro-drones. Miss Gibron here has been tagged-and-bagged. They have her audio sig and her facial print. You let her go, there is nowhere in

Florence—nowhere in Europe—she could run that the drones couldn't chase her. In the meantime, you and me could make a deal. We—"

The tall man turned but only slightly and fired once. The blond woman's Makarov skittered across the wood chips and sawdust and disappeared into a darkened corner.

The blonde paused, then said, "Or not."

Daria's hands were away from her torso. She waggled her fingers. She said, "Hallo," to the American man.

He turned his gun back on her.

"Daria Gibron." His voice was oddly pitched, as if being held under pristine control. He sounded like a man who badly wanted to shout or to cry or to howl in hysteria. "You killed Saito."

Daria nodded toward the one lone knee, bent and raised, unmoving, behind the rolls of insulation. "Saito being . . . ?"

"You've added to your body count of fine Americans. Good for you. But now you die."

Daria shrugged. "It's been one of those days."

The man had her at gunpoint but her mind raced toward the taunting woman behind her.

Tall, blond. Good with accents, good in a fight. Mercenary. The faintest tickle of a memory tried to assert itself.

The blond woman said, "Pardon me. May I add something?"

The man said, "What?"

"Suzanne Pleshette? The birds in Tippi Hedren's hair? Come on! Seriously?"

Daria and the American stranger ignored her. He attempted to smile. "It's . . . been a while. You probably thought I'd forget about you. About everything. But I didn't." He stood stock-still, gun aimed at her head. Not her chest, the center of her body mass. Calm and experienced gun hands go for the body-mass shot. Emotional people go for the head shot.

Daria kept thinking about the woman but blinked languidly at the American man. "Do I know you?"

Her words could have been made of pepper spray. The big man

staggered back. The lower half of his face, illuminated by the gigantic birthday candle of a pillar, seemed to dissolve as a hash of emotions fought for dominance.

"Do . . . do you know . . . ?"

The Hotel Criterion groaned and buckled and shuddered, sending a ripple of energy through the next-door livery building. Dust sifted from the overhead rafters.

The newcomer lost his footing. Daria shot out of her stance, hauling ass to her right. Toward the flaming pillar and closer to the gunman.

The man quickly regained his balance, but tracking Daria meant turning his dominant eye toward the flame. He got a shot off. He expected her to keep running in that direction—back toward the hotel. But Daria stopped after two steps, bent low, scooped up one of the circular saw blades from out of the wood chips, and hurled it Frisbee-style.

Her sandals skidded a bit in the sawdust. She skittered backward, reaching clumsily for the Makarov she'd dropped. She heard the laughing blonde scramble for her weapon, too.

Daria hit the floor with her shoulder and hip.

A bullet panged off the now much abused table saw. The blonde had won the arms race.

The woman's second shot slapped into the warped floor and threw up wood chips and dust. Daria grabbed the Makarov, fired toward the woman once, then rolled onto her back, brought her arms down, and shot between her raised knees, back toward the man. She raised both arms over her head and rolled yet again, chest down now, and got off two more quick shots to where the woman should be.

Shielded by the remains of the table saw, she took a little gamble. "Is this . . . Viorica?"

A beat, then she heard a musical laugh. "Ooooh, honey! I was hoping you'd heard of me."

Daria shouted, "We run in the same circles."

Another laugh. "Just us girls!" And two more shots panged off the table saw.

Daria waited. The fire crackled. No more shots.

Daria dared to look up again. She peered around the darkened floor, weirdly lit by flaming pillars like some sort of Viking great hall.

The laughing blonde was gone. So was the doctor's bag with the stolen technology.

Daria rose to her feet and turned her attention to the burning pillar. The tall American man was down but not out. He was on all fours, trying to gather his wits.

She glanced behind the insulation. The Asian American was missing part of his face.

Daria turned back to the blond man and noted the Glock by his side. A much better weapon. She tossed her stolen Makarov away and went to her haunches, retrieving the man's American-made .45 auto.

His left arm caved, and he toppled onto his shoulder. Daria studied his face. She had cut him badly with the thrown buzz-saw blade. Blood flowed from a wound that ran across his left cheek from the edge of his mouth to his ear. The left ear itself was bisected and bleeding badly.

One eye was clotted with blood. The other looked both dazed and crazed.

Daria patted him down and found a wallet. She found a temporary Italian driver's license and a passport. Owen Cain Thorson.

He gasped. "You . . ."

Daria stared into his good eye. She studied his face. "You look familiar. I'm sure we've met. Where do I know you from?"

His good eye bulged. His hands clamped into fists. "Fucking"—he gasped—"hate you!"

"You'll have to narrow it down."

She drove her elbow into his temple and his one open eye rolled upward, the white suddenly glowing from the overhead fire. She tossed down his wallet.

The building groaned again, the sawdust and wood chips on the floor dancing.

She turned and sprinted for the rubbish chute, pausing to grab the machine gun.

Daria got to the opening of the tough, plastic chute, held one arm out, barrel down, and emptied the magazine straight down. It was a simple enfilade. She didn't aim. She just let loose with a hailstorm of bullets.

When the machine gun clicked empty, she hiked one long leg up into the circular wooden opening, then the other, then leaped and slid, sliding blind, loving it.

Sixteen

The gathered men and women watched the many screens in the American Citadel subbasement. Fire spread upward through the Hotel Criterion de Medici. Smoke and debris billowed out of the windows and doors into the tight alley, then boiled upward into the sky.

Different lenses highlighted the images from each Mercutio drone: visible light, glowing green night vision, infrared. By glancing from one to another the Pentagon officials and the honchos from corporate could piece together what was happening to the hotel.

The hotel had not dragged down the livery building yet, but that was looking more and more likely.

On one of the screens the illustrated image of Daria Gibron faded and was replaced by a surveillance photo of a woman with a heart-shaped face, straight black hair, and extremely dark eyes. That photo showed just her head, neck, and shoulders. Smaller photos began popping onto the screen: the same woman, here in T-and-jeans, here in a dress; here running and here sitting at an outside cafe and laughing with someone unseen.

Snow's voice came over the PA system: "Interpol has her."

Statistics began scrolling beneath the array of photos. Daria Gibron was Israeli. She had served in the Israeli Defense Forces and Israeli intelligence. Later, in the States, with the FBI, DEA, and ATF.

Brevidge kept thinking this nightmare couldn't get any wore. Holy crap—they'd nuked a fed!

But he read on, and now the two guests were beside him, reading, too.

This Gibron woman was *formerly* attached to those agencies. These days she was *wanted* by those agencies.

General Cathcart and Colonel Crace studied the on-screen data. Then turned to each other. They seemed to communicate silently.

The general turned and glared into the eyes of Cyrus Acton until the thin man flinched away. The general turned, and this time glared at Todd Brevidge. Brevidge held the look.

Cathcart let his head swivel, taking in the room.

"Does anyone . . . anyone . . . doubt our next course of action here?"

One of the American Citadel managers raised a tentative hand. "I hope you're not thinking about—"

Colonel Crace interrupted the plump man. "Nobody likes an ultimatum, sir. Nobody wants to be told what to do by a psycho and a goddamn thief. But you can see for yourselves." She pointed to the scroll of data on the screen. "This Daria Gibron has been red flagged by the CIA. Even her own Israeli intelligence people won't touch her. She's screwed with U.S. interests before and, like it or not, the blonde was telling the truth. Gibron is, right now, right here, a threat to U.S. interests."

General Cathcart said, "Agreed."

After the shortest of beats, Cyrus Acton said, "Yes. Agreed." And of course Todd Brevidge quickly capitulated.

The general turned to them. "Well, then?"

Florence

The first thing Daria noted as she climbed out of the Dumpster was that the loquacious blonde was nowhere to be seen. She had called herself Major Arcana, but Daria had heard of her a few times over the years, working under the name Viorica. A mercenary and thief who often hired out to paramilitary groups. She had a fierce reputation.

The second thing Daria noted was that the Dumpster had been filled with soft foam packing peanuts. The blonde had had this exit well planned. The third thing she noted: about eight seconds after she climbed out of the Dumpster and was still pulling staticky foam peanuts and wood chips out of her hair, she heard a high-pitched *ping!* and turned to see the giant metal bin reverberate and shudder about half a foot.

The blonde had warned her about drones.

Daria sprinted down the alley, still seeing no sign of the tall woman. She got to the end of the alley, hung a quick left, and dashed through crowds that had gathered, wide-eyed, cell-phone cameras at the ready, to capture the destruction of the hotel.

A few caught a glimpse of the semiauto in her fist and shrank back.

Half a block from the narrow alley, a Birra Moretti parasol over an outdoor table splintered in two and toppled away. One of the tourists under the umbrella fell straight backward, a spiral of blood arcing in his wake.

Daria took a moment to check over her shoulder for a helicopter. She saw none. She dodged a cluster of Japanese tourists following a woman walking backward and talking into a minimicrophone and shoulder-slung speaker. She juked left around a newsstand, then right, pivoting quickly into a doorway.

The newsstand seemed to explode, lurid tabloids wafting into the air.

Inside the doorway Daria shouldered her way past a busboy, whose tray of dishes clattered to the floor. She saw stairs ahead of her and hit them hard, arms pumping, taking them two steps at a time. At the top of the stairs she found a perpendicular hallway lined with doors. Apartments, she thought, as she bounced off a wall, taking the brunt on her shoulder, and raced down the corridor.

The busboy behind her began cursing, then screamed. She heard his body hit the stairs.

Fucking hell! she thought, rising up, one foot out, and kicked a door at the end of the hall with all her weight and momentum. The cheap lock splintered and the door banged open. Daria was in, hurdling over an ottoman and shouldering aside an obviously drunk man with a massive belly and a Homer Simpson T-shirt. The man fell as Daria hit his kitchen, found his refrigerator, and slammed into it hard enough to bruise her shoulder. She opened the fridge door as wide as she could and sank to her haunches. She reached into her backpack and snagged her cell phone. She hit Diego's speed dial number and listened to it ring.

The fridge door rang like a chime and leaped, one of two hinges springing free. At her feet, a jar of pickles smashed to the floor, brine spraying.

Diego's number rang and rang.

The fridge door chimed again, and this time the bullet penetrated, two inches above Daria's head.

She shoved the Glock into her backpack. She smashed the door closed and sprinted for the kitchen window, phone in her fist, and sprang for the balcony. Another alley below. There was an old-fashioned collapsible fire ladder, and she kicked the ratchet release, watched the ladder clatter noisily under its own weight, and once it was down, turned and scampered down it not caring that the sundress was probably the wrong attire for climbing into an alley in sight of the half-dozen tables of the nearest restaurant. She heard someone whistle a catcall and applaud as she hit the pavement. She ran, hard, for the next street.

She paused long enough to turn and spot, not one, but two hummingbirds in the alley behind her. And now she remembered seeing them outside the Hotel Criterion. They hadn't registered before. As she watched, a hawklike figure, maybe thirty meters up, arced into the alley and a flicker of light erupted under it.

Daria turned as the brick wall by her head cratered and debris pecked at her hair.

Several blocks away, Diego's cell phone lay amid the shattered display of bathroom products, in the window of a pharmacy. Smashed in two, it didn't ring.

Twenty meters away, amid the dust and debris of not one, but *two* burning buildings, an American named Jake Kenner dragged Owen Cain Thorson clear. Thorson was bleeding heavily from his cheek and ear, and his boots barely scraped the asphalt. Kenner hauled him toward their white van.

Seventeen

John Broom, Calvin Pope, and two of the four interns stood around the congressional office. John's laptop was perched on a filing cabinet. They were watching a live stream from Al Jazeera English. Sitting next to it was Calvin's laptop. It was tuned to Sky News.

Both showed the fire and destruction of a hotel and adjacent building in Florence, Italy.

Calvin pointed to Sky News. "Russians are saying they lost some military attachés in the explosion."

One of the interns, Bryce, said, "Terrorism?"

John shrugged. "Looks like it." He glanced at Calvin Pope.

"Look. Just because your source called yesterday and said something was happening in Florence, doesn't mean—"

John's phone rang. He pulled it from his pocket and noted the international extension.

Italy.

"John Broom."

Instinctively, he put it on speaker. As he did so, Senator Singer Cavanaugh appeared from his office, wearing his bow tie and suspenders but no jacket.

"*John! It's Daria! The hotel attack—*"

They heard a clatter and rumble but her words faded. Singer stepped into their midst. John said, "Daria? Hello? Hey, we're watching it now. The Hotel Criterion. Is that the thing you—"

"They're drones, John! Micro-drones!" She sounded out of breath. *"Never seen anything like them. Hummingbirds for surveillance. Hawks have missiles and bullets! John, listen! They can track—"*

The line went dead.

"Daria? Daria!"

John looked at the senator. The man looked grim but not overly emotional, as if his staff received such calls every day. He turned and barely gestured toward Clara, his longtime secretary. The elderly woman hobbled over without Singer having spoken and handed him a cell phone.

Calvin Pope whistled. "Is this for real? Micro-drones?"

John said, "There's no such thing. On drawing boards, maybe. But not in the field. Not from any country."

"Then what . . . ?"

The senator spoke into the phone. "This is Senator Singer Cavanaugh. I need the White House chief of staff. Tell him it's a national emergency."

John's phone rang. A different phone number displayed but with the same international prefix. He answered and kept it on speaker.

Daria Gibron shouted, *"Bad guys are Serbs! Buyer in Belgrade! I'm going after them. There's a man called Diego. He's here, he'll help! Ask the Viking!"*

John said, "Daria? Can you find the U.S. embassy? Get there! Get inside! We're sending—"

"John! The drones have my voice pattern and face recognition! They can track cell phones. I'm trying a land line! They're . . . shit—!"

Everyone stood, eyes locked either on John's phone or on the devastation appearing live on the two laptop computers.

Singer said, "Edward? It's me. Need to speak to the president. Sorry: right now. It's about this thing in Florence."

Daria came back. *"John! Find out who controls the drones! Get to Serbia! I can't—"*

The line died.

Eighteen

Thirty thousand feet above sea level

John Broom always felt it was worth the money to fly business class. The extra legroom made all the difference.

This made his journey from North Carolina to Bologna, Italy, a little out of the ordinary. He was traveling in the cargo hold of a Hercules C-130 transport, thanks to a favor from a man known as the Viking. His seat was a canvas cot that folded down from the bare metal concave hull. He wore jeans and new hiking boots and a fleece-lined Hebrew Union College hooded sweatshirt under a waterproof, winter-weight coat. It was still July outside the Hercules, but inside it was Santa's workshop.

John had been lying on his side, his messenger bag turned into a pillow. He ached from the cold, and he hadn't been able to doze for more than a few stolen minutes. He sat up and groaned. The cargo hold was forty feet long and jammed with crates. The crates were unmarked, which meant they were filled with contraband.

John muttered, "John the Smuggler." His breath misted.

He peered through the frost-limned hatchway window. The sun was rising, lending a golden glow to the leading edge of the huge wing and both massive, barrel-shaped Allison T-56 turboprop engines.

He looked down. They were over land. John didn't know which country, and he wasn't sure which continent. Europe? Northern Africa?

He felt adrift. He had rarely been so out of his element.

It had been three days since anyone had heard from Daria Gibron.

Three days since a suspected terrorist organization (or organizations) had used highly sophisticated electronics to track Daria's phone calls. They apparently had tracked her with both a cell phone and, later, a landline phone at a bookstore that subsequently was fired upon and set ablaze.

Daria was a gifted urban fighter. She knew how to run. She knew how to hide. If the enemy was tracking her, that meant they knew the number she had called. They knew John's name.

John peered at his watch in the cargo hold's gloom. It was two and a half days since the U.S. State Department had declared the attack on the Hotel Criterion a terrorist incident. It was, in the parlance of State, a Black Swan Event: unpredicted but with huge international repercussions. It was being likened to the terrorist attacks on Spain and London.

Two and a half days since the CIA had taken operational control of the investigation. Two days since Daria Gibron had been positively ID'd by a CCTV camera at a Bancomat ATM a block from the hotel. Two days since her presence had galvanized the anti–Daria Gibron contingent at Langley, effectively freezing out any hope of an independent investigation by the Senate-House Joint Intelligence Committee.

A day and a half since John Broom had contacted the international criminal known as the Viking.

A day since John had resigned from the staff of Senator Singer Cavanaugh.

John—cold, exhausted, unshaven, and thirty thousand feet over God knows where—was unemployed.

Belgrade, Serbia

Dragan Petrovic stood just inside the door to the office of the Serbian foreign minister. The office was opulent and warmly adorned with

Swedish furniture and hunting prints. The desk was mammoth and boxy and currently empty of all paper. The wall behind the desk offered a cluster of framed diplomas and photographs of smiling children and a cherubic wife. The diplomas and children and wife weren't his.

Dragan Petrovic jammed his thick fists into his trouser pockets and stood, feet shoulder-length apart, as he often had stood on the factory floor during his Community Party days, or when watching his paramilitary troops march past him during the war.

A soft rap on the doorframe behind him alerted him that he was not alone. Dragan turned at the waist, without moving his feet, to find Veljko Tadic, chief of staff to the prime minister, standing behind him.

"Veljko."

The soft, slight, round man patted Dragan Petrovic on the shoulder. "Not the way I always envisioned you in this office."

Dragan took a step to his right so the chief of staff could fully enter. Veljko did, but only half a step, and peered around the office as if it were a museum exhibition.

"Josef was a great man. A great foreign minister. He understood the nuances of the past."

Dragan didn't know what that meant. But he nodded.

"He was a personal friend, you know. Maria and I had him to the house several times. He and Alena came up to the lake with us last summer."

Dragan did know all that. His intelligence assets were considerable.

Veljko Tadic sighed a second time. He always seemed to do everything in twos. Dragan expected a second comforting pat on the shoulder.

"The prime minister is grateful that you agreed to step up. More than grateful. Obviously, we can't be without a foreign minister. Not now with the EU talks, and with Greece spiraling into the abyss. There are the Turks, clamoring for more say in Europe. Stability, Dragan. Let that be our watchword now. Yes?"

Dragan intoned the word carefully. "Stability."

The chief of staff seemed pleased. "I'll let you get settled in, Mister Acting Foreign Minister."

"Thank you. Tell the PM I'll be at the Cabinet meeting. Three?"

Veljko Tadic checked his watch. "Three thirty, the way the PM's day is running. But shoot for three if you can."

He turned to exit, paused, and patted Dragan on the shoulder again.

Dragan let the man get five steps into the antechamber before speaking. "Veljko? What was Josef doing in Florence, meeting with Russian military?"

The chief of staff turned back and licked his thick lips. "Ah. Perhaps it would be best if the PM addresses that question?"

"Of course. Three o'clock."

The chief of staff waddled out.

As soon as he was gone, Dragan closed the office door and pulled out his cell phone. He hit the number one.

"You've reached the offices of *Skorpjo*. We're out plotting world domination and can't come to the phone right now. But your call is important to us. If you leave a—"

"You find this amusing?"

Major Arcana laughed. "I find it a *little* amusing."

He had no time for her humor. "The package is ready?"

"It's here. It's safe."

"The Americans?"

She said, "They'll play their part."

"You're sure?"

"The Americans are nothing if not predictable. Mister Foreign Minister."

Dragan permitted himself a shallow, off-kilter smile. "Acting Foreign Minister."

"Thank God someone's *acting*. It's what our country needs."

Dragan ran a fingertip over the desktop. No dust. He could smell lemon polish. "I don't for a minute believe you're Serbian."

She said, "Sure of that, are you?"

Dragan was not. Her accent was flawless. "Make the rendezvous."

"Of course."

He hung up. He turned on his heels, examining the office.

His office.

. . .

The blue-eyed blonde heard Dragan Petrovic hang up and tossed her burner phone onto the bed. She had checked into the Belgrade City Hotel, a little uphill from the train and bus stations, and paid extra for a double room because it had the space for her morning tai chi rituals.

She was not—so far—impressed by Belgrade. She had tried four restaurants since hitting town. The fare tended to begin and end with goulash. She had picked up a lovely college boy last night, a fair-haired art major whose singular ambition in life apparently was to be amiable if uncreative in bed. But that had been last night and now she was bored. It was always like this between operations. The waiting was the worst.

She retrieved the cell phone from the bed and dialed Kostic, the interrogator and her primary link to the penitentiary-bait ruffians she begrudgingly called her team.

When he answered, all she said was, "Daria Gibron."

She heard Kostic check with his partner, the laconic Lazarevic. "No," Kostic spoke into the phone. "No sign of the woman."

"You're sure?"

Kostic snorted. She could hear him fire up his lighter and suck down another Syrian cigarette. "We are sure. The border patrols in Croatia and Slovenia are ours. Everyone is handsomely paid. The smugglers all know what and who we will allow to cross our borders. Lazarevic sent some boys with lighter fluid and set a trucker on fire, just to be sure everyone knows we are serious. This Gibron cannot cross out of Italy. She cannot cross out of Germany. She is no longer a factor in this. I am not worried."

The blonde thanked him and disconnected. *That's 'cause you ain't read her file, sweetie pie,* she said to herself. She switched the phone from portrait to landscape mode, and typed: HOW'S TRIX?

Sandpoint, Idaho

Bryan Snow strolled through downtown Sandpoint, a copy of the Bonner County *Daily Bee* under his arm, wearing an Idaho Vandals baseball cap he'd picked up to blend in. He smiled. He whistled. This gig was terrific.

When it was all over, he might just buy a house on Lake Pend Oreille. Or have one built. With a water slide into the lake. And a seaplane. A seaplane would be cool.

Bryan Snow was a happy man.

He picked Connie's Cafe and Cocktails, his favorite eatery in town. The sign out front proudly announced PARKING IN THE REAR in pink neon.

He sat at a booth and ordered a Sprite. The waitress had started calling him Bryan, having memorized his name from his ATM card. She was quick and polite but not overly so. She didn't force conversation, but she knew he worked at American Citadel. Snow appreciated anyone who did his or her job well.

He felt the phone in his hip pocket vibrate just as the waitress brought his chicken potpie and a side salad with a little metal stand that held oil and vinegar bottles and matching salt and pepper shakers. She refilled his Sprite.

Snow used his fork to break the crust and steam rose out of the pastry. The edges were golden and scalloped. He smelled chicken and herbs.

Todd Brevidge had bitched incessantly about moving the R&D complex to the Idaho panhandle. Snow loved it. Sandpoint was clean, laid-back, and friendly. The views were spectacular. The residents ranged from aging hippies to retired LA County police officers. Snow had taken to attending legion baseball games on his days off. Also to hiking along the stunning Lake Pend Oreille or down south at Lake Coeur d'Alene.

The phone vibrated again. He pulled it out of his pocket and set it next to his plate.

He saw a text message. It read, HOW'S TRIX?

He sipped his drink, then typed with a single finger, slowly.

ARMY IN CHARGE. TODD = APOPLEXY.

He ate. The lettuce, cucumber, and tomato were fresh. The phone on the place mat danced a jig. SWELL. GIBRON?

M&H IN AIR 24/7. He didn't spell out Mercutio and Hotspur. MON-ITORING CELLS, LANDLINES. AIRLINES, ITALIAN POLICE. NADA.

He dug into the potpie. Succulent.

Vibrate: NADA-NADA?

He typed: NADA. GIBRON OFF GRID.

The waitress circled his way. "Your lunch okay, honey?"

The *honey* was cliché, but he liked it. "Sure is!"

She beamed, genuinely pleased. "How's work?"

"Good. Busy, but good."

"That basement add-on working out okay?"

"Basement . . . ?"

"The one they had excavated. Put three rooms down there? Retro'd the elevator? My uncle Terry worked on it."

Snow grinned at her, absolutely thrilled. Oh, god! If only that condescending asswipe Brevidge knew that his supersecret lair was the talk of the town!

Snow said, "It's great. Thanks."

The waitress refilled the Sprite and moved on.

Snow chuckled to himself and ate. Man, he loved this burg. He glanced at the silent phone. After a beat, he typed: STILL THERE?

Vibrate: YES.

GOOD NEWS. RIGHT? RE GIBRON.

He waited.

Vibrate: WE'LL SEE.

Six blocks away, Todd Brevidge hoovered up a generous line of cocaine in his second-story office.

No, wait. Not office. Cubbyhole? Not quite. Ah, yes. *Shithole.* Better.

That snooty, buttoned-down Colonel Olivia Crace had requisitioned Todd's spacious office. She and General Howard Cathcart had huddled after that psychotic fiasco in Florence. When they emerged they informed Cyrus Acton and the other American Citadel board members that some "new truths"—that's how they worded it: *new truths*—had replaced the old ones.

First, Cathcart and Crace would absolutely be touting the advan-

116

tages of the American Citadel micro air vehicles to the military intelligence black budget boys. If true, the company would be saved.

Second, the powers that be at American Citadel were in it up to their necks when it came to that flaming cluster-fuck in Italy. A Hotspur MAV had annihilated a hotel. Italian police, and then Italian intelligence, estimated sixteen dead, including seven representatives of the Russian military and a member of the Serbian Parliament. Plus, a respected Italian aerospace designer and two of her senior engineers.

Because the American Citadel brass was implicated, it was agreed that Colonel Olivia Crace would take command of the entire R&D offsite facility in Sandpoint for the duration. And the military defined *duration* as the elimination of the Israeli expat, Daria Gibron. That, plus the reacquisition of the woman calling herself Major Arcana. She would have to be eliminated, too.

Only thing was: both women had vanished.

General Cathcart had returned to Washington to coordinate the search—quietly, behind the scenes—with the CIA, which seemed most intent on finding this Gibron. America's allies in Europe were helping. Law enforcement had been called in, and all border crossings were on high alert.

Brevidge felt the coke flow through his nervous system. He waited for the drug to give him the perspective it always provided.

Sure: the Florence incident was one of the great screwups in the history of the world. It was the type of incident that ended not with people being fired but with firing squads. On the other hand, the covert war boys were impressed by Mercutio and Hotspur. The company looked to be solvent. The free world would remain safe from the forces of terrorism and communism.

Todd Brevidge almost couldn't believe he'd found the sweet spot between prison and profitability. But he had.

He tapped out another line of coke.

They say war is hell? Try sales.

Nineteen

The crew of the Hercules C-130 had spoken no English. The same was true for the trawler that took John across the Adriatic from the east coast of Italy to Slovenia.

The boat was maybe thirty feet long and sixty years old. The crew members were serious fishermen, and the trawler reeked of fish. The lower hull was filled with ice. John stayed inside the moldy wooden cabin on deck throughout the journey. It gave him plenty of time to think about Senator Singer Cavanaugh and the job John had thrown away.

John had arrived at the Cavanaughs' lush and tucked-away neighborhood at 7:00 A.M.

Adair Simon-Cavanaugh opened the cherry red door herself after John rang the bell. She didn't seem surprised to find her husband's aide at the door. "Hello, John. Please come in."

Mrs. Cavanaugh turned and led him into the house. She was sixty-five and wearing a crisp white blouse, slim black trousers, and red flats. She was the richest person John Broom had ever met, or was ever likely to meet. Singer was the brash New Orleans pol; Adair Simon came from very old Georgia money.

John entered in her wake. "I'm sorry to bother you at home."

Adair smiled. "It's fine, John. We were half expecting you."

John himself hadn't known he was coming until twenty minutes before he called the taxi.

Adair led him through the splendidly appointed town house and into the spacious kitchen. The senator stood near a many-paned window that looked out at the backyard. He started every day standing behind a plain wooden parson's lectern he had purchased four decades earlier. Its surface was big enough that Singer could lay out his newspapers with room for a bowl of oatmeal and a cup of coffee. He read eight newspapers every morning.

His reading glasses were perched low on his hawk nose, and he wore a starched white shirt; his bow tie was undone and laying against his clavicle, suspenders tight against his shoulders.

"John," he boomed.

Adair Simon-Cavanaugh poured John a cup of coffee.

"Thank you." He turned to the senator. "Sir, it's the Black Swan event in Florence."

Adair slid into the bench of the bright red and white breakfast nook with her own cup of coffee. She said, "I know about the hotel. I don't know the term *Black Swan*."

"It's an event—military, terrorism-related, political—that's big and brash and completely unexpected but which has strong repercussions afterward," John said. "It's a Latin expression."

Singer pretended to read his paper. "The poet Juvenal."

"Yes, sir. He said: all swans are white. So a black swan is, by definition, the rarest possible observation. A *rara avis*. It's where we get the term *rare bird*."

Adair stirred her coffee. "My goodness. The useless information you boys have in your noggins." But it was said with a smile, and John took it as just a wry jab, nothing more.

John took a deep breath and turned to the senator. "Sir, I think I need to resign."

Singer and Adair exchanged glances. Adair was a handsome woman, serene and even-tempered in public but known for her steely resolve.

She also was known as something of a poker player. John could not read her at all.

When the senator did not respond, John pushed on. "I'm sorry about this. But Daria made contact with me and asked for my help. She also suggested I contact a man to get me there through illegal means. For obvious reasons, I'm going. But I can't . . . we can't afford any of this to come back on you, or your staff, or the joint committee, or the party."

Singer nodded for him to continue.

"There's another factor. Whoever was tracking Daria's calls, they know she called me. So I need to inoculate your office from any blowback from that direction as well. I hope you understand."

Singer Cavanaugh pursed his lips. Adair busied herself with applying a spoonful of sugar to her coffee.

"Resignation accepted."

John stood there a moment. He had hoped the senator would put up a fight. "Thank you, sir. This is about the hardest thing I've ever done. You're a lion of Congress. Your reputation there, and as a prosecutor, and as FBI director, make you uniquely qualified to speak for all of Washington. For the nation."

Adair drawled, "Though apparently it would kill him to empty the dishwasher occasionally."

Singer pretended to glower at her. She smiled benignly.

John said, "I can't put that at risk, Senator."

Adair turned to their guest. "I'm on the board of directors for the International Red Cross. It's not common knowledge, but the IRC Subcommittee on Refugees is putting together a contact group for Croatia and Serbia."

John blinked at her. "Croatia and Serbia don't have a refugee problem."

She flashed him one of her famous high-octane smiles. "Then my friends at the Red Cross will need a contact group to study the great good fortune of Croatia and Serbia. They're looking for a freelance analyst to study the region. The sooner the better. We bypassed the request-for-proposal stage. The contract is yours. Congratulations and good luck."

John felt the world slip a little from beneath his feet. He wasn't used to being the second-quickest mind in any given room. Let alone third-quickest.

"Wait. I . . . you knew I'd suggest this?"

Singer waggled his bushy white eyebrows, looking pleased with himself. "We figured you'd get there on your own."

John felt his eyes tear up. "I don't know what to say."

Singer flipped a page of the *International Herald Tribune*. "Say yes and get the hell out of my kitchen so I can go serve the taxpayers."

Adair stood and reached for John's untouched coffee cup. "We won't be able to funnel too much money into this project. Not without raising some eyebrows. My secretary has a list of names and numbers for you. I'll have them messengered to your place inside an hour."

Singer peered over his glasses. "Or we could trust the CIA to do its job. You're sure we can't go that route, son?"

"Unfortunately, yes sir, I am. Daria did what she had to do last winter, but it resulted in the assistant director for antiterrorism taking early retirement. There was a field agent who was fired over the whole thing. Owen Cain Thorson. Daria made big enemies."

"Understood. You go do what you need to do. This Red Cross thing will provide you with resources so you don't have to worry about my office. But you have my personal cell phone if you need me."

John cleared his throat. He tamped down the outpouring of emotion.

"Go take care of your friend, son."

"Yes, sir."

Adair led John back through the spacious but understated living room and entry room to the front door. He was still reeling.

"Thank you."

"Singer thinks the world of you. And he trusts you. You go and get yourself killed over there, he'll never forgive himself. So don't do that."

"No, Ma'am."

"Good luck, John."

She bussed him on the cheek. John hunched his shoulders and hustled to the cab he'd left waiting.

. . .

Now here it was two days later and John was in . . . well, he wasn't sure. Slovenia, probably. The trawler had dropped anchor outside Opatija, overlooking a beautiful bay. The crew used an inflatable raft with a tiny outboard motor to get him ashore.

He found a man waiting for him by an ancient Austin Cooper. The man was dark, with shoulder-length black hair and the flat-planed face John associated with Central America. He wore jeans and a T-shirt, a cowboy hat, and dusty boots. He was tightly built and compact. He leaned on the Cooper. "Broom?"

"Yeah."

The guy climbed behind the wheel. John threw his messenger bag into what passed for a backseat. He sat. The dashboard was half missing and there were no seat belts.

Away from the icy trawler, John began unwinding himself from his winter clothes.

The guy said, "Diego."

"Hi."

"Friend of Daria."

John said, "Me, too."

The man put the Cooper into gear. "Better be."

It now was four days since anyone had heard from Daria.

John discovered he'd been put ashore in Croatia, not Slovenia. The quiet man drove south on a wildly winding road that dipped down to sea level near the towns and zoomed straight up the sides of mountains in between. The view was spectacular, the Adriatic glistening. Any other time and John would have enjoyed the road trip.

They drove for over an hour without speaking. John slipped into a quick nap, but the hairpin curves made that impossible to sustain.

At one point he rubbed at a severe kink in his neck and said, "Why are you doing this?"

Diego watched the road. He drove fast but carefully.

John said, "You're . . . what? Hired gun for the Viking?"

Diego downshifted through a precarious turn. "Who's the Viking?"

"Right. Sorry."

They drew closer to Split. The traffic wasn't too bad, although trucks got in the way a lot. John realized there was an elevated inland highway and wondered why the trucks weren't up there.

Twenty minutes later the driver said, "Let me guess. Daria saved your life."

"Me?"

Diego nodded.

"No. I'm not the kind of guy people have to save. I'm a lawyer. Biggest threat to my life is overaggressive air conditioning."

Diego seemed to absorb this, eyes on the road.

John said, "I guess, technically, I saved hers."

That took them another three kilometers.

"You saved Daria Gibron." Diego sounded incredulous.

"Yeah."

Four more kilometers. And Diego almost smiled. "Okay. I got to ask . . ."

"CIA hit squad. This was last November in Milan."

"She told me. She was sick."

"Damn near dead. And the CIA field team wanted her all the way dead. I intervened."

Diego upshifted, smoked a souped-up Z Car.

"How?"

"I found a legal loophole in CIA protocol. Once I did, killing Daria would have led to the mother of all paperwork storms. Bureaucratic nightmare. Not killing her became the easy way out."

They drove. The signs pointed them south to Dubrovnik and east to Bosnia-Herzegovina.

Diego shook his head. "You shitting me. You saved Daria with . . . paperwork?"

John leaned back. "I'm a D.C. lawyer. I could kill a water buffalo with paperwork."

And—miraculously—Diego gave him a full-fledged grin. "Damn."

Lago de Como, Italy

Brook Slate was the Man with the Plan.

A dishonorable discharge from the U.S. Navy might have ended the life of a lesser man but not Brook Slate's. In the fifteen years seen he'd been canned, he'd traveled around South America, Africa, and now Europe, doing a little armed robbery here, a little extortion there, and all the while picking up more tail than any man deserved.

What was his secret? A couple of things.

First, he was a keen observer of the human nature. He could spot potential talent from a nautical mile.

Second, like that line from *Apocalypse Now*: "Never get out of the boat."

Brook Slate rarely got out of the boat.

In his case, it was a forty-year-old, twenty-foot beaut currently parked in Lake Como, in the north of Italy near the Swiss border.

As for being a keen observer of human nature: take today. Brook sat outside a quaint restaurant on an arc of land that jutted into Lago de Como, just a tad north of the touristy town of Como. He drank a Heineken and wore his leathers well. Not a tall man—maybe five-six—he was economically built, he looked larger than he was. He should have been a movie star. That thought occurred to him virtually every day.

Como was gorgeous. He could look straight up and see crystalline blue. He could look a little lower and see the Alps. He could look lower and see forests. Even lower was the splintered dazzle of sunlight on one of the most beautiful lakes he'd ever seen. To the left were 1920s-era hotels and apartments, teeming with tourists. Or marks, depending on your point of view.

And look to the right, there was tonight's conquest.

She was maybe thirty. She had straight black hair, pulled back and tied with a bandana. She wore a rather simple sundress, but that didn't hide the high-octane bod beneath. She had a heart-shaped face and wore sunglasses.

Best yet, when the waiter came to her table, she had to point to a menu: no Italian.

Best-best yet, after she did, she rifled coins through a small change purse and looked nervous. She glanced around, furtive.

Brook sipped his beer, and then reached into the right pocket of his trousers. His fingers felt the comforting, familiar triangle of the Rohypnol tablet in its plastic packet.

He waited thirty minutes to make sure she was alone, then sauntered her way. He sat quickly at her table, tried to engage her in English small talk; it was clear she didn't understand the lingo. But she blushed and brushed stray hair away from her eyes and smiled at him. Brook thought: *And the crowd goes wild* . . .

He laughed about their language imbroglio. He bought her a prosecco, and one for himself to be suave. Then two more. He flashed paper bills to pay for their dinner, and they laughed and struggled with the language. She had a map, and they sat shoulder to shoulder and studied it.

Bubbly wine is good for date-rape drugs. The pill dissolves unseen.

She was a bit unsteady on her strappy sandals as they walked the curved shore of Como. He would point to objects and say their names, and she would repeat it. She would point to objects and say them in her language, whatever the fuck that was. And he mimicked her monkey sounds.

He showed her his houseboat. She seemed in awe of it. He took her hand and guided her onboard. Her legs wobbled a little, but then again, so did his. *Too many hours on land today*, Brook thought. He glanced around, and nobody looked their way. He noticed a blurring at the edge of his vision and wondered what was wrong.

Brook dreamed. The foreign chick using his kitchenette to make baked beans or coffee. The foreign chick doing tai chi in her underwear. The foreign chick poring over maps.

Daria sat on the side of the hide-a-bed onboard the houseboat, bored out of her mind. She'd read every book Brook Slate owned—both of them—and even scoured his porn magazines for reading material. He had satellite TV, thank God, and she watched Al Jazeera English and Sky News and the BBC.

On the fourth day she watched him come out of his Rohypnol stupor. It had been an interesting experiment, to see how much of the drug would keep a grown man unconscious without killing him. His eyes opened, pupils red. Daria said, "Can you hear me? Brook?"

"Wuzzzz . . . hppnnnnnn . . . ?"

"What's happening? Ah, very well. First rule of being a predator is: always be able to identify the other predators."

She shimmied on a pair of jeans that were just a tad short for her long legs. She shouldered her way into his Kid Rock T-shirt, pulling it over her torso. "I couldn't very well believe my luck. First, you were comically stupid. Then you turned out to be approximately my size. But a gender-neutral first name? Well, there you go."

"Cannnnn . . . moooove . . ."

"Either that will wear off or you'll suffer some sort of toxic side effect. I've really no idea. And it would be interesting to stay about and see, but I must scoot."

She slipped on a Hawaiian shirt Brook had picked up a couple of years ago. It was a favorite. She did her hair in a tight French braid, then moved to a mirror over his sink and tried on his straw porkpie hat. Brook tried to react—the hat had always been good luck in poker. He couldn't just lay there and let her take it.

She slid on some sunglasses, then picked up Brook's driver's license, studied it, studied herself in the mirror, turned a quarter this way and a quarter that.

She unfolded a paper clip and took a minute to scratch through the laminate of his driver's license, obscuring the M after *Gender*.

"Should do," she proclaimed. She threw Brook's wallet in a little black leather backpack with a fleur-de-lis stamp on it.

She knelt on the bed and bent low and kissed his sweaty forehead. "I'd have let you go. But I found the photo albums of your other *dates*. Souvenirs? That won't do. D'you understand me, Brook?"

He tried to swallow and nodded. His lips were cracked. His joints ached.

"The people who raised me wanted to ingrain a certain way of calculating into our brains. Aptitude tests, I suppose you'd call them. For instance, locking us in a sealed room with the ingredients for plastic explosives, a single match, and limited air supply."

His eyes pinballed wildly in his skull.

Daria shrugged. "Homeschooling."

She stood. "I'm about to scuttle your boat. It will sink. How long will that take? I don't know. Now: You're drugged. You likely will recover enough to get off the boat. How long will that take? I don't know. But my guess is: You're motivated to find out."

She checked her reflection in the mirror, and then walked to the door.

"Biiiiitch . . ."

Daria belted a musical laugh, her eyes scrunching tight. "Oh, I also have friends in the American FBI. I'm taking your souvenirs and mailing them from here. If you do get off the boat, then it's time for your next class in calculating. Bye. Thanks for dinner and the prosecco."

On the way to the bus depot, Daria found a post box and dropped off the photo albums of horrible assaults, addressed to Ray Calabrese, her former handler at the FBI.

Daria checked her reflection in a shop window. She disliked the hipster vibe, but it would suffice for the time. She had worked with facial recognition software before. She had no illusions that the Brook Slate ID would hold up once she got closer to the cities and the mass of CC cameras. But it was a start.

Twenty

John and Diego ate in the town of Split, a centuries-old trading village with Greek and Roman ancestry. They wound through the labyrinthine souk, through tall and tight oatmeal-colored walls, until they found a decent restaurant. John had been looking for an Internet connection. In just a few years, the term *Wi-Fi* had become ultrainternational.

He used an alias to check in with a contact at the International Red Cross, who would get word to Adair Simon-Cavanaugh that he was wheels-down in the Balkans and doing all right.

He sent a message to his contact at the IRC: ULTRA-LIGHT MAVS. GET INTERNS ON THIS: WHO MANUFACTURES BATTERIES? WHO MANUFACTURES CAMERA LENSES?

The questions had been bothering him all through the freezing flight across the Atlantic. Daria had described quick, tiny micro air vehicles chasing her and firing at her. And John had kicked himself that it had taken so long to ask the essential questions: Who was manufacturing and/or buying the batteries for such vehicles? Or the light but effective lenses for their cameras?

Find out who made the drones, and you just might figure out who was flying the drones.

From Split, John took the wheel, and they headed inland and up—steeply up—into Bosnia-Herzegovina.

A bored border guard took the two passports Diego handed him. Diego doffed his hat to expose his face. The guard glanced at them both, then pocketed the twice-folded euros, handed the passports back, and wished them *dobre deyn*.

John shoved the recalcitrant gearshift. "It means 'good day.'"

Diego slicked back his long hair with his hand and returned the cowboy hat. Diego said, "You speak Bosnian?"

"I learn five phrases, every country I get sent to: Hello and good-bye. Please and thank you. And, Where's the toilet."

A few kilometers in, Diego nodded. "Those're good."

The road to Mostar turned north and entered craggy stone canyons. In places rock strata rose crookedly, as if the gods had lifted one end of a geologic couch to vacuum underneath it. Ancient train tracks paralleled the road and dove into rounded, stone-framed tunnels. John could imagine the Orient Express, or its southernmost sibling, making the journey in the 1920s.

They passed through ramshackle lumber and mining towns that had started in hard times and fallen from there. Diego noted, on some of the winding and more luxuriously forested stretches, signs on trees with the skull and cross bones.

"Minefields," he said.

Every town they drove through had a minaret. "This is a Muslim country," John said.

"How'd that work out for them in the war?"

John grunted. Diego knew more than he let on.

They left the craggy, fractured Neretva Valley and entered the town of Mostar. John parked.

"You think Daria's here?"

"No." John climbed out, and after a moment, Diego did, too. "A woman who knows the ins and outs of politics in the region. She'll have information I don't."

Diego looked around the 1930s façade, at the graffiti and the clusters of bored teenagers. "So?"

"So information is power." John started walking, and Diego moved up beside him.

Diego said, "Only power's power, man."

The Turkish side of the Neretva River was one of the best marketplaces John had visited. Old men sipped sweet coffee from small bronze decanters on hammered-bronze saucers. Merchants sold metalworks and scarves, plus the ubiquitous paraphernalia of football clubs. John saw half a dozen very skinny, very black cats. He paused and knelt and scritched a couple behind their ears. Diego stood with his thumbs in his belt, his boots scuffed and dusty and low at the heel. John got the impression he saw everything and reacted to nothing.

Halfway to the ancient Stari Most, or Old Bridge, Diego nudged John and jutted his chin to the left. For a brief second the man's deep brown eyes were exposed to sunlight.

John followed his gaze. It was an abandoned building. Two large, vaguely round holes appeared in the wall, about twenty feet up.

Diego muttered, "Mortar fire."

"Yeah, and . . ." John pointed to a wall that looked like a giant Braille text. "Machine guns."

"The war?"

"It must've been bad here. My friend will know more."

They walked to the Stari Most, the bridge arched like a camel's back. Diego was not large and not angry looking. But city dwellers gave him a wide slip anyway. He just had that . . . John stumbled around for a description. Gravity well? Yes. As if bullets fired at him would enter his orbit instead of hitting him.

They crossed the bridge. All Turkish influence ended abruptly. Crossing the bridge wasn't easy: the builders had added one- to two-inch-high crossbars to the path. They made walking a chore. They found a flat flagstone at the end of the bridge that read REMEMBER 1993.

The civil war.

John said, "Before we get there: she's kind of abrupt. And caustic.

And just plain rude. Her name's Sylvia Rush. During the war, mid-nineties, she'd been part of the State Department's shuttle-diplomacy mission with Richard Holbrooke. Before that, she was a professor. She taught at the Kennedy School when I was there. After that and law school, I was an analyst for the CIA. Sylvia Rush was my go-to guy on the former Yugoslavia."

On the western side of the bridge, the remnants of the Neretva Canyon reasserted themselves. The place was vertical; it was the only way John could describe it. They came to an office and noticed a hotel ten feet below them, with a bridge ten feet below that, with a restaurant ten feet below that, with a cluster of shops ten feet above them.

Below it all was a trickle of a tributary of the mountain region. That trickle had needed a million years to dig such a ferocious trench. And the city had formed around it, hugging it, teetering precariously over it.

They came to a stout building and a dark wooden door with a placard in Bosnian and Arabic and English. It read: BOSNIAN-AMERICAN FELLOWSHIP FOUNDATION.

Diego snorted.

A young woman worked at the counter. John asked her if he could speak to Sylvia Rush.

Moments later an inner door opened and a human pixie emerged. She wasn't quite five feet tall and had a wild moss of kinky salt-and-pepper hair and crystal blue eyes. She looked tanned and taut, and John knew she was in her sixties. She wore jeans and soft suede booties and a frayed sweater, with half glasses hanging from a beaded lanyard.

She said, "Holy moly. John Broom."

She cackled and threw a hug around his shoulders. John had to bend over to receive it.

"Christ almighty. What a surprise! You should've said you were coming!"

John said, "We're flying under the radar. Sylvia Rush, you remember Professor Diego?"

Diego turned flat, chocolate eyes on John but didn't react.

The petite woman studied the Indio in the cowboy hat and boots. "Professor?"

John said, "He works in pain studies."

"Neurology?"

"Hoodlum."

Sylvia squinted up at John.

"What's going on?"

"Something big and bad is happening. Diego and I are trying to figure out what. I thought I'd start with you."

Sylvia Rush contemplated that. "You two eaten?"

"Not for a while."

"Come on. Nobody stays hungry in Mostar."

The restaurant had outdoor seating on gold-colored flagstones and under a flat stone awning. A plate of cheeses, olives, and quarter-sized, very red salami arrived, along with fresh bread and frosty pints of Bosnian beer. Sylvia Rush sat on one side, the men on the other.

Sylvia perched her half glasses on the end of her nose and peered over them. "Give me the Yugoslavia 101, John. It'll help calibrate where I need to start."

John picked out a green olive. "The intersection of empires," he said. "The Romans, the Ottomans, the Hapsburg Empire, the Eastern Orthodox. The first shot of World War I, the assassination of Archduke Ferdinand. The Nazis and the Soviets. General Tito tamped down all that hostility for four decades. But he died, and the old divisions came right back alive. The Serbs versus the Croats versus the Muslims. The civil war took up most of the 1990s, until the United States and NATO and the U.N. stepped in, leading to the Dayton Peace Accord."

Sylvia sipped her beer. "Very good." She turned to Diego. "During the civil war, the Serbs kept Sarajevo under siege for a thousand four hundred days. No fresh water, precious little food. Snipers picked off shoppers and children in playgrounds. In places like Srebercia, there was ethnic cleansing, with mass graves. Men, women, and children. Brutal."

She shivered. Diego watched her intently.

"But here's the thing to remember: The Croats did the same thing to the Serbs in World War II. You look at any atrocity in the former

Yugoslavia, then go back a hundred years, and I guarantee you you'll find its reciprocal event. Now go back a hundred more. And a hundred more. These are people who believe it's right and justified and *sane* to remain angry that a village was burned in the Year of Our Lord seven hundred. And then to be genuinely confused when the West condemns them for that."

Diego muttered, "*Dios.*"

"You're Indio, *Professor*?"

Diego nodded.

"You still pissed off—daily—about the Spanish decimating your land?"

Diego looked at John, then back at the diminutive woman. "No, Ma'am."

"The Serbs and Croats would look at you and see that as weakness. You have to understand that. Both of you." She turned to John. "How'd you get here?"

"Drove up from the coast."

"Then you saw the remnants of the war. The civil war is remembered as the Serbs and Bosnian Serbs versus the Croatians and the Bosnian Muslims. Tell me: who do you think threw the grenades and fired the machine guns into the buildings in Mostar?"

"The defenders?"

"It was Muslims on the east bank firing at the Croats on the west bank. It was both of the victims of so-called Serbian atrocity, who took the opportunity to lay into each other as well."

John and Diego exchanged looks.

Sylvia Rush ate a mouth full of potatoes. Downstairs, someone cheered for a shot on goal.

Sylvia said, "Welcome to the Balkans, boys."

Another round of beers, Sarajeveski Piva, followed the fish. Diego remained very quiet, but John sensed he was listening intently to Sylvia Rush.

John said, "*Skorpjo.*"

Sylvia said, "White Scorpions. Serb mafia. What about them?" She quaffed her beer with the vigor of a much larger person and smacked her lips.

"They were responsible for the bombing of that hotel in Florence."

Sylvia glared at him. "*Skorpjo* doesn't operate that far west."

"I know. But we have good witnesses."

Diego held up his right arm and pointed to it. "White scorpion tattoos."

"You're sure?"

Diego lifted his stein. "Friends died there. Yeah. We're sure."

John turned to him, surprised by the plural. "Friends?"

Diego turned only slightly in his direction. "Daria, maybe no. But they found the body of my friend Vince Guzman."

John didn't know how to respond, so he didn't.

Sylvia Rush went into the restaurant to pay.

When she was gone, Diego muttered. "As for Daria . . . ?" He gave a small flicker of a shrug. "Olsson got people in Slovenia, Croatia."

Fredrik Olsson was the Viking, but John wasn't necessarily supposed to know so, so again he said nothing.

Diego looked around to make sure no one could hear them. "Everyone's looking for Daria. Haven't found her. Been four days. Almost five."

"Doesn't mean she's dead. I told you she called me *after* the hotel blew up."

Diego finished the remains of his beer. "Said she called you under fire from them Flying Monkeys."

"Yeah."

The Indio shrugged again. "Five days. No word."

Sylvia emerged, her uncontrolled mass of gray hair bobbing and floating around her lined face. The men rose. Diego said, "Thank you, Ma'am."

John said, "Who do we see in Belgrade who can speak for *Skorpjo*?"

"I don't know. They used to be a government-backed paramilitary but not as much any more." Sylvia pointed up and to the right. "Pretty good hotel here. Quiet enough, until the call to prayer at five. Tomorrow you should head into Sarajevo. Go see Zoran Antic. He's a member of the Bosnia-Herzegovina Parliament. And a friend. He'll know more about *Skorpjo*. I'll call him in the morning."

John bent and kissed her cheek, webbed with deep, dry age lines. "Thanks. This is helpful."

She looked up at him with those startlingly blue eyes, eyes that didn't seem to fit into the midsixties face. "What are you hoping to accomplish, counselor?"

"Save a friend. Stop military tech from getting into the wrong hands."

She shook her head ruefully and patted him on the arm. "All these years, and you're still naïve."

He frowned in surprise.

"Military technology always gets in the wrong hands, John. That's what military technology is destined to do."

Twenty-One

The U.S. National Security Agency was the first organization to discover that Daria Gibron was still alive, due to an 85 percent match from a traffic camera on the A21 outside Turin, Italy.

The NSA alerted the CIA.

A disgruntled CIA employee informed former fair-haired boy and disgraced agent Owen Cain Thorson, who became the next to find out.

Thorson's surviving partner, Jake Kenner, had scored some morphine and patched up Thorson's blade-rent face the best he could. The two were waiting in a sweat-stink flophouse outside Florence. Stretch bandages held not-that-clean cotton swabs against the slice Daria had taken out of Thorson's cheek and ear. Kenner advised Thorson to stand down, but Thorson took note of the e-mail from Langley and dragged his body out of the camp cot.

Another person at the CIA leaked the information to the office and desk of General Howard Cathcart in army intelligence. Cathcart immediately contacted Colonel Olivia Crace in Sandpoint, Idaho. From there the drone pilots alerted the truck-and-trailer rig still based in Florence to get up on the A21, westbound, and to catch the bitch.

They had predicted she would head east from Florence, toward the

Italian border with Slovenia. Their intelligence apparently had been wrong.

Bryan Snow, chief engineer on the Hotspur and Mercutio projects, began punching in a Level 1 diagnostic for the drones into one of his consoles. His eyebrows V'd behind his Buddy Holly frames. "She was spotted near Turin?"

One of his in-house pilots said, "According to the NSA."

Snow shook his head. He couldn't help think that he'd heard the name of the town on the radio. Recently. "Why's that familiar . . . ?"

Behind the backs of his pilots, he typed in the information on a secure outside communications line. That line went directly to the woman working under the pseudonym Major Arcana.

Next to learn of Daria's resurrection was the Italian state security agency, the Agenzia informazioni e sicurezza interna, or AISI. Intelligence agents there also began forming on the east–west highway that bisects northern Italy.

A great deal of intelligence and firepower and anger were aimed at Daria Gibron.

As she had anticipated.

Major Arcana informed the White Scorpions, but in her usual cryptic manner: "Forecast calls for Hell."

Italian intelligence, or AISI, sent a request to the Carabinieri to monitor all of the closed-circuit cameras along the length of the A21 highway and throughout northwestern Italy. The notification went out at 8:00 A.M. on a Saturday.

When the state police had not responded inside of ninety minutes, AISI contacted the Carabinieri again. The response was harried. "We hear you! We hear you! Believe me, we've received nothing but requests for that whole section! Goddamnit, show a little patience!"

Besides guarding the Italian-Slovenian border, members of *Skorpjo* also sent three SUVs, armed like pirate ships, across the border into Italy. If they could intercept Daria before she hit the border, all the better.

The SUVs made it through Verona and got north of Milan before hitting temporary barricades set up by the Carabinieri. The gunhands of the White Scorpions stowed their obvious weapons, and the lead SUV coasted up to a motorcycle cop in a tunic, helmet, sunglasses, and Sam Browne belt. The driver lowered his window. He spoke Italian. "What's going on?"

The motorcycle cop shook his head. "You're kidding."

The driver glanced back at his cohorts, then at the cop again. "What?"

The motorcycle cop made a disparaging hand gesture. "Buy a fucking newspaper, Slav."

Sandpoint, Idaho

Colonel Olivia Crace had been tasked to the unnamed and officially nonexistent U.S. Army intelligence unit assigned to procure military tech because she knew much of the science the geeks always assumed was over the heads of the military brass. She also knew to share what she knew and what she suspected only with General Cathcart.

At the American Citadel R&D offsite complex in Idaho, Crace opted to remain in civvies. She knew she fooled no one, but it seemed a prudent precaution. Today she wore corduroy trousers and boots and a light T-shirt under a summer-weight blazer. She could actually *feel* the absence of a holster and the weight of a .45 on her hip.

She stepped into the observation lounge at almost exactly midnight. It was 8:00 A.M. in Italy.

She entered the underground observation lounge to find Todd Brevidge already there.

"Status?"

The PA system was active, so Bryan Snow and the pilots in the control room could communicate with the observers.

Brevidge looked like a guy trying desperately to control his bowels while looking calm. "Hi. We're getting into—"

Colonel Crace spoke louder. "Mr. Snow?"

Over the PA, Bryan Snow said, "We're moving the truck out of Florence. It's heading west, on an intercept for Gibron."

Brevidge opened his mouth to speak and Crace rode over him. "Time to intercept?"

Snow said, "The Away Team said they're hitting surprising traffic on the A21."

Crace closed her eyes. *Damn it. If I'd wanted traffic and weather . . .* She said, "Can I get a map?"

A few seconds later one of the screens that made up the full wall of the observation lounge popped to life. It showed much of northern Italy, stretching from Florence in the south, France in the west, the Alps to the north, and the Adriatic Sea in the east. Near the top of the map was a highway marked A21, which stretched along the route described by the northwest wedge of Italy and the southeast wedge of France. Between which was a serious mountain range.

Crace said, "That's a lot of territory."

Brevidge chortled. "It would be for a team of soldiers on the ground. Even for an armored platoon. But that's the beauty of Mercutio and Hotspur."

The colonel turned to him.

"If this chick is out there, then we can find her. She can't use any telephonic communication, because we can monitor all of them, landlines and cells. She can't pass any CCTV cameras, and European cities are busting out of their seams with closed circuit. She's traveling by highway, right? We control the airspace above the highways!"

Crace was impressed. The lethal reach and firepower of the micro air vehicles was becoming clearer. She was starting to be glad this Gibron woman was giving them a run for their money. She and Major Arcana might be the exact targets they needed to convince the brass to pour black-budget money into this tech.

She started brainstorming problems, looking for the weaknesses.

"What if Gibron gets around too many phones? Can't she max out the Mercutio's capacity to monitor comms?"

Before Brevidge could answer the godlike voice of Bryan Snow rained down from the ceiling-mounted PA system. "Negative, Colonel. We know how many cell towers there are in any given metropolitan area. And we've written an algorithm to monitor the traffic in the towers. Landlines are easier, of course. We actually just bribed phone company personnel rather than using technology to make sure we secure all those calls."

Crace nodded, as if Snow and the two in-house pilots could see her. "Outstanding. So she can't fool us by hiding among too many cell phones."

"Correct," Brevidge preened a bit. "She'd have to storm . . . I don't know, New York's Thanksgiving Day Parade or something. Otherwise, her ass is ours."

Turin, Italy

Paco Montoya took the steps two at a time down to the hotel exercise facility. He wore a scowl as thick as his mustache. He expected to find the youngest member of Team Tarantola warming up on a treadmill. At least, he was supposed to be on the treadmill. And if that idiot Docetti wasn't where he was supposed to be, then God help him.

Fortunately, he was. Gianni Docetti jogged methodically, wearing gym shorts and cross-trainers. He wore a black elastic headband to keep his long, wavy, sun-bleached hair out of his eyes. Like the rest of Team Tarantola, Docetti was long and lean, his legs much more finely defined than his upper body.

"Docetti!" the team manager bellowed.

The youngster stopped jogging and grinned. "Skipper! Feeling good. I got—"

"There's a girl." Paco Montoya jabbed a thumb in the direction he'd come. "Up in lobby. I tell her you not available. She insist. She very insistent."

Docetti let a smug smile alter the planes of his face. "She pretty, skipper?"

But Paco Montoya didn't find his enfant terrible all that charming. "Get your ass upstairs. Sign her autograph, get your photo taken. Whatever. But . . . !" He stabbed a stiff finger in the younger man's face. "No sex! You understand?"

Docetti said, "Sure, sure. I understand." He smiled warmly. One of the things he loved about Team Tarantola was how the skipper pretended not to like him. Docetti found it endearing.

Downstairs, Gianni Docetti pulled on a T-shirt with the team's colors and whisked off the headband. His thighs were sculpted like a Greek statue, and he loved the effect they had on people, so he didn't bother with sweatpants. He jogged easily up the stairs, feeling energized.

In the crazily crowded and cacophonous lobby of the hotel, he wended his way between fans, support personnel, and journalists, his eyes scanning for familiar faces. He almost missed her, because she wore a boyish Hawaiian shirt over a rocker T, with a straw porkpie, the brim turned up all around. He was used to seeing her dressed much more skimpily, or not at all.

"*Gatta!*"

Docetti whipped her up, lifting her feet off the carpet, his chest and arms sweat-slick and taut. He kissed her hard. Others in the lobby laughed, and a few snapped cell phone photos.

He broke the kiss and set her down. "You came!"

Daria was a little breathless from the hug and the kiss. "I did."

"You're here!"

"I am."

The twenty-year-old couldn't believe his fortune. "You're my good luck charm now! I will find you the best place to watch! When my team takes—"

Daria put both palms on his chest and kissed him quickly. When he'd shut up, she said, "I'm not here to watch."

His face turned quizzical. "Not watch? But everyone on earth watches!"

Daria shook her head. "No, thanks."

His eyes grew round. "You are here for love? I cannot! *Gatta!* My heart! Okay, but quickly, and not in my room. We—"

"I'm not here for sex, and I'm not here to watch."

Docetti blinked several times. "Then what?"

"I'm here to race."

Twenty-Two

Sarajevo

John was of an age that the very mention of the Bosnian city's name evoked a muted sense of loss and fatality, even though he had never been to this region of Central Europe. The four-year-plus siege of Sarajevo had been the longest urban assault in Europe since World War II.

As Diego drove up from the craggy Neretva Valley into the town ringed with hills, John could envision the mortar battery placements and the snipers that made the city a living hell for more than fourteen hundred days.

John must have been focusing intently on the morbid memories, because Diego had to ask him twice, "You okay?"

"Hmm?"

"Seeing ghosts?"

They drove toward the Old Town, or Bascarsija. "Seeing roses."

The soft dip of his hat brim meant *please explain*. John waited a couple of blocks, then pointed to an odd, rose-colored crater in a sidewalk. "See that? A Sarajevo Rose. A crater in a sidewalk where pedestrians were killed by mortar fire. After the war, they left the craters but filled them in with some kind of red resin. They're called Sarajevo Roses. To remember."

They began looking for parking.

"I was Army," the Mexican spoke softly, eyes on the traffic. "Force Recon."

"Yeah?"

"My problem: I see the value in a siege. See why it makes sense."

John was silent.

Diego found parking near the famed Latin Bridge. "Not saying it isn't shitty," he said, and opened his door. "Just saying I understand."

Zoran Antic was a very small man. He was maybe five-two and cypress thin, with a sharp widow's peak and steel-colored hair. Zoran Antic was an academic, a war veteran, and now a member of Parliament.

He met them at a coffee shop in the Bascarsija and under the shadow of a grand mosque. John had a thimbleful of strong coffee, Turkish style. Antic ordered peppermint tea, and Diego quietly smoked, sitting a bit apart from the other two.

John thanked the Bosnian for seeing them on short notice.

"Sylvia is a friend of mine, a friend of Bosnia-Herzegovina."

"Do I call you professor? Doctor? Delegate?"

Antic's skin seemed stretched over a skull too large for his thin neck. He smiled. "After all these years, you know, I still stop and turn if someone shouts 'Sergeant.'" He laughed silently, and his twiglike shoulders shook. "But it is a kindness of you to ask. Professor is nice."

Pedestrians passed: laughing children, beautiful European twenty-somethings, and somber older couples. Most men smoked. Some of the women, but not all of them, wore headscarves.

"A hotel blew up this week in Florence. Some Russians, the Serbian foreign minister, and a number of Italians were killed. You know about this?"

Zoran Antic nodded and blew across the surface of his tea.

John said, "*Skorpjo.*"

The old man's fluttering gestures ceased. He drew eyeglasses from a coat pocket: steel rimmed, perfectly round, and with curved earpieces. They were surprisingly antiquated, even for a man in his seventies. John had a sense that Antic used them as a prop, to buy him time to think.

"Go on, please."

"Eyewitness accounts. The scorpion tattoos. They were there to steal weapon technology from an Italian aerospace designer. I don't know why the White Scorpions were in Florence, and I don't know what a gang with no air force wants with aerospace technology. But a friend of ours is risking her life to figure it all out. She's asked us to meet her in Belgrade. If I'm going to help her, I need to know more about this situation."

As John spoke, Zoran Antic studied him.

"Tell me about this friend."

"Daria Gibron. She's been a soldier and a spy. Now she's . . . I'm not sure." John paused to think of a good word that described Daria. After a moment, he simply shrugged. "She gets involved. She's not a mercenary or a vigilante. She simply can't stand by and do nothing when something needs doing. I can't explain it better than that."

Antic said, "She sounds heroic."

"And Daria would be the first to laugh in your face for saying that. Nonetheless, she lived in my country for a while, and it's my opinion she acted heroically and wasn't treated very well by my government. So I aim to help her."

Zoran Antic nodded, as if weighing all that.

"I am a member of the Bosnian Parliament representing the Illyrian Party. Do you know of us, Mr. Broom?"

"No, sir."

"Hmm. The Illyrians were here before the Greeks. Before the Romans. The earliest organized society in this part of the world was the Illyrians. My party believes in a spiritual reunification of the region but not a political or military reunification. We don't want Yugoslavia back. But we don't want to be at each other's throats. You understand, yes?"

"I think so, sir."

Antic leaned forward, his thin neck elongating. "For too many centuries our people have been known as the keepers of grudges. A people who believe in the thousand-year-old feud. During the war, *Skorpjo* was a plague on Bosnia. Horrible, horrible war crimes. That this organization still exists in Serbia is terrible. But . . ." He raised one arthritic finger for emphasis. "The White Scorpions are not officially part of the Serbian regime today. They have been thoroughly denounced."

John had produced his Moleskine notepad and pen. He looked up and smiled. "'Officially?'"

Antic's eyes gleamed behind his round glasses. "Good, Mr. Broom. You pay attention to details. Officially, *Skorpjo* are just hoodlums. But they still carry out orders for some of those in power in Belgrade."

"Who?"

"I would start by keeping an eye on Dragan Petrovic. A member of the Serbian Parliament."

John wrote the name phonetically. "I assume this Petrovic would deny any knowledge of *Skorpjo*?"

Antic shrugged and puffed out his lower lip. "Of course! Mr. Petrovic is a man beyond reproach. A statesman, yes? He has impeccable taste, a beautiful wife, three lovely daughters. Such a man would know nothing of these hooligans."

John spoke fluent Diplomat. "Naturally."

"And if you were to get to Belgrade to ask him, I'm afraid he would be unavailable. Doubtless, Mr. Petrovic is quite busy these days."

"Busy?"

The old man nodded gravely. "Dragan Petrovic has been promoted to acting foreign minister of Serbia. After the untimely death of his predecessor. In a hotel in Florence, Italy."

John sat, his pen hovering over his notepad. Diego grunted, shook his head a little.

John said, "Holy shit . . . sir."

Zoran Antic laughed and reached across the table and patted the back of John's hand. "Yes. As you Americans put it so poetically, Mr. Broom. Holy shit indeed."

Washington, D.C.

The director of the CIA sat in the overstuffed chocolate leather chair in Senator Singer Cavanaugh's office and sipped the senator's coffee. It was 6:00 A.M.

Singer stood leaning on his cane. "The Gang wants to be sure we're getting the full report on this mess in Italy. You understand."

The director nodded. "Absolutely, Senator."

The Gang of Nine is the unofficial top echelon of decision makers on Capitol Hill when it comes to military and intelligence issues. They included the ranking Democrat and the ranking Republican in both the House and Senate; Singer Cavanaugh, as chair of the Joint Intelligence Committee; and the ranking Republicans and Democrats of the House Intelligence and Senate Intelligence Committees.

The director leaned forward, elbows on the knees of his Saville Row suit. "As soon as the Agency knows anything, we will pass it on to you. Guaranteed."

Singer sipped from his own cup. "And you've no word on this Daria Gibron?"

"Not that I've heard. But I think the Mossad is taking point on tracking her down. She was an Israeli intelligence asset originally. The Israelis are looking into what role she may or may not have played in the Florence thing."

"So when you find out about her . . . ?"

"I will call you, Senator." The director put extra emphasis on the words *I* and *you*, as opposed to *our agency* and *your office*.

Singer said, "Fine, fine. Thank you." His desk phone rang.

The director stood and handed the older man his cup, buttoning his suit coat. "We appreciate the support we get from you on the Hill, Senator."

Singer's phone rang again. "Of course. Say hello to Marjorie for me."

"I will, sir. Oh, she attended the gala that Adair organized for Johns Hopkins last week. Said it was a helluva time. A *helluva* time."

The phone rang a third time. The director of the CIA glanced toward it.

Singer set down the cups on his desk. "I'll let her know. Thanks again, Bruce."

"Any time, sir."

The phone rang a fourth time.

Singer drawled, "You might wanna get that."

The director blinked. "Senator?"

The phone rang a fifth time.

Singer limped around his desk. "The phone. I think it's for you."

As he settled himself into the desk chair, the director tentatively reached for the senator's desk phone, paused, then picked it up and identified himself.

"Yes . . . ? Admiral? How the hell . . . the Pentagon said . . . ? The budget is . . . A secret hold on *what?*"

The director stood, frozen. Singer used the side of his rough, calloused thumb to open the seam on an envelope and unfold the letter therein. The director listened. His face changed from pink to red to scarlet.

Singer began reading the letter in the envelope.

The director said, "I'll handle it . . . I said: I'll handle it!"

He slowly hung up the phone.

Singer held the letter in one hand and tapped it with the fingernails of the other. It was cheap paper, the kind found in any store. "Constituent mail. Nothing like it. Here's a woman in Ville Platte wants trees dug up along her street because their roots are raising the sidewalk pavers. But the city says 'no.' So she writes her senator."

The director of the CIA clenched his teeth so hard they ached. He withdrew his hand from the receiver and realized it was damp with sweat. He steeled himself, then spoke without separating his teeth. "Gibron was at the hotel. We suspect she was trying to steal an aeronautic prototype. We've examined the bodies and know she didn't die inside. She went to ground, but she's subsequently been spotted hitching a ride to the town of Turin, about six hours ago. IASI will pick her up for questioning. Our Rome station chief is en route, to participate in her interview."

Singer raised his bushy eyebrows. He had deliberately sat down when the other man was standing, so as not to tower over him. It was a trick Singer had picked up as a prosecutor: make the other guy think he's in the dominant position.

"No kidding! Bruce, that's fine. Thank you."

The director felt sweat prick his forehead and his upper lip. "That budget line item . . ."

Singer said, "Which line item?"

"The one . . ." There was no way he could say, *the black budget line item we didn't think you knew about*. He willed himself to breath. "Nothing, Senator."

"Anyway, thank you again, Bruce. You're a lifesaver. I'll be sure to tell the president."

The director chanted to himself *one . . . two . . . three . . .* then cleared his throat. "Thank you, Senator."

He walked stiffly to the door, moving as if his knees had forgotten how to bend.

Singer returned to reading about the sidewalk-destroying trees of Ville Platte.

It was just 4:00 A.M. Mountain Time. Colonel Olivia Crace had left the observation area to get some coffee and a bowl of oatmeal. She had no idea how long the day to come would last. The salesman, Todd Brevidge, and the American Citadel board members were nowhere to be seen at that hour.

She avoided the observation lounge and strolled confidently into the control room, rolling up one sleeve of her pale denim shirt.

Bryan Snow and his two in-house pilots blinked up from their screens as she entered the darkened room. One of the pilots had plugged his iPod into the PA system and was pumping out classic Tom Petty and the Heartbreakers.

"Status?"

Someone turned down the music. Snow and the pilots exchanged glances. The chief engineer said, "Didn't know anyone was still up."

The basement air was stuffy from hours of work and poor circulation, but Snow hadn't noticed it until that moment.

Crace stared at him and began rolling up the other sleeve with careful, symmetrical folds. She had asked a question. She would wait for an answer.

It took Snow close to six seconds to realize her greeting had been in the form of a question. "Oh. We're nearly there. The truck. It's nearly there."

Colonel Crace mulled the information. "Where?"

Snow adjusted his voice wand and tapped a key on one of the three keyboards before his chair. "Away Team: Hit your GPS, please."

He turned to one of his in-house pilots. "Gary, bring it up, please."

With a few clacks in the otherwise quiet control room, one of the screens before Snow's chair lit up. It showed a map of northwestern Italy with a red dot near the town of Turin. The map showed a mountainous region to the west, then a portion of southeastern France.

Snow's chair sat in the center of a dais, ten feet in diameter and six inches higher than the rest of the room. Crace stepped up onto the dais next to his chair.

"Traffic?"

"Yeah. It's slowed down the truck. Doesn't matter, though. We have two complete suites of Mercutio and Hotspur drones. We've sent one suite of both ahead of the truck. They can stay airborne for three hours. If the truck hasn't caught up to them, we just send those drones back and swap them out with the other suite while the first group recharges using the truck battery."

Crace stared at the one lit screen. She rested a hand on the back of his chair. Bryan Snow stiffened when he felt the chair swivel an inch.

"Why heavy traffic? It could be a factor."

Snow said, "It won't be. Probably. You know, there's a coffee machine in the break room. We can feed all the images into the observation lounge."

Crace said, "No thanks."

Snow inhaled, then swiveled his chair toward her. He knew it would swing the seat back out from under her hand.

"We'd prefer you observe from the observation lounge."

Crace turned and looked down at him. "Why?"

Snow couldn't say, *because Major Arcana could contact me at any time.* He stared directly up into her laser-precise vision. "Because I want controllers in my control room and observers in the observation lounge.

Because that's the way my team and I operate. Colonel." He gave it a pause before adding her rank.

Crace appreciated straight talk. She made him wait a couple of seconds, then crooked one corner of her lips into an almost smile. "Fair enough."

She stepped back down off the dais, and Snow silently exhaled. As she moved to the door, Colonel Crace spoke over her shoulder. "Let me know when the birds reach Gibron."

"Yes, ma'am."

"Also, find out what's going on in Turin that . . ."

Her voice faded. She stopped walking.

Snow turned to her.

She spun. "Turin?"

"Yeah. Like in 'Shroud of . . .' I think. I don't know—"

Crace marched back to him. "Bring up a news site. An international news site."

One of the pilots said, "We monitor all breaking news, as well as law enforcement and public safety Web sites, ma'am. We—"

She said, "Get me ESPN. Or Fox Sports."

One of the pilots began banging away at his keyboard. Seconds later a monitor blinked to life and quickly turned to a sports cable channel.

The other pilot squinted at the screen. "Wait. That's . . . is that Turin?"

Crace nodded. "It's the Tour."

"Tour?"

"Tour de France."

Twenty-Three

The Tour de France doesn't start in France. Not most years. It starts elsewhere, like England or Belgium or, that year, in Italy.

That year's Tour featured twenty-three teams. Each team had nine bicyclists. Each rider was wearing a transceiver low on his back, with an earjack that let him communicate with the team captain, as well as with the team managers traveling by car or motor home behind the two-hundred-plus scrum of riders called a peloton. The riders also could communicate with ancillary spotters who rode motorcycles in front, behind, and, quite often, amid the peloton.

Besides having talented and attentive drivers and riders, each team of bicycles and motorcycles and cars had its own communication frequency.

The Tour de France is one of the most widely covered sporting events in the world. That year's tour included credentialed newspaper, magazine, radio, television, and Web-based journalists from six continents and twenty-eight countries. It was estimated that one in five television microwave trucks in all of Europe was assigned to the Tour. The military and civilian airspace above each stage of it had to be carefully controlled by NATO to clear space for the helicopters, which would range from six to sixteen per day.

Fixed-wing airplanes also provided coverage.

In an increasingly homogenous journalism world, fans could watch the race online or on TV in virtually any language. That meant each team of journalists competed against the others. And each team used its own communications frequencies.

After the previous decade's terrorist attacks on the United States, England, and Spain all law enforcement, military, and intelligence agencies had determined that big public events like the Tour were especially vulnerable. For the Italian stage of the Tour, every public safety agency in a two-hundred-kilometer radius was on high alert. Every agency had personnel in the field or in the air. And each agency had its own frequencies.

It was estimated that each stage of the three-week tour would field anywhere from twenty thousand to forty thousand fans. Sometimes they lined the straightaways between the villages. Sometimes they braved the cold and wind of the uphill half of the mountain stages, waiting for the monolithic peloton, its two hundred bikes, ancillary motorbikes, and follow cars to lug past them, churning slowly, defying gravity. Sometimes the thousands of fans filled the villages to overflowing. For the townspeople along the route traffic would transform sleepy villages into bustling metropolises and back again, all inside twenty-four hours.

One in eight fans along the route would use Twitter. One in nine would use Facebook. One in seventeen would use Instagram. And one in 1.3 carried an active cell phone.

Which meant the cell towers were pushed far beyond endurance long before the first racing bike arrived.

The Tour de France did not tour.

It raged.

Sandpoint, Idaho

Bryan Snow attacked his keyboard. His two in-house pilots attacked their keyboards. Everyone leaned forward. The first acrid taint of flop sweat began to fill the control room.

Colonel Crace stood on Snow's dais and watched the screens. Her hands formed fists.

"Nothing!" Snow growled, and paused to wipe sweat off his upper lip. "Nothing. Jesus . . . nothing."

One of his pilots turned and, even in the bad lighting of the hidden subbasement, he looked pallid. "Confirmed," the pilot said. "As soon as the drones hit that goddamned race! All comms are off. We got nothin'. We are blind, deaf, and dumb."

Northern Italy

Daria watched the sky. There were no clouds, but the sky was filled with helicopters hovering between five hundred and one thousand feet, and with propeller-driven airplanes flying higher.

She stared through borrowed aviator glasses, but it was so bright she still squinted.

She had seen two hawks. And three hummingbirds. But that had been an hour earlier. They were nowhere to be seen now.

It was too hot to wear leathers, but Daria still wore the fuchsia-and-black uniform of Team Tarantola. The form-fitting bodysuit—leather trousers, tight leather bomber, riding boots—featured no fewer than ten company logos. Daria had gone into battle many times, but she had never before done so as a walking billboard for Amstel Beer or Barclays Bank.

Riders on the Tour de France do not wear leather, but the aides on motorbikes do.

Daria had explained to Gianni Docetti why she needed to ride one of the ancillary motorcycles during the race. It had taken some effort and flirtation to convince him.

Daria then explained it to team manager Paco Montoya. It had taken some talking and, admittedly, some threats regarding her hinted-at relationship with the U.S. Drug Enforcement Administration. She knew the right names to drop, she sprinkled the verb *doping* liberally, and he quickly saw the light.

Now Daria was assigned as a support rider. She would drive one of the team's tough little Moto Guzzi motorbikes while a small-boned but steady-handed Basque named Estebe carried a small video camera and sat behind her. They would ride slightly apace with, and sometimes ahead of, the peloton, shooting live video of the route and looking for obstructions or potential hazards or fans too stupid to get out of the way of the oncoming wall of riders. The video feed would be transmitted back to Paco Montoya and the coaches of Team Tarantola.

Daria would ride the one route in all of Western Europe that could keep her away from the eyes and the ears and the bullets and missiles of the micro-drones.

Not eighty meters to her left, a tempest rocked another group of participants: Team Rostelecom.

The Russian-telecom-financed team figured to do well in that year's Tour de France. The team had a world-class leader, exceptional secondary riders, a great manager, and one of the best fat-cat sponsors in all the world: Rostelecom, provider of more than 50 percent of the long-distance telephone service in Russia.

Despite that, the manager of Team Rostelecom sat in a Winnebago a mile behind the starting line pounding the walls and screaming obscenities in Russian. He had just lost communications with two of his outriders: men on Kawasaki motorcycles.

Behind a closed service station in Turin, Owen Cain Thorson and Jake Kenner pulled on leather jackets in the cream-and-teal colors of Team Rostelecom. The outriders wouldn't wake up before being found and transported to a hospital. By the time they did recover it would be too late for authorities to do anything about it.

Kenner kept one eye on Thorson. "You lost a lotta blood, dude. We should—"

Thorson gingerly slid on a motorcycle helmet, pulling outward on its edges as it slid painfully over his swollen cheek and oozing, possibly septic, ear.

"Pink and black," he rasped. "She's wearing pink and black."

"Yeah. I seen her."

Thorson was sweating, but then he'd been sweating since they left the safe house in Florence. His skin looked pinkish, and he radiated fever. "Hundreds of bikes," he said. With his swollen cheek, it came out *hunners abikes*. "Dozens of motorcycles. Thousands of fans. We hit her in the mountains. Don't worry about what I said earlier. About my talking to her. I don't need to talk to her."

Jake Kenner said, "Got it, man. But listen, let me do this. Okay? You're in no shape—"

Thorson said, "More than a hundred-mile ride. Five straightaways and seven climbs. Toughest climb is at the end. We get her in a pincer there. You take down her bike. I'll run her over. That doesn't work, we shoot her. Understood?"

"Confirmed. Listen, dude, Let me—"

Thorson slipped on smoked goggles, covering his red-rimmed, too bright eyes. "We kill her. Follow the plan. Kill her."

"I understand. We—"

"Kill her. We kill her."

Twenty-Four

The first stage of the Tour de France usually is a time trial. Each rider takes off one at a time, zips through a lovely village or city, and establishes his time for the day. But this year would start with a race day, beginning in Turin and crossing the border into France. The riders would zoom westward for almost two hundred kilometers and for four hours, into the heart of the Alps and into France. They would begin in the lowlands, with Italian towns such as Condove and Borgone Susa along the A32. There would be four fairly good climbs at this stage, ending with a tough 17 percent grade up the Col du Mont Carbonnel and a quick descent into the town of Romans-sur-Mercellen.

Estebe, the Basque cinematographer, was not happy about having a motorcycle driver he did not know, but Daria quickly demonstrated that she knew how to handle a cycle.

As the race commenced, Team Tarantola consisted of the nine riders in the middle of the pack plus the motorcycle, plus the team's Dodge Durango with the coaches and team medic, riding behind. The Durango's roof carried five extra bicycles, upside down. Every team was equipped more or less the same, meaning about twenty motorcycles would ride along.

The riders wore shorts and zippered, moisture-wicking short-sleeve tops, with reflective sunglasses and lightweight, honeycomb helmets. Daria, Estebe, and the others on motorcycles wore leathers with heavy helmets, transmitters on their belts, and microphones and receivers in their helmets.

For the first hour of the race, the peloton loped through the Italian, then French, lowlands, through farms and along a well-maintained highway. With the 102-horsepower engine, Daria had the luxury of roaming back away from the riders, then quickly gaining ground on them as needed. She often pulled behind the pack of riders and, from that angle, all she could see was a roiling mass of helmets and shoulders. They looked like the surface of rough seas bobbing up and down. From behind, the two-hundred-plus riders looked insanely close to each other; it was only when Estebe spoke into his mic and urged her to move forward that she could see the actual space between the riders. Even then, it didn't seem like much.

The man who sat behind Daria had his thighs on either side of her hips. His occasional nudge, as if she were a horse he was guiding through a turn, made Daria grin under her helmet. Estebe carried a small video camera that produced a remarkably clear image.

Paco Montoya and his three aides watched the race from the comfort of the Dodge Durango behind the riders, but they also watched the images being relayed from Estebe's camera.

With Ray-Bans and her helmet's black visor, Daria's vision was unimpaired. She watched the skies when she wasn't watching the bicycles, the other motorcycles, the follow cars, and the fans, who, in the villages, crowded perilously close to the racecourse.

Daria caught sight of a hawk-shaped micro-drone at one point and, as an experiment, spoke into the mic attached to her helmet. "How far to the final climb?"

The drone did not change course. It drifted to her right and soon fell out of view. It hadn't been able to hone in on her audio signal amid the mobile Tower of Babel.

Perfect.

Paco Montoya's voice came back in her earpiece in the helmet. "Twenty kilometers. It's a Category 1 ride: fifteen percent gradient, sometimes a little steeper. Three-thousand-foot elevation gain. The peloton will break up there. Over."

The peloton will break up there. Daria didn't know what that meant, but she was having too much fun to care overmuch.

She saw no more hummingbirds or hawks for the day.

The Team Rostelecom Kawasakis ridden by Owen Cain Thorson and Jake Kenner kept close enough to watch Daria as they crossed the border into France.

Sandpoint, Idaho

Todd Brevidge was roused from sleep to come observe the crisis. In the underground observation lounge, Colonel Crace watched live feeds from the Mercutio and Hotspur drones, although one of the screens had been dedicated to the actual television coverage of the Tour de France. The screen showed a gliding, amorphous blob of humanity whipping through picturesque valleys and mountains heavy with green forests.

As Brevidge entered, wiping coke from his upper lip, Crace turned to him. "You said the cameras couldn't lose her in a crowd."

"No!" The salesman tried to regain control of the situation. "I said our facial recognition system is the best in the business. It's not our fault if she's wearing a helmet."

"You also said we could track all her communications."

"I said she could be surrounded by a couple hundred cell phones and we could track her communications. Maybe thousands. Look!" Brevidge waved to the screens. "She's surrounded by tens of thousands of cell phones! Not to mention microwave trucks and helicopters!"

Bryan Snow's voice echoed from the PA system. He must have been listening in. "Speaking of which, we can't keep the Mercutios in the air over the racers. The helicopters are creating too much downdraft. I've had to pull them back. Plus, the support truck is still stuck in traffic in Turin. We've got about forty minutes, maybe forty-five, then we have to send these drones back. We can replace them, but understand: the chase is moving away from the support truck. That means the amount of time we can keep each suite of drones in the air is diminishing."

Crace looked ready to rip off someone's arm and beat them with it. She glowered at Brevidge. "I thought you said your drone system was the world's best!"

"It is!" he bleated, waving at the screens. "It's the very best! Ever! It's just . . ."

He gestured vainly at the living, surging snake of the peloton and its assemblage of follow cars and motorcycles and helicopters and rabid fans and journalists.

"It's just . . . we never anticipated this!"

Belgrade, Serbia

Kostic and Lazarevic came to Major Arcana's double room at the Belgrade City Hotel. "My source in America," she said. "They found Gibron."

"And the flying weapons? They're giving chase?" Kostic's polo shirt was, as ever, spotted with ashes from his cheap cigarettes.

"Yes." The blonde had jotted two sets of numbers and letters onto a sheet of hotel stationery. She ripped it off. "My source gave me coordinates. Find her."

The quiet, hulking Lazarevic set his laptop down on the room's desk and began keying in coordinates. The blonde had slipped on a short silk robe before the men appeared. Her hair was up in a loose knot behind her head, with icy tendrils framing her face. Kostic made a majestic effort not to stare at her long legs.

Lazarevic stabbed at his fingerprint-smudged screen. He frowned behind his thick mustache.

Kostic nodded. "Is funny."

"What?" The blonde crowded in behind him, peered over his shoulder.

"She is between France and Italy," Kostic said. "She is not coming here. She's running the opposite way from us. Smart. Smarter than I'd credited her for."

The tall blonde glared at the screen. And, slowly, her face morphed from a frown into a smile. The smile changed to a grin.

She giggled. It was an unsettling sound, making the two Serb hitters glance nervously at each other.

Kostic said, "Is problem?"

The tall blonde spoke English. "Oh, my stars and garters!" She laughed harder and used the back of her pale hand to wipe her lips. She switched to Serbian. "That's beautiful!"

Kostic said. "Ah . . . what is beautiful?"

Major Arcana pointed at the screen. "I know what she's doing. Punkin's using the Tour de France as camouflage. That's freaking brilliant!"

"So . . . are you saying she could escape the drones?"

The blonde shrugged. "Oh, she will. Trust me."

"So? Doesn't matter, for us. She is still running away. Yes?"

The blonde put one pale arm across his shoulder and leaned in. Kostic had spent his entire adult life hurting or killing people. Yet he flinched as she leaned in toward him.

"She's running. But not away." She grinned, leaned in, and whispered into his ear, "Around!"

The Western Alps

As the riders reached the Category 1 climb of Col du Mont Carbonnel, the racers split into three clusters.

Seven of the best young mountain riders made a mad dash for the higher elevations and quickly built up a lead of 3 minutes, 30 seconds over the rest of the bikes.

Twenty more riders formed what is called the chase group. They pulled 3 to 4 minutes ahead of the 180 riders in the peloton but still more than 3 minutes behind the seven leaders.

Then came the peloton. Going uphill, and struggling slowly, the scrum took on a compact, lozenge-shaped form. Once they hit the summit and began zooming downhill they would spread out into a snake shape.

The racers would stay like that for a while: Seven leaders, twenty chasers, and 180 in the peloton.

Daria and Estebe could hear Paco Montoya shouting, "Stay with the chasers! Stay with the chasers!" Team Tarantola had two riders in that center group.

Daria edged the Moto Guzzi around the peloton and rocketed uphill, past the perilously in-leaning fans and along the relative straightaways that lead to the summit. She quickly lost sight of the peloton and, within two minutes, caught up with the twenty chasers.

Owen Cain Thorson and Jake Keller also negotiated their way around the peloton and stayed with Daria. Once they headed toward the summit, and the crowds packed in around the riders, Daria would be vulnerable to their attack.

Twenty-Five

Three and a half hours into the four-hour race, and day one of the tour stayed broken into lead, chase, and peloton.

In front, the seven leaders were just summiting Col du Mont Carbonnel.

Behind them, twenty chasers pumped like madmen, gaining ground steadily on the leaders.

The 180 riders in the peloton fell back slowly and inexorably from the mountain climbers up ahead.

Daria and Estebe rode up with the twenty chasers.

Thorson and Keller stayed with Daria.

The Dodge Durango of Team Tarantola was stuck back behind all the bicyclists, along with the other cars.

The chasers were obviously straining. They rode vertical: standing up in the pedals, several inches between their crotches and the bike seats, and looked like gym-goers on elliptical machines.

The assent of Col du Mont Carbonnel was brutal, the elevation ranging from a 14 percent gradient up to a nasty 20 percent. The roads were more or less straight, curving only here and there. The riders' pace was such that fans could run alongside them for a few dozen paces, screaming, many waving national flags or dressed up as characters such as

Norsemen or comic book heroes or the pitchmen for products. Most of the crazies didn't seem to notice when they drew within an arm's reach of the riders. Daria had to dodge several of them, including a fool wearing the Kool-Aid red pitcher costume.

She gave the Kool-Aid pitcher an elbow, and the perfectly spherical costume rolled into the road's borrow ditch like a gutter ball in a bowling alley.

Estebe's voice rose a pitch over the helmet speaker. "The fuck are you doing?"

Daria spoke into the mic. "Knocking that fool out of my way."

"That's unsportsmanlike!"

Daria laughed, a high, lyrical laugh. "Who cares?"

The Basque said, "Think, woman! Do you bowl over everyone who's in your way in life?"

"Generally, yes. Why?"

Thorson and Keller pulled around to the left-hand side of the twenty chasers. They were behind Daria.

Jake Keller glanced to his left into the borrow ditch and watched a man in a round, red pitcher costume, like a beached whale, trying to roll enough to get his arms or legs beneath him. He shook his head in disgust.

"Fuckin' foreigners," he muttered. He'd adjusted their comms so he and Thorson could speak and hear each other but none of the rest of Team Rostelecom.

Thorson's voice echoed in his helmet. "Tire iron."

"I know, man."

They had agreed that Keller would ride ahead and knock over Daria's motorcycle by coming abreast and sliding a tire iron—currently holstered against his Kawasaki's gas tank and hidden by his right leg—into the spokes of her bike. Once she was down, Thorson would run over her. Or shoot her.

Or both.

Once Gibron was dead, the men could cut across the fields and hit farming roads that paralleled the highway. They'd be long gone before any authorities wound through the two-hundred-plus bikes and follow cars to the much-trampled crime scene.

"Brute of a climb!" Estebe grunted in Daria's ear. "They're stamping on the pedals!"

Daria could see what he meant: the twenty riders in the chase group were slamming their pedals downward, again and again, virtually willing their bikes forward, rising and falling, battling gravity as much as each other.

Out of the range of their vision, the seven leaders now were 3 minutes, 15 seconds ahead of the chase group. And the chase group was 3 minutes, 45 seconds ahead of the peloton.

Daria's radio crackled. "Leaders are summiting!" The seven riders up front had reached the top of the mountain.

Daria tucked her bike in close to the twenty chasers as they wound through the wall of screaming fans, leaning over the temporary barriers, waving flags, and screeching. She wore her wrist-length gloves with the thin gold zippers. Form-fitting leather sleeves wrapped around her forearms, leaving an inch of wrist exposed, along with the upper half of her throat and the lower half of her face. The rest of her was glistening black and fuchsia leather.

Daria glanced over her shoulder, aware that another motorcycle was closing the gap behind her. The rider wore teal and cream; she didn't know which team he represented.

They were two minutes from the top when Daria double-tapped her brakes and pulled sharply to her left. The road curved up ahead, overlooking a cliff, and thankfully the line of fans thinned out to nothing at the curve.

The twenty chasers began moving ahead of her as a solitary unit.

Over her shoulder, Estebe said, "The hell . . . ?"

The blue-and-cream motorcycle surged even with her.

Daria spoke into her microphone. "Look."

Keller reached for the tire iron in its side holster. Daria was even with him, on his left. The tire iron was on his dominant, right side. He reached across his gas tank and attempted to draw the tire iron with his left hand.

. . .

Daria had braked because one of the racers in the chase group had wobbled, the Herculean downward pressure on his pedals overcoming his forward momentum. Daria had seen it first, even through Estebe was an experienced hand at the European bike-racing scene.

The rider swerved and his front wheel connected with another rider.

Both bikes went down. Thanks to their momentum, when their front wheels collided both riders tumbled over the top of their handlebars.

Daria tapped her brake again. The chase group nudged ahead of her as a third, then a fourth rider slammed into the tumbling bikes and their fallen riders.

The motorcycle to her right pulled ahead a bit. And Daria saw the tire iron in the rider's left hand.

A fifth, sixth, and then a seventh bike collided with the twisted wreckage of wheels and arms and legs in the upward-facing road. The other riders either had passed the accident or began maneuvering around it, everyone just jostling for position and praying to miss their fallen comrades. An eighth bike tipped over.

All of the chasers had backup bikes, stowed and strapped down atop the follow cars, but the follow cars were four minutes back, behind the peloton.

With the collisions, the chase group, within site of the summit, dropped from twenty riders to twelve.

Daria goosed the Guzzi's eight-valve engine and jumped ahead.

The helmeted rider in teal-and-cream jabbed the tire iron at her front tire but missed, the point of the iron hitting her gas tank two inches in front of her kneecap. A spark flared and bounced off Daria's leather-encased breast.

Estebe shouted, "Idiot! What's he—"

Daria's right hand snapped out, toward the teal-and-cream rider. She reached under his neck and grabbed his helmet strap. A flick of her thumbnail, and the strap unbuckled.

Daria hit her brakes. Her cycle jerked back.

She held the attacker's helmet strap in her fist. The sudden change twisted his helmet and snapped his neck.

Owen Cain Thorson rode on, mind racing, directly behind Daria, now just passing the eight downed bicycles, his fevered mind trying to process the scene.

Jake Kenner and his Kawasaki drove forward. Jake's stiff leather jacket cocooned his body tightly, but Kenner himself was looking backward, hard over his left shoulder. And his mouth hung open.

He wasn't even looking ahead as his motorcycle rode straight and true for a dozen more feet. The highway began veering softly to the right. The motorcycle didn't.

The Kawasaki hit the guardrail and crashed through it and rode on before dropping off a cliff. His spine snapped, and he was dead before his bike went off the cliff.

Daria summited Col du Mont Carbonnel.

Twenty-Six

The television helicopters picked up bits and pieces of the melee on the mountain. Eight men landed on the asphalt, bike tires springing up here and there. And one of the motorcycles, from Team Rostelecom, careened off the road and began rolling downhill. It wasn't a truly treacherous cliff. The motorbike rumbled downhill for all of a couple dozen feet then simply fell over.

Sports fans and news directors don't care about the people on the motorcycles or in the follow cars; the TV cameras stayed either with the eight riders sprawled on the asphalt or with the few riders at the head of the now twelve-man chase pack. The chasers began hitting the summit, the fronts of their bikes dipping.

The racers themselves went from vertical to horizontal; from standing on their pedals to sloped low, grinding it out, all arched backs and tucked-in elbows, aerodynamic helmets snugged into the hollows of their spines.

Uphill, gravity is one of the great challenges. Downhill, too, but for the exact opposite reason.

The chasers began picking up speed as they raced downhill.

As Daria summited Col du Mont Carbonnel, a vast, emerald valley emerged. A pristine lake, Lac du Mont Carbonnel, glittered below her in the sun. The valley seemed impossibly low from her vantage point. There was no way this road could get them down that far in so short a linear distance.

That's when she saw the switchbacks ahead of them.

She glanced back behind Estebe and saw another teal-and-cream bike right on her tail.

She heard Estebe's shocked voice, an octave higher than before, through her earpiece. "Holy Mary! What in God's name happened back there?"

Daria spoke into her mic. "Not sure."

"That man tried to take us out with a crowbar!"

"Yes."

"Did . . . is he . . . *did you kill him?*"

"A bit. Hold on, please."

Downhill the look and nature of the race changed. The speeds picked up dramatically. The straightaway climb gave way to nasty, 180-degree switchbacks.

Ten kilometers meant that they would reach the finish line in about eleven minutes.

The twelve remaining chasers began gaining on the plucky seven in the lead group.

Daria cared about none of that. But it took her to the first harrowing switchback to realize that the second Kawasaki was still on her tail. She tucked in low and tight on her bike and pushed it hard through the hairpin. She quickly caught up to the chase group.

"Be careful!" Estebe shrieked through their mic. "You can stay behind them!"

Daria glanced at the tiny rearview mirror. The Kawasaki was on her six. And the rider was just now unzipping his leathers and reaching in for what she assumed was a handgun.

Daria leaned low and took the curve probably ten miles per hour too fast. Two of the bicycles veered to get out of her way.

"The fuck are you doing?" Estebe bellowed.

"Fond of that camera?" she shouted to be heard despite their mics.

"Am I . . . what? My camera?"

"Treasured heirloom?"

"*Look out!*"

Daria shifted her weight, lifted her thighs off the seat, and arched her back to power through the reverse hairpin curve. The Moto Guzzi heeled dangerously to the left, Daria's knee only inches from the asphalt. Estebe squeezed her tight. Bicyclists looked up as she whizzed past them on the tight downhill curve, a dangerous gambit.

Daria straightened out of the turn and now was a meter ahead of the chase group. The Kawasaki stayed on her tail, but it was riding even with the twelve bicycles.

The road straightened, and Daria toed her brakes—tap tap—quickly decelerating.

The Kawasaki was trapped: guardrail on his left, twelve chasers on his right, Daria dead ahead. He had no option but to return his gun hand to his handlebars and to brake back.

Daria then surged forward.

"Throw your camera!"

Estebe's voice rose yet another octave. "Throw . . . what? What did . . . ?"

The team manager, Paco Montoya, tried to cut in via the communications link. Daria reached behind her back, up under her leathers, and disconnected the transceiver. Estebe could still hear her but the Dodge Durango was cut off.

Daria kept one eye on the road and the bicycles, another on her rear view. "First Kawasaki tried to kill us. Second one is behind us! When I say, hit him with your camera!"

"Wait! What? Kill us?"

Daria said, "Okay, trying to kill me! Second rider has a gun! On my mark, hit him!"

"No! Are you insane! What . . . why would they be trying to kill you?"

Daria shrugged "Top three reasons . . . ?"

Before she could explain she stomped on the gas pedal and rocketed forward. Before the Kawasaki could react, she drew ahead of the first of twelve riders in the chase group. She slid to her right, directly in front of the bikes. She heard riders screaming at her in four languages. Once past, she tapped her brakes again and let the cluster of chasers pull even with her.

She was on the bicycles' right. The Kawasaki was on their left.

The Kawasaki rider didn't look like an idiot. That maneuver bought Daria no more than sixty seconds at best.

But then and there, and at that speed, sixty seconds equals most of a kilometer.

And the chasers were nine kilometers from the finish line, five kilometers from the edge of the village of Romans-sur-Mercellen.

And the return of the big crowds.

Daria said, "Estebe?"

"Y-yes?"

"When I say stop, I want you to dismount the bike. Ready?"

The Basque said, "W-why?"

"Because I have a gun in my backpack and I'll shoot you if you're not off this bike in three, two, one: now."

She braked hard. The man chasing her surged ahead, but to the left of the bicycles. He lost sight of her for a moment.

Daria screeched to a halt. Estebe dismounted the bike without comment.

Daria said, "Ciao," and peeled out.

The race now was down to the seven riders in the breakaway lead group and the twelve riders of the chase group.

The psychotic switchbacks of the downhill run began affecting the riders differently. The seven in the breakaway thinned out, three pulling way ahead, four falling back. The twelve chasers did the same, the head of the chase group drawing within visual distance of the four riders ahead of them. Instead of staying two distinct groups they were slowly morphing into one long, thin line of riders.

Daria played dodge 'em with the Kawasaki: breaking, gliding, drifting, using the thinned-out, fast-moving riders of the chase group much the way a bullfighter uses the red cape—to distract, to obscure, to confuse. Without Estebe's weight, she was much freer to maneuver.

But the Kawasaki didn't go anywhere. Daria stayed away from his gun hand, and her maneuvers forced him to keep his hands on his handlebars. But she couldn't shake him.

They hit the flatlands and flashed beneath the ridiculously tall and narrow arches of a Roman aqueduct. They drew within sight of the town, Romans-sur-Mercellen. The village consisted of white walls and tall red roofs, with a Germanic or at least alpine look to the three-story homes and the winding streets.

The nineteen riders began clustering closer together now that they were within the city limits.

Roaring through town, and through ever-growing throngs of screaming fans, the racers and the motorcycles passed beneath one of the inflatable latex arches over the road, indicating they were two kilometers from the finish line. Daria peered through the arch to the other side and caught sight of a roundabout.

Daria watched as the bicycles in front of her used the roundabout to curve gently to the left. The riders slipped clockwise along the shortest route toward the finish line.

Daria edged her Moto Guzzi toward the middle of the furious pack. She created a steady pace, right next to a cluster of five bikes. She had been watching, and she was pretty sure at least one of the bikes, and maybe more, would slide in tight behind her, drafting off the slipstream she was creating to cut their own wind resistance.

The Kawasaki pulled in behind her.

But he remained far enough back—and two of the bicyclists slipped closer to Daria's wake, letting her slice through the headwind for them.

The group hit the roundabout and the bicycles drifted to their left: clockwise, going from six o'clock to nine o'clock.

Daria hauled on the handlebars and veered sharply right. She arced quickly away from the pack. She was now heading counterclockwise, from six o'clock to the five o'clock position. Then four o'clock, three, two . . .

The Kawasaki had lost sight of her. It veered left with the bicycles. No longer fighting the mountain switchbacks, the rider had drawn his handgun but kept it low, against his thigh, where bicyclists and fans couldn't see it.

Daria took the roundabout too fast, leaning precariously. She reached out and let the tips of her fingers slide along the asphalt, an inch from her knee.

. . . one o'clock, noon, eleven . . .

The Tour riders sluiced through the roundabout to the nine o'clock position. The Kawasaki kept with them but slowed a bit, the attacker confused, having lost sight of Daria.

. . . ten, nine . . .

Like a fighter pilot coming out of the sun, Daria was in the Kawasaki's blind spot. He was looking ahead and to the left, his eyes following the bicycles, as she pulled in tight beside him and on his right.

She reached out with her left hand, grabbed his right hand and his Glock, and slid her much smaller finger through the trigger guard.

The attacker looked her way, eyes going wide. Daria noticed a dirty stretch bandage on his left cheek and his sky blue eyes under his helmet and visor.

She grinned and squeezed the trigger of his gun.

Daria put one bullet through the attacker's own thigh.

The Kawasaki bolted forward, the frightened attacker reacting by instinct and speeding up to escape the trap. Daria let go of his hand and gave her brakes the slightest of love taps.

The Kawasaki surged ahead, now out of control, and slipped between the upright, portable barriers, scattering screaming fans and gliding onto a sidewalk and through a plate-glass window, into a *boulangerie*.

Daria gunned it, catching the bicycles, blowing past them, bent low over her bars, elbows akimbo.

Thanks to the helmet and aviator shades, none of the Tour competitors got a good look at her. But several of them later would describe the ferocious, wolflike grin on the face of the madwoman who crossed the finish line of the first leg of the Tour de France.

Twenty-Seven

Without stopping, Daria peeled the Team Tarantola decals off the Moto Guzzi, the remnants floating away in her wake. She powered west, then north to Saint-Etienne-de-Cuines, which didn't amount to much more than a cluster of homes in a town known for decent football and peppermint-striped window frames on oatmeal-and-stone houses. A behind-the-times wayside like Saint-Etienne-de-Cuines was ideal for escaping the closed-circuit cameras that had become so ubiquitous, even in midsized European communities.

She stripped off the form-fitting leather jacket, with its array of team sponsors' logos, and rode in a sleeveless, ribbed white tank top, leather trousers, riding boots, and wrist gloves. The shirt exposed a swath of her midriff and the defined, concave frame of her lower spine. She kept the helmet and sunglasses for safety and for anonymity. But on the E70 northbound she drew more than her share of honked horns and suggestive hand gestures from truckers.

She pulled into a rest stop with a petrol station, a tiny convenience store with prepared foods in a freezer case, and a vaguely Chinese-looking picnic outbuilding with a tall, pointed roof. Only two cars were in the rest stop—two identical, generic white Audi sedans with tinted windows and German plates. A beefy man with a shaved skull and a Celtic neck tattoo rested against one of the Audis, reading *Le Monde*.

Daria booted down the kickstand and left the helmet on the cycle's seat. She slung the little Florentine backpack over one bare shoulder and strolled into the pagodalike picnic building. It had three red wood tables with benches. Only one visitor was there. He was painfully thin and almost translucently pale, with round glasses and hair worn short on the sides, foppishly long on top, and parted in the middle. His hair hung over his glasses, and he had a habit of snapping his neck to the side to clear his vision every few seconds.

He sat on one of the benches, his back to the table. His stick-thin legs were together and turned to the side, as if he rode sidesaddle. Twin aluminum crutches with perpendicular grips and forearm braces leaned against the bench.

As she walked over, Daria said, "Enter the Viking."

Fredrik Olsson smiled shyly behind his straight, limp, blond locks. "Hullo. You've captured the whole bad biker chick milieu rather nicely."

Daria bent to kiss him on the lips, then straddled the bench, boots on either side, her knees touching his thigh. She knew that he couldn't feel the touch.

The Viking produced a standard white envelope and a standard two-fold sheet of paper with Daria's distinctively bad handwriting. "Have you any idea how many years it's been since anyone wrote me an actual letter?" He spoke English but in his Swedish accent.

"The villains control telecommunications. I decided to go old school, as the Americans say."

Fredrik had brought coffee for both of them in lidded takeaway cups, plus a bag of prepackaged cheese sandwiches and packets of chips, along with two liters of water, for Daria. She rifled through the bag as Fredrik spoke. The childhood illness that had robbed him of the use of his legs also limited his lung capacity. He was always out of breath, even when not moving, and spoke in a raspy whisper.

"The Audi is fueled up. There's a bag with some travel essentials, a change of clothes." He eyed her cropped T-shirt and leathers. "Knowing your sartorial tangents, it's all very tasteful, of course."

Daria said, "Of course." Knowing Fredrik, the clothes would fit perfectly. The man was a master of the minor detail. It's how he'd made his fortune.

"You'll find money for tollbooths in the slot beneath the radio. Also three preloaded debit cards, some random cash for petrol and whatnot, and two mobile phones. Burners. You have a passport and driver's license, insurance papers. You bought the car used in Bonn. Maintenance records are in the glove box. It was a rush job, but it will do."

Daria was surprised. "That's an expensive package. You know I'm good for it. Can I—"

Fredrik waved her off as if it were the slightest of issues. "I never pictured you as the GPS sort, so there are maps of France, Switzerland, Liechtenstein, Austria, and Hungary. Also Serbia, obviously. I've marked a route. Border guards have been paid off, so please stick to the route. I have you crossing over at Subotica, Serbia. Take any other crossing and, I assure you, you'll be well and truly fucked. *Skorpjo* controls access to the entire country. I've bought you a three-hour window at the border, the day after tomorrow. That gives you about forty hours to cross Europe. Tight, I know."

Daria looked up from the paper bag, which she'd set between her thighs on the bench. "No chocolate?"

Fredrik reached into the pocket of his Windbreaker and produced three Toblerone bars. Daria's eyes sparkled.

"You do love me!"

Fredrik Olsson, known to the criminal element of Europe, Africa, and the Middle East as the Viking, looked down and let his lank hair obscure his eyes.

"Yes."

Daria let the moment pass. "My friends?"

"Diego and the American are in Serbia, or will be by this afternoon. Diego, I don't mind helping. I feel bad about the loss of his friend, Vince. Although Vince was an idiot."

"True."

"Not wild about helping the American. I've worked hard to avoid a reputation in the States."

She leaned in and kissed his cheek. "I understand. I trust John Broom. Thank you."

Fredrik twitched hair away from his eyeglasses. His was a terrible haircut, Daria mused. It wasn't out of style in that it had never been in style. His jacket and trousers had the look of a used-clothing bin. It was difficult to imagine that the Viking was filthy rich and had a hand in the infrastructure—transportation, funding, fencing—of half the major crime on the continent.

"Something else." Daria sipped her coffee. It was far too sweet but she didn't comment. "*Skorpjo* is working with a tall blonde. Quite lovely. Superb language skills. Silver eyes."

Fredrik grew very still. He seemed to be watching something on the cement floor of the picnic pagoda.

Daria sipped her coffee.

He lifted his hand and felt the shaft of one of the aluminum crutches, which made him look away from her. "Please, please tell me you're joking."

She knew that he knew where this was heading. "This woman certainly matches her description."

Fredrik twitched back his hair. "You just described ten thousand women in Europe."

"She beat me, soundly, in a fair fight."

He whispered, "Oh."

"Have you worked with her? Can you tell me what to expect if—"

Fredrik picked up his crutches and began the laborious process of standing. Daria didn't offer to help. "I would never discuss *you* with anyone else. You know that."

"But if it is Viorica . . . if she's in Belgrade . . ."

Fredrik levered himself upright. His legs hung uselessly from his narrow hips. He could never find belts small enough, and ten inches of leather tongue lolled to the left of the buckle.

"The key is in the ignition."

"Thank you. I owe you."

He said, "No. I found out that Asher Sahar planned to have me killed last winter, after I spirited him into France. If you hadn't stopped him in Milan, I wouldn't be here. So, thank you."

He edged toward the door and the bright rectangle of sunlight that spilled into the pagoda. It made his washed-out skin and dirty blond hair even less colorful.

Daria sat, straddling the bench. "I can't contact Diego and John Broom."

"True."

"If it is her, if she's there, you have to warn them."

He sighed as well as a man with diminished lung capacity can. "Daria . . ."

"You have to warn them." She turned to him. He kept his back to her. "At least Diego. He's your friend. If he knows who he's up against, if he's prepared—"

Fredrik Olsson, the Viking, wheezed a laugh. He rarely laughed, and it caught Daria off guard.

"Prepared? What if the roles were reversed? What if Diego faced you? Would being *prepared* save his life?"

Daria didn't answer. She didn't have to.

Fredrik looked back over his thin shoulder, hair bobbing in front of his lenses.

"You're mirror opposites. Viorica is everything you would have been if you'd been a true freelance and not working for this government and that. Always limited yourself to the *rules of the game.* You are everything she would have been if she'd stayed in the espionage business."

Daria stood. "Wait. Viorica was a spy? For whom?"

He studied her. She waited.

"I'm very fond of you," the Viking whispered. "I always have been. I'll not forgive myself if this ends badly. But I won't take sides."

"Warn Diego. Do it."

Fredrik gripped his crutches and tucked them tight under his spindly arms.

"Do it!"

"Go with God."

"Go to hell."

He smiled without offense. "I'm not the one driving to Serbia."

Twenty-Eight

John had this intrinsically American notion that you could drive from one Slavic capital to the next in a more or less straight line, à la the highways between, say, Sacramento and Salem.

Not so.

He and Diego filled the Cooper's gas tank and wound slowly north from Sarajevo, Bosnia-Herzegovina. They inched along narrow roads, gained and lost elevation frequently, and eventually made it to the shabby, industrial city of Tuzla. The main entrance to the town was a crossroads literally shadowed by massive nuclear cooling towers. From there they hit the border between Bosnia and Croatia. A quick right-hand turn onto a four-lane highway and, less than a half hour later, they passed out of Croatia and into Serbia for the first time.

Since each border featured two guard stations—one on each side—they handed over their fake passports four times in thirty minutes. And each time, John's heart raced. Especially entering Serbia.

But the guard in the blue Policja uniform waved them through with hardly a glance.

They were on a modern, well-paved highway now, and Belgrade loomed on the horizon far quicker than John had anticipated. Once in the city, past the vast banks of bland, Communist-era communal apartments and the hulking soccer stadium, John recommended finding a hotel in the triangle between the historic Stari Grad (or Old Town), Parliament, embassy row, and the historic train station, east of the Danube.

Diego spotted a hotel sign in English and pulled into the hilly central core of the city, which was aging and a little run-down. He said, "Figure she'll find us?"

"Don't know. But if we stay near the government offices, I guess we'll be more likely to stumble on each other."

Diego got out of the car and stared over the roof at John. His eyes were shaded by his hat. "Filling me with confidence."

"Well, I advise the U.S. Congress. Pulling a plan out of my ass comes naturally."

They checked in. After washing up, John headed to an Internet cafe on avenue Ozun Mirakova and bought sixty minutes of time on an aging, twelve-inch-deep computer monitor.

An e-mail awaited John at the address set up for him at the International Red Cross. It featured no letterhead and no signature: *DG alive. Seen near Turin, Italy. Lost her again.*

John just sat and breathed for a while. He realized he was grinning. He'd known deep in his heart that she was still alive. She had to be. This confirmation was a relief, though.

John found a second anonymous message on the IRC server: *Drones—found 3 makers lenses (plastic) and 6 makers batteries (hybrids). Only 1 cross match: Am Citadel.*

John thumped the table with his fist. American Citadel was a mid-range member of the military-industrial complex headquartered in Silicon Valley, California. In and of itself, the fact that they invested in research into lightweight camera lenses and lightweight batteries wasn't damning. But everybody in Washington knew that the company was facing crippling sanctions from the State Department, the Defense Department, and the Federal Trade Commission for violation of trade embargoes with more than one war-torn country.

For the past year or so, the rumor in D.C. was that American Citadel would get sold to one of the biggies—Boeing, maybe, or General

Electric—then strip-mined of its component parts to be sold off. Doubling down on under-the-table arms sales might provide enough capital to keep the wolves at bay for a while.

John sent an e-mail back to his contact at the Red Cross: *Where is R&D for Am Cit? Which state? Tell The Man.*

The Man being Senator Singer Cavanaugh.

John didn't know if this line of inquiry would help Daria. But it was a start.

Sandpoint, Idaho

Colonel Olivia Crace sat in the office she'd been allocated at the American Citadel R&D off-site facility and pulled a steel attaché case out from behind a large potted plant. She set the case on the desk and used the pads of both thumbs to dial the combination, then popped open the lid.

She pulled out a USB cable and plugged it into her cell phone. The attaché case's encryption technology began scrambling the signal even before she reached General Howard Cathcart in his office in the basement of the Pentagon.

Cathcart didn't bother with small talk. "We have her."

Crace tolerated her superior officer's penchant for ambiguity, but barely. "Which *her*, sir?"

"Major Arcana!" the gruff man barked, as if it should have been obvious to the junior officer. "She used an ATM with a security camera near the American embassy in Belgrade, Serbia. One hundred percent match, according to NSA."

"Okay. Well, the Citadel technicians found, then lost, Gibron. She used the Tour de France to flummox the drones."

Cathcart sounded incredulous. "The bike race?"

"Yes, sir. The drones are every bit as good as we hoped, but there was just too much signal-to-noise interference in the vicinity. I'm not happy that the American Citadel people lost her, but I think it speaks to her skills more than their ineptitude."

"Hmm."

"Gibron started in Italy. She's in France, to the best of our knowledge," she added.

"And Arcana's in Serbia. We would ask Sneaky Pete to interdict, normally, but given the obvious . . ." He let the thought drift away. *Sneaky Pete* was military parlance for the CIA, and *interdict* was a Washington nicety for assassination.

Crace sat in the salesman's chair, in the salesman's office, and studied the potted plants. "The micro-drones, sir?"

Cathcart had been thinking along the same lines. "Another urban demonstration. I've spoken to . . . parties here. We are close to an agreement. One more demonstration ought to seal the deal."

"I'll alert the crews here. They can get the truck to Serbia in, I don't know, a day, day and a half."

"Do it," Cathcart said. "We find this Major Arcana and handle her. Gibron is being hunted by every intelligence service in the West. She'll be out of our hair soon."

She heard him hang up. Crace disassembled the secure communication equipment, slid the steel case back behind the terra-cotta pot, and went to inform Bryan Snow and his pilots of the new target.

Twenty-Nine

Daria changed into a fresh T-shirt in the women's bathroom of the French roadside rest stop. When she emerged, one of the Audis and her borrowed motorbike were gone. So were the Viking and his bodyguard.

She checked the supplies in the other sedan, and headed north.

She ate cheese sandwiches and chips and drank bottled water as she curved east into Switzerland, past Bern and Zurich, along the E60.

She slept that night at a cheap motel outside Sanct, Switzerland.

In Hungary she began vectoring south, past Giyor, circumnavigating Budapest and catching the E75 toward Szeged. Along the way she stopped at border crossings and for gas, eating from vending machines and refrigerator cases in gas stations.

She stayed the night in Kistelek, Hungary. The hotel room was austere but clean, the bed linen taut and starched. She lay down fully clothed, an arm across her forehead, staring at the ceiling.

Girl, soldier. Bombs, blood. Pianist's fingers, nails shredded and bloody, reaching for her. Debris crushing ribs. Diggers screaming for help. The taste of dirt and blood. The smell of charred flesh. A woman's pitch-black eyes, the life in them fading. Lips moving, silent apologies.

Daria woke up under the bed, drenched in sweat, having dragged the covers and pillows down with her. It was 3:00 A.M.

It was the same dream that had dogged her since her youth. But the blast at the hotel in Florence had added fresh menace to it.

It was most annoying. Daria had survived blown-up buildings before. Daria had *blown up* buildings before. Why the nightmares were escalating, she could not say. She'd learned over the years that one of the only ways to stave them off was to sleep with someone—although that didn't always work. Daria didn't know anyone on the outskirts of Kistelek, so she woke up the proprietress and ordered a pot of strong black coffee, tipping her thrice the cost of the coffee to apologize for waking her. She sat up and drained the pot until dawn broke.

As the sun rose, she was sitting on the carpet in her panties, legs straight and spread wide, 160 degrees, in a dancer's stretch, feet arched and toes pointing, feeling the tension from the long road trip. She laid out a towel between her thighs and field stripped the Glock she'd stolen back in Florence. She made sure it was unloaded by removing the magazine and locking back the slide to check the barrel. She dry-fired the gun just to be sure.

As she cleaned the weapon she thought about the American she'd taken it from. Owen Cain Thorson, according to his wallet.

And it came to her: the second motorcycle rider, the man with the gun in the Tour de France. It was the American: Thorson.

She pictured the man in the livery building in Florence. He remained maddeningly familiar. For some reason, thinking of his face made Daria think of John Broom. She didn't know why, but it suggested that Thorson might have been involved in the battle in Milan. Or during her convalescence at Ramstein Air Base in Germany. Those were the only two places she had ever met Broom face-to-face. Daria had been delirious during parts of those days. Wide swaths of her recovery remained only vague and splintered memories.

It was funny. She thought of Broom as her friend. But in truth, he was a stranger. A stranger who had shelved protocol, had risked his career and even his own skin to help her, both in Milan and Ramstein.

Daria didn't trust that many souls. It was odd that a man she'd met only briefly, at the height of her illness, ended up being one of them.

Diego she had known for years, on and off. She'd known him in battle. He'd earned her trust the hard way.

Now those two men likely were in Belgrade, Serbia, awaiting her. Somewhere.

Then there was the tall blonde. Viorica.

In the espionage, gunrunning, and criminal circles of Europe, Daria had heard stories of the lovely blond polyglot with frost-blue eyes. She was a mercenary, a thief, and a killer. She had a reputation of success as crystalline as her eyes. Or so Daria had heard.

She had never given much thought to meeting this Viorica. But now here they were. Coming together over a situation Daria couldn't hope to pretend she understood. Fighting to stop *something* from happening, just because she'd made promises to people she hadn't kept.

She'd be in Belgrade later that morning. In just a few hours.

It was time to find out what this was all about.

Thirty

General Howard Cathcart returned from lunch to find mail waiting for him on the credenza outside his office, a soulless, anonymous little space in a subbasement of the Pentagon.

He froze, his eyes on the cheap, white, number ten envelope on the credenza.

In seven years assigned to black-budget weapons procurement, seven years in his tight little office buried deep in the deniability zone, General Cathcart had never, ever received any snail mail. E-mails, yes. Encrypted printouts from SigInt, yes. Summons from the three- and four-star gods of the building, always on their embossed stationery. Sure.

But a *letter*?

Cathcart picked it up. The address typed on a sticky label included Cathcart's name and rank and the room number of his office, a fact not wildly in circulation. He could see the rectangular card inside the cheap, almost transparent envelope. He ripped off a short end and shook the card out into his palm. In a flowery and distinctly feminine hand was the phrase, GREETINGS FROM WHITE CITY!

Below that was a URL. The http, the colon and slashes, and the www were followed by a seemingly random cluster of letters and numbers. The addressed ended in .cm, not .com.

Cathcart swiped his keycard to enter his office. He sat at his desk and glowered at the card. He looked at the back side. It was blank.

He pinched the envelope to open it further and squinted into it. It was otherwise empty.

His mood darkened. He made sure his door was shut, then wheeled his chair over to the computer workstation to the left of his desk. He held the card in one hand and gingerly typed in the alien URL. He checked it twice before he hit Return.

A prompt appeared, with the gray scale, woodcut image of the five-sided behemoth and the words The Pentagon, Washington D.C. The online launch page also warned him that he was about to enter an unsecured site and asking if he wanted to proceed.

He hit yes.

The screen changed. It showed a horizontal black rectangle. Beneath that was a button. Cathcart moved his cursor to the button and clicked it.

The screen lit up.

The image was the top of the tall blonde's head.

She was looking down but glanced up when her screen came alive. She wore reading glasses. Cathcart caught a reverse image of his own face reflected in her glasses, and he cursed himself for not thinking to deactivate his computer camera first.

"Oh! Hi! There you are!" She removed the glasses.

Cathcart felt his blood boil over. "What in Christ's name—"

"Please don't take the Lord's name in vain, you goddamned peasant."

Cathcart flinched back. But the blonde smiled and winked to take some of the vinegar out of her words.

"How did you get this address? What do you want?"

"First, you have a reputation as a historian, General. So I assumed you'd know 'Belgrade' translates as 'White City.' I also knew I couldn't easily hack into your computer but that you could dial out to any site you desired."

Cathcart floundered for an acerbic reply, but he was begrudgingly impressed by her tactic.

The tall blonde removed her reading glasses, and the general caught a glimpse of a hardback book under her monitor as she marked her page and closed it. She'd been online, waiting for him to make contact.

"Look. A few days ago, I swiped sixty seconds off your mini-drones in Florence to prove to my buyers that I could. I did it once. I can do it again."

Cathcart kept frowning but his mind raced: Was there a way to trace this signal?

"I am selling this technology to the Serbs," she said, and her quick-silver eyes sparkled. "Thing is: I'm an American. Oh, not a good one, mind you. I'm a cutthroat mercenary. I'd sell sunscreen to vampires."

"Scum like you—"

The tall blonde said, "Yes, yes. Got that out of your system? Good. I'm not the ingenue in this story, but I'm not the mustache-twirling villain, either. I don't particularly want these bloodthirsty grudge jock-eys to have state-of-the-art weaponry. For the same reason I wouldn't give my sister's toddler a cocked auto. You know?"

"What do you want?"

"Well!" The blonde smiled brightly and seemed to settle into her chair. "In a word: money. In two words: more money!"

The general gnashed his teeth.

"I don't go back on my word, General. I told the Serbs I'd sell them the backdoor access to the American Citadel drones, and I will. But!" She paused for dramatic effect. "I'll sell it to you, too! Armed with this knowledge you can buy the Citadel drones and reengineer the soft-ware breach that let me take command of them. I get my paydays and you get your top-secret weapons. God is in his heaven and all's right with the world!"

Cathcart's mind revved up into the red zone. The Mercutio and Hotspur drones were the best mobile weapons platforms he had ever seen. And there was no question that this blond bitch had taken com-mand of them. He needed to know how she'd done that.

He nodded. "Go on."

"Come to Belgrade. You, personally. I'll give you the intercept technology. You pay me . . . oh, let's say six million dollars, American."

"Six million."

"Pentagon black-budget weapons procurements? You can find six million in your vending machines, General. And we both know it. A cool six mil gets you complete access to the greatest covert weapons system on earth."

She waited for him to catch up.

"You have three options. You pay nothing and get nothing. You pay those ass-wipes at Citadel and get access to a tech that the thugocracy in Belgrade has, too. And you think that won't come back to bite you in the butt? Please. I have video of you at Citadel, remember? Or, you could go for what's behind door number three: pay Citadel, pay me, fuck the Serbs, and secure the peace for America and for Democracy. *Si vis pacem, para bellum.*"

Cathcart sat and scowled. "How do I know I can trust you?"

The woman reached forward, somewhere near her keyboard. A second later, the timer music from *Jeopardy!* sounded.

"Alright!" he snapped. His jaw was starting to ache from grinding his teeth. "I'll think about it. I'll contact you at this address within—"

"This address leads to a server farm in Cameroon. Which I'll scrap at the end of this conversation. Here's how it works. You check into the Belgrade City Hotel in the next forty-eight hours. Be ready to transfer my money to an electronic account. Fail to do so and watch Kosovo get bombed into the Stone Age. *Capice?*"

Cathcart said, "I'll need certain conditions. First, you must—"

The blonde waggled her fingers. "Hasta la bye-bye."

The screen went blank. A second later, and a scroll popped up: CAN-NOT OPEN PAGE BECAUSE SERVER CANNOT BE FOUND.

Cathcart muttered, "Bitch," and shut his computer down.

He thought about the situation for almost two minutes. Then he retrieved his secure communications rig and contacted Colonel Crace in Sandpoint.

She answered immediately.

"This line secure?"

"Yes, sir."

Cathcart said, "Major Arcana contacted me. She wants to sell me the bypass that let her hijack the drones."

Crace's normally impassive face showed her surprise. "How the hell did she—?"

"Focus! She was spotted in Belgrade yesterday. Any luck finding her again?"

"No, sir. But the truck with the drones will be there in about three hours."

"Okay. I'll meet her and draw her out. Have the drones ready. We eliminate her and move forward with securing the technology from Citadel."

Crace pinched her lower lip between her thumb and fingers. "Sir. It's a huge risk. There must be—"

"If you come up with a better plan before I get to Butt-Fuck Serbia, you have permission to speak freely. Cathcart out."

He hung up.

He didn't trust the blond mercenary. Not one second, not one inch. But as long as he controlled the drone technology—and if he took his own trusted cadre of people with him to ensure his safety—there was no reason to think this brouhaha couldn't be over in a day or two.

He called covert operations and arranged for six good Special Forces soldiers—men he'd used before—to be at his command. Then he arranged for transport to Europe.

Thirty-One

Belgrade is a city of 1.6 million people. It is one of the oldest continuously inhabited sites in Central Europe, sitting at the confluence of the Danube and Sava rivers.

Daria had come in from the north, on the E70 bridge across the Danube, and hit Avenue 29 Novembra. She drove around until she found a district with nightclubs and "gentlemen's clubs" and casinos. She observed a couple of women who, based on their attire, likely made a living offering succor for a flat fee. She followed them to a smoke-colored hotel, windows flush against the walls and unadorned by windowsills. Disturbingly, the walls reminded her of nothing so much as the material they use to make Presto Logs.

She pulled Serb dinars out of an ATM using one of the Viking's debit cards, then paid cash for a room for the night. The clerk, a thin and stooped sickle of a man, had to do the math with a pencil and pad to figure out the overnight rate.

He spoke behind shatterproof glass laced with wire, and through a mesh speaker. She and the clerk discovered a common tongue in Italian, and Daria paid a bit extra for a set of clean sheets and pillowcases. She trudged upstairs, stripped the old and supposedly clean sheets off the bed, piled them up in the hallway, and stretched on the new and supposedly clean sheets. Then she showered.

She remembered the advice of an old spymaster in Tel Aviv. "In a foreign city? Hide in a whorehouse. Nobody sees nobody in a whorehouse. Can you imagine an intelligence officer anywhere in the world saying to his superiors, 'You'll never guess who I saw with this hooker . . .'"

The shower water was tepid, the pressure anemic. Daria toweled off and sat on the newly made bed with a map of Belgrade that Fredrik Olsson had left in the car. The map showed a T-intersection of the Danube and Sava rivers. The ancient castle and Stari Grad were tucked tight up against the southeast corner of the T. Below that was the seat of government, including the Parliament building. South of that on Avenue Kralja Milana was an enormous Eastern Orthodox cathedral, St. Sava's. And between them, embassy row.

Target-rich environments for a psychotic mercenary, a criminal/terrorist cell, and a fleet of mobile weapons. The perfect place to start looking for trouble.

Outside, the old sheets were still piled in the hall. Daria took the stairs down to the crummy, chairless lobby—no CCTV cameras here, obviously—and stood just inside the door, holding her cell phone in both hands as if texting. The clerk watched her greedily. She stood like that as girls and clients passed by. Inbound, the girls and johns walked up the stairs together. Outbound, they descended the stairs alone. She waited until a Middle Eastern girl about Daria's size entered and trudged slowly up the stairs. Daria noted the clerk taking a phone call. While he was distracted, she tucked away her phone and followed the prostitute up the stairs.

On the third floor the girl rapped on a door, called out a name softly, then waited. After a bit, she unlocked the door and stepped in. She wore an acrylic dress, much of it transparent, and white boots with platforms and chunky heels. She didn't notice that the door did not close behind her as she tossed a worn-down hemp tote onto her bed.

Daria cleared her throat and the girl turned. She eyed Daria. Not warily, but wearily. "What?"

Daria held up a fan of dinars. Based on the girl's looks, she tried Arabic. "I have money."

The girl responded in Arabic with a Cairene accent. "I can see that. Can you find another girl? I'm dead."

"I need to borrow some of your clothes."

The girl yawned, willing herself to stay upright. "For how long?"

"The rest of the day."

The girl considered it a moment, then spat out a price. It was on the high side. Daria peeled off the bills and tossed them on the girl's bed.

"Why do you want my clothes?"

Daria opted for honesty. "To hunt down a woman in Belgrade and kill her."

"Oh." The Saudi girl thought about that. "Twenty percent more if you get blood stains on anything."

In a world of ever-shifting mores, values, and alliances, Daria had always appreciated the predictable, bottom-line sensibility of your garden-variety prostitute.

Two miles from the bordello, John Broom and Diego drank coffee and ate breakfast rolls that could have doubled as little sandbags in the event of a flood. John had bought new jeans and several generic, solid-colored T-shirts. Diego wore a T-shirt inscribed with the name *Chicharito* under a western-style, short-sleeved plaid shirt, untucked and unbuttoned.

Diego watched a football match on the restaurant's twelve-inch TV and sipped his coffee. He said, "Got a move?"

John chewed his roll. "Visit the U.S. embassy."

Diego didn't take his eyes off the flickering images. "How come?"

John held up a paper napkin and spat out the ball of indestructible dough. "I know a guy who works there."

Diego dragged his eyes off the game. He raised his eyebrows a quarter inch.

"I know," John said. "Coincidences bother me, too. The fact is, as an analyst for the CIA, I worked with State all the time. Those worlds aren't that large. It would be weird if I didn't know at least one person in any of the embassies in the former Yugoslavia."

Diego turned back to the football game. The sound was off. "How about the guy we were told about?"

"Acting Foreign Minister Dragan Petrovic. Okay, first, I don't know how we get on a foreign minister's calendar, but the guy I know at the U.S. embassy might. Second, what would we say if we met this Petrovic? 'Good morning, sir. I understand you're connected to a paramilitary death squad that helped kill your predecessor. How 'bout them Mets?'"

Diego nodded, but aimed it at the TV screen.

"We also have to remember: we're here to help Daria. If you know her as well as you claim to, you know she's not sitting around waiting for action. She'll instigate something. We need to be ready to back her play."

Diego said, "Okay."

"Also, I want to conduct a threat assessment of Belgrade. Let's assume we're here because of those Flying Monkeys you saw in Florence. If they're here now: Why? Is there a likely target? And if so, who controls the drones? Again: the guy I know at the embassy might give us a lead."

Diego sipped his coffee and peered at the screen.

John watched him. "Who's winning?"

"Don't know."

"Who's playing?"

"Don't know."

"Good match?"

Diego stood and reached for his hat. "Pretty good. *Vamonos güey.*"

The tall blonde waited in the half-finished parking garage near the Stari Grad. This time she waited with Kostic, her contact to the White Scorpions.

She wore skinny black denim jeans, boots with tall heels, and a white V-neck tank under a black jersey jacket. She leaned against the side of her stolen Volkswagen and smiled at the *Skorpjo* hitter.

Kostic nodded, then made eye contact with both of the snipers waiting overhead, at three and nine o'clock, hiding behind never-used cement parking bumpers on the open second story of the garage. He reached for his lapel mic and spoke to the men on roving patrol outside. He listened to their responses, then checked the Makarov auto in his shoulder holster to confirm he'd chambered a round. That done, he nodded back at the blonde.

She said, "Okay. The five best rock anthems of all time, involving cars. Ready . . . go."

Kostic blinked at her. "I'm sorry? I don't . . ."

The acting foreign minister's gleaming black Escalade and motorcycle outrider appeared. The tall blonde said, "Never mind."

The Escalade driver stepped out and, once again, the woman calling herself Major Arcana climbed into the SUV.

"Minister."

Dragan Petrovic wore a gray suit and a sky blue tie. He held himself with the posture of a man whom God would pick to lead other men.

"Where are we, 'Major'?"

She said, "Your drones have arrived. They have completed their first reconnaissance sortie over Belgrade. No sign of the Gibron woman."

Petrovic took a second to remember who "the Gibron woman" was. "The American from the hotel in Florence?"

"Not American. But yes."

"She no longer is a factor in this, I understand."

The blonde smiled languidly. "Oh, she's a factor."

Petrovic glanced at the concave curve of her lower abdomen. The low-rise jeans didn't quite touch her skin there, and he glimpsed scarlet panties.

He forced his mind back on course. "The Ameri— this woman. Gibron. I received a report that she was spotted heading into France."

"And I received a report that the meek shall inherit the earth." She shrugged. "Guess we'll see."

Dragan Petrovic waved this off as irrelevant. He glanced at his gold-inlaid watch. "The drones and the command-and-control truck—you've seen them?"

"Yes."

"Then we are ready for the next phase?"

"In twenty-four hours."

"This is the critical phase. I warn you—"

The blonde reached out to touch his thigh. Petrovic froze—surprised to be interrupted in midsentence; surprised by the familiarity of the physical contact.

"Let's not fall back on cliché, Mr. Acting Foreign Minister. We are at war. Every phase is critical. May I ask: What is the target?"

Petrovic willed his heart to slow down. He could still feel the point on his thigh where her hand had rested, ever so briefly. He steadied his eyes, his vision well away from her tightly bundled midriff.

He recited an address on avenue Kneza Milosa.

The woman smiled, and it somehow made the swirling silver light in her eyes glisten. "The U.S. ambassador's residence."

Petrovic's face betrayed his surprise. "How did you know?"

"I made a bet with myself about likely targets. The residence made my top-three list. It makes sense, given how close as it is to the old Chinese embassy. Or what's left of it, I should say."

Dragan Petrovic was not pleased but found himself preening a bit nonetheless. "You understand the symmetry of it? Good. I appreciate that."

"Thank you, Minister."

She looked into his eyes and smiled. The moment held. Then, appearing a bit flustered, she reached for the car door handle. "We'll be there, sir. On time. You have my word."

"And you have the unofficial gratitude of a besieged nation."

The blonde slipped out of the SUV. Before she could close the door, he leaned toward her to maintain eye contact. "And Major? You have my gratitude as well."

She smiled and bowed her head slowly in acknowledgment. "Once the mission is accomplished, perhaps we could discuss this further."

Dragan Petrovic said, "Oh, we will."

The strange woman closed the car door, and Teodore, Petrovic's driver, climbed back in. Petrovic's mobile vibrated. He checked the readout. It was his personal assistant.

"Yes?"

"The last details are being hammered out, Minister. The conference is on."

Petrovic smiled. He made a swirling motion with one upturned finger and Teodore turned over the engine.

"You're sure?"

"Yes, sir. The delegate from Bosnia-Herzegovina was the last to confirm. But we're ready."

"And the others?" The SUV pulled out of the parking garage and embraced the warmth of the July sun as it hit his face and neck.

"The delegates from Montenegro have arrived, sir. The delegates from Croatia and Slovenia were expected by noon."

That was four of the six republics that made up the former Yugoslavia, if you discount Kosovo, which Serbs do. Bosnia-Herzegovina and Serbia completed the list.

"The Americans will play host?"

His assistant laughed. "Oh, they leaped at the chance. They have orchestrated quite a media event, I'm told."

"Superb. And the Bosnian delegate?"

"Zoran Antic. MP from Sarajevo. Of the Illyrian Party. He'll be here."

The woman calling herself Major Arcana saw Dragan Petrovic answer his cell phone as his SUV roared out of the unfinished garage. She walked back to her stolen Volkswagen, the thick heels of her studded boots clacking. Her man, Kostic, was on his cell phone, too. He flipped it closed as she drew near.

He began to speak but the blonde let one heel skip-pop against the poured cement. The sound whip-cracked in the vast emptiness. She pivoted her hip, shimmied low, ran both hands through her icy locks, and snapped back upright, grinning.

Kostic gaped.

She danced, laughed, then squared her shoulders. "Oh, that was fun!"

Kostic blinked stupidly.

"Speak to me of good news, O Slavic one!"

The soldier lit up a Syrian Alhamra cigarette and sucked down a third of it in one blow. Blue smoke whirled around his squarish head. He did it to buy time until he found his voice.

"One of Lazarevic's guys. A whorehouse just off Trg Republike. A woman matching the description of Gibron checked in for a full night. Just as you predicted."

The tall blonde shook her head. "If I had a dime for every time I hid in a cathouse . . . Okay, grab her. Tell the guys to bring at least five good soldiers. Any fewer than that, and she'll make mincemeat out of them. Oh, and tell them I kind of want her alive."

Thirty-Two

When Daria rented the Saudi hooker's clothes, what she meant was the girl's laundry-day clothes: low-slung jeans faded chalky white down the front, with holes exposing one knee and her seat. Daria added a yoga tank and a cropped hoodie that zipped up the front. She did her hair in a loose bun behind her neck, pitch-black tendrils framing her face.

She grabbed her knife but left behind the stolen Glock. She'd be conducting reconnaissance too close to the federal government buildings to carry a firearm. She shrugged on the Florentine backpack.

The central core of the city was a fairly easy walk. The temperature climbed into the eighties, but Daria, born in the desert, tolerated heat better than most. She walked across the street from the Parliament building. It was a muddy gray building, three stories tall with arched windows, second-story columns, and a small dome that dominated the southeast corner. The red, blue, and white Serbian flag flew over the main door. Military guards in fatigues carrying semiautomatic weapons roamed the perimeter.

She studied the building from several angles. She also scanned the sky for hawks and hummingbirds but saw none. She nudged her fingertips into the front pockets of the jeans and stood with her weight on one hip. Parliament looked like a fine target. But . . . ?

She smiled wryly. As one of her Shin Bet handlers had hammered into her: "Focus on the 'Buts.'"

But . . . did *Skorpjo* have the drones?

But . . . did *Skorpjo* answer to Parliament? Or was the organization at odds with Parliament?

But but but . . . too many unknowns in the equation.

She heard laughter behind her. Three people speaking English with loud, broad Australian accents. Two guys and a girl, all midtwenties. They each had mobile phone cameras and were switching off taking photos, each of the other two.

Daria noticed soldiers on foot, vectoring their way. Daria moved toward the trio and chose a flat Midwestern American accent. "Here. Can I help with that?"

She took one of the phones, and the three Australians posed as the soldiers walked right past them. It was an old surveillance trick: by offering to shoot their photo, Daria morphed from a singleton to part of a youthful foursome. The guard might remember the four of them laughing but wouldn't report a lone female scouting out the Parliament building in his daily logs.

Daria took several shots of the Aussies. The girl giggled and thanked Daria, and they insisted on getting her photo, too. Daria borrowed the girl's large sunglasses and mugged wildly, so even if the vacation photos found their way into the hands of a border guard, Daria wouldn't look terribly much like Daria.

While flirting into the camera, cheek to cheek with a surfer boy with sun-dyed blond hair, Daria caught sight of the remnants of a large, two-block-long office building. It was six or seven stories high and designed with an austere, serious façade. Part of the surface remained but part had been sheared off and the upper floors demolished. It existed on both the north and south sides of a street with an articulated red trolley car running beneath what looked like the gaping maw of a former second-story skybridge, now missing. The grounds around the building were blocked off with tall, permanent walls, well graf-fitied.

Large, round holes appeared on the fourth floor of the building.

A memory clicked into place.

The Australian girl brushed long dishwater dreadlocks over her shoulder and caught Daria's glance. "What's that?"

Daria raked the oversized sunglasses up into her hair. She remem-bered her Midwestern accent. "The old Chinese embassy."

The younger guy, dark enough to be Aboriginal, snapped a gum bubble. "What happened to it, d'you think?"

"Wow. I don't know," Daria said, thinking, *Five American JDAM missiles. Fired from a very long way away and hitting a perfect bull's-eye.*

She remembered the Americans blasting the Chinese embassy dur-ing the 1990s, and then apologizing over and over again for the obvi-ous targeting error. *We hit the Chinese?* The American State Department had replied. *Holy cow! Who knew?*

The airstrike had been something of a legend in Israeli intelligence circles. Everyone knew the Chinese were providing signal intelligence to Serbian paramilitary groups. And everyone knew that signal intel-ligence had dried up right after the "accidental" airstrike. The Ameri-cans had publicly wrung their hands in despair and high-fived each other in private.

A jeep pulled up, and a soldier in green camouflage fatigues, a soft beret, and a white holster belt stepped out and moved directly between the Australians and the remains of the bombed-out embassy building. He did not smile. "Hallo. Are tourists? May I help?"

Daria smiled shyly and stayed clustered with her new friends. She lowered the borrowed shades as she checked out the man's PK machine gun. It was a Bulgarian Arsenal variant, an M6-1M. Inexpensive, but a fairly decent machine gun.

The soldier was unhappy to see tourists snapping pictures of the em-bassy. The ruined building hadn't been torn down after all these years in order to remind lawmakers of Western aggression. Not as a tourist stop.

The blond surfer lad apologized and the soldier glowered but returned to his jeep. Daria reached for the sunglasses, but the girl snapped a picture of her before she could remove them.

"They're you," she said, and popped a bright pink bubble with her gum. "Keep 'em."

The casual graciousness was touching. "I can't. Thanks."

The blond boy tucked an arm into Daria's. "Can't turn down a gift. It's bad luck, luv. Keep 'em." He turned to the others. "Who wants beer?"

The girl cheered.

Daria hugged them good-bye and thanked the girl for the glasses. She sidled away, one eye still on the jeep, as well as on the soldiers she'd seen on roving patrol. The blocks around Parliament were teeming with military. That made an armed assault on government row unlikely.

But the jagged round holes in the old and abandoned embassy were mute testimony to the power of an airstrike.

Two blocks south, John and Diego stood in front of the current U.S. embassy building. It occupied an entire block and looked more Victorian than John had anticipated. Diego turned to leave. He had no intention of entering this or any other government building.

John checked in at the U.S. marine pillbox in the turnaround in front of the building, then was escorted inside. His false passport once again passed muster.

The building was stout and had a tall, green, mansard roof, projected dormer windows, and decorative iron trim. John's trained eye could locate the modern security features, such as the hydraulic rampart that could rise and block traffic and the concealed CCTV cameras.

John asked to see Jay Kent and was told to wait amid the Serbians and Americans similarly waiting on church pew–style benches. The main room of the lobby maintained the building's turn-of-the-century feel, with morbidly dark wood paneling on the lower six feet of wall and mottled cream paint above.

John sat. Twenty minutes later a man with tight, curly brown hair, about John's age, appeared. He wore a sedate tie, chinos, and a pale blue shirt. John smiled. Jay Kent had worn chinos and a pale blue shirt to school every day when they'd studied law together at Harvard.

Kent held a Post-it note and peered around the waiting room. John rose and entered his line of sight.

"Excuse . . . hey! John Broom! Whoa, dude!"

Jay Kent pumped his hand.

"Wow, man. Welcome to Serbia. I didn't know . . . *you guys* were in town."

He meant CIA. Kent had lost track of John's career, and John thought maybe he could use that.

"We're not. And I'm the guy you're looking for." He nodded to the Post-it note with the false name.

Kent glanced at the note, then smiled. "Ah. Got it! Okay. C'mon back, amigo."

The offices in back were small and poorly ventilated. Jay Kent was the embassy public affairs counselor, a relatively low-level posting. He moved a video camera and several file folders out of a chair and nodded for John to sit. A cheap plastic fan was clipped to the office's disheveled bookshelf and shoved warm, moist air around.

"We don't have a Company representative," Kent apologized. "If you need a secure room, we'll find you something."

John had known that there was no permanent CIA presence in the Belgrade embassy. The upper half of the Balkan peninsula was considered a quiet spot on earth, espionage-wise.

They talked about Harvard Law a bit. John discovered that in the six or seven years since they'd seen each other face-to-face, Kent had been married, divorced, and married. He seemed to enjoy the life of a foreign service officer and didn't sound too eager to move up the ladder.

John asked about the office staff.

Kent picked up a used baseball. He'd pitched in high school, and as an undergraduate, and he often fiddled absentmindedly with a baseball when he was thinking. He said, "We're between ambassadors."

"Who's deputy chief of mission?"

"Allison Duffy."

Johns was mildly surprised. "She's good. She's not in Riyadh any more?"

"No, we stole her away when Prague got our old DCM. You're right about her: she's a gamer."

He went on to name the USAID director, the chiefs for economics and consular affairs, and the attachés for defense, commerce, and agriculture. John asked about the defense attaché but didn't recognize the name.

John went fishing. "Anything big going on around here?"

"Just the cocktail party. Which, I guess, is why the Company is here."

John maintained his poker face. "Tell me about it."

Kent focused on achieving a two-finger, split-seam grip on the baseball. He flexed his wrist, as if throwing in slow motion. "Croatia and Montenegro are here. Both foreign ministers. Slovenia arrives in about an hour. Deputy foreign minister. Ah, FYROM's sending their foreign minister, I think."

FYROM was the Former Yugoslavian Republic of Macedonia, a mouthful that had been negotiated with Greece, which had its own Macedonia.

John thought about the situation. "So, all foreign ministers or deputies?"

"No, I think Bosnia is sending a member of Parliament. One of the old guard from Sarajevo. You know how those guys are. They love their grudges."

"Sounds like a big deal."

"We'll have AJ-English taping. And State goes bat-shit crazy whenever they're around."

Al Jazeera had gone from a jihadi-apologist minor cable player a decade earlier to a respected news media outlet. Al Jazeera English was challenging Sky News in Europe and CNN elsewhere. And, of course, the Qatar-based news agency would care about long-latent peace talks that involved Muslims in places like Bosnia and Kosovo.

John's mind was racing. "Sure. Who's hosting from here?"

"Acting foreign minister."

"Petrovic?"

Kent leaned forward and scanned through a legal pad on his desk. "Ah, yeah. Dragan Petrovic. Newly appointed to the gig."

Petrovic was the man they'd been told might have connections to the White Scorpions. "Can I get myself invited to the cocktail party? Without any paper trail, of course."

"Of course! Hey, the Harvard Mafia's gotta be good for something, amigo. You got a suit?"

"Of course," John lied.

They chatted some more about their school days, and about idle gossip in State Department circles. John didn't like lying to an old acquaintance, and he was beginning to sweat through his T-shirt.

Kent walked him out and told him the shindig started at 8:00 P.M. John promised to return.

He wasn't outside thirty seconds before Diego ambled his way, head down, cowboy hat obscuring his face from the security cameras and Marines.

They walked a block to a bar and ordered cold beers. The place was a little loud and seemed to cater to Western tourists. It was perfect for a sotto voce conversation. John told him about the cocktail party for high-ranking delegates from all of the former Yugoslavian republics.

A trio of young Australians occupied the next booth and made enough noise to cover them. Diego leaned closer to John to speak. "Target?"

"Could be. If the drones are here, and if the White Scorpions are looking for targets, that's as good as any. More to the point, it's the kind of thing that would draw Daria's attention. We might have a chance of hooking up with her, even if the event isn't a target."

One of the Aussies in the next booth hopped up with her knees on her bench and leaned over into John and Diego's booth. She wore long dreads under a checkered scarf. She pointed to the ketchup bottle on their table. "D'you mind?"

"Of course." John handed it to her.

The girl giggled the way only a well and truly stoned person can giggle in public. She returned to her compatriots.

John mouthed words silently: *I think she likes you!*

Diego flipped him the bird. He changed the subject. "So. Antic, huh?"

John grinned. "Hmm?"

The Mexican shrugged. "You said Bosnia's sending a member of Parliament from Sarajevo. That's the little dude we met in Sarajevo, right? Zoran Antic?"

John blinked at the quiet man for a few seconds. Then spoke over the top of his beer, frozen halfway to his lips. "Son of a bitch."

Diego let a smile blink across his features but didn't gloat that he'd made the connection John hadn't.

"Let's just hope Daria's doing as good as us. Yeah?"

Three blocks away another camouflaged Jeep pulled up to the curb, and a soldier in fatigues and a beret stepped out. He wore a white holster belt and carried a Russian PK machine gun.

Daria had been walking on the sidewalk, making mental notes of the government buildings.

This soldier was older than the last one. "Excuse," he said in English. "May I help you?"

Daria opted to pick up the Australian accent she'd just heard. "Yeah. Is this city hall?"

The soldier adjusted the machine gun, which hung from a strap over his shoulder. "No. Is this way." He pointed.

Daria turned, noting that this man's gun was an actual PK, not the cheaper Bulgarian Arsenal knockoff she'd noticed earlier.

Before that thought had a chance to register, the soldier tucked a Taser hard against her back, just over her kidney. He pulled the trigger and Daria's legs folded. She was unconscious before she hit the pavement.

Two more men in fatigues and berets clamored out of the Jeep and picked her up. As they did so, both revealed white scorpion-shaped tattoos on their inner arms.

Thirty-Three

No mention of General Howard Cathcart and his special weapons procurement assignment would ever appear in the org charts for the U.S. armed forces. Nor would there be any mention of the budget for the transportation unit, which filed no flight plan, purchased no fuel, landed nowhere, but nonetheless dropped Cathcart off at the Belgrade airport using a civilian aircraft.

As for the six Special Forces soldiers he brought with him? They were ghosts.

Cathcart brought the strike team because he estimated the chances that the so-called Major Arcana was setting him up to be approximately 100 percent. Maybe she wasn't. Maybe she planned to sell Cathcart the technology that would patch the software glitch that had allowed her to wrest control of the drones in Florence.

Either she came through, and Cathcart's men killed her. Or she was the duplicitous thief he assumed, and his team would still kill her.

Howard Cathcart was ready either way.

Daria awoke in a warehouse. She sat restrained in a metal chair with white plastic flex-cuffs connecting her wrists to the iron arms of the chair and her ankles to the front legs. Her backpack and hoodie rested on a folding card table.

She blew tendrils of black hair away from her eyes and thought: *If you wake up once in a warehouse in bondage, it's just bad luck. Do it twice and it suggests some lifestyle changes. Three or more, and it's time to admit you have a problem.*

The tall blonde crouched before her. Behind her, two beefy Slavic men stood. One held a device that looked like a cobbled-together power strip with cables and duct tape.

The blonde reached out and gently slid a tendril of hair behind Daria's ear. "Hi!"

Daria opted to buy time. She spoke in English. "One question." Her eyes glided down to the woman's jacket. "Valentino?"

"Yes!" The blonde squeezed Daria's thigh. "I got it in Brussels, but on sale for . . . wait for it . . . five hundred euros!"

Daria said, "Oh, my God!"

"I know! Right?"

Daria looked down at herself and noted round, white adhesive bandages on the insides of her elbows and the insides of her knees. Beneath the bandages were something the general size and shape of macaroni noodles.

She tested her wrist restraints. The cuffs were tight enough to hold her but not tight enough to cut off circulation.

"I've longed to meet you, honey bunch. That shit you pulled with the Ulster Irish in Los Angeles? That was golden! Also: Calendar? Wow."

The blonde's intelligence was unsettlingly precise. Daria glanced around the darkened warehouse, trying not to think about the adhesive pads on her elbows and knees.

"Calendar?"

Viorica glanced over her shoulder at the Slav hitters. She spoke, but more softly. "He was good. He was my competition. We were always up for the same contracts. Not for nothing, but your putting him out of the game was most appreciated."

Daria had learned to pay attention to what people didn't say just as much as what they *did* say. It was impressive that Viorica knew about the incidents in Los Angeles and Montana. But they were hardly Daria's most recent adventure.

She took a shot in the dark. "And of course you know Asher Sahar."

The transformation was dramatic, despite being slow. The blonde's smile evaporated, the sparkle in those unsettling silver eyes dimmed.

She reached out and touched Daria's jaw gently with one knuckle. "Not as well as you," she whispered.

It was possible for the strange woman to know that Daria had stopped Asher Sahar's plot last November. But it was exceedingly unlikely she could have known that Daria and Asher had been orphans together in the Gaza Strip and were the only true family either had ever known.

The list of people who could have told Viorica all this was short.

Asher Sahar was on the list.

A heaviness seemed to invade the woman's lovely face. Her shoulders slumped under the jacket. But snap! The effect disappeared just like that, like a soap bubble popping or a conjurer's cards whisked away.

"Good times!"

The flex-cuffs around her ankles kept Daria's legs apart. They also allowed her to raise her legs straight up about six inches. Daria did so now, using her right hand to hitch up her right boot, then her left hand to hitch her left boot. She shook her head, black hair flying. She said, "Do I look all right? This next part's dramatic, I assume."

The blonde levered herself to her full height; considerable in the studded boots with four-inch heels. "Yummy. Kostic?"

The men behind her were *Skorpjo* for sure. Both were thick-necked, thick-bellied thugs; soldiers gone to seed. Both wore the white forearm tattoos. One was large and the other was damned large. The first held the cobbled-together power strip. He motioned toward his own elbows, and again Daria was reminded of the round adhesives on her joints.

"Squibs. Yes?" the mustached man said.

"Dunno that word, love."

Viorica said, "For Christ's sake, she's never even seen *The Birds*. Explain it to her." She switched to Serbian and turned to the large, laconic man. "Lazarevic, get the other one, please."

The silent mammoth rumbled out of the room.

The man with the mustache sucked down the last of a cigarette, dropped it, and ground it out with his heel. His shirt was flecked with ash. "You enjoy American movies? Bruce Willis, hero, is running. Always. Bad guys fire bullets. But they don't hit Bruce Willis. They hit walls, they hit street."

There was something rehearsed about the speech. Daria paid attention with only a portion of her mind. She also willed herself to forget about the connection between Viorica and Asher. She considered the power strip that had been lashed-up to make a remote control. Getting that out of the big man's hands seemed like priority number one.

"You have interrogation before, the Major say. You are tough. You don't talk. But there?" He mimed touching the inside of his own elbow, where the adhesives pinched Daria's skin. "Bruce Willis is not dodging bullets. There are no bullets." He waggled the long, narrow electric device in his right hand. "Squib. Small bomb. Goes boom in movie, it looks—"

"Got it. Thank you. We had another word for them in Shin Bet. We used them when we faked a hit. They . . . sorry." She rolled her eyes. "How rude of me. You were going somewhere with that. Please."

Kostic had expected fear. He'd expected anger, or attempts to free herself, or a quick capitulation and information. He had not expected the dark woman in the chair to so thoroughly underestimate the threat to her limbs.

Viorica said, "The next couple of hours are pivotal. You've been an FBI asset, of course. Also DEA, also ATF. Before all that, you were Shin Bet. And before that, you were IDF. And before *that*, you and Asher ran with . . . an interesting crowd. *Dick and Jane—Fun With Semtex*."

Daria's mind reeled. Her poker face abandoned, she allowed the tall blonde to see her shock. Viorica knew things she couldn't possibly know.

"But last year, you were a-hangin' with the CIA. First in Manhattan, then in Paris, then in Milan. The word on the street is: the CIA hates your guts. Which may be the case. Or it might be an elaborate cover to obscure a CIA asset. *Vous*."

"*Tu*," Daria corrected, opting for glib to cover her surprise. "You've tied me to a chair. You can use the familiar."

Viorica laughed. "Here's the kicker. Remember the blond hunk we stumbled into in that livery building in Florence? I hate coincidence. I looked into him. And presto: He's ex-CIA."

Viorica said, "Ladies and gentlemen: I present Owen Cain Thorson."

The silent mammoth in the straining polo shirt carried in a metal chair with arms, identical to Daria's chair. A full-grown man sat in it. The mammoth didn't appear to be straining much.

He set the chair down on the floor with a thunk. Daria recognized the blond American, although he had looked better. His hair was dirty, his skin a sickly jaundice. He wore a stretch bandage over his left cheek, and it had grown dirty, yellow, and damp with seepage. His left ear was bandaged and, from the misshapen lump of plaster, some of the ear was missing. From the tautness of his pant leg, Daria knew he wore a wrap around his right thigh. She had shot him there, on his motorcycle in the French village of Romans-sur-Mercellen. It must have been just a glancing wound.

The man wore white round adhesives on the insides of his elbows and knees.

"A *Skorpjo* team caught him sneaking from Italy into Slovenia," Viorica said. "You and the CIA, you and the CIA. Hmm . . . See? There's my whole thing with coincidence again."

Daria said, "Hallo," to the sickly American. She turned to Viorica. "Sorry. He and I never met before Florence."

Thorson spoke and sounded drugged. He didn't shout but spoke in a steady, reedy cadence. "I'll kill you. I will kill you. Fucking slut. Fucking terrorist spy bitch. I'll kill you." The left side of his face didn't move in accordance to the rest, as if he suffered nerve damage from the buzz saw Daria had thrown at him.

Daria said, "Not a fan, I think."

Viorica tsked. "Methinks thou doth protest too much."

"What is it you need to know?"

"Is the CIA here in Belgrade? If so, how large a contingent? And what do they know of the plan?"

As she spoke, Thorson did, too. He might not have realized anyone else was talking. His hooded eyes were locked on Daria. "Kill you. Goddamn spy. Syrian. Won' matter. Show 'em. Kill you. Bitch . . ."

Daria ignored him. "The CIA hates me. I'm involved in your business, first, because you killed a moron named Vince Guzman. A moron whose friend came to me to save him. Second, because I told Dr. Incantada that she'd be safe if she followed my lead, and she died badly."

"She died quickly," Viorica corrected. "Which is the most any of us can hope for. And your story doesn't ring true. If I were the CIA and needed an operative on European soil, you're exactly who I'd pick."

Daria shrugged. "Wish I could help you."

Viorica started to respond then reached into her back pocket and produced a mobile. It was vibrating. She checked an incoming text. Distracted, she said, "Is the CIA watching the ambassador's residence?"

"Dunno."

"Well. I have to skedaddle. Kostic?"

She took the hoodlum aside. They moved ten paces away.

The hulking, ever silent Lazarevic turned to watch them.

"Kill you," Thorson spoke in an emotionless monotone. Daria ignored him and adjusted her boots again. "Can't run. Track you down. Scum. For America. Get you . . ."

Across the room, Viorica whispered to Kostic, who lit another cigarette. They seemed to be arguing a little. Viorica began to turn away, and Kostic caught her attention one last time.

Kostic said, "Do not worry. We will find out what she knows. Lazarevic will have a bit of fun with the girl. Me, too. Then we make sure you never hear of her again."

He winked at Viorica.

And her face lost all of its twisted merriment. "I wouldn't. Were I you."

Kostic's waited, to see if she were joking.

"I'd watch her. From a distance. I'd keep guns on her. But I wouldn't fuck her. Then again," she patted the big man on the shoulder. "I'm not the boss of you."

She turned back to Daria and put on a bright smile. "Any-who . . . I'm off. Places to be, people to do."

"Must you go?"

Viorica nodded. "It was a pleasure to finally meet the great Daria Gibron. Take care. *Ciao.*"

She pivoted on one tall heel and strode out of the warehouse. Leaving Daria and the American in the chairs, facing Kostic and Lazarevic.

The Slavs began smiling at each other.

Daria's mind spun.

That, she mused, *made no sense whatsoever.*

Thirty-Four

Allison Duffy, deputy chief of mission for the U.S. embassy in Belgrade, had a to-do list as long as her femur. She'd been working on winnowing it down for the last seven hours, but the list had grown considerably longer in that time. Tick off one item and three more popped up.

Since the ambassador had been reassigned, Allison Duffy was in charge of the embassy for the foreseeable future. And the Tudor-style ambassador's residence, a half-block from the embassy, remained vacant. It was the perfect venue for an informal state affair.

A cocktail party with foreign ministers from the rest of the former Yugoslavia was a huge deal with serious ramifications, for good or ill. Carry it off, and this soiree could set the stage for a new round of formal trade negotiations for the region. Such talks could speed up Serbia's entrance into the European Union and Croatia's entrance into the Euro Zone. Both of which, in turn, could bolster negotiations between Serbia and the newly independent region of Kosovo.

Al Jazeera English would be on hand to film the reception, since any forward motion on peace talks in the Balkans was still considered a big deal within the Islamic world.

Then again, if the cocktail party went poorly, it could set back talks between the Serbs and Kosovars, or between the Serbs and its highly dysfunctional neighbor to the west, Bosnia-Herzegovina.

But sometimes a cocktail party is just a cocktail party. They didn't have to gain ground so long as they didn't lose any.

Still, her to-do list did not shrink.

Among the latest, a secure communiqué from the U.S. Department of Defense informing her that a man named Mr. Riordan would be attending. Mr. Riordan was an American businessman with an interest in agriculture.

The encrypted communiqué made a few things perfectly clear by making them perfectly muddy. For instance, by calling the new guest Mr. Riordan, Defense was informing Allison that he was a military officer working under cover. By leaving out his first name, Defense informed her that he was of high rank. By mentioning agriculture, Defense informed her that Mr. Riordan cared about anything other than agriculture.

Great, Allison thought. She would be saddled with an intelligence officer from the Pentagon.

The other new addition to her to-do list came from Jay Kent, her public affairs counselor. Jay—a genial but lackluster foreign service officer—told her that an old college friend now employed by the Central Intelligence Agency would be attending the cocktail party. Also under a false name.

Another spook, she thought. *And from a different shop than Mr. Riordan. Oh, good.*

Allison Duffy added to her to-do list: *Check bona fides of Jay's friend w/Langley*.

Then she began the task of worrying about her dress and shoes for the event.

General Howard Cathcart showered and shaved and shined his shoes. He opened the windows in his room at the Belgrade City Hotel to let out the steam. Then he used his attaché case with its secure communications rig to inform Colonel Crace in Sandpoint, Idaho, that he was on the ground.

He also told her that the woman calling herself Major Arcana had left him a bouquet of flowers, a cell phone, and a note telling him to meet her at a cocktail party at the U.S. ambassador's residence.

Cathcart had to admit it was a clever stratagem. No way he could drag his six Special Forces soldiers with him. Not inside a home that was, essentially, embassy grounds.

Cathcart contacted his support personnel back at the Pentagon and arranged to attend the party as a Mr. Riordan.

He would play the blonde's game.

For now.

Dragan Petrovic had Teodore pick him up early so he could shower and change before the cocktail party. He left the Parliament building early, even though he had no intention of arriving at the U.S. ambassador's residence on time. But during the inevitable investigation, it would appear odd if he hadn't left early.

He also wanted to remind Adrijana and his daughters that he would not be home for dinner. He tried to eat dinner at home no fewer than four nights per week.

He barely made it into the family room when Adrijana appeared and threw a hug around his shoulders. She kissed him. He was surprised but pleased.

"A good day?" he asked, setting down his case.

"You devil! A good day!" She kissed him again.

His eldest daughter, Sofija, raced into the family room. And she hugged him as well.

"Mother told us! Thank you!"

Dragan hugged her back. "Ah . . . ?"

Adrijana made a clucking noise. "Was it supposed to be a surprise? I'm sorry, darling. The invitation arrived at noon. We were just thrilled!"

"Invitation?"

"To the American embassy affair!"

The edges of Petrovic's vision began to blur.

"Sofija and Ana are beside themselves! We had to get new gowns. Ljubica said she wouldn't be caught dead in a gown. I'll count it as a victory if we get her to bathe! I'm wearing the blue thing, from my brother's wedding. You remember."

His wife and daughter bustled away. Dragan Petrovic stood where he was, rooted, throat dry, heart bursting through his ribs.

He spotted the invitation on the coffee table. It had come from the American deputy chief of mission herself. It contained Adrijana's name, and the names of their daughters.

They were expected.

Their absence would be noted.

Especially afterward. During the investigation.

Dragan Petrovic felt his world crumble under his feet.

Thirty-Five

Kostic stepped up behind Daria's chair and reached around to squeeze her breasts roughly through the Lycra yoga tank.

"We will be friends. Yes?"

Daria winced in pain. "Looks that way."

The silent Lazarevic returned with a bottle of vodka. He took a swig, handed it to Kostic who did the same, then handed it back. Kostic circled the metal chair.

Owen Cain Thorson watched the scene, still muttering to himself. His face had taken on a sheen of perspiration, and his hair was matted with sweat. The bandage on his cheek had begun to reek. He never turned away from Daria and never stopped his soft rant.

Kostic lit a cheap cigarette and took a lungful of smoke. He stood in front of Daria's chair, their knees touching. Daria looked up at him, her face at his belt height.

"You remember squibs." Kostic touched his own elbows. "You behave. You be good or we blow off an arm. What you good for now, we don't need arms. Yes?"

He reached for his belt.

He watched as Daria lifted her arm.

He blinked.

That arm could not be lifted. It was tied down.

In her hand, she held an old-fashioned, steel, straight razor. Which she couldn't possibly hold.

Daria slashed horizontally. Kostic took a stumbling step backward.

Daria lifted her left wrist an inch and used the razor to slice through the left flex-cuff.

Kostic took another step back. He began to speak, and a pink bubble of blood popped at the corner of his lips.

Daria used the blade to sever her ankle cuffs before Lazarevic realized something was wrong.

Kostic tried to call out, and a flow of bubbling, aerated blood drooled over the edge of his lips and down his double chin.

Lazarevic realized something was wrong. When he saw Daria rise, he let the vodka bottle drop and reached back for the holster on his hip. He grabbed it and swung back around.

Daria was on her feet and across the room in under a second. She slashed horizontally with the razor. Fully open and locked, the cutthroat razor gave her eight inches of extra reach.

Lazarevic's .9 millimeter Makarov clattered to the floor. He glanced down and saw the exposed bones of his wrist.

Daria reversed the blade and thrust it upward. The Spanish steel handle smashed into the bottom of Lazarevic's nose. His neck snapped back, and the huge man tumbled like a felled log.

Dazed, Lazarevic lay like that for a little over three minutes. His vision cleared. He had slammed his skull into the floor when he landed. Coming around, he realized he was losing copious amounts of blood. He cradled his right arm against his chest and felt the hand flop like a dead fish. He blinked stupidly, trying to clear his head.

The Israeli stood over him. Where had she gotten a straight razor? She'd been searched by Major Arcana!

The Israeli held the cobbled-together power strip that served as a remote control for the squibs. Speaking no Serbian, she cleared her throat and pointed.

Lazarevic raised his aching head. She'd broken his nose, and he spat blood out of his mouth. He looked down the length of his massive body.

The squibs now were adhered to his trousers, in the region around his genitals.

The crazy woman placed a thumb on one of the remote control toggles. Her knuckle turned a little bit white as she began to apply steady, even pressure.

"English," the silent Lazarevic said. "I speak most excellent English. Perfect English. I answer anything. Anything you ask. You ask and I answer. It is that simple. Anything."

She said, "You're a dear."

Smiling, she turned to the fading ghost of the American agent strapped to his chair. He watched her, eyes haunted. He'd stopped ranting.

"Be good," she told him. "I'll get to you next."

Viorica walked to the silver van her team had parked next to a corrugated metal utility shed, behind a padlocked gate and just off Avenue Kralja Milana. There she met her two compatriots, Winslow and Danziger, who had been with her since long before the Serbian contract.

There wasn't much room in the van, especially since more than two-thirds of the interior had been transformed into a tightly packed replica of Bryan Snow's workstation back in Sandpoint, Idaho.

Winslow, a hyperactive caffeine addict with bulging eyes, sat in the bolted-down chair. Danziger rested against one of the computer monitors. All of the monitors were dark. Danziger, a brusque bull of a man, six foot five with a boxer's cauliflower ears, wore a shoulder holster with a silenced SIG. He took up far more than his share of the interior of the van.

Winslow said, "Did we get the drones, then?"

Viorica had created a little closet space in the van for her change of clothes. It included a mirror on an articulating arm, which she could maneuver as needed. She whisked off the jersey jacket, then yanked the white tank up and over her head.

Danziger had seen mercenary work in Sudan, Rwanda, and Pakistan.

He did not shock easily. Winslow averted his eyes and pretended to play with his smartphone.

Viorica toed off her platform boots and shimmied out of the jeans and thong. She said, "The Americans are parked on the other side of the Danube. The drones can be here in under a minute."

For the first time in weeks, she spoke with her native accent.

The hulking Danziger watched while she selected underwear from the closet. Winslow turned three shades of red, eyes averted, and tapped the icon for a game on his phone. He said, "And . . . er . . . the . . . ah . . . the Israeli?"

"What of her?" She pulled a black Lycra garter out of the closet. She wrapped it around her right leg and pressed on the Velcro. It clung tightly to her upper thigh.

From within the little closet she selected an Italian switchblade stiletto with a blood-red handle. She touched the stud, and the slate-gray knife popped forward, bayonet-style, rather than rotating on a hinge. It was six inches long. The tapered blade and the handle were hammered steel. A touch of the stud and the blade retracted. Viorica slid it into the Lycra band around her thigh, on the inside, where it wouldn't bulge under clothes.

She pulled out a black leather Armani skirt and snugged it up her legs. It covered the stiletto and the Lycra band.

Her tech expert frowned but kept his eyes averted from her long, lean body. He'd noted the old, well-healed bullet wounds, of course. They were hard to ignore. "You have her? She's out of the way?"

Viorica shrugged on a black silk camisole. Then a tight leather tunic, supple and black, with squared shoulders and a plain, round collar. "I supposed that depends."

"On . . . ?"

"I left her with Kostic and Lazarevic. I told them to keep away from her, and to keep guns aimed at her. She has a blade in her boot. A blade she can reach. If they followed my suggestions, she's out of the way."

She added a very wide black-leather belt that cinched her waist tight. It made the tunic and pencil skirt look a bit military. If the military wore Alexander McQueen.

The men waited. Danziger shook his head a little—for him, the equivalent of a tantrum—and sipped coffee from a metal travel mug. Winslow moaned. "Please tell me they listened to you."

Viorica shrugged. "Not likely." She dug into a Marks & Spencer gift bag and found a small glass vial of lip gloss. She used the pad of her little finger to apply it. "Probably not."

The young Englishman looked pained. "So you let Gibron have her way with them. Even though we have her at eight-to-one odds as the most significant threat to the plan."

"Yes."

"Then . . . what?"

She slid on strappy black stilettos. She set a foot on Winslow's chair, between his knees, and did the wide leather strap around her ankle. Winslow blushed and played with his phone. Danziger, annoyed with her constant flirting, drank his coffee.

Viorica ran her fingers through her icy locks. "Then I guess the boys learned a valuable lesson."

Danziger sipped his coffee and spoke for the first time. "A lethal lesson."

She beamed at the guys. "The best ones often are."

Thirty-Six

The floodlights limned the façade of the U.S. ambassador's residence in Belgrade and made it look like a wedding cake. It was only a block from the embassy and was within the security perimeter jointly maintained by the U.S. Marines, the Serbian military, and the Belgrade Policja. Parking isn't allowed in front of embassies or their ancillary buildings for fear of car bombs, so attendees of the foreign ministers' gathering parked two blocks away and were escorted to the building. Or they took taxis.

General Howard Cathcart arrived by taxi and was furious—he hadn't bothered to ask the front desk how far the embassy and residence were. He waited twenty minutes for the cab, and then the journey took four minutes.

Cathcart paid the driver, thinking, *None of this bullshit would be happening if I'd stayed in my damn office to begin with!*

A hundred meters behind Cathcart, a *Skorpjo* soldier spoke into a wrist-cuff mic. "He has arrived. Over."

To the right of the soldier, a Jeep Navigator arrived in the designated parking and began to disgorge the film crew from Al Jazeera English. The crew included two camera men, an audio tech, a rigger, and a typically lovely TV presenter who fluffed her hair and straightened her dress and beamed at all of the lights as if she were there to accept her well-deserved Oscar.

Thirty meters from the Al Jazeera film crew, a hired limousine glided to a halt, directed by a Policja traffic officer. It was a large enough sedan that six people climbed out. Five were low-level bureaucrats of the Bosnian-Herzegovinian Parliament.

Professor Zoran Antic, soldier turned academic turned politician, eased his way out last. The seventy-year-old man looked hobbit-sized next to his aides.

The sun was an hour from setting, and Antic's aides retrieved sunglasses. One junior adjutant offered his glasses to the MP, who waved him off. "I prefer to see the world's true colors."

Antic eschewed a cane, so the two-block walk took a while. Antic had broken a hip eighteen months earlier, and his doctor had assured him that one more such break would result in a wheelchair. He walked gingerly. The aides, all in their forties or fifties, inched along as if they were meditating and walking a labyrinth.

John Broom watched them approach. He'd emptied his International Red Cross piggy bank to buy a new suit, shirt, and tie, and he felt like himself for the first time since hitting the Balkan peninsula. Diego had split off to reconnoiter the embassy and the ambassador's residence. They still had hopes of running into Daria.

Zoran Antic's leather face crinkled. "Mr. Broom!"

"Professor."

The old man offered John his hand. It felt weightless; all sinew and no muscle. "Did you find what you were looking for?"

"Maybe. Professor? Please don't attend this party."

The aides looked concerned. Zoran Antic look merely bemused.

John said, "Sir, my friend and I are here to stop a terrorist attack. Remember the bombing of the hotel in Florence? We believe the weapons that did that are here in Belgrade. We're trying to track down our friend—the one we told you about. If we're right, and if trouble is coming, then a gathering of foreign ministers is a tempting target for terrorists."

Antic scrunched his bushy white eyebrows. His aides grumbled. One tried to step between John and the old man, but Antic waved him aside.

"Mr. Broom, I have to be at this affair. It may seem frivolous to you, a cocktail party. It may seem a mere frippery."

The old man stepped away from his party a couple of paces, and John backed up to accommodate him. "You are not here solely for your friend, Miss Gibron. Yes?" Antic patted John's hand. "You are also the patriot, I think."

"Well, yes. That's part of it. U.S. technology might be hijacked, and I want to stop that as much as I want to help my friend."

"You treat the symptom."

Antic held John's hand in both of his, the way men of a certain generation do. Maybe it was camaraderie, and maybe it was support for an old man too vain to use a walker.

"John . . . it is John, yes? Not Jonathan?"

"John."

"John. My new friend. You say the White Scorpions have stolen weaponry? The White Scorpions, or criminals such as they, made hay with stolen weaponry during the civil war. During the Tito years. During World War II. During World War I. That is a very old song in the Balkans. You say the attack on the hotel in Florence was terrible, and now you are running about, searching the skies, fearful of seeing the words *Made in the USA*. John, the Americans have played that game—apologizing for old threats, reacting to current threats, oblivious to future ones—for generations! This is nothing new. Your friend is captured, and you want to ride to the rescue: the American cavalry!"

He wheezed a laugh, eyes disappearing into leathery folds of his skin. John started to react, and Antic squeezed his hand. "I don't poke jest, John. I admire this. But it is as I say: you react to symptoms only. Not to diseases. You believe America played a hand in the current calm because of the Dayton Peace Plan, but Dayton did not stop the hatred anymore than the iron fist of General Tito did. John, you are in the old Yugoslavia. You are in the Balkans. You and I? We are in the crosshairs of history."

John begrudgingly understood the truth of the professor's words. "I know this, sir. I do. I'm not generally naïve. I'm only naïve by Balkan standards."

The old man laughed, filmy eyes twinkling, and for a second John saw the vigor of the man's youth.

"Come in with me. Hear what our Serbian hosts are suggesting. Then think about the future, John. Think about—"

"Excuse me?" A woman slipped in next to John. He glanced in her direction, back to Antic, then did a double take. Crisis it might be, but a knockout's a knockout.

She was ice blond with eyes like quicksilver. She wore a gorgeous suit, a bit risqué for an embassy gathering, maybe, but stunning.

"Professor Antic? I am such a fan." She spoke English with a cultured German accent but switched quickly to a Balkan dialect John couldn't understand. She spoke of something that sounded like political victories. The old man preened a bit. The aides instantly warmed to her but continued to shoot daggers at John.

The tall blonde gripped Antic's papyrus hand in both of hers, spoke a few more sentences, then turned to John. "Forgive the interruption, please." The German accent turned back on. "Professor? An honor."

She turned to walk toward the entrance to the ambassador's residence. John watched her walk away. Who wouldn't?

Antic chuckled and patted his arm. "To be young again . . ."

John snapped back to reality. "Sir, I honestly think—"

"Mr. Broom." He spoke firmly but not unkindly. "I need to be in that room tonight. I need to hear what our host country is proposing. I'm sorry. I understand your warning, but I can't let it sway me. However, if you'd care to join me . . . ?"

John started to laugh. He had just told this crazy old coot that it wasn't safe in the U.S. ambassador's residence. Now he . . .

But John checked himself. Who was he fooling? He'd spent the last of his cash on a suit. Of course he was going into the residence.

When have I ever let being an idiot get in my way?

Besides: his number one job now was to find Daria Gibron. And if not in the eye of a shit storm, where else?

Ahead of them, a U.S. Marine captain let a cable film crew through, checking their heavy metal boxes carefully.

Next in line—and looking none too patient at the delay—was a Mr. Riordan. The Marine captain was a battle-hardened veteran of Iraq and Afghanistan. He looked at the taut man with the steely eyes and brush-cut hair and thought, *If this guy's a civilian, I'm a Quaker.*

"Go right in, sir."

The military officer nodded curtly and barged through the metal detector, which was inlaid subtly into the doorframe.

The next group on the list was a handsome, somewhat regal woman in her forties with three blond, teenage girls who were clearly her daughters. Her ID read Adrijana Petrovic. She had ID cards ready for her daughters, too. The Marine waved them in.

As he did, his ear jack chirped. A Marine at the camera monitor station said, "Captain? Guy on the sidewalk, on your ten, black suit and brown hair."

The captain scanned the growing crowd outside the ambassador's residence. He saw the person in question, a man standing with a small, white-haired, elderly gentleman. "I see him."

The captain's ear jack crackled a bit. "That's the guy showed up earlier. His CIA creds were a bust, sir. Orders are to let him through, then detain him in the basement for questioning."

The captain nodded. "Okay. Swenson, Gerardo: haul ass. Bring your sidearms."

The crowd for the ambassador's residence soiree appeared to be in the scores, John thought. Possibly a hundred or more. He hoped like hell he was wrong about the threat assessment.

The throng logjammed at the tall double doors and on the three stairs leading up to them. John noted the uniformed Marine at the door. The man wasn't armed, which was no surprise. Marines assigned to American embassies rarely carry handguns.

The partygoers clustered outside the door. The Marine captain was not happy about that. He was aware that two of his guys had pulled up behind him, ready for action.

People were pushing a bit now, anxious to get inside. *And not for the canapés*, John thought. People understood that the most dangerous place at any given embassy is outside, nearest the traffic.

John was two steps from the front door when a woman to his left stumbled as if pushed. She fell forward, toppling a young couple, who in turn toppled another man.

Diego grabbed John's arm and yanked him back from the door, and from the stumbling partygoers.

"Viking. Your fake ID got tagged. They made you. Go."

John looked past the quiet man and realized that two of the three Marines in the entryway were armed. They began wading out of the building, into the stumbling scrum of well-dressed people. Heading right for John.

Smiling, Diego turned to the Marine captain on duty at the door and punched him in the nose.

Thirty-Seven

John was pushed free of the scrum and saw the Marine captain at the residence door fall straight back. Diego followed him in, wailing on the man. John stumbled down the half-circle stairs and was jostled by partygoers.

He reoriented himself in time to see one of the Marines pistol-whip Diego, just before the double doors slammed shut.

John further extracted himself from the throng and kept the people between himself and the Marine pillbox on the embassy grounds. He stumbled out onto a side street and kept moving, until he couldn't see the residence or the embassy, or their ubiquitous surveillance cameras.

As near as he could tell, Zoran Antic and the Bosnia-Herzegovina delegates got inside the residence before Diego's well-timed dustup.

Leaving John free to . . .

. . . what?

Teodore held open the door to the Escalade. "The ambassador's residence, Minister?"

Dragan Petrovic climbed up into the seat. He probably smelled of scotch but didn't care. His eyes were shadowed, a little too much white showing around the irises.

"No. Parliament."

Teodore paused for only a split second, then closed the door. He drove quickly to the stately Parliament building, with its fluttering flag and soldiers on roving duty.

Petrovic entered through the front door and stepped straight through the metal detector—no queue at this hour. He worked enough nights that the soldiers on duty recognized him. One of the soldiers jokingly asked about his ever-present attaché case, but Petrovic stumbled past him without a word.

One of the guards lifted a fist near his lips, thumb out, and tipped—the international sign for "drunk." The men stifled laughter.

Petrovic rode up to his floor, and used his swipe card to open both the anteroom and the door to his office.

His office. The office of the Serbian foreign minister. An office that had become tragically vacant after . . .

Petrovic went to his side table and splashed scotch whiskey into a tumbler. Some missed the glass, hitting his hand. Liquor seeped under his gold Philippe Patek. He gulped the straight drink. It stung, going down. He poured more.

He walked, stiff-legged, to the arched window overlooking Avenue Kralja Milana. By his own order, the bombed-out Chinese embassy remained brightly lit with harsh, ground-floor floods. The setting sun made the formerly flavorless and colorless office building appear a vivid oyster pink. The gaping, jagged, round holes from the American missiles looked like three zombie eyes, their insides hollow and black as hell.

Dragan Petrovic gulped his whiskey. More liquor seeped coldly under his Swiss watch. He set down his drink, unclasped the watch, and spinning around, hurled it at the foreign minister's desk.

He missed. The heavy gold watch hit a portrait of the late minister, his widow, and their children. The glass shattered. The tumbling frame took out two more family photos.

He glowered at the destruction, breathing shallow, almost hyperventilating. He turned back and stared at the cadaver of the Chinese embassy.

For a second he thought one of the missile holes on the fourth floor winked at him.

The Americans. First, interfering in a civil war that was none of their business. Raining death down on Petrovic's troops surrounding the Muslim enclaves of Srebrenica and Gorazde. Then on the soldiers bravely holding out around Sarajevo. Then interfering with the border dispute with Kosovo. The damn Americans breaching protocol in 1999 by dropping missiles on Belgrade! On this oldest and most historic of cities! Bombing the embassy of a valued ally not three hundred meters from Parliament!

The Americans had laughed at Serbia.

Dragan Petrovic had arranged for a fitting end to that laughter, tonight. A strike on an American asset, using illegal American weapons, that could never be linked back to Serbia. A blow that would smack down the grinning cowboys of Washington while simultaneously sending a strategic loss to the Croats and the Muslim Bosnians.

It was a grand master's play, a coup de grace.

And Adrijana had waltzed blithely into the midst of it. Adrijana and their beloved Sofija, Ana, and Ljubica.

He pulled the disposable mobile phone out of his pocket and stared at the inert, meaningless block of plastic. He could use it. It would be easy. Only one phone number had ever been accessed from this phone. *Major Arcana.* That unsettling blond witch with the inhuman eyes.

Press Redial and Adrijana and the girls survive. Nothing could be easier. In his years as a soldier, Dragan Petrovic had never been asked to make a simpler life-or-death decision than that.

Redial. Call it off.

Petrovic held his phone in one hand, thumb hovering over the lit rectangle marked Redial.

He drained his drink.

Sandpoint, Idaho

It was just past noon as the unmarked Longbow Apache looped in low over Lake Pend Oreille and touched down flawlessly at the Sandpoint airfield. Stripped of its gun and rocket arms, the Boeing helicopter looked more mantislike than usual. It settled quickly and smoothly next to a Lexus SUV.

Colonel Olivia Crace stood at attention beside the Lexus. Three military men stepped out of the Longbow and duck-marched beneath the propellers. All three wore black trousers and button-down shirts under gray Windbreakers with shiny black shoes.

Crace opened the front and rear passenger-side doors. Two of the men rode in back and one in front. The one in front, a redhead with hazel eyes, was armed. He wasn't from the Joint Chiefs. He was part of the crew of killers General Cathcart had at his disposal.

Crace circled the Lexus and climbed behind the wheel.

She did not speak until spoken to. One man said, "Status?" He was the highest-ranking man in the car. He was also the highest-ranking officer Crace had ever addressed.

"The weapons platform is solid, sir."

They motored through the sparse noon traffic toward the American Citadel off-site research facility.

"And these idiots here?"

"Dangerous, sir. Huge risks." She slowed and hit her turn indicator.

The men from the Pentagon exchanged looks. The man in front spoke for the first time. "Is it worth it? For us to even be here?"

Crace turned into the parking lot. She hesitated longer than protocol allowed.

The third man said, "Colonel?"

"Huge risk, sir. Huge reward."

"How huge?"

Crace unbuckled her seat belt. "Sir, American Citadel can't be trusted. Doing business with them is doing business with the Devil. This wouldn't be the kind of deal that ends in scandal. It's the kind of deal that ends with life sentences in Leavenworth, best-case scenario. Worst-case? War crime trials in The Hague."

Before she could reach for her door handle, the highest-ranking man said, "Then why are we even here, Colonel?"

"The finest drone tech on earth. Period."

Thirty-Eight

Daria had a long and productive talk with the silent Serb soldier, Lazarevic.

He sat on the floor of the warehouse. She threw him a greasy shop towel to bandage his badly bleeding wrist but wouldn't let him touch the squibs and the round, medical plasters she'd adhered to the crotch of his trousers. The big man's eyes flickered in a three-part pattern: from the explosives over his dick, to the remote in Daria's hand, to the pool of blood coagulating in an almost perfect circle around Kostic's head, shoulders, and torso. Daria's lightning-fast blow had severed Kostic's windpipe and his carotid, and it had been a race to see if he'd suffocate or bleed out first.

Kostic was the toughest son of a bitch Lazarevic had ever served with. Against the dark-skinned, tightly muscled woman, it hadn't even been a contest.

The American man tied to the second chair had stopped mumbling. His eyes roved jarringly from Daria to the corpse of Kostic, who lay on his back, arms straight out. He'd waved his arms a few times in his death throes, and the arced pattern on the cement floor looked like he'd tried to make blood angels.

The ever quiet Lazarevic occasionally spat gobs of blood from his broken nose but otherwise talked a blue streak. He told Daria about Acting Foreign Minister Dragan Petrovic, about the unpredictable and probably insane Major Arcana. He told Daria about the attack on the hotel in Florence and about that evening's attack on the U.S. ambassador's residence in Belgrade.

Daria crouched on her haunches, leaning forward, unmoving, her heels up under her bum, all her weight on the balls of her boots. She didn't blink, and she didn't stop smiling, and Lazarevic thought she looked more like a raptor than those damned drones ever did.

He talked until the blood loss from his wrist caught up to him. His eyelids drooped and he keeled over.

Daria held the remote detonator carefully and reached down to feel his pulse. Satisfied, she remove the makeshift bandage from the sleeping man's wrist. She reached into her back pocket and flicked open the cutthroat razor. A snap, and Lazarevic began bleeding from his other wrist.

She picked up the metal chair and moved it to face the American. His breathing was shallow and wet. His eyes almost glowed. Daria sat opposite him. She reached out and removed the squibs and adhesives from his elbows and knees, scrunching them in her fist.

"You were waiting for me in Florence. You tracked me to the Tour de France."

The American watched her.

"Thorson? Something-something Thorson. Sorry, I'm not good with names."

His lips were cracked and sand-dry. He licked them but appeared to have no spare saliva.

"Hate you . . ."

"Yes. Were you in Milan? In November?"

With an insane burst of energy and anger, Thorson suddenly thrashed. He yanked violently on his flex-cuffs. He strained, muscles in his neck and shoulders standing in relief. The iron legs of the chair danced a little staccato jig on the cement. The plastic cuffs split the skin at his bound wrists.

Daria waited.

He fought until he couldn't, then seemed to deflate in the chair. His head lolled. He gasped for breath. His head down, he maintained eye contact by looking up from under his brows. Sweat and snot dripped onto his lap.

Daria stood and went to a window. She peered out. Seeing nothing, she crossed behind Thorson's chair and checked the opposite window. They were alone. She walked back to him. "Were you with Asher's people? Were you CIA?"

She was behind him, so he hung his head and gulped what meager breath his sodden lungs could handle.

Daria could smell the infection wafting up from his wounds. "I have to stop that blond woman from attacking the Americans. If I let you go, would you stop chasing me?"

"Fuck you . . ."

She stood behind him and rested a cool hand on the nape of his neck. It should have been comforting. Thorson's long muscles tightened.

"Mr. Thorson? My life is such that I tend to make enemies. I'm sorry I don't remember you."

She moved away from him and knelt by the Serb mobsters. Lazarevic had bled out. She took his Makarov auto and a magazine. It was the longer, twelve-round mag, not the usual eight. She rose and crossed to Kostic, searching for his weapon and spare clips, working one-handed, holding onto the remote control with the other. She also found a SIG that she assumed was Thorson's weapon. Running out of hands, she set the automatic on a workbench by her side.

"Kill you . . ."

Daria knelt with her back to him. "You're obviously not well. The humanitarian in me tells me it would be cruel to kill a man suffering from a fevered mind. Then again, one of my old instructors in Shin Bet used to say: *Zol er krenken un gedenken.* 'Let him suffer and remember.' It's Yiddish. By Jewish standards, it's considered cruel."

She rose, drew her cutthroat blade, and turned on Thorson. He ground his teeth, but she quickly shredded his plastic bindings. A deft flick of her wrist and the razor closed up into its metal handle.

He was free.

"Go your way, Mr. Thorson. Take up a cause. Find God. May we never meet again."

She turned away and began shoving the Russian-made guns and magazines into her leather backpack, next to the oversized sunglasses the trio of Australian tourists had given her.

Behind her, Thorson rose shakily to his feet. His eyes were locked on the SIG-Sauer Daria had left on the worktable.

Daria slipped the lilac hoody over the Lycra top but didn't zip it. "Good luck getting out of Serbia, Mr. Thorson."

Thorson reached for the gun, whisked it up, and raked back the slide, aimed at Daria's back, and pulled the trigger.

Even fevered, he realized two things:

The gun was empty.

And he'd felt a skin-tugging adhesive at the nape of his neck.

"Never let it be said I was cruel." Daria flicked the switches, firing the four squibs she'd adhered to the base of his skull.

Beheadings are quick.

As Viorica had said, it's the most any of us can hope for.

Thirty-Nine

The United States did not currently have an ambassador to Serbia, but it did pay for an opulent ambassador's residence.

The first floor was decked out in Victorian furniture and Oriental rugs. The wall art was by contemporary Serbian artists, and each came with a card written in English and Serbian, describing the piece and its creator. Chandeliers hung from the scalloped ceilings.

There had been a to-do at the front door, twenty minutes earlier, but the Marines on duty had taken care of it so quickly that none of the guests knew quite what to make of it. Protesters, probably. It was quickly forgotten.

Cathcart carried a cell phone in the left-hand pocket of his suit coat and a second phone in the right-hand pocket. The one on the left vibrated, and he shifted a canapé to the other hand to check it.

2ND FLOOR BALCONY. 20 MIN. *ALONE*!

A television crew was setting up, including a camera operator, an audio operator, and a stout man in an American-style baseball cap adorned with Cyrillic letters. He was on his knees laying cable and using blue painters' tape to lock it down. Cathcart maneuvered himself around the rigger and into an alcove with some privacy. He put away Major Arcana's phone and dug out his own.

Cathcart texted Colonel Crace, back in Idaho, and let her know.

The information circuit was circular, as it so often is in war: General Cathcart in Belgrade informed Colonel Olivia Crace in the American Citadel observation lounge. Crace told chief engineer Bryan Snow in the control room, who informed the guys sitting in the truck-and-trailer on the north side of the Danube in Belgrade.

They released a suite of eight Mercutio spotters and three Hotspur shooter drones. The micro air vehicles shot away from the truck and vectored due south toward the heart of the Serbian government.

Twenty minutes from sunset, and nobody on the streets of Belgrade noticed the mechanical birds.

Bryan Snow informed the American Citadel brass, plus the three newcomers from the Pentagon, that the drones were airborne.

He then switched to the communication frequency known only to himself and informed Major Arcana that everything was a go: he was prepared to hijack his own drones at her command.

John Broom had rarely felt so helpless.

He'd been spirited to Serbia under the steam of a mysterious international criminal known as the Viking. John's only contact with the Viking was Diego, who had just sacrificed himself to keep John out of the hands of the U.S. Marines.

John was in Serbia to assist Daria Gibron. But standing on Avenue Kralja Milana at sunset, John had no earthly idea how to reach Daria. Or if she was even in the country.

He had information for her, information she badly needed, but in a city of 1.6 million people, John was at a complete loss. What had he suggested to Diego? Just hit the center of government and hope they stumbled on Daria. What the hell had he been thinking? How could—

Daria Gibron slipped her arm through his and bussed him on the cheek. "Hallo, John!"

John's voice climbed about an octave. "You just gave me a freaking heart attack!"

Daria laughed. "A girl never gets tired of hearing that!"

She wore sunglasses, a thin lilac hoodie unzipped over a stretchy jog top, and weirdly faded ripped jeans. She carried a small black leather backpack over one shoulder.

She took John by the arm and led him off the street and into an *apoteka*, or pharmacy.

The clerk wore earbuds and was engrossed in a Hollywood magazine. She didn't look up. Daria pulled John deeper into the shop. As they passed the window, the darkened silhouette of two humming-birds flicked past.

They both saw the drones. "Crap. The Flying Monkeys are here."

Daria grinned. "Flying Monkeys? I like that." She led him down an aisle, away from the window.

"What do we—?"

The first thing Daria did was to grab John by both lapels of his fine suit and kiss him, hard, on the lips.

John froze, not kissing back but not pulling away.

Daria smiled at him. "You're an absolute love, John Broom. I can't believe you're here."

"Having a little trouble believing it myself."

"There's much to tell and no bloody time to tell it. Sorry." She dropped to her haunches, unzipped the backpack, and withdrew two matching pistols. She slid the sunglasses up into her hair.

John knew nothing of the make and model of handguns. She also dug out two magazines. John checked the clerk, who hadn't looked up. He knelt.

Daria began fieldstripping one of the guns. "Diego?"

"Under arrest in the U.S. ambassador's residence. He made a big play to get me free."

"Bollocks." Her fingers moved deftly, breaking a gun down to its component parts, then reassembling it. She did it while looking at it, but also while looking at John, and her hands didn't move any slower during the latter bits.

238

"Right, then. Briefly: fellow named Petro-something hired a mercenary to steal the Flying Monkeys from the Americans and to blow up the ambassador's residence. The mercenary is quite good. Named Viorica. Nom de guerre: Major Arcana. Blond girl, silver eyes? Might've passed this way. The target is some big thing at the residence. Wish I knew more, but—"

John said, "Petrovic, Dragan Petrovic, member of Parliament, front man for the White Scorpions. The *big thing* is a gathering of foreign ministers from the former Yugoslavia. And your mercenary: Tall, ice blonde? Gorgeous?"

Daria wrinkled her nose. "If you fancy that sort of thing."

John gave her a smile. "I wrote the CIA file on you. You fancy that sort of thing."

She giggled. "I do, a bit."

Daria started in on the other gun. She was disheartened: neither had ever been properly cleaned. She could understand a man's decision to be a killer, a mercenary, or even a terrorist. But a person who lets their weapons go unmaintained should be keelhauled.

"I saw blondie at the residence."

"Good, then. That's a start. What have we here?"

She held up one of the bullets from the magazine, closing one eye and peering through the other. "Damn."

"What?"

"Russian overpressure variants. I've never used them. I hate using weaponry in a fight I've not practiced with."

"Who doesn't? Listen—"

"Tell me about the drones. They're using the things so they can lay the blame on the Americans, I assume? Clever. They could kill hundreds."

"I know."

"We have to do two things. Find Viorica and warn the people in the residence."

"Yeah. Listen, we—"

"You speak Politics. You take the residence. I chatted up a most helpful fellow, one of the White Scorpions. He gave me an idea where to find this Petrovic. We get him to call it all off. Yes?"

"Fine, but—"

She jammed magazines into both guns, then returned them to her backpack. She stood, and John did, too. Near the cash register, the clerk languidly turned a page in her periodical and blew a gum bubble.

"Not much time, John. Shall we?"

John said, "Hold it!"

Daria had been about to move out, but paused. "What?"

"Petrovic isn't the bad guy!"

Daria blinked at him. "'Course he is."

"Nope. Even *he* thinks he is. But he's not. And the ambassador's residence isn't the target."

Daria stared into his eyes. John stared right back.

"If that's not the target, what is?"

The mobile in Dragan Petrovic's hand lit up a split second before it vibrated. He noticed that and thought it odd; the light happens first, then the vibration. He drained his stiff scotch whiskey and splashed more into his glass. He thumbed the Answer button and lifted the phone to his ear but did not speak.

Major Arcana said, "It's now or never," in a singsong voice that Petrovic recognized vaguely from American pop music.

Petrovic drank whiskey. His stomach considered rejecting it. He moved to the window. From there the former Chinese embassy was fully limned by the ground-floor floods. Two blocks beyond it was the façade of the U.S. embassy and, behind that, the ambassador's residence. Both were lit like Christmas trees.

Major Arcana said, "It's your call, Acting Foreign Minister."

Petrovic looked back at the tidy desk and the constellation of family photos and diplomas on the wall, courtesy of his predecessor in office. He looked at the ones he'd broken. Petrovic's brilliant plan had included murdering that man.

God's judgment is swift, Petrovic thought. He faced the question: Carry out his plans for the sake of all Serbia? Or save Adrijana and their daughters?

Sacrifice the battle? Sacrifice his family?

Major Arcana didn't interrupt him. The silence stretched a full minute.

Petrovic gulped whiskey. Bile rose in his throat.

He said, "Proceed."

She said, "You're sure?" And the words were a soft purr.

He turned to the window, eyes down the avenue at the American buildings. "Do it."

"Come what may?"

"Yes."

Viorica said, "Very good, Acting Foreign Minister." She disconnected the line and hit the next speed dial. Bryan Snow, her bought-and-paid-for engineer in Sandpoint, Idaho, answered without speaking.

Viorica adopted a deep, cartoony baritone. "Release the hounds!"

Before they stepped out of the *apoteka*, John grabbed Daria's sleeve. "If I'm right about the drones, the second that one of them locks onto your face or your voice, you're tagged. We go out there, there's a good chance we're screwed."

"Can't stay here."

"Okay. But the U.S. Marines and the State Department know I tried to sneak onto the embassy grounds with a fake ID, so they won't help us. And Petrovic probably knows you're here and on the loose, so the Serbian military will be looking for us. Plus, he runs the White Scorpions. Plus, there's the Belgrade police. Plus, there's this Viorica of yours."

Daria adjusted her backpack full of guns. "And your point?"

"Making small talk."

She led him out onto the gloomy street. It was still overly warm and a bit muggy. John wished he'd doffed his suit jacket, although the blackness of it might come in handy in the dark. Street lights had popped on and shop windows cast shadows over the sidewalk. They moved away from the pharmacy. Belgrade is a pedestrian's city, and the sidewalks were full, mostly with teens and twenty-somethings, but also with working men and women taking their time to stroll home or to a pub on a warm evening.

Daria frowned. "Does the name Thorson mean anything to you? Owen—"

"—Cain Thorson? Sure. I know him. We both do."

She turned, eyebrows arched.

"CIA guy. Headed up Pegasus."

"The thing in Manhattan?"

John smiled and studied her eyes to see if she was having him on. "Yes. The thing in Manhattan. When you ash-canned his career. Also the takedown in Milan. The guy aiming his gun at you. Okay, aiming his gun at you through me. Big, blond, good bone structure?"

Daria wrinkled her nose. "If you fancy *that* sort of thing."

"Which again . . ."

She patted his arm. "Now, now. Be nice, John." Her eyes darted as she put together the pieces. "So Thorson was CIA. Then he was freelance . . ."

John shrugged. "Guess so. I lost track of . . . Wait. *Was* freelance?"

Daria turned raven-black eyes on him.

John said, "If he *was* freelance, what is he now?"

"Room temperature."

John took a second to get there. "Ah, God. Dee. You didn't. The CIA's deal was to leave you alone so long as you left them alone. Killing even an ex-agent is—"

"Tomorrow's problem. Tell me about this Petrovic. He's today's problem."

John opted to leave the lecture for later. "So my guess is: Petrovic thinks he hired Viorica. And *Skorpjo* thinks they work for Petrovic through Viorica. But she's playing a different game."

"We agree on that part." Daria tucked into John suddenly, as lovers might, turning him and pointing at the display of cashmere sweaters in a store window. A camouflaged jeep rolled past them. "I got away just now because I had a blade in my boot. There's no way Viorica didn't frisk me and find it. She knew I was armed and didn't warn the White Scorpions. She's definitely playing a different game."

The jeep didn't stop. Daria and John started moving again.

"Diego and I met this guy in Sarajevo, a member of the Bosnian

Parliament. Zoran Antic. I ran into Antic tonight, going into the U.S. ambassador's residence for the event."

"You couldn't talk him out of it?" She scanned the skies for drones and the street for police and soldiers.

"Tried. He wouldn't budge. He also knew you'd been captured."

Daria stopped in her tracks and turned to him.

"Yeah. He told me you'd been captured. He also said I was 'searching the skies and fearful of the words *Made in America.*' Which means he knows about the drones. Which means he's been in contact with this Viorica. Who, by the way, I saw tonight. She stopped and talked to Antic outside the residence. They're in cahoots."

She blinked at him. "*Ca-Hoots?*"

"Cahoots. It means to work together. Nineteenth-century western slang."

She nodded. "Thank you. So: Viorica and . . . a Bosnian?"

"A Bosnian who first pointed us in the direction of Dragan Petrovic, couple days ago in Sarajevo. This guy Antic survived the siege of Sarajevo. Petrovic was a general in the war. Antic's got plenty of reason to hate him. So Antic sets up a Serb strongman with ties to organized crime because, hey, when are those guys not good villains? And the ambassador's residence isn't the target, because Antic insisted on going in there. Your tall blonde? After she talked to Antic, I saw her talking to a media crew outside the cocktail party. My guess: Antic controls Viorica, and Viorica controls the Flying Monkeys. Which, by the way, probably are the creation of a company called American Citadel that's manufacturing and marketing drones without the okay of State, or Defense, or the Federal Trade Commission."

Daria said, "Good lord. You *have* been busy."

"Yeah."

She wrinkled her nose. "God. When I was tied up, Viorica asked me if the CIA was watching the ambassador's residence. She asked this, knowing I had a blade in my boot. She practically drew me a map."

"Misdirection."

She sighed. "Must be nice, being the clever one once in a while."

"Okay. So Viorica let slip the *ambassador's residence* to lure you there.

243

Zoran Antic's plan calls for him to be inside the ambassador's residence. We agree that something's getting blown up, but it ain't Petrovic's target, the residence. Which means . . ."

He let her get there.

"It's Petrovic."

"Sure."

Daria said, "Fuck."

"Pretty much, yeah."

Forty

Allison Duffy, U.S. deputy chief of mission, had switched to a simple black dress. She wore kitten heels. She looked both professional and elegant, a tough tightrope to walk.

She had transferred her daunting to-do list to her smartphone, which she carried in lieu of a clutch. She had winnowed the list down considerably but had not tamed it. Not completely. The roughhouse at the front entrance to the ambassador's residence had complicated matters, but only for a minute. The Marine contingent had dealt quickly with the party crasher, who now was in handcuffs and secured in the residence's wine cellar under armed guard. He'd stay there until the soiree ended.

Duffy checked with the caterers to make sure the hors d'oeuvres and champagne were flowing. One of her aides had already checked. Twice. Duffy recognized the symptoms of micromanagement, even in herself, but couldn't help it.

She ticked an item off the to-do list on her phone and checked with the camera crew: a cameraman, an audio man, and a technician, plus the ubiquitous talking-head bottle blonde. They had set up an alcove with a neutral background for interviews and had been given permission to roam the party with a steady cam, so long as they didn't record any conversations. They could use audio only in the alcove. Allison Duffy had insisted.

She watched the rigger kneel and hook his camera and audio equipment into the residence's communications array. The residence was, for all intents and purposes, part of the U.S. embassy, which meant they were on U.S. soil and had to obey all State Department rules. One of the things the Qatari-based film crew had negotiated was permission to use the residence's satellite dish and transmitters to bounce a high-res signal back home.

A signal that strong might screw with Serbia's RTS 1 station or the Kopernikus Cable Network, but the news directors for both stations had never shown the West much love. Allison Duffy could live with that.

The camera and audio crew spoke mostly Arabic. Her own Arabic was fairly good, but she listened to them for a minute and realized the technical specifics of a TV setup were way beyond her.

The presenter held a cordless mic and stepped forward, sweeping perfectly coiffed hair away from her face. She had that stereotypical Hollywood look that Allison Duffy had come to associate with almost all TV news reporters around the globe: perfect in a bland, Botox-and-Pilates sort of way. The California Every-Girl look.

"Hello. I'm Allison Duffy. Deputy chief of mission." She spoke in high Arabic. "So, is everything all right?"

"Yes. Is splendid." The presenter chose English but with a Russian accent.

Allison went with English, too. "So far six people have agreed to be interviewed. I've asked them to come to you. You understand? They will come here; you can't record in the rest of the mansion."

The presenter waved Allison off as if she were a waitress asking if she needed a refill.

"Yes, yes."

The rigger, on his knees, spat an insult at the presenter, who was standing with her stilettos on either side of a power cord. She stepped around the cord with an eye roll that Allison sometimes got from her own teenage daughters.

Allison stepped fully in the Russian's way and bobbed her head to force eye contact. "We are clear on that?"

The presenter offered a contrite nod. "Of course. Hospitality is greatly and also appreciated. You are . . . *super helpful*." She seemed proud to have mastered the lexicon of Los Angeles.

Mollified, Allison walked away. She nodded at the embassy's public affairs liaison, Jay Kent, who'd been tasked with keeping an eye on the news crew.

Allison's agile mind drifted for a second to the likelihood of a Russian aerobics instructor somehow becoming a presenter for an Arabic cable channel. She had wanted to say, *How's the silicone holding up, dear?* But a career in diplomacy turned the snarky aside into a fun but finely tucked-away thought.

Allison also found her academic upbringing interfering with her snarkiness. The word *Caucasian* came from the Caucasus mountain range, which was the seat of a very large Islamic community.

Which would explain the presenter's ice blond hair and silvery blue eyes.

You cannot easily slip a covert comms unit into a U.S. embassy building. Ask any spy. It's difficult.

Viorica slipped her microphone into the U.S. ambassador's residence by disguising it as a microphone.

Got your Purloined Letter right here, sweetie, she thought, as the officious DCM marched away from her.

Viorica lifted the wireless mic to her pink lips and said, "We are clear."

In the silver van, Viorica's tech guru, Winslow, saw that their equipment now was lashed into the embassy's rooftop transceiver array. He adjusted his head set. "Ah. Got it. Lovely."

He heard Viorica switch to her Russian accent and say, "Testing . . . testing . . ." One of the partygoers must have passed close to her and the team of mercenaries posing as a film crew.

"Where are my drones?" Winslow asked.

"Patience. We'll have them in two minutes."

Winslow sat in the fixed chair before the array of flat-screen monitors laid out before him. He didn't have the room that Bryan Snow and his pilots luxuriated in back in Sandpoint, but he had all the technology at his fingers. Anything Snow could do with his micro air vehicles, Winslow could do as well once Snow passed the baton to them by disabling the American Citadel system in Idaho.

And that would be fine, so long as nobody reactivated the American Citadel controls.

Winslow heard her voice over his comms. "Has Danziger checked in?"

"He's on patrol," the Englishman said. "I assume we are expecting opposition?"

"Could be."

One by one, his monitors began to come alive. Each screen showed a different bird's-eye view of Belgrade.

"Mr. Snow came through," he drawled. "We have ourselves an air force."

Viorica said, "Well done. I called Petrovic. I asked him if he was sure—absolutely sure—that he wanted to go through with this."

Winslow adjusted his controls and smiled at the thought. "His grand plan for the attack on the residence? Even though his wife and children are inside?"

"I'm looking at them right now."

"And our beloved acting foreign minister said yes, didn't he?"

"He most certainly did."

"Bloody wanker."

Viorica laughed. "We gave him his out. What happens next is on him."

Winslow reached for his joysticks.

Sandpoint, Idaho

Colonel Olivia Crace entered the control room, but not alone. She brought one of the three military men, the redhead with hazel eyes. And a Colt .45.

Bryan Snow stood behind his two pilots, who sat at their workstations. They were attempting to run a diagnostic to find the problem in the command-and-control of the drone suite in Serbia.

Snow adjusted his black plastic frames and looked annoyed at the disturbance. "Can you give us a minute?"

The black woman ignored him. She held a small, rectangular device that Snow, at first, mistook for a cell phone. Only when she stepped closer did he notice the short, blunt antenna.

That's when he noticed the Colt .45 as well.

"Hey, hey, hey!" Snow felt panic rise. "What's this? You two have to leave. Right now."

Crace studied her handheld device. "If he speaks again, kneecap him."

The redhead didn't bother responding.

Snow's pilots sat frozen.

Olivia Crace finally looked up. "You lost control of the drones for sixty seconds in Florence. Since then you've run every test you can dream up to explain the glitch. Every test but one."

The pilots looked from the newcomers and the massive Colt to Snow.

Snow said, "Hey. I don't know—"

"I had the NSA bring us this device so I could see if any unauthorized radio transmissions were leaving this building. Your offshore bank accounts also were flagged, Snow."

One of the pilots said, "Offshore accounts? Bryan?"

Snow tried to gut it out. "You need to leave. This is my—"

Crace said, "Kneecap only."

The redhead stepped forward.

Snow said, "Okayokayokay! Fine, yes! C'mon, please!"

Crace said, "Thank you. Please put us back in control of the drones. Do it now."

Belgrade

Dragan Petrovic gulped whiskey, his vision blurring with tears. He stared out the window, past the ruined Chinese embassy, at the

American buildings two blocks away. He pictured his beloved Adrijana and their three daughters in their festive frocks, laughing, the girls with bows in their hair and flutes of sparkling pear cider. Adrijana, his beautiful butterfly, in her element.

Petrovic offered a silent prayer to St. Siva to accept the terrible blood offering he made on behalf of all . . .

He squinted. He wiped tears away from his eyes.

A hawk arced into view.

Heading directly toward him.

Petrovic saw a splinter of light flash beneath the mechanical bird.

His window shattered.

Despite the gloom of dust and the penumbra of the street lights, both Daria and John glimpsed the Hotspur drone. Both saw the flicker of light from the belly of the hawk. A second later they heard the tinkle of breaking glass coming from the Parliament building.

Daria said, "It's started."

"So what do we do?"

"The fellow I interrogated said . . . Hold on."

She deftly hopped up on an iron garbage can that was welded to the sidewalk. Passersby gasped as she straddled the can, balanced on both boots. Teenage boys hooted.

John had a working understanding of the term *undercover* and thought probably this wasn't that.

She pointed. "There!" She faced the graffiti-laden security wall around the remains of the old Chinese embassy. The wall featured a padlocked gate beyond which lay a corrugated maintenance outbuilding. Parked next to the shed was a newish silver van featuring a small but advanced telecommunications transceiver on the roof.

She hopped down. "The van. That's them."

John checked his watch. "I'll get to Parliament, tell the guards they're under attack."

"No." She turned to him and smiled. "You're much smarter than I. I need you to go find Zoran Antic. He's been ten steps ahead of everyone, me, the Serbs, *Skorpjo*. I need you to check him. Go."

John blanched. "Go? Into the ambassador's residence? With the armed Marines who already know I tried to sneak in before?"

Daria pulled a Makarov out of her backpack. "Yes."

"The fuck am I supposed to do that?"

She grinned. "That's where the *smarter than I* part comes in. Good luck."

She sprinted for the bombed-out Chinese embassy and the silver van.

Winslow squinted at the centermost plasma monitors. The .22 had made only a modest hole in the window of Dragan Petrovic's office but a more sizable hole in Petrovic himself. The man had fallen fast, but the blood spatter on the window was most gratifying.

The hawk drone was not firing incendiary rounds, he noted. Unlike the attack in Florence. Otherwise, Petrovic's corpse would be smoldering.

Winslow made a gun of his forefinger and blew on it, gunslinger style. He reached for his controls and toggled the suite of hawk drones, two of which were equipped with American Citadel's miniature pyrophoric rockets.

He targeted the Parliament building.

A red warning light flickered on a screen. He almost missed it.

First his hummingbird watcher drones began vectoring away from Parliament. Then the hawks followed.

"Hold on . . ." Winslow muttered, trying to determine the problem. Had Sandpoint reacquired control of the MAVs?

A new screen popped up. It took Winslow a moment to realize it was an audio monitor. He peered at the time stamp and GPS location. The search parameters had been fed into the Mercutio drones days earlier. And in Italy.

One of his speakers crackled:

"No. You're much smarter than I. I need you to go find Zoran Antic. He's been ten steps ahead of everyone, me, the Serbs, *Skorpjo*. I need you to check him. Go."

A head-and-shoulders mug shot appeared on the screen. The woman with a heart-shaped face and straight black hair.

"Ah, we are holding," Winslow spoke into his mic.

Viorica's voice came back quickly. "Problem?"

"The Mercutios were tasked to find your Miss Gibron. I think they just did."

A second audio signature appeared on the monitor. The words *Target 2* blinked to life next to it.

"Go? Into the ambassador's residence? With the armed Marines who already know I tried to sneak in before?"

"Yes."

"The fuck am I supposed to do that?"

Winslow said, "Gibron's here. And she has a friend."

Viorica said, "Where's 'here'? Be specific."

But it was the dour Afrikaaner, Danziger, who broke into their comms first. "Here is here," he said. "She's at the fence."

Forty-One

The Chinese embassy had been seven or eight stories tall, a brick-fronted slab of bureaucratic and Communist sobriety and efficiency. The grounds originally had been paved over with cement, but waxy grasses had reasserted themselves, pushing up here and there, displacing entire ten-foot-by-ten-foot pavers, raising the corners of some to create a tilted, cracked public area. The grounds were littered with fast-food bags and cigarette packs and hypodermic needles and random bits of clothing. Government officials may have thought the cadaver of the building was mute testament to Western aggression. Belgrade citizens were using the grounds as a blockwide trash bin.

The corrugated-tin maintenance shed on the grounds was dilapidated and rusted-out and the frame so warped that the double doors were as crooked as a snaggled tooth.

Only the silver van was new. That, and the telecommunications array on its roof.

Daria hopped down from the fence and jogged into the grounds as a big, pale man with a square, jowly face and shaved skull stepped out from behind the shed and fired a single silenced shot at her. The .45 bullet snapped off the raised, ruptured cement and sent a tuft of caked dirt and hearty weeds into the air.

Daria changed tack, turning on a dime, seeking cover behind a tall breaker box that was standing like a dull gray casket in the middle of the grounds.

She had time to register the gunman when a second bullet panged into the ground and coughed up crumbled cement. But this shot came from behind her.

Behind her and above her.

A hawk drone swooped past her, arcing over the van and gaining elevation for a second pass. Daria crouched behind the breaker box, adjusted her backpack, and dug out a stolen Makarov. She glanced at the sky and found two hovering hummingbirds, unblinking plastic eyes locked on her.

Two more hawks circled for position.

Hummingbirds are spotters. Hawks are shooters. The combat analysis flashed through Daria's mind without any conscious effort. *Hummingbirds hover. Hawks swoop. Hummingbirds can operate stationary. Hawks need a glide pattern facing their target.*

The pale man fired his sound-suppressed SIG, and a bullet smashed a hole clean through the breaker box, a meter over her head. Daria spat, "Shite!" and bolted.

A movement caught her eye. No time to analyze it.

She sprinted for the body of a rusted-out Russian Kamaz truck. Long abandoned and slumped on disfigured rims, the midseventies vehicle had the aerodynamics of an anvil.

The pale shooter's SIG coughed again, and the bullet cratered the Kamaz's radiator. Daria ducked behind the snub-nosed truck, landing on her ass. A hawk made a pass for her, but she'd changed position before it could adjust its diving run.

Her years of combat training fed her a continuous stream of subconscious analysis. *You can't aim the guns on the hawks. You can only aim the hawks themselves.*

Fat lot of good that would do her if any of the shooter drones were carrying missiles. And given their target—the Parliament building—she assumed at least one of them was.

. . .

Simultaneously—both in Sandpoint, Idaho, and inside the silver van sixty paces from Daria's redoubt—Bryan Snow and the hacker, Winslow, attempted to regain control of the drones.

Snow, in Idaho, did so with an army officer's handgun aimed at the back of his skull. He was sweating heavily and in fear of losing control of his bladder. His two pilots stood frozen, their faces a combination of helplessness and slowly evolving anger, as they realized Snow's role in the crisis.

Snow's fingers flew over his keyboards. "I can't . . ." he bleated. "I can't get 'em back!"

Colonel Crace said, "Why not?"

"Their signal is too strong! They're . . . Jesus, I don't know! They've boosted their signal somehow. They're blocking me out! I don't know!"

A little over a thousand kilometers to the east Winslow breathed a thankful prayer that Viorica had boosted their signal through the communications array of the ambassador's residence. The added gain was more than enough to disrupt the signals beaming from the Idaho panhandle.

"American Citadel attempting to reacquire," he spoke calmly. "And failing."

Viorica's voice came over his headset. She spoke from inside the residence. "Do we have control of the drones?"

"They were programmed to find Gibron amid a crowd, to isolate her and to kill her. That program is running."

Viorica said, "All of the drones?"

"Yes."

"Well, get the missile birds back on target!" she hissed. "Mission number one is the destruction of the Parliament building."

Winslow allowed himself a smile. "I'd say mission number one is keeping that crazy woman away from me and this trailer, thank you very much."

But he began to reprogram the two drones carrying missiles.

Daria squatted with one boot under her, the other leg extended and ready to provide her with balance if she moved left or right. She gripped the Makarov in both hands.

When she was behind the breaker box, she'd sworn out loud and noticed that both of the hummingbirds froze. Those beasts were the ones tracking her voice print.

She inhaled deeply, let it out, breathed in again, and shouted:

"My country tiiiiiis of thee . . . !"

The Afrikaaner, Danziger, had moved up from the shed to seek cover behind the silver van. He got ready to move again, to pin down the Israeli, when he heard a song: off-key, bellowed.

". . . sweet land of liiiiiiberty! . . ."

The two hummingbirds reacted to Daria's acoustic signature and vectored for her position. They found her and hovered, sending telemetry via satellite directly to the hawks.

Daria bleated, ". . . of theeee I—"

She rose, spun, and snapped off two shots, then dropped to her haunches again.

She heard the sounds of sparks jumping and metal clattering to the cement. *Funny*, she thought: she hadn't realized she'd had that song stuck in her head.

In the U.S. ambassador's residence, Viorica stood in her shimmering black leather outfit and stilettos, beaming vapidly, waiting for the latest faux interview to end. She thanked her subject in high Arabic and watched as her rigger escorted the Bosnian businessman away from the alcove.

She heard Winslow over her earjack. "Christ!"

She flipped the frequency of her hand-held cordless mic. "Trouble?"

Winslow's voice sounded in her ear jack, "I . . . wait . . ."

"Talk to me."

"Two Mercutios are down!"

"Two?"

"Ah . . . yes. They were tracking the woman. Then . . . no signal."

Viorica squeezed her eyes shut. "She's going for the drones. Winslow: you have six more Mercutios. Get them back on task. Danziger: kill her."

Across the elegant drawing room, Viorica made eye contact with Zoran Antic, the little Bosnian diplomat in the too-large suit. She nodded.

He made a show of glowering and looking at his wristwatch.

Sure enough: Daria's stolen Makarov jammed.

When she had fieldstripped the weapons in the pharmacy, she realized the *Skorpjo* hitters had not taken good care of them. She'd been expecting the cheap gun to jam.

The big man across the way leaned out and fired at her, then ducked back.

Daria pegged him at six-five and three hundred pounds. She preferred not to go hand-to-hand against a gorilla. But if it ended up being a hand-to-hand fight, Daria wanted it to be on her terms. The man was right-handed but also right-eyed—he lined up his gun with that eye. And right-footed: from the way he moved, the man would strongly favor going to his right.

Knowing that wasn't much of an advantage, but a little advantage often is enough.

Daria drew the second Makarov from her backpack. She reached up and gripped the long whip aerial of the rusted-out Russian truck. She placed the gun barrel against the base of the antenna and fired once.

She hunkered down again, now holding almost six feet of wiry antenna in her left hand.

Forty-Two

In the van, Winslow retasked the drones to head for the Parliament building. That meant removing two of the three Hotspurs, the birds that were loaded with the ten-inch-long pyrophoric rockets. He left one Hotspur behind for the annoying Israeli. That drone had fired twice—once at Petrovic, once at Daria—and still had four rounds left.

Daria had "killed" two of the Mercutio spotters, leaving six. Winslow assigned four to go with the rocket-launching drones, leaving two to find Daria.

The Chinese embassy grounds are across the street and one block down from Parliament. It took his drones less than fifteen seconds to get back on target.

Both Hotspur drones arced toward the capital building. One drone fired. Relieved of the additional weight, it arced sharply upward.

Dragan Petrovic had been the last established target, so the missile defaulted and aimed for Petrovic's office.

The explosion knocked out windows in a two-block radius.

The missile's external blast-fragmentation sleeves disintegrated on impact, multiplying the effects of the carnage. The pyrophoric nature of the weapon meant that everything in the foreign minister's office—including Dragan Petrovic—instantly ignited.

. . .

Daria, hunkered behind the Kamaz truck, went to her knees, and covered her ears as the office in the Parliament building disintegrated. She listened as glass and concrete and plastic and metal clattered into the street. Cars began smashing into each other in blind panic.

The explosions shook the ambassador's residence. The lights flickered, failed, then stuttered back on. Marines and Deputy Chief of Mission Allison Duffy were the first to react.

The blond TV presenter in high-fashion leather ensemble and stilettos hardly reacted at all. Same for her camera crew. They'd been waiting for the explosion.

Serbians older than thirty know the sound of buildings exploding. People began streaming for the exits.

Not knowing if the embassy was under attack, the Marine captain in charge of security decided the best bet was to get out of the way of the civilians who wanted to flee. He spoke into his shoulder mic, and his men threw open the double doors to the front of the residence.

Some guests and staff streamed out. Some stayed inside, hoping that was the safer bet.

None of the Marines noticed John Broom, dressed like everyone else, slip into the courtyard, then into the embassy, amid the tumult. He stumbled on a tote bag a woman must have dropped as she fled. John rummaged through it and found a cell phone. He dialed an international number from memory.

It was 2:00 in the afternoon D.C. time. One of the four summer interns in Senator Singer Cavanaugh's office answered. Before she could go through her greeting ritual, John shouted, "It's Broom! I'm in Serbia! I'm in trouble!"

"John! It's Piper. We miss you! What—"

He found a walk-in coat closet that provided a modicum of privacy. "Kinda under fire here, Piper! I need help, quick!"

"You need the senator?" she asked.

"Nope. I need you! And Bryce and Ryder and Paige!"

Among the people who did not panic was the seniormost

representative from the government of Bosnia-Herzegovina. Professor Zoran Antic limped gingerly over to the TV news crew. Both camera operators snapped on their lights, lifted their rigs to their shoulders, and aimed at the old man.

Viorica moved past him without a word. She wended her way deftly between jittery civilians. She got to the stairs that led upward.

Seconds later, General Howard Cathcart raced downstairs. He'd been up on the second story balcony, looking for the so-called Major Arcana to show. At the foot of the stairs he skidded to a halt in his well-shined shoes, mouth agape, seeing the woman he'd been looking for.

"General. Hello!" she said in English, flashing her radiant smile. "Are you ready for your close-up?"

She pivoted and kicked him in the knee. The joint hyperextended, the anterior cruciate ligament tearing.

The general fell like a guillotine.

The Afrikaaner hitman, Danziger, was safe enough behind the silver van. He'd shielded his ears when the first drone strike had destroyed the third-story office, kitty-corner from his position.

The hacker, Winslow, was doing his part. Time for Danziger to do his.

Danziger peeked out from behind the van. The Israeli woman fired. Danziger ducked back behind the van. She couldn't hit him, but she kept on firing. Five shots. Eight. Ten.

Amateur! he thought. *Dumb enough to waste bullets on a man hiding behind a van. What could she have been . . . ?*

The pure stupidity of his position hit him like the physical blow.

The Israeli wasn't firing at him, hiding behind the van. She was firing *at* the van.

It's fine to hide behind a van during a firefight. But not inside one. Few .45s can penetrate both walls of a van but most can penetrate one. Danziger scrambled for the front passengerside door of the van, ripped it open, clamored in.

Too-white light from the ground-floor floods poured in through holes in the van's wall. Winslow lay on the floor, holding his upper thigh, keening in pain. Blood oozed from between his clutching fingers.

Inky, acidic smoke curled up from three of his ruined monitors.

Danziger screamed into his head set. "Winslow's down! She's taking out the computers!"

In the ambassador's residence, Viorica heard the call. She made eye contact with her camera crew, tossed the microphone to the rigger, and sprinted for the door.

She passed John Broom without recognizing him.

John was talking on the stolen cell phone. He recognized her but was too late to stop her.

Daria emptied the second Makarov into the side of the silver van. She tossed the weapon aside. Nothing to do now but wait.

She'd hoped she'd done enough damage to the van—the transceiver array on the roof suggested that that was how they were directing the Flying Monkeys. But she hugged herself against the tireless rim of a truck wheel as one of the hawks swooped in and fired a .22 into the ground, an inch from her knee.

She could only see one hawk now. The other two must be vectoring for the Parliament building.

There had been no further explosions. That counted as some sort of good news.

She heard the unartful pounding of the big man's size-fifteen boots tearing across the ruptured cement patio. The man fired a few rounds in the general direction of the Russian truck to keep Daria pinned down. His plan was to overpower her with his speed, size, and weapon while the drone overhead circled and set up for a shot.

The man would come in on her left, on his right. She'd seen it in the way he moved. Right-handed, right-footed, right-eyed. The fellow wouldn't go to his left to get out of a burning building.

Daria calculated the gyre of the hawk—ten seconds to get back into a shooting glide path.

Danziger rounded the bulky, rusted-out Kamaz, expecting to be shot at any second. He was a very, very big man, capable of running very,

very fast. Shooting a big, fast man rarely stops him in his tracks. They still tend to move forward, even if wounded. And he was willing to bet his life he could round the truck and be on top of the damned Israeli before she fired a killing shot.

He fired one more blind bullet to keep her head down, roared out his rage, and sprinted around the truck.

There was no way she could tell which direction he'd come from. Chances were, she'd be facing away from him.

She wasn't.

And insanely, the Israeli had moved *toward him*, not away.

Danziger's brain registered pain. Lightning hit him, and his body spasmed, feet landing wrong, momentum turned from friend to foe in the blink of a thought. His vision blurred and his pain receptors maxed out. He plowed, headfirst like a base-stealer, into the raised and ruined cement pavers. He skidded, his nose breaking. His SIG clattering away.

He had no idea what she'd done to him.

Daria used the whip aerial from the truck as if it were a real whip. The springy metal antenna, six feet long, sliced into Danziger's face, from the upper left to the lower right, and across his chest and his right biceps. With Daria's full weight behind the blow, the aerial had sliced through skin and tendons, and scored bones.

The man crash-landed. His head ricocheted off the cement and blood spattered in a hundred-degree arc.

Daria counted down in her head. The hawk would be back in five seconds.

She turned and snapped the whip antenna again, this time severing the man's carotid artery. The blood geyser was most impressive.

Daria circled the pulsing gush of blood, gathered the man's SIG, and hauled ass toward the silver van. Her boots chewed up the distance.

The hawk would be back in two seconds.

She ran and the hawk completed its turn, firing at her from above.

But she'd made her run crosswise to its gyre—running to the inside of its circular course. That forced the hawk into too tight a turn, and it couldn't compensate for the moving target.

The bullet embedded itself in a paver three meters behind her.

Ten more seconds for the bird to come around again.

Daria got to the van, threw open the back door, gun aimed inside.

She found a smallish man, dressed as a civilian, lying on his side, screaming bloody murder, his arms and legs soaked with blood.

She glanced out just in time to see Viorica, wearing haute couture and impossible heels, sprint across Avenue Kralja Milana. The tall blonde drew a Glock from a handbag—a nice Prada piece, Daria noted wryly.

Viorica hit the gate of the security fence and it flew open.

Daria ducked into the van, thinking, *Splendid. Spring heroically over the gate, you bloody great idiot. Don't bother to check if it's locked.*

Forty-Three

In the U.S. ambassador's residence Zoran Antic told the camera operator to start rolling.

The film crew looked at each other. "The major's orders were to wait for the full explosions."

"And she has run off to assure that they happen," the old man hissed. He had ordered his entourage to line up behind him. "We are running out of time. Begin the broadcast."

The rigger knelt and began adjusting controls on his portable production unit. The speech from inside the ambassador's residence would be broadcast, live, throughout Central Europe. Thanks to the lash-up to the embassy's own communications array.

The same array through which the drones were being run.

Daria ducked low behind the van's computer array as Viorica's bullets began penetrating the side of the van. The embassy's powerful floodlights were on that side of the van, and each bullet hole produced a conical blast of light, illuminating the growing haze of acrid smoke from the burned-out computers.

The Englishman lay in the fetal position and howled in pain. The amount of blood he'd lost suggested Daria had clipped his femoral artery. A lucky shot.

Daria checked the stolen SIG-Sauer. The big man had fired a feverish fusillade at her when she'd hidden behind the old truck. He'd emptied the magazine. She tossed the gun aside, drew the cutthroat blade from her backpack, and began hacking through the power cords behind the computers. One by one, they shut down. Daria hadn't noticed them hum until they stopped.

The Englishman sobbed. "God, Jesus! Oh God, pleeeeeaase!" The oozing of blood around his hands was diminishing.

"If I destroy the computers, do you lose control of the damn drones?"

Viorica fired another bullet through the van wall.

"Oh God! Pleeeease . . . !"

"Answer me and I'll save you!" she lied.

"Yes! Computers . . . ah, God! This hurts!"

"Tell me!"

"We . . . Incantada . . . command module. It's, oh, Jesus Christ!"

"What command module? The bag Viorica stole? In Florence?"

"Yes!"

"What's it do?"

"Override for the drones!" He sobbed. "Help me!"

Daria felt the shock absorbers dip a bit. Someone—Viorica?—had climbed into the cab up front. Daria rose to her knees and scrambled for the rear door.

"Wait!" the Englishman wailed. "Please!"

Daria hit the door with her shoulder and rolled out, making a tight bundle, a smallish target, as she hit the cement.

The tall blonde had been in the cab but was no longer. She was dashing away, hauling a maple-colored, pebbled leather doctor's bag with twin buckled straps. Daria recognized the bag; Dr. Gabriella Incantada had carried it into the Hotel Criterion in Florence.

Daria sprinted after the blonde.

They were heading for the smashed husk of the Chinese embassy building.

. . .

"My friends. My name is Zoran Antic."

The old man spoke in Bosnian. He looked dignified and somber, his lined face humorless, pained but humble.

"Today, as we speak, Western forces are attacking the government of Serbia. Using the same drone technology that has terrorized Afghanistan. Terrorized Pakistan. And Sudan, and Libya.

"Today, as I speak, the West is bombing Belgrade. As they did a decade before. And a decade before that.

"I am not Serbian. I am a Bosnian. A Catholic. I have fought against the Serbians. But today, I stand with my brethren, with the Balkan people, against Western aggression."

Professor Antic motioned to his left, and the camera operator panned that way. General Cathcart had risen to one knee, his left leg useless. He'd never experienced such pain as the torn ACL in his knee.

"This is General Howard Cathcart, U.S. Army. He is in charge of the aerial bombardment of the civilian government of Belgrade. He and his forces currently are smashing the Parliament building, in the heart of the city, endangering civilians. Once again.

"I speak to you from the U.S. embassy, from which General Cathcart controlled this humanitarian nightmare. I could not stand by and watch the slaughter of government officials, of women and children on Serbian streets. I stood up. I am an old man, but I stood up!"

Antic waved to his entourage in the background.

"These people have stood up. They are Serbian. They are Bosnian. They are Croatian. They stood up. They are Catholic and Muslim and Eastern Orthodox. And they stood up!

"American occupation of Afghanistan went unanswered by the world. American occupation of Iraq went unanswered. American aggression in Libya and Egypt and Syria went unanswered. So now the Americans turn to the former Yugoslavia. But we stand up. We cannot—"

"Hi! Hello! Hey!"

An American jumped up next to Antic, standing shoulder to

shoulder—although much taller. The old man was startled. The camera operators weren't sure how to react, so they kept shooting.

It took the professor a second to realize it was John Broom.

John faced the camera but spoke to Antic. "I'm CIA. I used to be. I'm ex-CIA. Tell them, sir. Please."

"What?"

"Talk to the people. Tell them!"

Antic's plan to frame the Americans, and to lure General Cathcart to the scene of the crime, had worked brilliantly. Now the rash young American, the one he'd met in Sarajevo, had stepped in. But not to stop the plan; the young fool was adding to it! Antic realized that John didn't speak his language. The idiot thought he was helping.

"This man is CIA!" the professor told the live audience. "He said so! He just admitted as such! The CIA and the U.S. Army, both here! Proof!"

"Thank you!" John hugged the old man—actually hugged him! He spoke in rushed English. He held up a cell phone.

"YouTube!" he shouted into the microphones hooked to the cameras. "YouTube! Twitter! This is trending. You understand? Trending?"

The rigger, on his knees by the production controls, knew enough English to realize John wasn't acting the fool. He drew a smartphone and accessed his YouTube account.

Daria had been trained by the best spy agencies in the world. And before that, she'd been raised as a child into the world of espionage. Consequently, she was proud of her many amazing abilities.

Not the least of which was her skill at running in stilettos.

As the tall blonde reached the gutted hulk of the Chinese embassy, Daria admitted she was no slouch either.

Daria slammed after Viorica. Her lungs began to burn and she could feel the stress in her legs. A year ago, she could have done this fight-and-flight festival without a noteworthy change in her beats per minute. But that had been before the damned superflu.

She pumped her arms and doubled down and sprinted after the mercenary.

• • •

Above the fight, the Hotspur and Mercutio drones waited five minutes for their next orders. The Hotspurs soared in circles; the Mercutios hovered.

At the five-minute mark, when no further orders were received from their controllers—in the silver van, across the river in the American Citadel truck and trailer, or from Idaho—the drones reverted to the previous order.

All three shooters and all six spotters turned their attention to finding the last declared target: Daria Gibron.

Forty-Four

Viorica made it to a vertical rupture in the ground floor of the Chinese embassy and ducked inside. The bright, low floodlights created harsh, theatrical light outside but made the interior obsidian black. She made it to the craggy gap in the wall and disappeared as utterly as if she'd been teleported aboard a spaceship.

It took her a moment to adjust from the harsh glare of the street-level floodlights to the gloom of the Chinese embassy. The building wasn't terribly wide, maybe only forty yards front to back, but it stretched the whole block. The ragged egress she'd spotted from the cab of her team's van was at the narrow northern end of the ruptured structure.

Once her eyes adjusted she realized that the interior was lit from without by the floodlights, through cracks and holes in the masonry, and from within by burn barrels. She spotted two of them as her eyes dilated. Human forms hovered around them, some standing, some sitting. She heard music: American rap. Her eyes adjusted. The people were young, scruffy, and stick thin.

Viorica thought she must have looked like a hallucination to them, in her tight leather tunic and skirt, her stilettos, and her doctor's bag.

She said, "Hello!" in Serbian.

A few shuffled forward. One was a young girl with stringy dirt-blond hair and sunken cheeks. Viorica noted the glowing Sterno stoves at their feet and the discarded plastic water bottles.

She set down the doctor's bag on the overturned skeleton of a shopping cart. She undid her wide leather belt and began undoing the stiff tunic.

One of the youths drew a box cutter from jeans that barely hung from his bony hips. "Who are you?"

Viorica dropped the tunic to the filthy, cracked floor. She wore a black silk camisole. "I'm from the Temperance League," she said. "Just say no to drugs."

She drew her Glock and shot the stoned girl in the heart.

Daria dodged as she heard the shot. She was still twenty paces from the gutted building. Some part of her reptilian brain told her she wasn't under fire, so she motored on.

She heard the whir of the hummingbirds coming from behind her; this far from the avenue traffic, she could distinguish their sound. One over her left shoulder; then a second over her right.

She hadn't heard any more explosions from Parliament.

She thought, *Uh oh*, and sped up.

She hit the tall V-shaped gap in the building wall and leaped through, then immediately juked to her left. She crouched, eyes useless.

She expected to be shot at. She expected the drones to home in on her. She expected a physical assault.

She did not expect her lungs to seize and her hands to begin shaking, blood pressure spiking, knees buckling.

It was the same panic attack she'd felt at the Florentine hotel.

. . . girl, soldiers, bombs, blood. Debris crushing ribs. Sounds: her own ragged breathing, diggers begging for help. Tastes: dirt and blood and adrenaline. Smells: charred flesh and plastique. Images: pitch-black eyes, pianist's fingers with cracked nails, lips pleading, apologizing, silent.

Her nightmares. The howling, haunting specter of all her fears, came to the fore.

She squeezed both fists against her temples. She shut her eyes tight, willed her breathing to calm down.

She crouched, tight and low amid the shadows.

She remembered where she was. She willed herself to calm down. It was like being dunked deep in a body of water, then needing to figure out which way was up.

The old fears were nowhere nearly as buried as she often hoped.

Combine that with her winded state, and she was in trouble. Viorica had been running like an Olympian. Daria's knees twitched and her lungs still heaved. It was the remnants of Asher Sahar's superflu.

. . . her Asher. Her childhood Asher. Whom Viorica knew . . .

Daria had warned Diego, back in Caladri, that she wasn't 100 percent.

Oh, she was close, to be sure. Eighty percent of normal? Eighty-five? Still more than a match for a lot of foes. But against someone like Viorica?

The calculus of chaos rarely favors the foolish.

She stood. Darkness receded. She saw shafts of harsh white light through punched-out holes in the wall. She saw two burn barrels. She saw nobody else. She could smell fresh cigarette and marijuana smoke. Others had been here, frightened off when Viorica fired that single shot, doubtless. Fired at . . . what?

As her eyes adjusted, she caught sight of the body. It was a girl, on her back, chest wound glistening in the glow of the fires in the rusted barrels. Her eyes were open. She lay spread-eagled. Lying next to her were a supple leather tunic and belt, plus a pair of four-inch Louboutin heels, the soles devil red. The dead girl was barefoot.

So much for chasing a lass in stilettos, Daria thought. *My luck's rarely that good.*

She looked around. The first floor of the old embassy was a shambles. The floor had buckled in several places. One of the second-story walkways had snapped under the impact of the American's JDAM missiles, all those years ago. The northern half of the walkway had slammed into the ground floor, creating a sort of ramp to the second floor. Daria caught sight of marks on the canted surface, where dust and debris had been swept away.

She turned in a full circle, eyes up. A decent gun with a full magazine would have been a boon. But here and now, that was like wishing for a pony.

Daria could see holes in the ceiling, glimpses of the second floor. If Viorica chose to fire from up there she'd be a—what was the Americanism? *Shooting goose?*

She doffed the hoodie; lilac, it glowed in the horizontal shafts of smoky light from the floods outside. The racer-back jog top was black. Better for skulking.

Daria studied the floor around the burn barrels. Several discarded water bottles, some still with water; others with a gooey brown-and-white sludge. She saw packages of cold pills, a dozen boxes still shrink-wrapped together, the tops of three boxes ripped open. A few pills had spilled to the filthy cement, lying amid the cigarette butts, used condoms, fire-blackened soup spoons, and hypodermic needles. She spotted a grease-stained cardboard box containing drain cleaner, camp stove fuel, batteries, and a red metal can of starter fluid. Also, one of those instant cold packs one buys for a sprained wrist or a backache.

Daria looked at her hands. The shaking was obvious. And not just from the flash image of her lifelong nightmares.

She knelt in the shadow of a burn barrel, grabbed a bottle of water, sniffed it first, and gulped some. It was warm and stale. She poured out the rest on the floor, then emptied two more bottles. She began adding ingredients from the cardboard box.

She studied the instant cold pack. It was a good source of ammonium nitrate. *Clever young felons,* she thought.

The so-called *shake-and-bake* school of producing methamphetamine had been known by soldiers throughout the world for years. It had obvious downsides. One—drug abuse—was obvious. The other less so, unless you knew what you were doing.

She smashed a handful of the cold pills, using the cracked half moon of a tea saucer as a mortar and the handle of the straight razor as a pestle. In the flickering darkness, she guessed about the quantities.

But last time she'd done this had been under the plummeting glare of Fajr-3 rockets in Lebanon. She'd guessed then, too.

She filled three bottles with the nasty potion, carefully screwing on two of the caps and tightening them down, really tightening them, until her muscles strained. She couldn't afford any additional oxygen seeping into the bottles.

She paused, still on her haunches, checked the crumbling ceiling one last time, then gulped from the third bottle.

She winced. It was horrid. She fought back her gag reflex.

In low dosages, meth can increase energy levels, alertness, and concentration. The effects are fleeting. The damage to the nervous system is a real threat.

She squeezed her eyes shut, willed herself not to vomit.

She sealed the third bottle and stuffed all three in her backpack. There wasn't room for everything, so she threw away the sunglasses she'd been given by the Australian tourist.

Daria grinned, exposing her canines.

She grabbed her cutthroat razor, the blade enclosed in the steel handle, and leaped up, jumping onto the half-felled walkway and scrambling up to the second floor, using both her boots and her hands.

Forty-Five

Viorica's borrowed Chuck Taylor All Stars were red canvas and lacked laces. They looked silly with the twelve-hundred-dollar slit-leather skirt and nine-hundred-dollar satin camisole. She could forgive Daria Gibron for screwing with her scheme. But ruining her ensemble?

The situation had grown more complicated but not unmanageable. Daria appeared to have killed or wounded two of her oldest, most reliable associates. But Viorica had always had a utilitarian outlook on friends: don't use anyone you're not willing to lose.

It goes that way if you stay in the game. Everyone knows that.

Viorica harbored no burning hatred for Daria. Some annoyance, sure, but it was tempered by admiration. The Israeli was every bit as good as her reputation.

She remembered all the stories Asher Sahar had told her about the legendary wild child of the Shin Bet. She would be dishonest if she said she hadn't felt more than a bit of jealousy whenever Asher talked of Daria. No lovers could ever have quite the same bond as orphans who adopted each other on the streets to survive. Daria touched something vital in Asher that Viorica never could.

Now Viorica hoped to touch something vital in Daria. Any major artery would do.

The second story of the Chinese embassy was far riskier than the ground floor. It was structurally unsound, with fallen support beams, aging loops of dangling wires, and loose rubble everywhere.

Viorica had exceptional night vision, which was helpful as she snaked under a droopy air duct that looked like a giant's Slinky covered in metallic cloth. The air glistened in the remnants of the floodlights below. She hoped it was dust. More likely it was asbestos.

She found an exposed structural column; the sheet rock had been knocked off and exposed a crisscross of iron support grids.

Viorica loosened one of the twin straps on the doctor's bag and slid her weapon halfway in, as if it were holstered. The arced leather handle was wide enough that she could slide her hand through the loop, letting the heavy bag hang from her wrist. She slid a toe of one sneaker into the diamond-shaped cavity between the iron supports, reached up to grab another, and began hoisting herself up to the third floor.

At this point her mission was simple: keep Daria Gibron distracted. Keep her away from the real mission: Professor Zoran Antic's televised call to arms back at the ambassador's residence.

That was the only place the Israeli could do any real damage.

The camera operator didn't speak English, and wasn't sure what John Broom was babbling about. But he held a smartphone toward the camera, and one of the operators shrugged and focused on it.

The man was a hired gun. Nobody paid him to make critical decisions.

The rigger had opened his own smartphone. He peered up at John Broom's phone, then turned back and used his thumbs to tap the controls. He scrolled through some YouTube feeds.

"—the cause of Slavic hegemony!" Zoran Antic was addressing the camera, as well as the audio operator with the long-handled boom mic. "This man kneeling here is American Army."

He gestured to General Cathcart, who held his rapidly swelling knee in both hands.

"This man is CIA." He gestured toward John, who, incongruously, winked at him. John understood little of the Bosnian polemic but got the initials *C. I.* and *A.*

"You tell 'em, Prof. Keep 'em focused on me."

Antic couldn't believe that the American idiot was being so helpful. Behind the cameraman, the rigger's eyes bulged.

The broadcast was going out, and was being picked up around the globe. But on Twitter the hashtags were . . .

#Oldsoldier? #Crankydude?
#Yugoslobbering?

The old man was being made to look like an ancient, babbling idiot! The rigger shot a glance at the grinning American. He understood.

"Wait!" he burst out, interrupting the professor. "Stop talking! Stop!"

The rigger went to his tool kit and drew a screwdriver. It was the only "weapon" he'd been able to get past the Marines and their metal detectors.

He advanced on John Broom.

But every eye in the room turned to a scuffle near the door. Two figures emerged. One was a uniformed Marine, at the top of a stairwell that likely led to a wine cellar. The man was on his knees, bleeding freely from a badly broken nose.

The other was Diego, sans cowboy hat, wrists cuffed behind his back. He had a splotch of blood on his forehead—from the Marine's broken nose, John figured.

Diego's wild hair flew as he dug his cowboy boots into the carpet and sprinted for the alcove with the TV cameras and lights.

The camera operator, confused, went with his role and kept filming.

The rigger held his screwdriver like a combat knife and advanced on John. Diego leaped and caught the guy in a midair cross-body block. Diego and the rigger smashed into the audio operator and the three men fell in a scrum.

Professor Antic surged forward, eyes on the cameraman. "Wait! Stop! The broadcast—"

The rigger rose first. Diego, cuffed, lay on the floor. The handle of the screwdriver emerged from his stomach, and blood began seeping around the wound.

Silent in his pain, Diego kicked out with one foot, his Spanish heel catching the rigger in the teeth. Blood and broken teeth gushed. The rigger toppled back, unconscious.

John fell to his knees, tearing off his new suit coat, and applied pressure to Diego's stomach wound.

Diego grit his teeth, tears running down his scarred, pocked cheeks.

To Zoran Antic's dismay, the camera operator caught the whole melee on live broadcast.

Daria clamored up to the second floor like a little kid going the wrong way up a playground slide. She spotted the truncated remnants of a support column, now no taller than she, and skittered behind it. As a desert dweller she'd always been proud of her visual acuity in the brightest sunlight. That skill was less handy in the old embassy. But her eyes were growing accustomed to the dark.

She recognized the meth rush—the blast of euphoria that swept away her fatigue and her aches. She knew it wouldn't last. It never did on the battlefield.

Daria rose and crossed quickly but cautiously down the blocklong floor. Once upon a time there had been offices up here. The walls between them had been cheaply made, and had crumbled under the assault of the American missiles. Stand in the right place and you could see the entire distance of the building to the rectangular hole that might have been an overpass to the next building a dozen-plus years ago. Daria could see city lights through the opening.

Big, round holes, two to three meters in diameter, dominated the ceiling and the floor. That's where the American missiles had cut through, back in the day.

She pivoted, never moving in a straight line, going from busted wall, to still-standing water pipe, to the remnants of a stairwell. Neither her knees nor her hands shook any longer, but her heart was racing abnormally fast. Aftereffects of the shot of meth she'd gulped.

A shot rang out.

A .45 bullet ripped through the stairwell drywall as if it were cheese-cloth. Daria zipped back to the water pipe—not very wide, but tall and iron. She stood ramrod straight behind it, doffed the backpack, holding it by the shoulder strap. She took out one of the water bottles.

The shot had come from above, from the third floor.

"Viorica?"

A disembodied voice echoed from three directions. "Well, if I've learned anything from all this, it's that one person *can* make a differ-ence!"

The psychotic was in full blossom, Daria thought.

"Punkin? Did you kill Winslow and Danziger?"

Daria shook the water bottle very hard. She spoke to cover the noise. "Which ones are Winslow and Danziger?"

"Nerd in the van? Guy built like a bison?"

"Ah. Yes. Sorry."

"No, no. Just doing your job."

Daria let go of the backpack. She gripped the bottle and the bottle top, gingerly applying a hint of pressure. Then a hint more. She had secured the top well, and it held. She spied a largish hole in the ceiling leading to the third floor.

She saw dust filter down from the ceiling. Viorica was moving.

The bottle top gave a bit. Daria felt the soft plastic in her hand ex-pand, as the tiniest gasp of air slipped into the bottle. The plastic started to grow warm.

Daria stepped out and underhanded the bottle upward, toward the hole in the ceiling.

A bullet snapped off the water pipe at face height. Sparks and rusty bits of shrapnel flew, temporarily blinding her. Daria fell straight down, making a tiny target, head between her knees, arm over her shoulder.

The water bottle arced through the hole, and the volatile metham-phetamine within erupted in a caustic, white-hot fireball.

The ceiling reverberated. Dust and debris clattered. Something hard and heavy clipped Daria's hip on its way down. The floorboards under her sagged.

She waited. When she lifted her head, the vision in her right eye was fine. Her left eye was slick with blood. Shrapnel had dug into her skin in a parenthesis above, around, and under her left eye.

It had spared her eye, though. *Another day, another scar.*

She listened to the clatter of falling debris realigning itself.

The lyrical voice rang out. "Holy freakin' fuck-balls!"

Daria wiped blood away from her eye. The wounds didn't hurt. Yet. She saw an exposed iron-grid support behind smashed drywall. It could double as a perfectly fine ladder. She sprinted for it and started climbing.

"Shake-and-bake meth!" Viorica laughed, high and brittle-bright. "No wonder crackheads stopped using that method! Get the ingredients cooking, add a little oxygen, and boom! You got a firebomb! And I left you on the ground floor with all the ingredients. Wotta ma-*roon!*"

Daria cleared the third floor, landing and rolling as fast as she could behind a little aluminum rectangle, four feet high. It took her a moment to recognize it as a water fountain.

Completely and hopelessly nonbulletproof. But beggars, choosers, and what have you.

She used her bare shoulder to wipe blood away from her left eye. She felt tiny flaps of facial skin rub against her shoulder. That was going to leave a scar. She peeked out from behind the water cooler.

Daria saw the leather skirt and long legs and ridiculous red canvas sneakers disappearing up a stairwell, headed to the fourth floor.

Daria gave chase.

A thought nagged at her: Why are we chasing? Why did Viorica run in here in the first place? Surely she's noticed I've not fired at her.

Was this all misdirection? Was Daria being led into a trap?

She couldn't be bothered to work it out just now. She started up the stairs, blade folded and in her fist.

Fully extended, the cutthroat razor made a lovely hand-to-hand weapon, because it increased her reach and because it was so sharp that even incidental contact drew blood. But it was useless as a throwing blade. The damn thing spun unpredictably, like a child's toy boomerang.

She drew the second of the three meth bottles out of her backpack, held it in two hands: one gripping the bottle, the other ready to release the cap and introduce air to the volatile mixture.

Many—perhaps most—of the risers and steps were broken or missing. Especially in the center. Daria had to stick to the wall, handrail pressed against her hip, and sidle slowly up. The stairs curved twice in forty-five-degree right twists. She rounded each quickly, body low. Nothing.

She got to the top.

The devastation here was much worse: you could see that the third floor had once been office space. But not so the fourth floor. Here was an expanse of utter desolation. No interior walls remained. No water pipes, no doors. It was just an open space, forty yards wide and a whole block long, filled with mounds of knee- to hip-high debris. The western wall was perforated with three vaguely round holes, six feet wide, each with a few standing bricks that looked like teeth in a screaming cadaverous maw.

The entire space was a jagged, meter-deep playground of downed walls and wires and cabinets and desks and ceiling joists and crossbeams and bits of shiny, concave shrapnel that might have been pieces of the missiles' fragmentation sleeves.

Up here, the light, which had entered the lower floors almost horizontally, shown in from below. Serbian dignity had insisted on nighttime spotlights hitting each round strike point. They cast weird, undulating shadows amid razor-sharp cones of light. They made Daria's depth perception falter.

She saw no way up to the remnants of the upper floors. But then again, the evidence before her suggested that the upper floors were right here, that they'd pancaked down to the fourth level when the missiles hit.

Viorica wasn't doing any more climbing.

She was somewhere on this floor.

Forty-Six

Viorica had studied ballet as a child, gymnastics as a teen, and tai chi in her twenties. They served her well. Moving silently through the thigh-high landfill of the Chinese embassy's fourth floor took a combination of balance, strength, and stealth.

The footing was completely unreliable. The debris was rusty and jagged and shifted under her weight. The American missiles had smashed out the flooring, leaving the thick piles of debris painfully and precariously balanced on the metal crossbeams that had supported the flooring. It was the world's biggest Jenga game. Guess wrong, and plummet to the third floor. Or all the way to the bottom. Worse yet: you'd likely take a metric ton of debris with you.

Viorica had a flash image of Wile E. Coyote and an anvil, both falling from a cliff at more or less the same rate of descent: thirty-two feet per second per second. If she guessed wrong and fell through the floor, would she land atop the sharp shrapnel of a long-gone war? Or would it land atop her?

The good news: Daria didn't seem to have a gun.

The bad news: Daria had firebombs.

Viorica was a chess devotee. She liked to lay out fifteen, twenty scenarios well in advance, then use her natural intelligence to pick and choose from the best. She detested improvisation, which she always thought was the lazy person's term for dumb luck.

She saw movement by the stairwell: Daria, wearing a black jog top and holey jeans. The left side of her face glistened with blood. She appeared but ducked for cover too quickly for Viorica to spot up on her.

Dark skin, dark hair, dark clothes, and fighting in the dark. Viorica had platinum locks and Nordic skin tones. Less helpful.

She hunkered low behind an overturned desk that was torn in half. She noted gobs of decades-old chewing gum still adhered to the underside of it. Icky. The ground-floor floods cast crazy arcs of light and shadow on the remnants of the ceiling, reflecting it down on their madcap playground.

The Israeli's low voice rang out. "What are we doing up here?" She spoke with no known accent: or maybe with the mélange of every accent Viorica had ever heard.

"Two crazy kids? Caught up in the moment?"

"No. I mean: What are we doing *here*? Why did you lead me on a merry chase to this spot? You're too fucking smart to be chased into a dead end."

Viorica grinned. A pretty woman, she banked on being underestimated by opponents. She almost always was.

Daria Gibron probably relied on the same. Check.

"There's this guy from Sarajevo. He's gotta be three hundred years old. Weighs in at about twelve pounds soaking wet. This guy paid me a commission to set up a number of variables."

Viorica slowly, quietly cocked her auto. If a shot came, quarter-seconds would make the difference.

"The variables included a naïve, bitter Serb soldier turned politico. Some dim-witted American military types. A software genius from the military-industrial complex looking to snare a couple million bucks, tax-free. And some wicked-bad drone tech."

Viorica heard clatter; the sound may have come from her two o'clock, but the confined debris field and the three round, gaping holes in the western wall confused the acoustics.

Daria's voice came from two directions at once, bouncing madly off the jagged metal briar patch of the fourth floor. "So? What's your end game?"

"The drones are the bee's knees. But Incantada's remote control circuitry is every bit as cool. This bit of electro-doohicky can be retro-engineered to all manner of drones. All's you need is a powerful enough broadcast."

Daria maneuvered a little. Detritus slid from beneath her feet and clattered down to the floor below. She winced, the picture of Viorica's scam becoming clearer.

"God," she moaned. "The U.S. ambassador's residence."

"Oh, yeah! You got it, Punkin. That old guy is making his speech there. He needed the boosted signal from the American's satellite transceiver to reach the Faithful throughout Europe. I needed the transceiver to override any effort to block the Incantada device from controlling the drones. Have you got any idea how much money I'm gonna make off this thing? It's, like, the Ginsu knives of terrorism!"

"Strong enough signal, that thing in the doctor's bag could override any drone on earth."

Viorica yelped. "So cool! Ain't it just?" She heard something thin and aluminum clatter. She raised her head and her gun over the top of an overturned desk chair, its starfish legs spread in the gloom.

Nada.

Viorica shifted carefully, Converse All Stars on an exposed crossbeam. She could see through the matrix of debris to the third flood below.

Daria shouted, "What is the old man saying?"

"Who cares? He's probably telling the true believers that the Americans have gone crazy. Afghanistan. Iraq. Can I have democracy from Column A and peace from Column B? And does that come with Arab Spring Rolls?"

She ducked under a low loop of wires. A fine crust of dust had formed along the top, like cheap, preshredded Parmesan. Viorica didn't want to sneeze. She crouched low, arced her long, lean body under the wires, sidled slowly up on the far side of them. She caught a glimpse of skin across the room. She looked down long enough to position her sneakers on two semistable crossbeams.

Daria shouted: "You know Asher."

The tall blonde thought: *Ah ha!*

"Oh, yes." She straightened slowly so as not to disturb debris. She kept her weight evenly distributed on two apparently stable floor joists.

"He lives?"

"Since your reunion in Milan? Yes. He lives. No thanks to you."

Viorica peered over the chaotic mounds of crap. The skin she was seeing was a neck and shoulder and a bit of long arm. She sighted up on it.

Shadows swooshed past at two of the three round missile holes in the wall.

Two Mercutio drones ducked into the building, humming. They held station, twisting this way and that. Seeking.

The outside light flickered as two hawks cruised by the third hole: one heading south, the other arcing west.

They were hunting.

Viorica considered the situation. Before this fight they had been tasked with finding Dragan Petrovic and the Serbian embassy. Before that: Daria Gibron, on the loose in northern Italy.

And before that? Both Daria and Viorica. In a livery building in Florence.

So which program were they following now?

Forty-Seven

John Broom pressed his jacket against Diego's stomach wound. Blood spattered the sleeves of his new white shirt and his pant leg. Diego lay on his side, wrists cuffed behind his back. A Marine finally arrived. He had captain's insignia.

Diego moaned. "This . . . a hell of a plan of yours."

"Going better than expected." John turned to the Marines and noticed that the camera and audio men had fled, leaving their equipment behind. The rigger—the man Diego had savagely kicked, the man with no front teeth—lay on the floor, wrists tightly cuffed at the low of his back, the captain's knee on the his spine.

John said, "Get a doctor!"

The captain said, "That dude's in custody."

"Throw him in the stockade. *Build* a stockade. Just get a fucking doctor!"

"Soldier." General Cathcart grabbed an ornate white chair and levered himself to his feet. His left pant leg was stretched tight over his ruined knee, and his skin was blotchy and sweaty.

The Marine captain said, "Have a seat, sir. We'll get that leg looked after."

"I need to leave. Now," Cathcart growled.

The captain shook his head. "Not till I figure out who's who here. Please have a seat."

"Soldier! I'm ordering you to—"

"I'm not a soldier. I'm a Marine. Sit your ass down . . . sir."

A sergeant hustled over a civilian with deft eyes and dexterous fingers who carried the presence of a man well used to trauma. He brought the residence's well-stocked medical kit. He and the sergeant hustled John out of the way and began working on Diego's stomach wound.

John almost tripped on the video equipment, backing away. He adjusted the camera and audio boom, making room for the doctor and sergeant. Finished, he sat on the floor, back against a wall, knees up, arms out over his knees. His hands and forearms were bloody, his shirt ruined.

He spotted Professor Zoran Antic and, releasing a gust of exhausted breath, waved the old man over.

The small old man in the too large suit looked well pleased with himself. He eased himself down into the chair next to John. He wheezed a little.

The two of them watched the doctor and the Marine sergeant work on Diego.

John said, "Why? Please. Professor. I need to know why."

Professor Antic sat ramrod straight, his body hardly seeming to weigh anything on the antique chair.

"Muslim holy wars around the globe. The utter failure of the euro. The first President Bush leads Europe into a land war in the Middle East, then the second President Bush does it again! Europe learns nothing. American arrogance, European weakness. What do these things have in common, Mr. Broom?"

John waited.

"The fall of the Soviet Union."

He couldn't help himself: John actually snorted a little laugh. The blood on his arms and hands was turning stiff but remained tacky.

The old man shook his large head. "Oh, we are not stupid, Mr. Broom. We know that the Soviet model was corrupt and an economic joke.

But the concept! The idea! A strong East, to counterbalance the blustering West. A European superpower to curb the American cowboys. It would have saved the last quarter century from so much bloodshed."

"The Illyrian Party?"

"The Illyrian *League*, Mr. Broom. My counterparts throughout the former Soviet Union are taking up the banner. Romania and Hungary. In the Czech Republic and Slovakia. In Poland and Ukraine." The old man allowed himself to preen a bit. He patted one spindly leg, the way a man might applaud while holding a wineglass.

"The fuse is lit. As with the assassination of Archduke Ferdinand in Sarajevo, in 1914. So today. We fan the flames of European independence and liberty."

John wiped his left hand on his pant leg—the new suit was ruined anyway—then gingerly drew his stolen phone out of his pocket. He activated it, creating a perfect bloody thumbprint on the screen. He nudged his chin toward the man with the flattop haircut and badly swollen knee. The guy was sweating and in a great deal of pain but was trying to be stoic.

"That schmuck? He's American military. You lured him here?"

Antic chuckled. "Like shooting a barrel of monkeys."

"Shooting fish in a barrel," John sighed. "Fun as a barrel of monkeys."

"I'm sorry?"

"Nothing. Give me your hand."

John wiped blood off his. Then raised it.

Antic studied the younger man's hand warily.

"I'm serious. I see you're the grandmaster here. Give me your hand."

Antic's distaste was obvious.

"Is it because you want to avoid blood on your hands?" John laughed. "'Cause, I gotta say: That ship's sailed. C'mon."

"I admire you as a student of politics, Mr. Broom. I do."

"But . . . ?"

The old man shrugged apologetically. "You're just a Jew."

John shrugged. "I'll buy that."

But he didn't lower his hand. And after a beat, Antic took it. A simple, weightless, gripless up and down. Antic performed it the way one might shake a hound's paw: he's a lower species. He doesn't understand.

John nestled back against the wall. He closed his eyes.

"Boy. Hell of a day."

To Antic, it looked like the young American was just giving up. The old man felt vindicated. He felt young.

"You're an anti-Semite."

Antic shrugged as if to say, *Isn't everyone?*

"The Muslims of Bosnia and Kosovo?"

"They will rise with us now, when we need them. Later, like children, they will need to be put in their place."

"You're a neofascist?"

"Let us not mince euphemisms, Mr. Broom. I was a Nazi."

John held up the stolen cell phone and waggled it a bit. The old man glanced at it.

"You should see this," John said.

The old man took the phone from John, peering myopically at the screen. His breathing grew thin.

"What . . . what is this . . . ?"

"Bunch of really smart twenty-something interns in Washington." John leaned his head back against the wall and watched the doctor work on Diego. "They're crazy-good with the Internet. They created a bunch of hashtags and markers telling young people to watch your broadcast. They pushed it out on every social media platform. Then they located your original feed from here. And they're rebroadcasting it throughout Europe."

The professor's face fell. His rheumy eyes flashed from John's phone to the video camera and audio boom.

Which lay on the floor. Facing them.

"You're still live, Professor. You and the discredited CIA agent you just shook hands with. Smile for your fans."

Forty-Eight

Daria studied the floating hummingbirds framed in the harsh oval light as if they were lead performers, dead center onstage in their designated follow spots. They hummed. When they didn't move, they didn't look much like hummingbirds. More like badminton birdies with four horizontal plastic wings and miniature helicopter rotors at the end of each wing. Their downdrafts sent up billows of dust and paper debris.

Outside the hawks swooped past the aging missile holes.

Daria held one of her incendiary meth bottles in both hands, one hand wrapped around the cap. She stood on the remnants of a filing cabinet, on its side, straddling it like it was a surfboard. She could see the curled remnants of tile flooring beneath it, but also holes that plunged all the way down to the third and second levels as well.

"Those," Viorica's voice echoed, "are Mercutio. I think they like you."

"And the hawks?" When Daria spoke, both hummingbirds snapped in her direction but held themselves motionless in the middle of the white beams from the ground-floor floods.

"Hotspur. Made illegally by a company called American Citadel. A company that, collectively, is peeing its pants right now."

The Mercutio drones did not sight up on Viorica when she spoke. Daria cursed silently. Flying fucking Monkeys.

"We need to get them out of here."

"How come, Punkin?"

"Because—"

A shot rang out from outside. A .22 bullet raced into the confining, confusing space, through the centermost of three missile holes. Subsonic, the bullet made a zipping sound before it embedded itself in a downed ceiling support column, inches from Daria's right shoulder. She twisted back, hissing in pain. The bullet missed but blood bloomed from the talons of wooden shrapnel driven into her shoulder.

In the shock of impact, she'd jostled the lid of the water bottle. Daria felt it begin to expand.

She threw it clumsily, left-handed, without room to wind up and really heave. The bottle lobbed about five feet in a high arc.

Daria ducked.

Viorica spied the bottle and rolled up and over a pile of debris.

The fireball erupted.

Wood and copper and ceramic shrapnel rained down from the ceiling. Already twisted debris twisted more. Mounds of detritus crumbled, falling through the missile holes to the floor below. A cyclone of dust and asbestos and bits of paper and plastic swirled around the floor.

Both spotter drones crashed into the wall and fell to the floor.

Viorica had scrambled over debris and almost tumbled into a great hole in the floor. It was almost six feet in diameter, the rim cluttered with felled bits of building and office equipment. It was almost round.

Viorica teetered precariously on the edge of the round abyss, grabbing onto a truncated length of water pipe, her left foot dangling for a moment. Her Glock bounced off an old coat rack and glittered as it fell to the floor below.

The dust was suffocating. Both women hacked coughs.

Daria rose and clambered unartfully over an mound of insulation, moving clockwise from Viorica's presumed position, finding a new hiding place. She couldn't know that Viorica had dropped her weapon. Daria's right arm throbbed as long slivers gouged against the hardworking muscles. Blood from the cuts around her left eye again obscured her vision. She found a depression behind a remnant of a chalkboard that now served as a pretty good duck blind.

She hunkered down, the backpack dragging in her wake. Volatile meth bombs had seemed like a good idea down on the first floor. Now they felt like a ticking time bomb strapped to her back.

She rubbed blood away from her left eye and let her finger just brush the handle of the cutthroat blade in her boot.

She glanced at the chalkboard. Miraculously, it still held writing, even after all these years. It looked like the ghost of a Venn diagram with Cyrillic scribbling around it.

Only ten feet away, Viorica swung one of her red canvas sneakers up and snagged a jagged bit of copper pipe around the edge of the abyss. The pipe held. She levered herself back up and put her other shoe on the last viable floor support she could see.

"You . . . wanna not . . . do that again," she gasped, flexing her left arm. In stopping her fall, she'd jolted her rotator cuff.

Daria was surprised by the proximity of the blonde's voice. They were almost atop each other. She said. "Can you call them off?"

"Can I what?"

"The doctor's bag." Daria levered herself to her knees. "Dr. Incantada's bag. Call off the drones."

Viorica laughed. "Why should I?"

Daria rose to her haunches. Blood oozed from the long splinters in her shoulder. "You should call them off because there was only one explosion from Parliament. The hawks with the rockets stopped hunting. And if they can't get me with bullets . . ."

She waited.

In the swirl of dust and gloom, Viorica whispered.

"Oh, shit."

Outside, another Hotspur glided past the three round openings, casting a rolling shadow from the ground floor floodlights.

Would the shadow, the threat of the rocket-hawks, distract Viorica? One way to find out.

Daria vaulted over the chalkboard, scrambling like mad. She spotted the blonde only a few feet away, standing on the precipice of a whacking great hole, almost two meters wide. The pebbled leather doctor's bag sat atop an overturned water heater.

Daria landed on the far side of the round hole, reached for hanging wires, and swung out over the emptiness. Her fist connected with Viorica's mouth.

The blonde spun as well as she could, one foot on a floor support, one leg outstretched, and the sole of her stolen sneaker on the jagged end of a copper pipe. Blood spurted from a split lip.

Daria swung on the overhead wires, drawing closer, fist flying.

Viorica ducked, threw a sharp elbow into the glistening blood seeping from Daria's bare right shoulder. Daria grunted. Hanging by one arm, she swung back to the far side of the six-foot hole.

Viorica grabbed another section of the overhead wires—they hung like a giant letter W—and swung toward the middle of the hole. She gambled that the wires would hold both their weight. She made a blade of the large, middle knuckles of her right hand, fingers tightly together, fingertips curled in toward her palm, and drove the knuckles into her enemy's side.

Daria felt a rib crack.

They swung over the precipice, both finding new footholds. If they had been at twelve and six o'clock before, now they were at three and nine.

They dangled, each from one arm, and eyed each other, looking for weakness. Both gasped.

Viorica swung out, kicking, going for Daria's gut. She missed, but by inches. Daria floated across the void, too, her elbow slamming into Viorica's ribs. They spun, hanging by one fist each, and scrabbled again for new footholds.

They stood, panting, feet finding precious little purchase, on separate sides of the vaguely round missile hole in the floor. They'd both gone halfway around the ominous hole.

They eyed each other on the far side of the gap.

Viorica wiped blood from her lip with the back of her free hand. "Suppose it ends here."

"Suppose so." Daria struggled not to inhale too deeply, her newly broken rib screaming at her. She let go of the overhead wires, half turning, both hands scrambling for purchase amid the overturned desks and chairs and trash bins.

Viorica took a gamble: she relinquished her overhead handhold, which provided reach and maneuverability. And she averted her eyes from the enemy. In a fight, doing that begs for defeat. But she reckoned the payoff was worth it. She hiked up her skirt and yanked at the Velcro holding together a black Lycra garter. Tucked into the band was an Italian switchblade stiletto with a hammered-steel blade and oxblood-red handle.

She grinned at Daria. "Round Two?"

Daria looked up from across the abyss.

And grinned, too. Her wolfish smile exposed her canines. She showed her left hand. It held the last of her meth-bombs. She shook the plastic bottle vigorously.

"You can't kill me with a bomb, Punkin. Not this close. You'll kill us both."

"Might," Daria shifted her weight. She revealed Gabriella Incantada's leather bag. It was open, in her other hand.

"Don't!" Viorica shouted.

Daria felt the plastic water bottle expand a bit. She stuffed it in the doctor's bag, snapped the bag shut, and hurled it back across the abyss.

In midair, the bag stretched comically, as round as a beach ball, and fire glowed from beneath the handle and the double straps. Streamers of fire began to emerge from seams. Viorica tried to spike it out of the air, but some of the meth clipped her forearms, fire spreading. She screamed.

Outside the Chinese embassy, in the warm, still air of Belgrade, the drones were robbed of their brains.

The Mercutio drones hovered in midair, awaiting instructions. They could stay like that for another ninety minutes, give or take. Then they would simply fall to earth.

The Hotspur drones still swooped. But now, blind and deaf. They smashed mindlessly into the Chinese embassy.

Daria leaped feetfirst into the hole in the floor. She could not see how far down it went.

Above her, the pyrophoric missiles housed inside the hawks detonated. A firestorm engulfed the fourth floor.

Forty-Nine

Chaos held the reins, dragging the Belgrade first responders and Serbian military and intelligence forces along for the ride.

The madness up and down Avenue Kralja Milana left civilian, municipal, and federal officials stumbling over each other. The main north-south thoroughfare became a parking lot, smoke roiling from the damaged Parliament building on the left; the upper floors of the long-abandoned Chinese embassy pancaking in on themselves to the right; and the city's political elite fleeing the U.S. ambassador's residence back on the left.

It didn't help that a large contingent of the nation's infamous and greatly hated White Scorpion gang had shown up at the Parliament building. They had been tipped off in advance that something would be happening. Some street fighting broke out with police. *Skorpjo* was there to stir up trouble. As if trouble needed any help.

Amid the police cars, ambulances, fire trucks, and military vehicles parked randomly up and down the avenue, the biggest and baddest beast was a camouflaged Vystrel two-axel tank that roared up from the south, roof hatch open, a soldier in the black fatigues and black beret of Special Forces riding beside the roof-mounted, rotating weapons platform.

The Vystrel—a BPM-97 armored personnel carrier designed by the Russians—is a thundering leviathan: ten tons of armored hull, 240 horses, and large enough for a crew of twelve. This particular vehicle included a turret fitted with a 30 mm cannon and automatic grenade launchers. Every other responder with a lick of sense got out of its way that night.

The war wagon ground its way up Kralja Milana and stopped first in front of the U.S. embassy. The soldier who rode up above half emerged through the open roof hatch and deftly hopped down. The smoked, bulletproof glass of the armored personnel carrier obscured the remainder of the crew.

The soldier didn't walk, he stalked: shoulders straight and a little forward, chest out, arms straight, and never far from his low-slung belt holster. He was pale and blond. He wore a major's insignia. His hair was spiked with sweat and his athletic form was bulked up by a ballistic vest and a web belt. He exchanged IDs with police and U.S. Marines at the ambassador's resident.

Under armed guard, he took a handcuffed John Broom to the tank. Two U.S. Marines with a stretcher brought out a bandaged and unconscious Diego.

Captives in hand, the battle tank roared up the street to the gutted Chinese embassy.

Smoke curled out from the hulking ruin. Everything above the third floor was either crumbling or in flames. Most of the devastation was internal, so it wouldn't be until the light of morning that officials realized the damage there was far greater than that of the Parliament building.

The Vystrel chewed up tarmac, coming to a halt before the former embassy. A Belgrade police officer wisely rolled his cruiser back to let the military vehicle through. The driver whacked the partially open main gate of the security fence, then rumbled through.

Once on the grounds the side doors of the tank sprang open and two more soldiers, one a woman, joined the lead soldier with the major's stripes. The woman had roughly chopped black hair and moved as if she'd been born in combat armor. A dark-skinned man, as small and as compact as a bullet, dashed to the gate, machine gun in both hands, to keep out the police and fire trucks. The Special Forces soldiers' cheeks were blackened by angry slashes of charcoal, à la American football.

The taller man and the woman began a methodical search of the grounds, working quickly and concisely. They spoke little. They were disciplined and, more importantly, had worked together often enough to interpret each other's movements and silence. They moved like Army ants: all purpose, no distractions.

They found a dead man behind a tireless Russian truck with a four-foot slash across his face and chest. He had bled out. They found another man in a silver van with burned-out electronics. The inside stank, a nasty funk of melted plastic. He'd died of a leg wound.

They approached the rapidly disintegrating Chinese embassy. The soldiers could see that the building was nearing imminent collapse.

They reached a wide, vertical gap in the wall, acrid smoke billowing from within.

A form stepped out.

The soldiers drew closer, machine guns raised.

It was a woman. She stood with her feet planted far apart for balance. She held something in both hands. The major moved forward and peered into the greasy bank of smoke.

The woman held twin power cables.

"English?" Her voice rasped, smoke damaged. "French?"

The major stepped forward and nodded. "English."

"I've disconnected the building's main generator. It won't explode. If I reconnect the power . . . well, then we shall see."

The soldiers apparently understood. Both slung their weapons, hands raised, palms up.

Daria stepped out of the smoke. Blood soaked the left side of her face and her right shoulder. She was sooty and bruised. She had kohl-black eyes.

"Weapons down. I need your vehicle."

The male and female soldiers exchanged looks.

"Now!" Daria brought the two power cables within an inch of each other.

The major turned to look at the massive tank, then back at Daria. He shrugged.

And when he spoke, it was with an American southern drawl.

"That old thing? Name your price, darlin'."

The woman soldier rolled her eyes. She sounded British. "Pay him no mind, love. The Viking sent us."

Daria dropped the two power cables. They turned out to be random bits of heavy-duty wiring connected to nothing.

The "soldiers" all but carried her to the stolen armored personnel carrier. The darker man dashed to the cab and the engine roared to life.

Daria found John Broom sitting inside, shirt and arms brown with dried blood.

Diego lay on a gurney, bandaged, sedated, and breathing.

The man up front revved the engine and hit the vehicle's red and blue flashers that were embedded behind a steel grille.

John hugged Daria. She hissed in pain.

"Sorry!" He pulled back, studied her bloody temple, her ripped shoulder. She was gasping, eyes dilated, swaying as the ten-ton Russian rhino smashed its way out of the embassy grounds and back onto the avenue.

Daria eased herself down, sitting on Diego's gurney. John supported her, and she let him. She had tucked a bundle of black cloth into her belt, into the indentation before her hip. John noticed but didn't ask.

Daria peered around the darkened interior, lit by red combat lights. "My."

She recognized the soldiers now. They appeared to be about a decade older than she'd initially thought. She'd met them less than a block away. The blond man with major's insignia no longer looked like a surfer. The woman had lost her long dishwater dreadlocks. The dark-skinned man driving the Russian carrier like a race-course professional no longer appeared aboriginal.

They'd lost their Australian accents, too.

"The sunglasses," Daria said, and now, away from the rumble of the dying embassy, they could tell she was slurring her words. "The ones you gave me on the street. Trackers?"

The woman removed her black beret and, with it, the poorly cut black wig. Strawberry blond hair was pinned in tight to her skull. "Sorry about that. Kitschy, I know."

The blond man smiled, and it immediately changed the contours of his face. He was rakishly handsome behind the grit and sweat. "The captain's turned off the seat belt sign. You're free to move about the tank."

He sounded like he came from the deep American South. He studied Daria. "You doing okay, sugar?"

Daria shrugged, although that, alone, caused blinding pain.

"You saw Viorica?"

Daria leaned against John. "She was inside. Might've made it. Dunno. Didn't see her die."

John felt her body tremble as her wounds began to take their toll. He thought she sounded concussed. He said, "Look, guys. It's not that we're not grateful. But do you mind telling me how we're getting out of Serbia?"

The British woman gave him a crooked smile. She unpinned her strawberry locks and shook them free. "Never fear. Ever hear of the Black Harts?"

John said, "Nope."

The man winked. "Which is as it should be. Anyway, we'll get y'all out. And all for a fairly reasonable fee."

Daria leaned back against John. Around her, the red interior lights faded and the voices grew tinny. She felt herself melt against John's side.

She said, "Tell Viking . . . I'm good for it . . ."

And blacked out.

Fifty

A great many things occurred next.

Mostly they occurred amid a smog of confusion. It was days, and sometimes weeks or months, before some of them became clear. Some never did.

At the Parliament building, terrorism was the first and most obvious theory regarding the explosion and fire in the foreign minister's office.

But building guards reported that Dragan Petrovic had arrived alone that night, although he'd been scheduled down the street at the American soiree. He had been obviously drunk. No other bodies were found in the burned-out office.

Investigators reluctantly began to believe that Petrovic himself had delivered a bomb, which went off prematurely. Further investigations turned up direct links between Petrovic and the dreaded *Skorpjo* gang.

Right-wing Web blogs and anti-immigration TV stations from Montenegro north to Estonia broadcast a live announcement from a member of the Illyrian Party of Bosnia-Herzegovina. Professor Zoran Antic claimed the attack on the Serbian Parliament was the work of American strikes similar to the illegal and internationally denounced ones in Pakistan, Sudan, and Libya.

The professor gave a rousing, barn-burning speech from the grounds of the U.S. ambassador's residence, urging anti-Western and pro-Slavic forces to rise to the defense of their Serbian brethren. The speech was all the more moving since Antic had been a foe of the Serbs during the civil war and had suffered under their four-year bombardment of Sarajevo.

But then, amazingly, the old man kept talking. Dozens of hidden supporters were posting the speech live on YouTube. They watched as Antic sat in a chair with the brown-haired man he'd just accused of being a CIA spy and laid out his true intentions, his Fascist roots, and his anti-Semitism in excruciating details. He then shook the man's hand, conspiratorially.

In country after country, groups calling themselves the Illyrian League popped up. Often within hours of Antic's live broadcast. Throughout the western and southern boundaries of the old Soviet Union a new coalition quickly formed in opposition to American aggression.

But as quickly as it rose, it also was hindered by the bizarre and inexplicable story of Zoran Antic, and by the lack of any drones being found in Belgrade. While the notion of an Illyrian League spread quickly, most of its leaders soon distanced themselves from the seventy-year-old Bosnian. Political scientists would spend the next year studying the seismic impact of the new movement. But the name Zoran Antic quickly faded into obscurity.

He died ten months later of heart failure.

Despite the rocky start, the political movement was huge, secretly well organized, and it caught Western observers unawares. It was being compared to the Arab Spring. It was, in the parlance of State, a Black Swan event.

The brown-haired man sitting with Zoran Antic on the live speech was identified as a John Broom, an adviser for the International Red Cross Subcommittee on Refugees. The Central Intelligence Agency took the unusual step of identifying John not as a CIA agent but as a lawyer and analyst who had worked for the agency but who had resigned the previous year.

Red Cross officials confirmed John's identity. His name appeared quite a bit in the first two days of the crisis, sporadically by the third day, and not at all by the fourth day.

He dropped out of the limelight.

At American Citadel LLC, teams from Homeland Security investigated the entire board of directors and a tier of top administrators. Charges likely were drawn up, but a shroud of national security secrecy fell over the entire incident. Rumors had it that members of the board, and one of the board's top salesmen, Todd Brevidge, were relocated to Guantánamo Bay, Cuba.

The R&D offsite facility in Sandpoint, Idaho, was closed down. Every stick of furniture was removed. The computers were degaussed, then recycled for spare parts.

A tech named Bryan Snow was interviewed. Then interviewed again. And again. It soon became clear he had been the brains behind the micro-drones.

He was not transferred to Guantánamo. He was offered a job.

By the fall, reports began to seep in from Pakistan's Hindu Kush region and western Waziristan regarding new, quiet micro-drones that had begun targeting Al Qaeda and Taliban forces.

The U.S. Department of Defense denied any knowledge of these new drones.

A court-martial tribunal was scheduled for General Howard Cathcart and Colonel Olivia Crace.

But both died in an auto accident in Washington, D.C., when the car they were riding in slid into Rock Creek Park and burst into flames.

No one on the Joint Chiefs of Staff was ever connected to the American Citadel incident.

Fifty-One

The day after the fight in the Chinese embassy, Daria Gibron woke up in a farmhouse.

She lay in a huge, downy bed, beneath a comforter. The walls were white, the molding a faint and pleasant mint, the bed enormous, the sheets cheap but clean and thoroughly starched.

She could hear farm implements in the fields. Someone was plowing. She could smell overturned earth. She'd read somewhere that farmers actually like the aroma of turned earth. To her, the smell meant foxholes or funerals.

She tried to rise and broken ribs disabused her of the notion. She felt her face with her fingertips. Bandages overlapped above, beside, and below her left eye, in a C-shape. They felt fresh and dry. Her right shoulder was bandaged and almost immobile.

She drifted back to sleep.

She had no nightmares about being a child buried in a crumbling building. She had just clawed herself out of yet another such building.

For now, at least, the nightmares were satisfied.

She awoke after the sun had set and come up again. She was beyond thirsty. John Broom sat in a chair. He was framed by the bedroom window, in a rocking chair, reading a document.

Daria licked cracked lips and dredged up some saliva. "Hallo, John."

John got her water. He also made her swallow pain pills, although swallowing was torture. He didn't say much. Daria must have slept again, because the next thing she realized, John had produced a powder-blue electric kettle, a mug, and a little jar of bullion cubes and made her a steaming cup of beef broth.

He helped her sit up, and Daria took the mug of soup gratefully.

"What were you reading?"

John glanced at the rocking chair. "The owner's manual for a water heater. It's the only thing in English. I was bored."

She sipped the warm broth.

"Our rescuers?"

"The American guy wants to talk to you. Can I ask him to come up?"

Daria didn't laugh, because that would have hurt like hell. She thought, *Lady Gibron will see you now.* "Please."

John left, and Daria waited. The broth tasted heavenly. She scanned the room for makeshift weapons, but the clock radio and reading lamp had been moved away from the bed. She looked straight up. A framed print hung over her head. Jesus dangled on the cross, upside down from her perspective, palm and foot wounds bleeding upward. She reached up with her good arm and touched the image. She felt cheap canvas under her fingertips. No glass to turn into a makeshift blade. The Black Harts had a good eye for detail.

The smiling American entered with John. He'd changed into jeans and a navy sweater. He wore clothes exceptionally well and moved like a dancer. He didn't look anything like an Australian surfer dude, and he didn't look anything like a Slavic professional soldier, but he'd totally fooled Daria both times they'd met.

He wore his blond hair longish and swept back in the style of another era. He had wicked blue eyes and a mischievous grin. He looked like a boy getting away with something.

Daria said, "Mercer Gaudette."

"Gracious," he drawled. "Reputations, preceeding and otherwise. Miss Gibron? A pleasure." He shook her hand.

John Broom said. "What am I missing? You said something about black hearts?"

"Hart." Daria said. "Like the deer. There's a bar called the Black Hart. It's where you go if you want to hire—"

Mercer jumped in. "—a support group for people suffering from, ah, possessive-compulsive disorder."

John laughed. "Thieves?"

Mercer sniffed. "Gauche." He turned to Daria but nodded toward John. "May I . . . ?"

Daria sipped her broth. "He's with me."

John reacted to that but pretended not to.

"Lucky boy. The Viking hired us. Old Freddie felt sorta bad about getting both you and Viorica into Serbia. He hired us in to watch you gals. And to throw you a lifeline, if it came to that. But not to interfere."

John said, "He sent thieves?"

Mercer winked at him. "He sent folks who specialize in the art of the egress, Mr. Broom."

Daria mulled that over. "Fair enough. And Diego?"

"Bleeding internally. Sally—you remember Sally?" Daria nodded, thinking of the woman in the battle tank with the strawberry blond hair. "She's as close to a doc as we got, which ain't enough. She got your guy stabilized. Gian stole a plane and flew him to Stuttgart. Fredrik had transport awaitin' there."

John said, "Gian being your other guy?"

Mercer said, "I can neither confirm nor deny . . ."

John moved toward the door. "Okay, okay. I'm getting coffee." He turned to Daria. "Are you alright?"

Daria nodded. John stepped out.

Mercer Gaudette watched him leave, then sighed theatrically. "Any chance he's . . . ?"

"Straight."

Mercer made a show of snapping his fingers. "Shucks. Anyway, military's hunting you. Those *Skorpjo* gentlemen, too."

Daria said, "What now?"

"Sally and I take a train south to Greece. You and the Dreamboat stay here another forty-eight hours for that concussion of yours. Got a nice stolen car out front, with passable fake papers. You two drive north, across the border into Hungary. There's a hospital in Prague with orders to take you in and to ask no questions. Fredrik's paying up front. He'll bill you later. It'll be ridiculously exorbitant."

"Good to know. And my bill for your services? I like to put 'paid' to my debts."

Mercer laughed. "You'll owe us one, Miss Gibron. Got a feeling that could come in handy someday."

He took her hand, kissed her knuckle.

John returned with a steaming mug of coffee. Mercer checked John's ass in passing, *tsked* in disappointment, and left.

John whistled. "Wowza."

"Indeed." Daria set down her soup. "He said there's a stolen car out front."

"There's a Renault, yeah."

"As soon as they leave, so do we."

"You're concussed. We—"

"We'd best be gone, John."

"Don't trust him?"

Daria winked at him. "Do you?"

Fifty-Two

The Hungarian countryside bustled with massive farm machinery in fields to the left and to the right of the M5 highway. Neither Daria nor John came from farming stock, and neither could identify the massive combines. Getting through the border had been harrowing, and the queue agonizingly long. But they did get through. John turned the Renault north toward Kecskemet and, beyond, Budapest.

It was a fine July day with few feathering clouds in the sky. Daria wore new cargo trousers and a light, horizontally striped sweater, and suede moccasins with no socks. The mysterious Sally had provided a first-aid kit for Daria and a generic carryall with a few changes of clothing for both of them.

Her only other possession—right then and right there—was a roll of stretchy black Lycra that John handed her when they climbed into the car. "You had this on you. When we found you in Belgrade."

Daria held the roll a moment, then let it unfurl. A hammered steel tube fell into her other palm. Six inches long, it was oxblood red. A stud bulged near one end, but only slightly raised. If you weren't looking for it, you'd miss it.

John said, "Looks old."

"I think it is."

She depressed it with the pad of her thumb. A steel stiletto, six inches long, popped straight out of the handle. Tapered to a point, with two razor-sharp edges. She held it gingerly and flexed it. The metal held firm.

She touched the stud and the bayonet-style blade evaporated as if by a conjurer's decree.

John said, "Yikes."

Daria said, "Indeed. Now, all I need are sunglasses."

"What kind of sunglasses?"

She blinked at him a moment.

"Right. Expensive. Hold on."

Twenty minutes into the drive, John stopped at a highway *benzin-kut*, a combination gas station, market, coffee shop, and car wash. John returned with a bottled water for her, a lidded coffee for himself, and an oversized pair of shades that, truly, weren't that terrible given that they were in rural Hungary and not on the rue de Rivoli. She slid them on, lowered the sunshade, and checked the mirror. With her curtain of straight black hair, the facial bandages were nicely hidden.

"Not bad, Mr. Broom."

"You're not the first girl I've shopped for." He nestled his coffee in the cup holder, adjusted his safety belt, and pulled back into the highway.

"We left Belgrade too fast to pick up your bags," he observed, blending into the traffic.

"I haven't any." Daria tilted the seat back and rolled down her window, smiling as Hungary whipped by.

"Whatever happened to your condo in LA?"

She looked a bit startled. "You know, I never inquired."

"What did you have with you in Italy?"

"A duffel bag, some clothes. Some credit and debit cards."

"Where are they now?"

"A bordello."

"Ask a stupid question . . ."

They veered northwest toward Ocsa and Dunaharaszti. Traffic picked up—more family cars, fewer cross-border freight haulers. Massive, asymmetrical hayricks stood like tribal huts in fields.

Daria might have been asleep until she asked, "How bad is it?"

John had been waiting until she asked for a debriefing. "Zebra-shit bad." He deactivated the cruise control to conform to urban traffic. "I've been in contact with my senator. Singer Cavanaugh. I had to resign to come out here and do this stuff, but he thinks the worst is past and I could be back on the payroll by August. Anyway, he's—"

"You quit your job to come get me?"

John kept his eyes on the traffic and his speedometer. "The stuff you do. You understand. I couldn't let any of that splash on the senator."

She studied him from behind her shades. "I do understand." And she meant it. "Thank you, John. Yet again."

"Sure." He tried and failed to sound nonchalant. "Anyway, Singer's keeping track of the CIA for us. Owen Thorson's body was found, along with two thugs from the White Scorpions. And, um, I hear Owen was a little shorter than usual."

Daria kept her head back against the cushy leather rest, chin tilted up. "That happens with age."

"Ye-eah. Anyway, the agency had washed its hands of Owen. And that would be doubly so if he'd fallen in with *Skorpjo*. But here's the thing: a second ex-CIA spook, guy named Derrick Saito, was found dead near that hotel in Florence, where you were positively ID'd. I didn't know Saito from my time at the agency, but his rep wasn't good. And a third ex-agent, Jake Kenner, was found with a severed spine and a stolen motorcycle on a mountain pass in France. The agency has confirmed your involvement in the race. I knew Kenner a little. Nobody's missing him."

Daria put her injured arm up on the window frame and made a flat plane of her straight palm, letting it ride wind eddies as the Renault cruised along. The small movements, pushed by the wind, felt good as they stretched her torn muscles. "So my peace accord with the CIA is null and void."

"If I were to guess, I'd say ninety-five percent of the CIA wants to forget you ever existed. And five percent wants your head in a lunch box."

"Five percent of the U.S. Central Intelligence Agency is a considerable foe."

"Won't lie. It is. Mercer back there said the medical clinic in Prague is safe. After that . . . ?"

Daria let her flat, horizontal hand glide up and down with the wind.

"Which brings me to this: Ray Calabrese is gonna beat me senseless if he doesn't get to see you."

"Ray!" Daria turned abruptly, and a sunrise smile burst across her heart-shaped face. She had wondered why her former handler in the FBI Los Angeles field office hadn't contacted her, but of course he couldn't, given the circumstances. Ray was another one of those men who seemed forever in Daria's camp. And another who had suffered because of it. "How is he?"

"He's good. But I'm trying to keep him out of this thing, in case there are international repercussions. You understand?"

Daria bit her lip and thought about it. "Yes. Quite right. I'll contact Ray when I can do so without hurting his career. Thank you."

John made another deft hustle around some slower cars. "Then there's this Illyrian League." The night before he had told her about the continentwide right-wing movement Zoran Antic had helped launch. "They were counting on the drones to hammer home their anti-American screed. No one's found any drones in Belgrade. And from what I hear, they blame you for that."

"So, to clarify: A portion of American intelligence wants me dead. And a portion of this anti-American movement wants me dead."

John said, "Yeah."

"The enemies I made earlier—the ones who drove me into hiding in Italy—they're not going away any time soon. And they're blackballing me among other Western intelligence agencies."

"Yeah."

They drove a bit. John thumped a nervous beat on the steering wheel.

"At least you've still got me."

Daria said, "No," and reached out to cup his hand on the gearshift. "I'm . . . yes. You do."

She removed her sunglasses, then reached out and removed his. She didn't let it register that the movement stressed her ribs and bad shoulder. She made eye contact with John.

"No. Your first instincts regarding your senator were right. I'm running in illegal and highly visible circles. You can't be part of his world and mine. And you can do a hell of a lot more there. It's where you're most needed."

He drove for a time, watching for signs to the E60 to Bratislava, where they could jump on the E65 into the Czech Republic.

John obviously had told himself the exact same thing. He cleared his throat.

"So what have you got?"

Daria gave it some thought. "A bit of money squirreled away. An Italian assassin's stiletto. A pocketful of favors I'm owed. Fast friends— who need to stay mum, lest I call!"

John ground his teeth. "Yes, Ma'am."

She slid the sunglasses back on, lowered the visor again, and checked her reflection. She ran her tongue over her lips and her fingertips through her hair.

Then she leaned back.

"And I've spanking new sunglasses."

John didn't want to, but he laughed. "They are pretty fetching."

"See?" Daria leaned back, eyes closed, and relaxed. "Things are looking up."